Lady
LIMBO

Lady
LIMBO
Consuelo
ROLAND

First published by Jacana Media (Pty) Ltd in 2012

10 Orange Street
Sunnyside
Auckland Park 2092
South Africa
+2711 628 3200
www.jacana.co.za

ISBN 978-1-4314-0508-4

Set in Sabon 11/15pt
Printed by Ultra Litho (Pty) Ltd, Johannesburg
Job no. 001847
Cover design by publicide
Editorial assistance from Lynette Paterson, Winnie Thomson and Fiona Zerbst

See a complete list of Jacana titles at www.jacana.co.za

*For my mother, who brought an unusual
story back from her travels*

~

*Thanks to Eric Clapton, K.D. Lang, Youssou N'Dour,
Bob Marley, Édith Piaf, R.E.M., Cat Stevens,
Giuseppe Verdi, for the music*

*Thanks to Mitch Albom, John Fowles,
Milan Kundera, William Shakespeare,
Sun Tzu, Thornton Wilder, for the classics*

Limbo has a rich literary history, in honor of which I hope the pope and his International Theological Commission will refrain from exiling this amiably ambiguous realm.

Hell, Purgatory and Heaven may seem rather strictly demarcated and limited destinations, without Limbo as an interesting outrider. In the Italian Renaissance poet Luduvico Ariosto's 'Orlando Furioso', the knight Astolfo visits the moon's Limbo and discovers there all of earth's wastages: talents locked up in named vases, bribes hanging on gold hooks, and much else besides.

– HAROLD BLOOM, FROM
'PARADISE FOUND, LIMBO LOST:
A STORIED STATE', INTERNATIONAL
HERALD TRIBUNE, 2 JANUARY 2006

What a human being possesses deep within him of the lost, of the tragic, of the 'blinding wonder' can be found again nowhere but in bed.

– GEORGES BATAILLE, FROM
THE SECOND SEX,
SIMONE DE BEAUVOIR

Contents

Prologue

17 May 1994. Hello. I am a 32-year-old single woman who wants to have a baby in the natural way. I have been told that Real Man Inc. provides a professional vetting service and an excellent list of potential candidates for copulation. Has anybody out there used the services of Real Man Inc.? Any information will be treated in strict confidence. Lady Limbo (ladylimbo@aup.extramural.edu)

WHAT KIND OF A DUMB, *attention-getting name was that? It didn't seem right that somebody should be trading on a concept like Limbo. She read it several times before it made any sense to her. There was an organisation somewhere in the world that permitted women to select and copulate with the fathers of their unborn kids-to-be, and allowed them, nay, encouraged them, to walk away without so much as a 'see-ya-later'. The site went crazy for a few days, but Lady Limbo didn't come on again while she was keeping an eye on it.*

Thanks to an enthusiastic visiting American lecturer, that's what Psychology I students spent much of their time doing that year: dialling into the online social bulletin boards that were exploding into existence, virtual agony columns for the delusional and dejected, trying to figure out if theirs was a cry for help or just consolation or if they were looking for rejection. Islands of despair on the world wide web. This one had her interested. She'd followed the 'Iwanttohaveababy' thread that day looking for something tragic for a class assignment and slipped through the controls to an 'open' unmoderated forum that dealt with more racy subject matter: sex, drugs and dating. Lady Limbo wasn't tragic enough for her immediate needs, so she logged off muttering, 'Where the hell is Lady Macbeth when you need her?'

But Lady Limbo's little problem was perfect for another purpose. Nicky was delighted with her thoughtful gift, brought back to him after lectures. The message was indeed a delectable novelty (that was what he said as he licked and kissed her honey-dipped fingertips). She was gratified that her offering had been so well received.

Daniel was there too that night, head cocked to one side, surrounded by plumes of blue smoke, smiling at her as she read the message out loud for his benefit. Later, the three of them lay on Nicky's emperor bed and became horribly inebriated on Drambuie and Coke. Daniel made Comanche Indian smoke signals that rose to the ceiling and dispersed.

I

PERFECT RECALL

Man
Overboard

THE FIRST TIME DANIEL did a real vanishing trick, he was on a cruise ship to St Helena. My mobile rang while I was washing my hands in the cloakroom of our Johannesburg office, en route to the monthly project managers' meeting.

'Damn.'

The caller number wasn't local. I dried up quickly and moved into the passage, shifting my folder so that I could walk faster.

A woman's voice. Plenty of static and crackle. It could just as well have been a call from the moon.

'Paola Dante speaking.' Using my maiden name at work had made the transition to married life fluid and comment-free.

'Am I speaking to … is that Mrs de Luc?'

'Yes, that's right. Could you speak up?'

'Mrs Daniel de Luc?' The voice was louder, insistent.

'Yes, I'm Daniel de Luc's wife. Is there a problem?' There is no reason to panic. You don't know anything is wrong. Breathe. Stay calm.

'This is Commander Kapa at the St Helena police station. I've just been in radio communication with Captain Becker of the

RMS *St Helena*. I am very sorry to have to tell you that your husband is missing.'

Oh Daniel, not again. Please, not again.

The words washed over me like an oil slick. They glued me to the woollen carpet in the corridor of the three-storey building. The only sounds I heard in the encapsulated space were the distant voice and a booming thud that I took to be my own heart.

'Mrs de Luc? Are you there? I realise that this must be a great shock for you, but as you can appreciate, time is of the essence with a disappearance at sea. The captain would like to know if you have any idea where he might have gone.'

I wanted to laugh; it was funny after all: the captain asking me if I knew where my husband was when I was the one on land and he was the one on the ship. I told the voice to hold on while I found the closest empty office and shut the door.

'Who reported him missing?'

'A cabin attendant. It seems that the bed was not slept in although everything else appears to be intact – his suitcase and his belongings, even a mobile phone and some notebooks. But Mr de Luc himself and the clothes he was wearing when last seen are missing. Does he have diabetes or asthma, something that might have caused him to collapse? What about medication?'

'No! Nothing like that. Definitely not. He dislikes medication of any sort.'

'I hope you will pardon my asking, but did the two of you argue over anything before he left?'

'Look, the answer is no. Categorically, no! Is that clear enough? You're wasting valuable time, Commander. Why aren't you on a helicopter flying out to the ship?'

'I assure you we are doing everything within our power to find him. The island's rescue helicopter has been sent out to search the area at the co-ordinates where your husband is believed to have been seen last.'

'The ship – why aren't they searching the ship? Maybe he fell asleep in a life raft – has anyone checked the life rafts?'

'Mrs de Luc, I realise how difficult this is, but your husband's life may depend on your co-operation. Now, has he ever suffered from depression or displayed any suicidal tendencies? What about his alcohol consumption? Would you say he sometimes overdoes it?'

'Daniel does not *overdo it*, Commander Whatever-your-name-is. And he does not suffer from depression or suicidal tendencies. He's a writer so he likes to dramatise, but I don't know how that's going to help you find him.'

'He's a journalist? Is that why he was travelling alone?'

So that's what was on her mind.

'An author,' I corrected her shortly. 'It was a field trip for a new book. You're looking in all the wrong places. Somebody must have seen him. A grown man can't just disappear overnight.'

'They have already searched the ship several times. There is no trace of your husband. He appears to have done exactly what you say is not possible – disappeared into thin air from a ship in the middle of the ocean. And I'm afraid that may mean only one thing.'

The implication echoed up the line. She wasn't to know I'd been here before.

'What about the South African Police? Why aren't they calling me?'

'The South African authorities have passed the case on to us after consulting with the ship owners. It is not easy to turn a cruise ship back when it is full of paying passengers. We have about four days until the ship docks.'

That made me sit up. '*Four days*? Are you serious?'

'The RMS *St Helena* operates according to a strict schedule. Unfortunately, half the world's press will be blocking our communication lines by then ...' Her momentary irritation tapered off mid-ocean.

'What about the helicopter?'

'We considered lowering a detective onto the ship, but weather reports predict gale-force winds. It wouldn't be safe. We'll be waiting to go on board when the ship docks.'

'But what if one of the passengers ...?'

'The captain has already conducted his own preliminary investigations. A ship's officer saw your husband entering his cabin after boarding. Two elderly passengers thought they might have seen him smoking a cigarette on deck later last night. Nobody else has come forward. Security personnel on the ship have secured the cabin. On disembarkation, all the passengers will be asked to leave details of where they will be staying, and later each passenger will be questioned. St Helena is a small island. There is nowhere for them to go.'

The smug tone annoyed me. 'I'd be careful if I were you, Commander. It might be contagious, people disappearing on your watch.'

'I certainly hope not.'

She was quiet for a moment. 'Mrs de Luc ...'

They were probably calling my mobile from the meeting room to find out where I was, and getting an engaged tone.

'What?'

The woman on the other side spoke in a more kindly voice.

'If there is anything I should know, it would be best for you to tell me now, otherwise it may be too late to help your husband.'

'There's nothing you need to know.'

Through the window I could see the distant skyline of the City of Gold with its mine dumps and high-rise buildings. There wasn't a cloud in the sky. Damn it, Daniel, I have a career. You can't keep doing this to me. Where are you this time?

A burst of garbled static came down the line. Somewhere out in the Atlantic Ocean, a storm was building up.

'You'll have to repeat ... I didn't get that.'

'Do you have somewhere to go? Is there anyone I should contact on your behalf?' She came through loud and clear this time.

'I'm fine. I'll be even more fine when you find Daniel.'

'Very well. This is not the right time, but we may need to talk again about the assignment he was on.'

'He's not a journalist.' A crackle of static drowned us both out for a moment.

'... anything at all – that might assist us, please contact the St Helena station immediately. Goodbye, Mrs de Luc.'

The conversation ended there. In the far distance, a tiny plane streaked across the empty sky, trailing a plume of white smoke in its wake, until that too vanished. Maybe I should have said more about Daniel's books. But what would I have said? That as far as I knew they were French crime fiction paperbacks? That my Internet searches had yielded nothing? That even his agent's messages were lost in translation?

In the early days of our renewed acquaintance, both lying naked on my bed on a hot summer's night under the gaze of an amber moon, I'd asked where I could buy his books. It was one of those post-coital conversations that remain embedded in memory. While he stroked my breasts, Daniel said that the book publishing world and its pandering to the mass public for profit was a death knell to creativity. He'd watched with interest as my nipples hardened. '*Incroyable*!' he'd exclaimed softly. For this reason, it was a principle of his never to see the published book, he said, before setting off down my naked body, his tongue now roped into the game. In the same way, he said after stopping briefly at my belly button, discussing one's writing with others would be like a man discussing a woman he loved with another man. My last rational thought was to wonder whether a woman might view her privacy in the same light.

I flew home to Cape Town the day after the call from St Helena. There was still no word.

On the Saturday morning, the sparrow Daniel fed was at the window, hopping around on matchstick legs. I crumbled some toast onto the sill. A whistle from the street below made me glance down. A teenage girl in faded jeans and a grey hoodie was sitting at the bus stop watching me. The last bus into the city had come past thirty minutes ago. When I checked five minutes later, she was gone. There'd been something hostile about her targeted stare. But I was probably imagining things. Daniel's continued absence was making me nervous.

At around midday, I was informed by the Cape Town harbourmaster that my husband, the missing author whose picture was in the weekend papers, had just walked into the Mission to Seafarers.

I found him sitting alone at a table. He shifted his rucksack off a plastic chair to make space for me next to him.

'Bonjour mon amour. Est-ce que tu as faim?'

Daniel behaved as if it was perfectly normal for him to be sitting in the Seafarers' cafeteria eating soup.

The St Helena Tribune, International Edition, Friday July 22, 2005

AUTHOR DISAPPEARS ON CRUISE TO ST HELENA

A St Helena police spokesman has confirmed that the whereabouts of French author Daniel de Luc, 32, a passenger on the RMS *St Helena*, remain unknown. De Luc was reported missing from his cabin on Tuesday July 19, the morning after passengers embarked at Cape Town harbour for the two-week round trip to St Helena. His absence from the Captain's dinner the evening before had been put down to a bout of seasickness. De Luc was travelling alone. Foul play is not suspected.

As the remote island where French emperor Napoleon Bonaparte was ignominiously exiled and later died in 1821, St Helena's place in history is assured. But in the past few years several tragic incidents have again put our remote island in the news.

In 1998, a luxury yacht owned by the Swiss stockbroking magnate Bernard Chevalier, 72, went up in flames in James Bay. In spite of quick action by harbour officials and local boatmen, all occupants on board, including Chevalier and his wife, acclaimed actress Sophie Kahlo-Chevalier, 25, who was pregnant with their first child at the time, perished in the fire.

Six months ago, a young woman from the UK, Sarah Wheelan, 30, a bird researcher on the island, committed suicide by poison. It was alleged that she mixed the poison herself. No note was found. Ms Wheelan's family remain in the dark about the reasons for her death.

Her sister, who agreed at the time to speak to our reporter, mentioned a failed marriage and multiple miscarriages as a possible reason. 'But I thought she had put that all behind her and moved on. She was so happy to start a new life on St Helena. We are very grateful to the people of St Helena for allowing us to bury her in the Christian cemetery. Perhaps she will find peace here.' The Saints (island population) have a long history of tolerance towards suicide.

De Luc, a French citizen based in Cape Town, is the author of several crime novels published under the popular Pocket Policiers label. According to his wife, the voyage to St Helena was part of research for his first English-language crime paperback.

Shipping in a 100km nautical area has been alerted and Air Force helicopters have been requested from the South African National Defence Force to assist with the search at sea.

9

Pasta alla Carbonara

On Friday, 9 September 2005, the day he disappeared properly, my husband, Daniel de Luc, was about to make pasta alla carbonara. I'd rung his mobile but he hadn't replied. Minutes later he'd called back. I'd asked him what was for supper, and he'd replied it was my favourite pasta dish. He'd bought fresh parmesan cheese and some of the imported salt-cured pancetta that made all the difference at Giovanni's, the Green Point deli. One of Daniel's many talents was cooking.

'Patrice left a message again looking for you. Why don't you call him back, Daniel?'

'Patrice is an intolerable cretin. What time will you be home?'

Sometimes I thought I'd become so used to Daniel putting me off that I made it easy for him to avoid my questions. I couldn't be sure which had come first: his unwillingness to discuss his writing or my acceptance of the situation. It remained obscure to me – the desire to write a book and then have no interest in the finished product. But I'd decided that my husband's penchant for mystery was harmless and had backed off gracefully.

'I've still got the project weekly report to do. It's been a hectic day, meetings and more meetings.'

'Mon amour, sweet love-of-my-life, it's Friday – get that pretty butt of yours home smartly. I have put a special bottle of wine to chill – a Chianti should not be drunk too warm – and I am about to create a meal so sublime you will remember it on your deathbed. And who knows what might happen after the meal? It will be an unforgettable evening! Spell "hippopotamus" for me.'

It was Daniel's idea of a pleasurable diversion. Elephant, aardvark or hippopotamus. On any SWOT analysis I'd ever done, spelling could be found under 'weak points'.

'You're a sadist. I'm far too tired to spell "hippopotamus".'

'Exactly my point. Bring the laptop home; you can work on Sunday.'

No one else had ever managed to talk me out of work the way Daniel did. I put the receiver down and sat there for a moment, high-backed chair swivelled around to face the mountain, wondering at the speed with which the tablecloth of cloud descended. I was trying to ignore a tight feeling in my windpipe that had been there for days, as if a very small, annoying fish-bone were jammed in there. It was probably indigestion. Maybe an early evening would be a good idea.

That was it. All the warning I had.

Things are perfect. Daniel is the perfect househusband. The natural order of things has been restored in the last few weeks.

Or has it? Have I missed something? It's understandable that a writer busy with a new book should be distracted. And the playful come-hither Daniel of our phone call was the Daniel of old. After all, I hadn't committed to being home early. But where is he?

I sit on the balcony in a tracksuit, watching the road, but at night the cars and headlights all look the same. I ask myself why I haven't been to the police, but he's gone away before, and he's always come back.

Breathe, just breathe. If you stop breathing you'll never find him.

It's not clear why but while other people get stomach aches, I have difficulty breathing. He's always said something, or had a

11

reason before. There's something ominous about the dry dishes waiting to be packed away and the white bed sheets left on the rooftop washing line, billowing spooks in the evening wind. In the study, his desk is tidy. No loose papers lying around, no cups of half-drunk coffee, no pencils or pens.

The first attempt I'd made to file a missing person report was also the last attempt. Daniel had been away three nights without calling me. I'd gone to the police station on Beach Road, where I was given a form to complete. The overweight desk sergeant sounded like a pre-recorded message: 'We'll check the description against accident and crime reports. If anything turns up, we'll contact you at the number you've provided, otherwise you can enquire about the progress of your case after forty-eight hours. Sign here.' She made me feel that a missing husband was a run-of-the-mill event, that husbands walked out on their wives every day, that I shouldn't be such a cry-baby. Shit happens.

'You know what? I've changed my mind. My husband's not missing after all.' I'd torn up my statement and marched out of the police station. The policewoman probably just shrugged. Another spoilt white woman with an exaggerated view of her own importance.

Out at sea, ships wait to come into the harbour. One of them glitters like a distant Christmas tree in a darkened room. It could be a luxury floating hotel, a container ship, or an oil rig. On this fog-enshrouded night I can't tell. Where does it hail from? What is its next port of call? There is no way of knowing.

Alien
Abductions

'YOU MISERABLE, SLIMY BASTARD!' I yell at Gregory August, private eye, shaking him by the lapels. Daniel's disappearance is pushing me over the edge.

After two weeks had gone by without a sign of the man missing from my life, I was forced to admit that I needed help. But my earlier police station experience hadn't exactly engendered confidence. An online search revealed plenty of private investigators in my home city. But the smarmy predictability of phrases like 'clandestine investigation' and 'cheating spouse' made me cringe. The situation seemed unreal to me. Why not just close my eyes and see where it took me? That's how I found the unfortunate Gregory August. With a single squeamish jab of the finger at the Yellow Pages directory. Private Investigator. Reasonable Rates. References Provided. I told him he had three days.

August spent the first morning visiting Home Affairs. I went round to his office on the way back from a client. Apparently there were some 'anomalies' concerning Daniel's French-born parents – Marie-France and Antoine de Luc. That could mean anything. Daniel had always refused to talk about his family, simply saying that he'd left home at a young age and had lost contact with them. When we were deciding on witnesses for our civil marriage, he'd laughingly said I should check how many people could fit into one small office. Luckily there was no one to invite from his side.

'What anomalies? Could you be more specific?'

August shrugged and said foreigners were always tricky; it was something to do with them being on a different system. There wasn't anything more he could do 'with his hands tied behind his back'. The reference to my condition that no one should know that Daniel was missing infuriated me.

'What about your flight to Durban tomorrow? You know, the one *I* paid for so *you* could visit the town where my husband was born?'

A thin sheen of sweat broke out on his forehead.

'You said they call you The Rottweiler!' I snapped. 'I thought you never gave up on a case?'

The perspiring August scratched his armpit. A high-society divorce case had come up – a government minister.

'The wife's lawyer wants him caught on camera in flagrante delicto. Preferably with one of the street kids he takes to the baths. They're looking to double the payout.'

It was clear my PI wanted out, but I wasn't in the mood to be accommodating.

'Goodness! Maybe you could bring the government down?' I suggested sweetly. 'Isn't sodomising a child illegal? One of those cases you're legally obliged to report?'

He pretended he hadn't heard. 'If I was you, I'd get on with my life, Mrs de Luc. If you'll pardon me saying so – and I've got some experience in these matters – if there's no body and no suicide note, Mr de Luc doesn't want to be found. Marriage isn't everybody's cup of tea ... and a Frenchie ...' He shook his head in sympathy.

That's when I leaned over the desk and grabbed him by the shiny lapels.

'You know nothing about my husband, Mr August. How could a dung beetle like you ...?'

The telephone rang. Once. Twice. Three times. Between rings,

I heard Gregory August panting like a phlegmy animal.

'I ... know ... some ... one.'

Croup chest. I recognised the sound. My mother eschewing hospitals, sitting on a floor mat with my skinny, wheezing brother, potent fumes from a bubbling mixture on a camping stove escaping from a large blanket draped over the kitchen table, like a medicine woman's tepee.

The telephone stopped ringing. My grip loosened. What was I doing? This was another Paola, the Paola that I'd carefully deconstructed in my teenage years. I was never going to be my loopy mother. I let the shoddy piece of humanity with bulging eyes fall back into the chair. I needed another PI.

August took one of those miniature liquor bottles out of a jacket pocket and slugged the contents back, then started fishing around in a drawer. A friend of his specialised in finding missing people, he panted. Dead or alive.

'He's had some ... health problems. Bloom sometimes uses unorthodox methods, but he gets ... results.'

Later, in the car, I interrogated myself: What if he'd had a gun in the drawer? Who would have looked for Daniel? But I'd taken the battered business card August had held out between two nicotine-stained fingers and paid the hefty daily fee he'd negotiated up front. On my way out, I'd ripped a clean page from the notepad on his desk and written, 'This man will let you down,' before handing the note to a head-scarfed woman waiting on a chair in the corridor. If she hadn't been there I'd have nailed it to his door. That's the kind of woman I was becoming.

'Specialist in extraterrestrial phenomena, alien abductions and unexplained disappearances.' That was the blurb Bloom had on the back of his business card. I made an out-of-character decision to ignore the misplaced sense of humour and drove straight into the chaos of lunchtime city traffic to look for his office. The card led me to a street number on Long Street. A sign pronounced it to be the premises of W&W&W, a second-hand bookshop I'd never noticed before.

A shop assistant in baggy black pants and jersey led me among shelves heaving with books, and up some narrow stairs. 'He's gone to Lefty's. He'll be back now,' the anaemic-looking youth said as we reached a small office in the roof. 'Who shall I say is calling?' He had a very red mouth and appeared to be wearing eyeliner.

I waited in a worn faux-leather armchair. A mug of unfinished, cold coffee graced the horseracing page of the *Cape Times*. It took me back to the Dante breakfast table, a glass of freshly squeezed orange juice at each place, my father waiting for my mother to leave before winking at me and turning to the page with the horses in full graceful gallop, their big, powerful necks straining towards the winning post.

Two scuffed filing cabinets stood against one wall and a rough pin-board with newspaper cuttings dominated the other wall. They were mostly crime reports and missing people bulletins. But the centrepiece was a newspaper photograph of a street child wearing a beanie leaning against a graffiti-covered wall. The unknown artist had used large capital letters dripping with black blood for maximum dramatic effect:

I HAVE OF
LATE, WHERE
FOR I KNOW
NOT, LOST ALL
MY MIRTH

The words sounded familiar, as if I should have known their source, but I didn't. Daniel would have known.

'I apologise. I manage the bookshop for a friend.' I swung around to find washed-blue eyes regarding me. 'Occasionally I have business to do. We have a flexible arrangement.' Bloom wore black-rimmed spectacles with huge flat-screen lenses and his excessively freckled face was topped by carrot-red hair. He reminded me of the Little Prince sitting on his planet, in the book our French teacher had read to us before I gave up French for a science syllabus.

'How may I be of assistance, Mrs Dante-de Luc?' Bloom asked, glancing at my business card in his hand.

I'd never liked introducing myself as Mrs anything before Daniel's disappearing trick, preferring to simply call myself Paola Dante. I'd made a point of retaining my maiden name. Now I'd had new cards printed. Being identified as Mrs Dante-de Luc was no longer confining; it meant Daniel wasn't a figment of my imagination.

'Paola is fine.'

'Of course. I'm Elijah.'

I placed a photo of Daniel, taken at our wedding lunch, on the desk facing him. 'I want you to find my husband. He's been gone since the ninth of September.'

'Have you reported him missing to the police?'

'No.'

'I see.' Do you? 'And you're only hiring a detective now? I suppose you've been going it alone,' he said. So I told him about Gregory August. He nodded, but didn't comment.

Instead, Elijah Bloom asked if I had a lawyer. He said that my number-one priority should be to protect my interests. He strongly recommended that I report my husband missing because he had found it was almost always best to operate within the parameters of the law. Things became messy otherwise. Certain avenues were no longer open to one – like police records – and private notices in newspapers were a hit-and-miss affair. Publicity around unsolved police cases was often one's best ally in the field. It was amazing what weevils a well-placed newspaper report could bring out from their hiding places.

I let him give me the standard cover-your-backside speech, his face half-turned away from me as he watched a pigeon's antics on the ledge outside. Then I told him I didn't want the police involved. Daniel didn't like policemen. Anyway, it was already too late. I would automatically be the prime suspect because I hadn't reported the disappearance straight away. And I had no alibi for that night. It wouldn't help anybody if the police got sidetracked and sabotaged any chance we had of finding Daniel. This was one of those 'almost' cases. He'd have to take my word for it. And – I took a deep breath – he should know that as far as I was concerned, there was only one priority: to find my husband.

Elijah swung around to face me. I returned his steady look, not giving an inch. The small voice had won. My new PI didn't have to know everything, especially not about the caller in the night who'd insisted my husband had another name and that I shouldn't call the police. Going missing was not a crime. I was bending the rules, and I didn't care. I was here to hire a private investigator who specialised in alien abductions to find my missing husband. There was no doubt in my mind that I was laying myself wide open to whatever the universe was planning to throw at me.

'You are exposing yourself to the darkness,' Elijah agreed, rubbing his hands together as if my proposition was beginning to appeal to him.

Is he reading my mind? I'm going mad. The darkness?

'And from me, you are asking for an act of faith,' he continued, inclining his head with a certain gravitas. 'I confess to being intrigued but perhaps I should clarify my position at this point.' I followed his gaze to the ceiling. It was dotted with pencils, hanging awkwardly like one-legged yellow bats. I imagined him sharpening the points and hurling them heavenward like rockets sent up to ward off misery and recall mirth.

'I'm a drunk, Mrs de Luc. Once I start, I don't know how to stop. I've been going to AA for a year now, and I've been clean for ten months. That's the truth of it. I'm a recovering alcoholic. A has-been PI in anybody's book.'

I guessed him to be about forty – young for a has-been. If I was interviewing this person for a position, based on his confession I'd make sure he received a formal letter: 'We regret to inform you that your application has been unsuccessful.' No reason given. Explanations lead to lawsuits. Now my entire life felt like one of those pencils, something far too light to keep clinging to, and I had nothing to go on besides instincts half-frozen with disuse and misuse.

'Mr August says you have a talent for finding missing people. Do you?' Something in the slimeball's tone had made me come to see Elijah Bloom for myself. I thought I'd detected grudging respect.

Bloom glanced sideways at me. 'I've been doing routine stuff to keep going: lost relatives, debt fugitives, a missing dog – the reward on that case paid the rent for three months.'

'For a *dog*?'

'Miniature poodle, actually. On her way to a show in Dubai. Escaped from her cage at Joburg International and survived for a week on her own. Clever little thing.'

'What makes you an expert on missing *people*?'

'I suppose you're not interested in poodles.' He carried on, smiling at me. 'Gregory and I used to do the big cases: kidnapping and murder.'

'Oh, he's still into the big ones. The bigger the payout, the better,' I murmured.

Elijah acted as if he hadn't heard. 'We worked together with the police on the ones nobody else could solve. Gregory did the background research; I looked for things the police had missed.'

'What kind of things?'

He scratched his head thoughtfully. 'Mostly it's about patience: I'm good at working out what makes people tick, at finding what others have overlooked. Sometimes the answer lies in the lacunae, what is *not* said or done, rather than what is.'

Elijah Bloom got out of his chair and stood by the window, staring out at the city skyline, hands clasped behind his back.

'We had a case once where a schoolgirl disappeared from the toilets in a shopping mall. The parents were desperate and the police had no leads. I interviewed the security guards again myself. There was one of them, a bit cocky, whose palm wasn't sweaty when we shook hands. He had a rock-solid alibi and he'd won company awards but I had a feeling about him. After a week of undercover surveillance, we photographed him meeting with a young woman who supervised the shopping centre cleaning operations. That's how they'd done it – she hid the kid in a cleaner's trolley under rolls of toilet paper. They were going to get married and put a deposit on a house with the payout. We found the girl – heavily drugged but alive – in a caravan park. They had instructions to take her to a private airstrip once the fuss died down.'

Elijah took his seat again. 'The thing about a body is that that person's gone, you can't get them back. With a missing person, there's always a chance you'll find them. I get hunches about these things.'

I considered the pale red-haired warrior whose battlefront was the outer frontier of missing and absconded souls. Imperturbable blue lenses returned my gaze. I found my voice.

'That's good enough for me. Mr Bloom, will you take my case?'

'Very well, I am at your service,' he said simply.

'There is one thing. I don't want you wasting your energy on anything weird, like alien abduction or paranormal disappearance theories. Your brief is to find Daniel de Luc, my husband, on planet Earth. Are we clear on this?'

'I absolutely understand,' said Elijah Bloom, leaning forward with hands clasped, eyes glinting. 'But I shall need to do things my way if we are to find him. Are we in agreement?' He offered me his outstretched hand across the desk with the peculiar gentleness that was always to unsettle me in our relations. We shook on it.

'Since you refuse to go to the police officially, we shall have to avail ourselves of their services unofficially. I know somebody who might be willing to help when the time comes. What was Gregory able to come up with?'

'Basically nothing.' I handed him the documents. Our marriage certificate. A copy of Daniel's birth certificate. His parents' birth certificates.

'Your husband's full name is Daniel de Luc?'

'Yes.'

'How long have you known him?'

'Almost twelve years, on and off.'

'Has he ever to your knowledge used another name in the time that you have known him?'

'No, not to my personal knowledge.' I stuck to the truth as I knew it.

He scribbled something on the block-pad in front of him. When he went to the filing cabinet to get some forms, I turned the pad around and read the note he had written to himself: 'Follow the name!'

'You'd be surprised how often missing people use their own name,' was the only remark he made as I returned the notepad to its original position.

We agreed on an hourly rate plus expenses, progress to be detailed in a weekly report and emailed to me, and a considerable mission-accomplished fee, for finding the person or producing proof of his whereabouts. He preferred working like this because it gave him a monetary incentive, and it put the client's mind at ease, giving him the space to operate freely and do what he did best – locate missing people. Our next meeting would be at my apartment the following day.

I tripped down the bookshop stairs with the agility and speed of a mountain goat and asked Count Dracula if he had a moleskin journal. His response involved a guided tour. As he led me down tight corridors, between floor-to-ceiling shelves, outlandish titles flashed by: *Diary of a Psychic*, *Survival Kit for the Hereafter*, *New Age Living*, *Shamans of New York*, *Almanac of Alien Visitations*, *Encyclopaedia of the Paranormal*, *White Magic for Beginners*. Once or twice I lost him in the gloom, only to have him reappear ahead of me again. My head was spinning in the dank, airless space with the odour of second-hand, forgotten books; I heard myself ask if I could sit down for a moment.

'Uriah, a chair, if you would.' Elijah Bloom's tranquil voice sounded very far away.

A chair materialised from the crowded shadows.

'A little sugar will work wonders.'

A cup of tea with three biscuits on the saucer appeared in my hand.

'Are you a magician too?' How had he known I was lightheaded with hunger?

'I considered that profession once,' he smiled. 'But it seemed too precarious an existence.'

After the hot tea I felt better, and Elijah turned to re-ascend the stairs to his office. 'Tomorrow we start with the day your husband disappeared,' he said. 'Even the smallest detail may be useful. I'll need you to take me through every conversation, every argument, every word or action you remember, step by step. And I will need an inventory of what he took with him. Do you think you can do that?' He held my gaze. He was asking me to tell the truth.

'Yes. Of course. Goodbye, Mr Bloom.'

'Elijah. All my clients call me Elijah.'

'Elijah. Till tomorrow, then.'

'Goodbye, Paola.'

After a while, I got up and bought a maroon hardcover notebook with lined pages from a stand next to the till. On the first blank page I wrote the day and date, Monday, 26 September 2005, and the words: 'Hired Elijah Bloom. Follow the name!'

On the way home, I had to pull into a service station, overcome by a fit of hysterical giggling. What if Elijah Bloom told me Daniel had been abducted in a flying saucer and he could prove it?

It was all too much. Anybody passing would have seen a demented woman attacking her steering wheel. Why couldn't I sob and howl like a normal woman? After I'd calmed down, I thought I should eat something, so I bought a hamburger. I drove up Kloof Nek Road, turned left towards the cable-car station and carried on driving to the very end, where the winding road turned to gravel and came to a stop against the mountainside. It was a deserted spot where Daniel and I had come often in the early days, with pizza and a bottle of wine. The spectacular view over the pulsating city lights was as good as an outdoor drive-in cinema. After necking like teenagers, we usually ended up on the back seat, something we hadn't done in a while. I sat in my car eating the cold burger, the looming mountain behind me the bedrock of memory, and pondered what it was about marriage that changed things.

Déjà Vu

EIGHTEEN DAYS AFTER MY HUSBAND had planned to cook spaghetti alla carbonara, Elijah Bloom sat in the kitchen of our apartment and took me back to that night. He asked me to tell him everything I remembered.

I visualise the face of the kitchen clock quite clearly. I hear the click of the battery-operated hand moving to the next notch with the precision of a metronome reverberating in the empty kitchen. The short hand is on the six and the long hand on the four; it is exactly 6.20 pm, earlier than usual. The calendar page for September 2005 is Pablo Picasso's *Grande baigneuse au livre, 1937*. The block for Friday the ninth is clear. What can I see? Snap. Snap. Snap. Under Elijah's expert probing, my mind retrieved images from an entire album of what it apparently recognised as important signs of Daniel's presence in my life. The chilled Chianti. A clean wine glass. A knife on the meat-cutting board.

'Perfect recall' is what my recently appointed specialist PI called it. According to him, in the case of a flash-like premonition, the subconscious mind took over. The subject registered everything with a heightened state of perception. Elijah said the mind was better than any surveillance system if one could tap into these memories, because human beings had six senses. *Six? There is no scientific proof for six.* I groaned inwardly.

Elijah Bloom insisted on knowing the smallest details.

'What is the first thing you do?'

The woman I once was picks up the knife and runs her index finger along the blade. The edge is as smooth and sharp as a rapier. Was that the kind of information a private investigator grappled with? Should I tell him Daniel took inordinate pleasure in the sharpening of a knife?

There is nothing like a sharp blade, ma chérie! I was born to be a swordsman. En garde!

Paola giggling while she tries to parry Daniel's epée thrust is already nearly another puddle in the tundra, so I don't mention it. Daniel's capacity to make me laugh. Watching *The Three Musketeers* with Daniel, all the versions ever made.

Wondering if I would ever watch another movie with Daniel made me careless. Blood dripped onto the white tiled floor, my thin skin so easily penetrated. I sat on the high stool and watched numbly as Elijah disinfected my hand and bandaged it. When he'd finished, he wiped the blood off the floor with a kitchen towel, in the same calm and efficient way he'd handled my fainting spell the day before, as if it was all part of a PI's job. Now where could he find some tea? I pointed out a Chinese tin where Daniel kept some green tea. But not for me, I wanted to get this over with.

Elijah scratched his forehead. 'Right, of course. Let's leave the tea for later.'

'I must have missed it,' I reflected aloud. 'He was going to tell me he was going – that's why he wanted me to come home early. He's always said something before.'

'It's happened before?' Elijah didn't hide his surprise.

It had to come out at some stage. So I told him about the time I found Daniel on a park bench with a stranger's handkerchief around his bleeding arm.

'Daniel called them field trips,' I explained. 'He said it was undercover research for the new book. Usually it was just overnight, sometimes it was a few days. I never knew when he'd be back.'

Elijah Bloom made an involuntary noise, but when I looked at him enquiringly, he shook his head. 'Just a frog in my throat. Please carry on.'

'About a year ago, he called me to say he'd been mugged. But he couldn't explain why he was in the park, or what had happened.'

It was months now since Daniel had phoned to ask if I could collect him at the kids' park in Woodstock, the one near the bridge. I'd snapped that if he was going to keep wandering off, the least he could do was organise his own transport home.

'I've been mugged,' he'd said. 'You should probably bring some bandages.'

The line went dead. *I don't know what blood group he is.* I'd dropped everything, told the project secretary not to expect me back, hurtled down three floors of escalators, careered into the pharmacy on the ground floor, and probably broke the land speed record for inner-city traffic getting to him. I'd found him sitting upright on the bench next to the playground roundabout, a blood-soaked handkerchief tied around his upper arm. He'd refused to go to the emergency clinic at the city hospital so I'd taken him to my GP Carrie Fischer – the three of us went back a long way.

'You look worse than he does,' she'd said to me. 'I'm going to give you a script for Valerian. It's a mild homeopathic sedative. You can both use it.'

She was right. Daniel was as cool as a block of permafrost. The day after, I'd driven around the neighbourhood where I'd picked him up, wondering why the muggers hadn't taken his wallet. On impulse, I'd stopped at the park and gone over to a woman watching a small boy playing on the swings. I'd enquired about a public callbox, and she'd replied that there was one at the railway station down the road, next to the footbridge where the homeless people slept. Had she noticed a tall, dark-haired man at the park? My husband had been mugged here – I was trying to find out what had happened.

'Mugged? That is terrible. There is a white man who comes here sometimes. He sits and watches the children play and then he gets up and leaves.' She'd squinted up at me, a plump, honey-skinned woman with a black scarf wound around her head and neck, her voice kind. Had we lost a child? Lost a child? No, I didn't think so.

'Did you believe him?' Elijah's voice brought me back to the present. 'About not remembering?'

An obvious question, you'd think. I tried to answer honestly. 'I don't know. The doctor said temporary loss of memory was a normal response to trauma.' There was no reason not to believe him. He was my husband. And he was the smartest, most interesting man I knew. And therein lay the rub. I wanted to believe him.

'She also said I might notice behavioural changes, and I should just be patient.'

'And? Did you?'

'He stopped shaving. And he started chain-smoking again.'

How to explain it all? Words don't always capture the situation. Daniel also stopped having regular showers. And he kept the door to the bathroom open while he was peeing, like a boy or an old man. And he didn't bother putting the toilet seat down any more, as if he was a bachelor again. And he left his dirty ashtrays everywhere.

I felt a peculiar shame. I had hated the scruffy beard and what it stood for. The new aromas of unwashed, smoky skin and cigarette stubs in our bedroom. In a lucid moment, Daniel had offered to shave his beard off if I disliked it. But I wanted to protect us both from whatever was threatening us, so I said I'd get used to it. Once, I asked him to close the bathroom door next time and he looked at me coldly as if I'd crossed some sort of line.

'And you're sure it had nothing to do with the new book? I believe it's not uncommon for writers to become so involved with their characters that they start to live the part.'

'I can't say. He wouldn't talk to me.'

'Did you report the incident to the police?'

'He said it was just a scratch. I took him to a friend who's a doctor, and she cleaned it up and put stitches in. My friends know that Daniel writes crime thrillers.'

I was mainly referring to the few university friends that still lived and worked in the same city as I did. Not that I had seen much of any of them lately. They'd said we made a perfect couple.

At my kitchen-tea-cum-lingerie party, after copious amounts of alcohol and ribald laughter, Susanna had surprised me. 'How do you do it, Paola? Land with your bum in the butter every time? I don't get it. You get born with brains and looks, and you find a dishy Frenchman who stays home and does the housework and the cooking while you climb the corporate ladder. There's something abnormal about it. Sometimes I worry about you.' Everybody had agreed, amidst shrieks of laughter. Ditzy, glamour-puss Sue had a point: he was a real hunk.

My mother, on the other hand, said straight out that she thought Daniel was a saint to take me on: it wasn't natural for a woman to commit herself to a career and work the hours I did. That's my mother for you, an opinionated woman who claims never to have recovered from the blow of my undiluted capitalist orientation. Not a word about my father's duplicity that turned her to art and a socialist brand of capitalism, at an age when most of her friends were turning to religion and charity work.

'What is a mother to do?' she used to say before Daniel came on the scene. 'Resort to finding her clever daughter a husband in the park?' I knew she was referring to those Japanese parents who congregated in city parks to swap photos and histories of their super-intelligent progeny in the hope of a relationship blossoming, because she'd given me the *National Geographic* with a pointed allusion to the article in question. What possible chance did a career-obsessed, commitment-averse young woman have of making a marriage work? 'These days it's young women living together and young men living together. Who is going to make children?' my Italian mother would pontificate. Most times I managed to ignore her.

She'd adored Daniel from the moment she set eyes on him. Which was strange, because the redoubtable Mrs Dante, owner of Dante's Art Gallery, who'd thrown herself headlong into her work as a patron of the arts after my brother Massimo's death, didn't adore people easily. Art, yes; people, no. There were many occasions when I understood why my father had chosen to create a separate life for himself. She'd say things to Daniel like: 'We artists understand each other.' Or, 'As one artist to another ...' On the other hand, all women adored Daniel, so why should my mother be any different?

Elijah was watching me with a pensive expression on his face. 'So, occasionally he took off without warning but the park was the only time he actually went missing?'

'No. There was another time. It was much worse. He disappeared off a ship.'

Elijah's eyes shone brighter with each new revelation.

'Was it a passenger liner?'

'The RMS *St Helena*, to be exact. Daniel was struggling with his book. His agent Patrice arranged it. He said St Helena might make a good location, but it wasn't that – he thought I was a distraction. Daniel didn't want to go, but he said Patrice was his bread and butter. I told him he should just say no, we'd manage, but he went anyway.'

'Patrice shouldn't have forced him; that's why Daniel left the ship, he was under too much pressure.'

'Have you been in touch with this Patrice?'

Patrice. It's Paola here. I know you can speak English. Daniel is taking a long break. He hasn't been well. Please don't keep phoning. He will contact you when he is ready.

'I left a message on the answering machine and he stopped calling. Hold on, here's the number.' I held my mobile out for Elijah to see.

Months before, I wake to a beeping mobile long before first light. Next to me Daniel breathes with the regularity of a tree in a dark forest. Has he forgotten? It takes me forty minutes to shower, dress, finish packing and gather my things together. Five minutes has been allowed for the act of a minor god, so a ladder in my pantyhose causes no delay. I buy new pairs in packs of six. By 6.30 am I will be on a flight to Johannesburg.

'Daniel, I'm going. Have a good trip. Did you find out if they have mobile reception?'

My husband groans and rolls over as I sit down.

'Mmm. Mon amour, I'm not going to the Antarctica. Tout va bien. I'm only going to St Helena. I'll use the normal phone if the mobile doesn't work. I will probably be very bored, but I shall have to make the best of things.'

The warmth that comes from him burrowed deep in the blankets nearly overcomes me, as if heat is rising off volcanic rock. He kisses me on the lips, taking his time, enticing me to stay, to climb back into the warm bed with him. When he sees it's no use, he tells me to be careful, to make sure I stick to the main routes – the newspapers are full of hijackings in the City of Gold. In return, I instruct him sardonically to behave himself, which is shorthand for staying far away from every entertaining woman on the ship, even though it's pointless. I know it will start as he strides up the gangplank, his dark hair gleaming in the sunlight, the glinting eyes of the women on deck hidden behind tinted sunglasses. It is a lovers' game we play. Jealousy is not my thing.

'He's a regular Houdini, this husband of yours.' Elijah's voice brought me back to the present, his nose twitching as he scribbled, but the way he said it made it sound as if he relished the thought of reeling Daniel in, like a rogue fish. 'So who found him that time?'

'He must have slipped off the ship without anybody noticing before they left port. That's where he was found. At the Mission to Seafarers. The chaplain called the harbourmaster. He recognised Daniel from the photograph in the newspaper.'

Elijah looked thoughtful. 'Am I right in thinking there was an Arab dhow in the background of that photo?'

Yesterday's island mirage.

'It was taken in Zanzibar. How did you know?'

'I recall reading the news report,' Elijah said. 'It was an odd case.'

'Well, anyway,' I continued, 'the ship's captain agreed to log a report with the St Helena police, and they were happy to close the case. Missing passengers aren't good for the tourism industry. Daniel had no recollection of anything. He couldn't give an explanation for why he'd left the ship. I told the authorities he suffered from occasional blackouts, and that seemed to satisfy them.'

'Was he hurt?'

'No, just hungry and disoriented. He'd been missing for four days.'

'What was he dressed in?'

'The same clothes he was wearing when he boarded the ship.'

My Daniel, who loved French cologne, had smelt like a rubbish heap.

'Did he recognise you?'

'Oh, yes. I suppose it was rather like having your husband come back from a war. He knew who I was, but his mind was elsewhere.'

I wanted Elijah Bloom to understand that waiting for Daniel to come back home time after time had made me re-evaluate what I thought I understood about him. My girlfriends – what *exactly* did it mean when they refused to meet my eyes? What had my own mother meant with her annoying comment, 'I wouldn't have thought you were his type'?

'I keep on coming back to that question. Why me? Since he's disappeared for good, I've been even worse.'

I am shrivelling up without answers. I am no longer a ripe plum.

'You don't know that for sure,' Elijah Bloom interrupted. 'That he's disappeared for good.'

'Oh, but I do,' I replied, 'this time I do.' My finger was starting to throb. 'What if he's dead?'

Elijah fiddled with his glasses and smiled at me. 'Let's talk about you. What makes you get out of bed in the morning?'

I had to think about that. 'The project I'm busy with,' I acknowledged. 'In Time and On Budget. That's my mantra.'

'That's something to work with,' he said.

Of course, I'm not always so morbid. Most days I manage to talk enough sense into myself to drag my body under a hot shower, get dressed, and roll the futon. Some days I leave the futon. It's heartbreak work; an extra-thick marriage-bed futon is designed for love. Its construction assumes there'll be two of you doing the rolling. '*Why can't you move on! Move on! Move on!*' I rant at myself all the way to work, oblivious to the traffic and the early morning DJs with their brain-deadening breakfast shows. Occasionally I have a really bad day, obsessed with interpreting messages from the universe. One morning, elegant script on the back windscreen of a minibus taxi at the robot in front of me proclaims ALL IS WELL. When the robot changes to green, the taxi lurches forward, the rear axle bent low by a full load of passengers. I wait to play God. On the cliff road, around the next bend, I flick the taxi over the barrier and look down stonily as upside-down passengers scream. I go further: I tip it over the edge with my pinkie and watch it plummet onto the rocks below, flipping over and over as if it were a dinky car, until it crashes into the churning ocean and sinks.

Very little is well in the world on any given day, Mr Taxi Driver. You suffer from an immense delusion. '*Nothing is well!*' I wail through gritted teeth, bashing the steering wheel. I steer off the tar onto the dirt roadside without using my indicator and come to a shaky halt. Motorists hoot as they veer past. I open the window all the way down, the electric whirr a cutting block of sound, and sit there for minutes, folded over the steering wheel with my head down and both arms holding on, sucking fresh, chilled air into my lungs and blowing used air out, waiting for my breathing to grow easier and the sick emptiness in my stomach to go away.

Oh, for God's sake, get it together, Paola! I manage complex projects with large teams, I deal with MDs and CEOs, I travel all over the world. Last year I collected enough Hilton Hotel guest stamps for a free weekend for two at any Hilton Hotel in the world. When there's a tough project, they bring Ms Dante in. As it happened, I forfeited that weekend and our first overseas holiday together because of a last-minute proposal to a major client. If I hadn't stayed, Emma Patterson would have gone ahead in her usual gung-ho fashion, committing to unrealistic project schedules to get licence sales. As new recruits, we were told that no woman had ever been made a shareholding partner before the age of thirty-five. I knew what she was after.

Once, when he thought I was out of earshot, I heard Andrew Morton say that clients didn't stand a chance when 'Super-bitch Dante' was around. It had a kind of ring to it. Andrew Morton and I went back a few projects. I took it as a compliment.

Every office has an Andrew Morton. Andrew understands the nature of favours: one does a favour so that when the time comes, one can cash it in. If a human sacrifice to the gods of capitalism is required, Andrew finds someone else to do his dirty work. I've done him a few favours along the way. He owes me big time.

'Tell me about how you were recruited,' Elijah asked. 'At this stage everything is equally important,' he responded to my questioning look. 'Until we know more.'

'I was handpicked from university, straight firsts with an alpha-type personality profile. That got me onto the shortlist of twelve.'

What I didn't tell Elijah was how I had done my homework. After whittling a shortlist of five companies down to one, using a simple point system based on ten factors, I'd selected Picador & Plexus, kingdom of high-tech project management with a young, progressive image (among 'Ten Best Companies to Work For' three years in a row) combined with a strong results-orientated philosophy, as the corporation that was going to hire me. I drew up partner profiles and created computer models of the company's market share and share prices over a rolling three-year period. I joined a student employment agency and eventually landed an after-hours receptionist position at the gym across the road from the P&P city headquarters. The P&P consultants in their corporate gym kit made easy targets. During breaks, I struck up conversations and learnt to blend in and speak the jargon. For a while, I went out with one of the senior managers who was in the middle of a messy long-distance divorce, but things became complicated. Office politics meant we couldn't be seen together and he was too needy; I didn't want extra ballast. Still, he was generous with his insider advice, and thanks to him I learnt to play passable blackjack at the casino tables. From then on, I stuck to friendships and associations. After a gruelling week of psychometric tests culminating in a panel interview with four partners, I was in – one of five graduates to receive three months training at the P&P Academy in Montreal before being guided and coached through a real project, with the prospect of one day becoming partner dangled in front of all of us at every right turn, and the threat of being kicked out hanging over us if we took a wrong turn. The carrot and stick philosophy. *Fit in or go home.* There are cruder versions, but the polite one will do just as well.

With all of that, you'd think Super-bitch Dante could find one lost husband, wouldn't you?

'Any rivalries in the company?'

'Have I mentioned Emma Patterson?'

No, Elijah Bloom confirmed, I had not mentioned anybody by that name. 'What about Ms Patterson?'

Emma Patterson was one of the other graduates from my year selected by P&P. She had always been under my feet. At university, we'd vied over who would be chairperson of the Residence Committee. The position came with a monthly stipend, a fully furnished flat with a separate entrance, all of which I'd set my mind on from the first day in residence. Emmie the populist won. We'd competed over who would graduate cum laude (we both did), and over a position with P&P (we were both recruited). It wasn't surprising they grabbed Emma as an account manager. Along with good people skills and a high IQ, she had firm bouncing breasts that she treated like priceless assets, putting them on judicious display to keep their value up. One besotted CEO of a client company was heard to say 'Breathtaking!' every time she walked past.

Our business is as full of image spin as the next. The professional women I associate with choose their suits carefully as they clamber up the career rungs. Fine nuances between fabrics, colours and hemlines elevate a work suit to a power suit. Fabrics that are too soft and clingy are rejected, colours that are too dewy or bright are rejected, hemlines are never too short. The trick is to come across as feminine but hard-assed. Emma acted as if she were oblivious of the unwritten fashion edicts. Her signature look was platform heels worn with skimpy skirts and diaphanous blouses in luminous fabrics that created the impression she was permanently ready for a party. I once made a comment about her TGIF look and she looked thoughtful before asking if I didn't think suits were 'so over'.

'Emma Patterson was born to drive me crazy,' I told Elijah. 'That's all. She has the emotional intelligence of a five-year-old.'

Elijah chewed on his pencil. He used the old-fashioned type, sharpening them often with the metal sharpener he carried around in his shirt pocket. Apparently clutch pencils had proved unreliable. He glanced dubiously at the glass receptacle I pushed across for his wood shavings. He wasn't to know that the hand-blown *objet d'art* with its swirls of igneous red and smoky white was one of the few possessions Daniel had carted with him into married life.

Once, in a fit of peevishness, I ask why such a supposedly refined object is being used to harbour filth. It is after the park bench incident when Daniel has reverted to smoking. The whole apartment stinks.

'You'll get emphysema. I'll get emphysema.'

Daniel's eyes glitter serpent-green. 'Beauty is not something one puts on a shelf not to touch, ma chérie,' my unshaven husband replies evenly, as he lightly taps ash into the concave form.

'Go ahead,' I said. 'Daniel used it as an ashtray.'

'Perhaps we can return to Ms Patterson another time. Tell me what happened after you spoke to Daniel on the phone the day he disappeared.'

'Patrice left another message on my office answering machine; I gathered there was no reply at the apartment. I tried a couple of times myself and then gave up. I decided Daniel had probably gone for a walk on the beach to avoid Patrice.'

Our apartment block was one road up from Camps Bay beach. In the old days, when we were barefooted *laaities* burnt the colour of brown sugar by the blazing sun, Camps Bay was a beach for lazy bathers, dog-walkers, treasure hunters and fishermen, a peaceful enclave for those in the know, protected by steep cliffs and poor roads. It was our favourite beach because of the rocks and the tidal pool. These days, it was part of the city's outer ring. Family hideaways and beach shacks with front stoeps had been transformed into pristine, glass-fronted mansions with sea views. The old Dolphin Hotel with its sea memorabilia bar had long since been bought up by developers, morphing into a low-impact designer block with sundowner terraces and rim-flow pools that regularly appeared in trendy décor magazines.

All the special occasions of my youth had been commemorated on the Camps Bay rocks with a bottle of bubbly and the waves lapping below. In our student days, we'd watched the sunsets with wine and pizza. These days it was a more sanitised experience; any form of alcohol was strictly prohibited on the beach and fireworks were outlawed. Any recollection of those heady, exhilarating nights where the whole community headed for the beach now induced heartburn that could be traced back to the combo of pleasure and guilt that flooded the adrenal glands.

Occasionally, I wondered what had happened to Generaal de Wet, the Dolphin Hotel's parrot who terrorised guests by yelling out '*Jou robbish*!' as they walked past. If anybody else noticed that there were hardly any seashells left, they were staying *tjoepstil*; silence was golden when business was this good.

A young, funky crowd with plenty of ready cash moved in, and a host of eateries and clubs sprang up. Almost overnight, Camps Bay went from being a tranquil local beach to an architecturally revamped, upmarket recreation area catering for everybody from the taxied and bussed-in crowds to visiting celebrities and royals from abroad. It remained beautiful, with its palm-tree promenade and the tranquil aquamarine bay, a picture-perfect idyll on constant standby for a photographer's lens.

Our two-bedroom apartment was part of a 1960s three-storey block of holiday flats awaiting reinvention. The price was relatively low, the rooms were airy, spacious and full of light, and, via Kloof Nek, it was only seven minutes from the city outside peak-hour traffic. I called Francesca Goldmann, a friend of my mother's in the local property business. She said we were doing the right thing, buying a run-down property in a desirable area.

Daniel had been difficult to convince. 'A *desirable* area?' he scoffed. 'A woman is desirable – this is *le désir* – not an area! This is estate-agent-speak for expensive. It's a yuppie place. Not for you and me.'

We'd have Camps Bay beach on our doorstep, I countered, reminding him of our student days. In the end, he'd given in. Maybe it was the dolphins in the crescent bay and the cool white sand percolating between his toes that won him over. Or it could have been the spectacular sunset show from the huge west-facing balcony. I'd learnt to appeal to the romantic in my husband-to-be.

We signed all the papers, grinning at each other like idiots. Later we went for a walk on the beach, striding out like property tycoons. When we came back, we stopped at Angelo's for strawberries and cream and watched the sunset.

'Do you know the palm-tree promenade?' I asked Elijah.

'Yes,' he nodded. 'I had a case there just the other day, a woman cheating on her husband. I'm not much of a beach person, but it gave me the chance to use my metal detector,' he confessed. I could see him walking up and down the beach fully clothed, checked shirt with a big pocket, beige trousers, sturdy brown PI shoes, metal detector in hand – eccentricity the perfect disguise for keeping a careful eye on an adulteress and her paramour.

'Daniel always calls it Sunset Boulevard. It gives me a funny feeling, like skating on glass, the way he says it, as if he's looking at another boulevard, some other place.'

Elijah Bloom gave me a sympathetic look. I held his gaze for a moment. 'I don't know he's dead, do I?'

'Please carry on.'

'We talked at 4.10 pm. I had checked my call records. He knew the earliest I'd be home was some time after 6 pm. It was already dark, after 7 pm, when I drove down to the beach – maybe he'd stopped for the sunset on the way back – but he wasn't there.'

I'm back in that surreal night sitting on a bench under a lamp surrounded by a cloud of insects, trying to work out where he might have gone, why he hasn't phoned. There's nobody I can call. Daniel doesn't have any male friends that I know of. Not any more, anyway.

Elijah Bloom jotted down a few words.

'He'd been away from South Africa for so many years. All our mutual friends are work friends or couples. Anyway, I wasn't panicking yet. I told myself he'd probably gone to buy something he'd forgotten for supper and lost track of time listening to his CDs. He's crazy about R.E.M. And jazz and African music.'

'His car was gone?'

'Yes. There's only one garage, so he parks in a visitor's parking bay. Sometimes he parks around the block if Mrs Shimansky complains, but it wasn't there either.'

Daniel had once told me that when he was in France he ached with longing for Africa, and it was there that he'd discovered the music of Youssou N'Dour at an open-air concert. He'd listen to his music as we drove at night. He talked about elemental music patterns that acted as a bridge between Africa and Europe, saying that African music was closer to the beating of a heart than Western music. High office towers rose above us in the moving darkness. The mountain, one of the seven spiritual sites in the world, loomed in the background. It could have been a game of dodgem cars, directed by some master of the galaxy – the city, our little car, just one of many racing by with their own little destinations in mind. We were all play tokens, zipping around, occasionally colliding, hypnotised without knowing it. In the grip of this fantasy, I'd feel an eerie, pregnant silence pushing against our bubble of music. Daniel liked to be driven at night, his mind far away from me. There were times when I felt he was fighting the inclination to sit in the back like a passenger and shut me out completely, but I told myself I was imagining things.

'He doesn't really like driving,' I said. 'He says it requires too much concentration. Sometimes he'll stop the car and I'll take over. Or if he can't sleep, I'll suggest a drive. When we get back home, he'll make us a plate of pasta and open a bottle of red wine, and then we'll make love until the morning. Red wine makes him horny.'

Elijah Bloom cleared his throat as if a rusty nail was sticking there. Maybe it was more than he needed to know. The more I spoke about Daniel, the more a sense of loss overwhelmed me. I did not think it was grief. Grief and loss are different, I feel sure. Perhaps grief will follow later. Elijah was very patient with me.

'I'll need more details on the car,' he said. 'A car is often easier to track down than a man.'

'Yes, of course. So, anyway, after I don't see Daniel on the beach I decide to go back home and wait for him. I found myself wishing we hadn't given Brutus away.'

'Brutus?'

'Our dog – my dog – a dog I once had. The body corporate rules don't allow dogs.'

'Why is the dog important?'

'That was when it started.'

Et Tu, Brute?

I COLLECTED BRUTUS FROM THE SPCA in my early P&P single days when I rented a city duplex with a tiny garden, in an area that turned out to be plagued by night-time robberies.

'Something big that looks vicious,' I said to the young woman with the strong, capable calves who accompanied me past the rows of lost and destitute dogs. 'And it must be vaccinated and neutered; I don't want to come back.' We stopped in front of a cage. Brutus was leaning his whole body up against the fence as if he was trying to push his way out. It was difficult to relate him to any dog species that I knew of.

'He looks pretty vicious, don't you think?' the young girl said with false enthusiasm. I could see she was wishing that the ugly brindled giant would stop wagging its tail. Even though her face was obscured by dyed blue-black hair escaping from a pink plastic barrette, I got the feeling she was watching me.

In the office, she fumbled through the filing cabinet drawers. The necessary forms eventually emerged, but she kept a broad, dirty-nailed hand firmly on top as she passed them across. 'I think you should know – it's our policy to warn people – the other staff

39

call him the kamikaze dog. This will be his,' she flipped through the papers, '*third* home. He keeps on getting out and running into traffic. That kind of thing runs up some awful vet bills.' She sounded as sad as I'd ever heard anyone sound about a troublesome dog.

Just my luck to run into the Florence Nightingale of the animal kingdom. Still, I didn't want to be rude to a kind-hearted girl who, for some unfathomable reason, didn't want me to have the dog I'd chosen. I decided to change the direction of the conversation. 'What do you call it?'

'He's got his own name. The name he came in with. We stick to that name.'

'Okay.' I tried to help her along, but she didn't respond. 'So what is it?'

'Brutus,' she said. 'He had a litter-brother called Marcus. Marcus was run over on Rhodes Drive, just below the memorial. You know, the same place where those buck are always getting run over? I think that's why Brutus keeps on running away. To look for Marcus.'

I considered disillusioning her, explaining that in strict historical terms Brutus was a cad and a skunk and a traitor. He probably led Marcus into the traffic. But it was too complicated. Anyway, she didn't want to know. To her, Brutus was a cuddly teddy bear who needed love.

I felt a little sorry for her. We were about to enter into a business transaction. She should have been pleased I was about to pay her for letting me take a stray off her hands. Brutus was going to get a blanket and food and clean water every day. If I was out of town, I'd get somebody to come in and feed him. What else did she want from me?

'It'll be fine,' I reassured her. 'The place where I live has a fence and a gate. Look, I'm in a hurry, so can I sign those forms and pay you?'

Reluctantly, she lifted her hand and let me take the forms. Once I had signed everything, she took the pen from me and tucked it behind her ear with a strand of blue hair. She looked close to tears. 'I'll get him out for you.'

I'd worried about how to get the dog into the car, but it turned out to be easy. The creature bounded onto the back seat as if I was the escape plan it had been banking on. The next time it got into the car was when I moved from the city duplex to Monica's garden flat in Camps Bay.

Honestly, I took the dog because it was the biggest and ugliest dog on the row that day. Its fur was patchy and one ear was lopped off, but it looked as if it could easily knock a man off his feet. I never believed it was going to frighten anyone off, not with that wagging tail, but I'd set off with a purpose that day, and I wasn't one to turn around once a decision had been made. That made it easy for me to give the dog away once we got married and moved into our Camps Bay apartment. Daniel couldn't believe I'd actually known about the No Dogs rule. I tried explaining it to him. I hadn't invested emotionally in the dog; I'd just acquired a temporary guard dog. What I hadn't anticipated was Daniel and the ugly mutt becoming big mates.

We left the dog behind with my landlady while Daniel set out to find Brutus a new home. He asked around and stuck pictures up on noticeboards at the vet and the local supermarket, but nobody called. When the bored animal nearly caused an accident after digging its way to freedom under a ramshackle fence, Daniel finally had to acknowledge defeat.

In the end, it was Daniel who took the dog back to the SPCA, with its collar and lead and bowls. He borrowed a trailer to take the kennel as well. It was just a packing crate he'd put a makeshift roof on, but he said they'd give it to someone who couldn't afford a kennel.

There are times in one's life when one doesn't expect to feel bad, and then one does. I had never felt any need to have pets like other people did. It was a bit like having children: time-consuming and pointless. But watching Brutus leave with his tail between his legs, reluctant to jump into the car that was going to take him back to the doggy version of death row, had not made me feel proud of myself. Still, I hadn't expected Daniel to be so unsettled by the whole thing.

After he got back from the SPCA he jammed on his headphones and listened to R.E.M.: '*Tell me why, tell me whyyyy.*' When I called him for supper, he said he wasn't hungry. We ended up arguing. I told him he was being childish; he told me I lacked feelings and stormed out, banging the door behind him. I'd made paella with Mozambique prawns to show him I'd forgiven him for making such a fuss over a dog. The paella ended up in the dustbin, the prawns floating to the top to spite me. But the next evening, I came home to find the apartment cleaned up and Daniel back. He said he'd bumped into some people he knew at the Buddha Bar and slept on somebody's couch. It was nobody I knew, just casual acquaintances.

We didn't ever talk about Brutus after that. We were busy settling into our new sea-view apartment, and with all the unpacking Daniel seemed to forget about the dog.

At Elijah's suggestion, we had adjourned to the comfort of the lounge, where he'd let me get Brutus's story off my chest without interruption. I had to smile a little. Here I was, spilling my guts to a PI. This must be what it felt like to visit a psychologist, delving into the small shitty details of your life, getting it out of your system. The Dante family had never been big on therapy.

I pondered Elijah's tranquil approach from the couch as I sipped boiled green water from a hot mug cradled between my good hand and the bandaged one. There was a time when I would have refused the grassy liquid. But I had come to the point where I was prepared to relinquish some control, content to let someone else make small decisions for me within that enclosed space.

Elijah was waiting for his tea to get cold. He kept on looking around him, almost sniffing the air. 'We'll need a good copy of your fingerprints and Mr de Luc's,' he said, 'for us to match against in the future. Do you have something he used that hasn't been washed, like a glass?'

'His mug is on the window in the study. I haven't touched it.'

'The pencil sketches are very accomplished,' Elijah commented on his return from the study, the mug carefully sealed away in a plastic bag.

I knew he was referring to the year planner on the desk, covered in Daniel's drawings.

'Sometimes on a Sunday he does these quick sketches at the beach – like the street artists in Venice – and people come over to take a look. At first nobody makes a sound – it's just squiggles – but then you see something taking shape, as if you're looking through the squiggles, and then people start to gasp. From one moment to the next you can see what he's drawn. Most of the time he just gives them away. He said – says – it's relaxing, that a writer needs a diversion. Once he said that real life has its own pull.'

'Truly a man of many talents,' said Elijah, without a trace of irony. 'Do you mind if I take a quick squiz into the drawers and cupboards?' he asked hopefully. 'It seems the study was where he spent most of his time.'

I gave my permission and he went trundling off again, a bloodhound on the search. Background noises filtered through. He was trying hard not to sound like an intruder, but it wasn't quite working. It didn't matter; he wouldn't find anything. Daniel was too careful of his privacy.

'Nothing,' announced Elijah on his return, sitting at the opposite end of the couch.

Nothing. Such a desolate word. Not a trace of my husband's whereabouts. What had Elijah been hoping to find? I could have told him: there is nothing in this apartment that could explain why my husband would abandon ship, get stabbed in a park, or just plain vanish.

'Absolutely nothing,' he repeated, as if I hadn't got it the first time.

I was suddenly exhausted. 'Is that it? Are we done?'

Elijah glanced at his wrist. His watch looked as if it had been built to explore the furthest corners of outer space. 'I've overstayed,' he declared, springing to his feet.

I stood up and went over to my laptop bag. 'Here: the list of what he took with him. Basically one set of clothes and his wallet.'

'What about a credit card?' he asked.

'He didn't have one.'

He nodded, scanning the sheet of paper before folding it and sliding it into an inside pocket. On an impulse, I handed him his newspaper. He folded that too and made it disappear.

'Good night, Paola,' said Elijah, patting his jacket pockets to make sure he had everything. It struck me that an oversized houndstooth jacket must be a very useful item in a sleuth's wardrobe.

In bed that night, I brooded over the word 'absolutely', a word I had never trusted or liked. Was it permissible to conjoin the word 'nothing' with 'absolutely'? Even though 'nothing' was strictly 'nothing' and not a jot more.

When day finally broke, I donned running shoes and tracksuit, and set off on a slow jog in the chilly morning air, something I'd always watched others do with enormous indifference. After a youth spent in delightful, enforced indolence, I'd never seen any necessity to acquire the habit of regular physical activity. That first run of my life, I hardly knew how to move my stiff limbs, shuffling like a cuckoo bird emerging on an ungreased mechanism. But once I made it halfway round the block, each step forward began to amplify the oddly pleasant warmth that pulsed through my veins. And later, after a steaming hot shower and a cup of coffee with toast and Marmite, a peaceful languor settled over me. The tightness beneath my breastbone seemed to have eased.

A Simple
Theory

Some information would only have distracted Elijah.

I never mentioned the small mystery that had presented itself the morning after I lost Daniel. An annoyed Mrs Shimansky arrived at my door to complain about a burnt patch on the brick paving. The security guard had seen Daniel making a pyramid of sticks and paper and setting it alight.

'He's away,' I'd said calmly. 'It couldn't be him. The security guard must have mistaken someone else for him.'

'Someone else?' Mrs Shimansky snorted. 'It's always someone else. Is it a ghost that feeds the pigeons on the entrance pathway? Is it a ghost that puts his chair in the corridor to watch the sun come up?' She walked off, shaking her head.

Later, on the way to my car, I'd furtively sought out the blackened paving in the parking area. The image of the hooded girl at the bus stop flashed through my mind. Could a teenage vandal have slipped past security into the yard? Mrs Shimansky was a senile old bat.

Late at night, when I reviewed the question-and-answer sessions with Elijah, whole sections seemed more like long underground conversations with myself.

What do I know about Daniel's background? To answer that, I'd have to tell you about Nicky. But I find myself unable to do that just yet.

'I knew Daniel from university,' I had replied to Elijah's question. 'He was a friend of a friend. He left a year before I finished. Anyway, we went our separate ways. You know what it's like: everybody says, "Let's keep in touch", and then nobody does. Somebody from our old crowd said he was living in France and he'd become a writer. So you can imagine my surprise when I bumped into him at the laundromat just around the corner from where I was staying.'

He'd phoned me. The switchboard operator put the call through to the conference room just as an important meeting was about to start. It was terrible. The awkwardness of two old friends, their past a monster in a jar as they talked in muted voices. He'd found me on the P&P website. I asked him to phone me back later. He made me wait for days before following me into the laundromat. I was nearly crazy by then. I had even dreamt it was Nicky who'd called me from the other side, pretending to be Daniel.

When Daniel stepped back into my life, I had moved from the duplex to a garden flat in Camps Bay. It was a cheap lock-up-and-go arrangement that suited me as I was away during the week. My landlady fed the dog. On Saturdays I escaped the other tenants by going to the laundromat. There were the usual creeps but nobody hit on you if you looked scruffy and bad-tempered, something I managed with ease. One day my white load came out sherbet pink, thanks to a red lace G-string I'd missed that belonged to Monica, my landlady.

I went ballistic. 'Shit! Why can't she wear normal underwear like the rest of us?'

Someone behind me snickered and handed me a laundry basket.

I turn around and Daniel was standing there grinning at me. My first thought was that I'd forgotten how beautiful his eyes were. In that moment we are back on the emperor bed. I have turned away from my daredevil blond boyfriend to laugh conspiratorially into the dark-haired boy's intense eyes.

'The same Paola,' Daniel murmured. 'La jolie brune déterminée. Still trying to control the world.' Then he'd kissed me on both cheeks, French-style, elegant and contained. He said he'd spotted me crossing the road a few weeks ago, and then he'd called at the office but I'd been absorbed, so here he was. What about a cup of coffee at the café around the corner? He'd moved back to Cape Town recently – he wasn't sure for how long – and he visited the city bowl often, he said.

'You don't stay here?'

'No, I live out of town.'

I remembered waiting for him to say more, and then becoming impatient. You always had to worm things out of Daniel.

'Where out of town?'

'Bulldog Beach.'

'Bulldog Beach? Where's that?'

'It's a private beach on the West Coast,' he explained. 'The original land belonged to a childless English couple who developed the property and bred bulldogs. They would dress their dogs up and walk them along the beach in male and female pairs. Soon every property owner had their own cute little bulldog pair with matching outfits.'

'You're making this up.'

'Pas du tout. This is a dinkum story. You see how straight my face is?'

I must have still looked disbelieving because Daniel lowered his voice for dramatic effect and leaned closer. 'But there is more. Eventually all cute little bulldogs grow up into oestrogen- and testosterone-driven sex machines. Can you imagine the spectacular sunset mating rituals on that protected beach? Et voilà! C'est comme ça que le nom est arrivé. And so the beach gets its name.'

At that point, I'd dissolved into laughter.

Elijah's voice broke into my reverie. He was asking for a physical description.

'He has incredible hands with long fingers,' I said.

I recalled thinking how charming this new sophisticated Daniel was, in his crisp linen shirt. He spoke English with a slight French accent now, and his voice was more vibrant than I'd remembered, more confident. The boy was gone. He had gained muscle weight and grown taller, the way some men do in their twenties, and the thick, wavy brown hair was worn longer, in the continental way, but he had the same striking dark-green eyes and playful grin.

How to explain Daniel's peculiar male beauty? It was unusual in a man. And it wasn't only my bones he turned to quivering jelly, women of all ages were fascinated by him. My friends could hardly take their eyes off him, and then they were embarrassed by their own lecherous thoughts.

'Whatever he does, you notice his hands,' I said again, 'the way he touches things, and holds them. Even when he folds washing. There's a delicacy about them – for a man.'

Sheona, my best friend and a psychology major, had said he was Edgy. I could hear the capitalised word.

'Edgy? Is that good or bad?' I had asked. She'd said some men exuded sexual energy, and it could go both ways. She called me a sexual neophyte – borrowed from her textbook – and implied that Daniel was just the man to enlighten me. Call it what you will, I'd shrugged, annoyed with her know-it-all attitude.

'Basically, he's extremely hot,' she acknowledged.

'I'll need a clear colour photo, as current as possible,' Elijah said briskly. 'A full-body standing shot is always useful. Let's move on to the coffee shop. It was your first meeting after how many years?'

'Eight years. He was twenty-two and I was eighteen when I last saw him.'

Down the road from the laundromat, waiting for our coffee, I watch impatiently for him to light up a cigarette. I feel the fascination the abstainer feels for the overtly reckless sinner. The Daniel I know and remember was always surrounded by plumes of smoke. When

I can't bear it any longer I ask. He says he woke up one morning and stopped, just like that. Comme ça! with a click of his fingers in the air between us. Why do I find it so incongruous? There had always been something about him that struck one as worldly and ingenuous at the same time. Now that he is older it is easy to imagine him as the lover with a hat in a monochrome movie classic, the music score fading away and the woman leaving on the train. He has that elusive air about him. It's as if he's the one who escapes even though he's the man on the platform.

'He talked about France and the wonderful cuisine and the wine terroirs, and I talked about my work and the overseas countries I'd travelled to.'

'Anything else?'

I've never had a man recite poetry to me before, and I've only recently started reading novels again – there at the laundromat, where they keep a shelf full of books left behind by customers. Daniel is speaking words of fiery beauty.

Elijah can't see us at that coffee shop, how Daniel murmurs 'courtesy of William Blake', as he helps me put my jacket on against the winter elements that beat and wail against the windows of the coffee shop. It could be yesterday.

'I had a paperback copy of *The Collector* with me that day. Daniel made some comment about Fowles being a butterfly collector as a boy, how that had influenced his writing. Then he said he remembered how I ate books up, that it showed my ferocious side, and that there was one particular poem that always made him think of me.'

'A poem?' Elijah probed.

'"Tyger! Tyger! burning bright ... Did he who made the Lamb make thee?" That's all I remember – two lines.'

'He recited poetry in English?' Elijah sounded impressed.

'His English was always excellent. As a student, his plan was to do a doctorate in English Literature at Oxford University one day.'

'So he was born in South Africa? He regards it as his home?'

'He was born here, but his parents came from France.' I hesitated. How to describe the change I'd seen in Daniel. 'Now he says all Europeans speak several languages. But he's still passionate about English poetry.'

'Could I have a copy of the poem?' Elijah asked.

Daniel and I hadn't made a particular appointment to see each other again, not in so many words. In spite of our history, we were now strangers to each other, with so many years gone by. Yet I was so certain that he'd be there the following week, I went to George the Genius, Monica's hairdresser.

'This is glorious hair, woman! Hair to be flaunted, not hidden!' George the Genius walked around me in one direction and then came back in the other, running his fingers through my thick brown hair, lifting it up and letting it drop again, as if it transmitted something inaudible to his fingers. Then he got right on the job. He whipped my boxy don't-mess-with-me-I'm-a-professional-woman bob, perfect for a tight ponytail, into a stylish mass of soft dark curls that bounced as I walked. George whizzed the hand mirror around behind my head with the panache of a matador, revealing a new more adventurous me in supersonic blurs.

'This is the look,' he said, waving a hair magazine in front of my nose. The pouting girl with 'the look' sported my new swinger's hairstyle and a pair of gladiator stilettos that defied gravity.

'We will let it grow. I'll show you how to pin it up for work. It will be a new, softer look that will turn heads,' pronounced George. It seemed that my new hairdresser and I were in this together.

'Swankyyy, girl!' Monica wolf-whistled when I walked in. 'Go get him!'

'I feel like a walking shampoo commercial.'

She grinned. 'If he doesn't notice, you can always hit The Bronx with me on Saturday night.'

Daniel noticed. He looked at me in wonder, as if he'd never seen my hair before.

'Well, if that isn't something to behold,' he said. 'I can't think of a poem that would do justice to hair like that.' I blushed like a schoolgirl, and he grinned with satisfaction.

'Daniel has a way of knowing what I'm really thinking, even

when no one else does,' I said. 'The last person who was able to do that was my father – before he screwed up big-time.'

Elijah Bloom jotted a few words down – I imagined something succinct, like *Father – follow up!!!* – and then paged back and forth, tapping with his pencil, going over what he had so far.

Elijah Bloom's low-tech approach to the nightmare of Daniel's disappearance was educational. My job was to lead project teams in the race to implement state-of-the-art technology that gave companies a competitive edge. In our time-is-money business, you had to be an adrenalin junkie. In theory, an IT project is akin to a warzone, and a good project manager, like a good general, wins the war by making calculated, intelligent decisions. The reality was that proven, time-worn principles often fell by the wayside. At university, I'd researched the ancient arts of problem and conflict resolution, studying what good generals did to keep their troops resolute under adverse conditions and in the most terrifying circumstances. My role models were Napoleon, Hannibal and Shackleton, leaders adept in the strategies of warfare and survival, and my personal guru was the most revered general of them all: Sun Tzu.

It seemed to me that Elijah had a lot in common with the legendary strategist and author of *The Art of War*, who taught that achieving victory required not only foresight but a certain amount of insight: 'If you do not know others and do not know yourself, you are destined for failure in every battle.'

I'd progressed in a different direction. In addition to being Ms Iceberg, I could wield a pool stick like a pro and hold my alcohol as well as most of the men I worked with. A dead brother and father had to be good for something. The best compliment I'd ever received before I met Daniel was, 'You've got balls,' delivered in slack-jawed awe by a company director on a project that entailed playing darts in the client bar after hours. I'd just beaten him 2–1 on a three-series round of Killer. He wasn't to know my father had taught me to win, no matter what the game or who the opponent. My brother had taught me that a humiliated opponent loses the will to live. And that was why I resisted the impulse to inflict total annihilation and allowed the company director to win one series.

'That's all there was to it in the beginning,' I continued. 'We'd wander off to have a cup of coffee while our washing spun round and round.' I could have been reliving a dream or a previous life. 'Could we take a break?'

'There was just something I wanted to go back to.' He flipped back in the notepad. 'You spoke about a mutual university friend. Would he be somebody who might have kept in touch with Daniel?'

'Nicky? No, he wouldn't have kept in touch.'

'You're certain?'

'Dead certain.'

'What is his full name? Just in case it comes up in the investigation.' His hand was poised over the notebook, his blue eyes almost wistful. A case was not just a case to Elijah. It was a mission to unexplored realms.

I submitted to what had to be. 'Nikos van den Bogen. He's dead.'

When I returned from the bathroom, Elijah was busy making sandwiches. 'Supplies,' he'd said by way of announcing his arrival that morning, shoving a brown paper bag into my hands. I sat on the bar stool and watched. His sandwiches were the hearty type, with thick slices of fresh brown bread and blocks of cheese.

'Gherkin?' He extracted a dripping swamp-green object from a jar.

'Do you actually eat those disgusting things?'

'Every day,' he said. 'Okey dokey, fresh tomatoes ...' He slapped three slices of tomato on top of the cheese, added some salt and pepper, and compressed the sandwich as he cut it in half.

'Do you ever get a feeling of déjà vu?' I asked, getting two plates out of a cupboard. 'It happened to me just now, as if I'd been at exactly this point of my life before.'

'Most people say it's dreams,' he replied between bites. 'Others say it's a hallucination, something that seems real but isn't. Sometimes a chemical imbalance can do that.'

'Some cosmologists believe that déjà vu is actually the collision of parallel realities,' I mused. 'But that's just mathematical models. Anyway, ever since Daniel left I've had the feeling that I'm reliving an episode I've experienced before. As if I should know what's going to happen next, but it doesn't matter how much I think about it, the significance escapes me. It wriggles away, always one step out of reach.'

'The brain is a mystery,' Elijah said sagely.

Maybe he's at home waiting for me in another dimension.

'Sometimes I have to question people who say they've been abducted by aliens.' He gave me a sideways look and enough time to stop him. But what the hell, I was curious, so I let him go on. 'There's the occasional fraud or mentally unstable person, but most of the time you can tell they're sincere.

'Once we got called out because a swing in a kids' play park wouldn't stop swinging. Every other swing in that play park stopped when the kids got off but not that one. A little girl had disappeared in the area a few months before; some people said it was her ghost. Eventually they dismantled the swing.'

'Who's "we"?'

'The Intergalactic Detective Society.'

I just carried on eating so he continued. 'Then there's a small village in the Karoo that's had unexplained electrical fires for years. They've had experts from all over the world trying to come up with a rational explanation for why their toasters and microwaves explode, but no one has any idea. There's a real belief among the townspeople that aliens are running tests from outer space. These days, most of them avoid anything electrical, hoping that the aliens will lose interest in them.'

'It's weird, but it still doesn't prove anything.'

'That's the problem. After all these years, I still don't know for sure. Not in a scientific sense. The bottom line is: I've never seen a flying saucer.'

'So why do you do it?'

'They say you've either got faith or you haven't. You can't trick yourself into believing. Conversely, you can't stop yourself believing if you have faith.'

'But that doesn't make it true,' I observed.

'No, it doesn't,' Elijah agreed.

We finished eating our sandwiches in contemplative silence.

'Shall we continue?'

Talking to Elijah had started up a rollercoaster of memories. I edited everything as I went along. It was not necessary for Elijah Bloom to know the extent to which the chemistry between Daniel de Luc and Paola Dante was still there. We both knew it from the moment I turned around and looked into his eyes. I was once again an explorer in a mysterious, dark-green jungle, unable to resist the powerful vine that wrapped itself around my ankles. Monica knew right away – her unashamedly sexually liberated lifestyle had resulted in extraordinarily well-developed antennae where matters of lust were concerned. When I offered to do her washing at the laundromat, she became instantly suspicious.

'I'm enjoying the time to myself – catching up on all the reading I've been missing out on.'

'Oh yeah, sure!' Monica said. 'Be my guest.'

A leisurely walk past the laundromat was all she needed to put one and one together. 'So, who's the stud?' she wanted to know when I returned. 'What are you waiting for, girl?' she said, after wheedling the story out of me. 'I might even nab him if you don't do something about it.'

But I couldn't, or wouldn't. It could have been the past that was holding me back, but more likely it was the future. I enjoyed our weekly rendezvous, spending the time of a wash cycle together over a cappuccino, Daniel's eyes blazing as he talked about books and films and politics. But our relationship was going nowhere fast. Perhaps it was just one of those things that wasn't meant to be. I hid behind lame clichés. 'When Daniel came into my life again, I hadn't been in a relationship for a while.' Elijah Bloom looked up as he noted the resonance in the word *again*.

When the away project I was on reached completion, I was given a choice of assignments: Zurich on a bank project, hand-holding the client through the three month start-up phase of a multinational project; or Cape Town, as programme manager for an oil company. My superior, Piet van den Berg, a principal at P&P, enjoyed offering two-option scenarios. That way the illusion of consensual decision-making was maintained.

But our discussion didn't pan out as expected. He sat opposite me, blinking with bemusement. What was I up to, choosing the cushy overseas gap option instead of the local career-advancement opportunity? Was I suffering from burnout? His stubby ginger lashes blinked rapidly as he processed the implications: he'd have to find someone else capable of handling a heavyweight client for the Cape Town project; the project estimates would have to be recalculated; my CV, which had already been given out as part of the original proposal, would have to be pulled back.

Too bad, Pietie.

'I need a change, that's all. I've never been to Switzerland.'

'Emma is the account manager for the Swiss project. She'll be your contact person. You sure about this?'

'Relax, Piet. You never know, Emma and I might be buddies by the end of the project. Besides, I *adore* Swiss chocolate.'

I smiled at him sweetly. His flabbergasted expression was comical.

Later I heard he'd taken a bet with Andrew that I'd choose the home option. Ordinarily, he'd have been right. I was tired of out-of-town commuting, and I avoided doing projects with Emma if I could help it. To Ms Patterson, a project was merely an extension of a smoothly honed sales campaign to win hearts and minds. The reality of implementing state-of-the-art systems went right over her ambitious account manager head.

'So, why did you choose Zurich?' Elijah asked.

'Patience is not one of my virtues. I was getting tired of meeting Daniel once a week for coffee. Maybe I was hoping to shake him up. I've always had a contrary streak.'

Maria, Maria, cosi contraria, how does your garden grow? Before our family fell apart, my father used to sing that all the time. My second name was Maria, after my paternal grandmother. He preferred it to Paola, I think. He had a saying: *You've got to keep shaking those dice; you never know what might turn up.* That was my inheritance. My father was a closet gambler, and in the end he gambled everything away. Including his wife and daughter.

I don't know what I expected, but Daniel acted as if he was pleased for me about The Swiss Opportunity, as he came to call it.

'Three months? All expenses paid? Allez! C'est fantastique!'

When Daniel de Luc said goodbye to his old friend Paola Dante he sounded wistful.

'I'll be here, same laundromat, when you get back.' Maybe he held on to her hand a little longer than necessary, and maybe something passed between them. She offered her cheeks, first left and then right, for the standard two kisses. When he stepped back, he looked as cool and debonair as ever.

We were nothing more than laundromat pals. There'd been no exchange of phone numbers. I wasn't even sure he had a mobile phone in those days – he'd never used one in front of me – and I kept mine on silent in my time off. I decided to move out of the garden flat and away from the area on my return. I told myself things weren't working out with Monica & Co. Much as I liked the incorrigible Monica, I'd run out of patience with the affairs of passion that rocked our communal abode. We'd become accustomed to being woken up by Monica's current love interest, local model and TV soapie star Gloria Quina, screaming 'Fucking psycho bitch!' in the small hours at the top of her voice. Enraged by the sultry Gloria's promiscuous exploits, Monica would dump her belongings on the pavement in front of the house. Later, Gloria would ring the bell and promise never to do it again, and by that evening she'd have moved back in. When I asked why she put up with it, Monica grinned and said making up was worth it.

The truth was that I chose The Swiss Opportunity because I couldn't stand the weekly proximity to a man who made me feel that I existed for a higher purpose.

Piet was right about one thing. Emma Patterson and I were two incompatible human beings. A clash was inevitable, particularly since I hadn't been involved in the original proposal and presentations to the client. It took me forty-eight hours to familiarise myself with the project, and another three extended days to produce a feasible project plan and revised budget. When Emma heard about the changes, we practically had a stand-up fight, both of us up on our feet snarling at each other over the bemused client's head. It was certainly not a professional exchange. Finally, Emma set up a teleconference with Piet. His opinion was that the matter was better tackled up front than later. Did she need him to get involved? Emma glanced at me and said that, no, that wouldn't be necessary; we'd manage the situation ourselves. I'd won.

But watching her negotiate her way through the acrimonious project board meeting on the only sunny day since I'd arrived in Zurich, I found it hard to feel triumphant. I even experienced a twinge of sympathy as the chairman and his executives ripped her carefully constructed cage apart like sharks in a feeding frenzy. I found myself wondering what Daniel was doing today. When my turn came, I felt curiously detached. I didn't give them a choice. Did they want a successful project? As I looked at the smooth, bloated faces of the men around the table, I thought how different Daniel was.

That evening, in a far-away winter city, a project manager walks into a warmly lit hotel after a hectic sixteen-hour kick-off day and spots a colleague in sales sitting alone at the bar in the foyer. The Puss-in-Boots outfit is unmistakable. I curse softly under my breath. The barman is shaking his head and pointing at a hotel sign, pointedly ignoring the slim manicured hand and its empty glass.

'Emma, it's past closing time. Let's go,' I say.

'Oh, it's Miss Goody Flat-shoes. I don't want to go. My bed's too cold. Unless you want to sleep with me?'

'We'll put the heating on.'

'I can't breathe when the heater's on.' Ms Puss-in-Boots turns back to the barman. 'So, if I don't get a drink, where do I find a warm-blooded male in this ice palace?'

'I'll ask housekeeping for a hot-water bottle,' I say quickly, before he can respond.

'Loser!' Ms Puss-in-Boots mouths at him.

'Come on, Emmie.'

'Mmm. You haven't called me that for a long time.' There are dark smudges under the red eyes. 'They're great, huh?' Ms Puss-in-Boots sticks a booted leg out and giggles. 'Those wankers today couldn't stop ogling.'

'No, they couldn't,' I agree evenly.

The red eyes narrow. 'I want some Horlicks too.'

'I'll see what I can do.' I shift my laptop to the other shoulder. 'You're right. Swiss hot chocolate tastes like shit. Now let's go.'

'Shit!' Ms Puss-in-Boots mouths at the bartender before standing up unsteadily and letting me put an arm around her waist.

It's almost like we are first-years again, I think. Almost.

'Next time, you refuse her a drink before she gets drunk,' I hiss at the barman over my shoulder. He just shrugs and takes the empty glass back.

When Paola Dante finally gets Ms Puss-in-Boots into bed and switches the light off, a quiet voice comes out of the darkness.

'You were a real bitch today.'

A week later, Emma was on her way back to Cape Town. I was free to do things my way.

During the days, I practised total control and fine-tuned schedules with OCD precision. But in the nocturnal hours, with the lamp-lit streets of Zurich deserted except for a few late-night revellers and city cleaners, the lifelike mannequins in luxury ensembles my only company, I'd see my wakeful reflection in a lit-up display window. She would stare back at me as we kept pace and I'd wonder who this other woman was, the woman in a thrall I didn't recognise. Crossing empty squares, pausing at icicled fountains and watching swans glide by under stone bridges, I inhabited her frozen glittering dream.

Whose bed was he in tonight? Why hadn't I taken his number? And what would I say? My body longs for you every second of every day of every week of every month that I'm away? The thought of you makes me so crazy, I can't concentrate? Let's talk about what happened to Nicky?

That wasn't my style. I was behaving like a besotted schoolgirl. There was only one way to handle the situation. And that was to walk away from it.

There was so much I didn't tell Elijah, but he seemed to fill in most of the gaps for himself. Later, when we knew each other better, he told me that he'd come up with a simple theory: Everybody wanted somebody to love and they wanted to be loved back. 'Sounds pretty cheesy,' was my comment. Elijah said I should read *Tuesdays with Morrie*.

'Who's Morrie?'

'It's a book. Morrie's a dying professor.'

'I can't wait.'

'There's even a movie.'

Risking
Absurdity

FOUR MONTHS AND SIX DAYS after leaving for Zurich, I was back in the sun-baked Mother City, the winter displays of Europe a remote memory. The big news in the office was that Emma Patterson was pregnant.

'It's a case of the immaculate conception,' gossiped Andrew.

'Why do you say that?'

'Didn't you know? Her husband's got some motor-neuron disease. That's why she's always alone at the office functions.'

'I didn't know she was married.'

I'd found a temporary flat, but it was stuffy and depressingly dark, so I'd already arranged to go back to Monica's. Nothing else had changed in all that time. When I heard Daniel's voice on the phone, I had to sit down.

'The circus?'

Drums roll, cymbals crash, lions roar, a thousand white doves lift off in a flurry of wings, a Chinese doll with a parasol cycles on a slim cable suspended in space, the flying Olsens do a triple trapeze somersault, Tikkie the dwarf-clown bounces off a circus-tent pole and flattens Bozo on the canvas – all in a breath-taking instant.

Who could have remained standing through that? It wasn't just his voice – in a more innocent time I'd had a thing for the circus. I was the child who clapped and laughed all the way through the clowns' act, no matter how absurdly sad or slapstick they were, the same child who insisted on going to every circus that ever came to town. Now the laundromat man was asking me to go to the circus with him.

'Yes. The Moscow Circus is in town. There's a new act with twenty trained cats. And a talking cat never before seen outside of Russia.'

I remained silent. I wasn't sure what to make of this. Was he playing the fool with me?

'Are we going alone?'

'Why, was there someone else you wanted to invite?' He didn't miss a beat.

I was too annoyed with him to say anything.

A snigger came down the line. 'You can relax. I am not divorced and there are no little petits so you will not have to share your popcorn.'

I found my voice. 'So can you read minds, or what?'

'Only yours. Say you will come. I bet you have never seen twenty cats on a seesaw.'

'How did you get my mobile number?'

'Your friend, Monica. I went round to the house when you didn't reappear at the laundromat. I phoned around – a frighteningly efficient woman on the ratepayers' association gave me the address.'

I had told him about Monica Stratos and the dilapidated rose-washed house with the ground-floor flat leading into a rambling garden over one of our coffees. I'd mentioned it was on a list of historic protected properties in the area. He'd gone to all that trouble to find me? Had I deliberately left a trail to lead him to me? I called Monica, who confirmed that asking me to the circus definitely qualified as a date, although it wasn't a *romantic* one. It was her way of managing my expectations. But Monica was wrong. We couldn't keep our hands off each other. Someone had opened the floodgates and the dam burst. That was all it took – I just needed to know he wanted to be with me. Lying together in the huge old bath later that night, facing each other, he said he'd wanted to ask me out months before but I'd acted as if my work was the only thing I cared about. When I came up with The Swiss Opportunity he'd almost given up on me. But he couldn't get me out of his head so he'd called the P&P offices when the three months was up. Nobody there could tell him when I'd be back. He'd finally come round to wondering *why* I'd wanted to put distance between us. That maybe I was testing him.

It was so typical of a man to think like that, I burst out.

'You are here, are you not?' he reminded me, smiling lasciviously as he ran his foot up the inside of my thighs.

A Cat Stevens song line came back to me: '*I swam upon the devil's lake*'.

I shut my legs tightly, crossing ankles, arresting the movement of that climbing foot. 'What was the circus thing about?' I demanded. 'How did you know?' There was a moment's silence. *Nicky*.

We are having lunch. My father is giving my rich boyfriend insider tips. He tells him how much I love the circus, how I once dragged my baby brother up to the big cats' cage and he peed in his pants. I say rudely, That was right about when you left, wasn't it?

Daniel improvised, looking straight into my eyes across a lake of bubbled water. The circus? Ah, oui, he really loved circuses, always had, always would, so he figured if I really loved circuses too, then maybe I was the girl for him.

I grabbed a towel and climbed out of the bath. I told him it was time for him to go and handed him a towel. He got dressed and I let him out. I was standing with my back against the closed door when he knocked softly. I flung it open. He kissed me with the intensity of a man who had nothing to lose.

I love you. I always have. Nicky is in the past. I heard the words as clearly as if he'd uttered them aloud.

The next day, he went back to meet the cat master and his

feline friends and helped them pack up to leave town. The cat master swore the cat he used for his ventriloquist act was the direct descendant of a real talking cat. *On ne sait pas quand il retournera.*

Over time, and during our marriage, I discovered I had misjudged him. It was only a half-lie to protect me. Daniel truly did love circuses. After that first date we never missed a visiting circus and he always bought ringside seats. Sometimes he went alone to the matinee shows and visited with the circus people after the show. He once commented that his mother hadn't believed in circuses but didn't elaborate.

One day, Madame Zingara's Theatre of Dreams comes to town. This time there are no cats but a trapeze star from Budapest, blond wavy hair to his shoulders, defies gravity with a virtuoso solo performance on the high wire. Diaghilev's snow music peaks in symphonic rapture as Count Laszlo loses his footing. In the split second that death enters the tent – the audience gasps and holds its collective breath – almost no one notices the woman shoot up, her face bloodless, or that she sits down again just as abruptly, when the handsome blond youth dangles before them. Scattered applause breaks out as the performer regains terra firma and raises his arms. His sculpted physique is so graceful, his apology so tenderly executed that she can barely breathe.

On the way home the husband says, 'The poet like an acrobat climbs on rime to a high wire of his own making.'

'Should that mean something to me?'

'A true artist must constantly risk absurdity and death. The boy will always be mediocre. Nothing more. That's what Ferlinghetti meant.'

'You're being ridiculous, Daniel. He would have died tonight if he wasn't wearing that safety wire. Would you have preferred that?'

'Infinitely.'

When she finally retires to bed she turns her back stiffly to him but her husband, who is still awake, pulls her towards him.

'Dove sta amore
Where lies love
Dove sta amore
Here lies love,' he whispers in her ear.

The woman feels she can't love the man just then – she can only imagine plummeting bodies and split-second timing – but as he moves lower beneath the blanket, she thinks she would rather die guilty than have his mouth and tongue stop what they are doing.

Occasionally, when I'm utterly alone and my absconded husband might as well be a puff of conjuror's smoke, it's only his tinny circus music that convinces me any of it happened. I've started to see us from a distance. Daniel always said the heart has its own intelligence. The rest of me is preoccupied with day-to-day survival but my heart remembers.

I know what real love is now. It's when you can't keep your hands off each other, and you can't let the other person out of your sight without feeling as if part of you has walked away. It's when a kiss is a kind of near-drowning experience where you break to the surface gasping for air, oxygen rushing to the head like champagne. It's when you look into a crowd at a wedding reception and feel the beloved's gaze pull at you from across the room; or turn a corner in the park and the first thing your eyes light upon is him sitting against a tree trunk, the canopy of leaves vibrating oxygen green; or walk down an escalator into a crowded shopping mall and, undirected, your eyes fall upon him. It's as if a magnet were permanently engaged between two entirely separate corporeal realities.

I held on to that. It was real. Whatever we felt, it was real. Just then at that time, I was certain of that.

He couldn't stop loving me, any more than he could stop loving the circus. That's what I told myself. But I knew as well as anyone that we humans are prone to ideas, and that one contrary idea could have far-reaching consequences.

I began to remember all kinds of things.

Perdition

BESIDES THE OCCASIONAL DISAPPEARANCE, Daniel seemed happy as a lark on the marital bough. One morning I woke up and a year had passed, and it was weirdly nice to find him snuggled against me on the futon, an arm and a leg flung possessively over me.

We had a fight at the weekend. In the great books of literature, we women are not shown as petty, sniping prima donnas. From the pens of the literary giants we acquire beauty and majesty, and, best of all, a mysterious allure that draws men to us and keeps them enthralled. But in real life we call the men with whom we share the rites of intimacy 'old women' when they keep us waiting, and tell them they're worse than our mothers, who couldn't be punctual if their lives depended on it.

Daniel didn't retaliate immediately – that wasn't Daniel's way – and he played the role of the loyal husband at the year-end work function I dragged him to, smiling graciously as he was introduced and being impeccably polite all evening. But he punished me mercilessly by flirting with Emma Patterson, who was back in shape, cling-wrapped in a provocative red number with a plunging back. I responded by engaging in animated conversation with big Theo van de Watt, who was sans petite blonde wife. Theo was the CEO of a major client where I regularly consulted; he had the physique of a rugby player and exuded the confidence and sex appeal of an exceptionally well-travelled man who enjoyed wielding power. He'd made it clear from day one that I was fair game by inviting me for sundowners at Blues after work. I'd politely declined, of course; I had no intention of getting into an awkward situation with an important client. That was Emma's speciality. And she did it so well! On the other hand, an occasional game of darts or drinks on company premises wasn't flirting; it was taking care of business. I agreed to meet Theo in the P&P bar later that week to discuss 'project progress' not long after Emma put a slim, well-manicured hand on Daniel's arm.

Daniel drove home with a locked jaw, acting as if he didn't know me. Of course he didn't know me. Jealousy wasn't my style.

I'd regretted the patronising words almost instantly, but what has been exposed to air cannot be recaptured and taken back. And then it hadn't been so much the words that sprang Daniel and me apart but the rancid bossiness of an older woman's voice striking from within the voice of the beloved. How many steps to perdition?

The day after the work function was a Saturday, so we went to the Salt River fresh produce market to stock up. Daniel relished these outings. I'd teased him once, in the early days, saying that in his previous life he must have been a chef in France. He'd stopped then and given me an odd look, considering my words. On this Saturday morning in December, just the right time for fat, juicy plums, he headed straight for the fruit.

'I have eaten the plums that were in the icebox,' he said, offering me a purple-red globe, 'and which you were probably saving for breakfast.' It took me a moment to realise he was spouting poetry again. He used his finger to clean the corner of my mouth where the sweet juice dripped.

'Forgive me,' he said, 'they were delicious so sweet and so cold.'

That poem is transcribed in my pillow book now. By William Carlos Williams, it says.

* * *

Three days after Elijah came to our apartment he had news for me relating to the copy of Daniel's birth certificate I'd kept with our wedding papers. Mother: Marie-France de Luc. Father: Antoine de Luc. Gregory had changed his mind: that was all Elijah ever said. August had taken the trip to Empangeni, the stated town of birth, on Elijah's behalf. Municipal records and local newspapers of the time had been pored over, but to no avail. Parish priests had been visited and church and synagogue records examined, but no evidence was found of any religious ceremony ever having been performed on a boy named Daniel de Luc. No parents. No teachers that remembered him. No school records. No hospital visits. No friends. No Marie-France de Luc or Antoine de Luc. No family. No neighbours. August had not been able to find a single thing that proved the corporeal existence of Daniel de Luc.

Elijah's investigations led him back to Home Affairs. The details on the birth certificate matched the information on archived computer files. The identity number of a dead man with the same birthdate as my husband had been 'borrowed'. The only way they'd found it was because his contact still had access to the old system; records weren't moved over to the new if the person had been dead for more than ten years.

'And, hey presto, Mr de Luc gets an ID record that's practically the genuine article,' Elijah said gently, putting two photocopied records down on the kitchen counter so I could see them. I could feel him watching me to see how I'd take it. 'It was a smart move; it's not easy to pick up those kinds of frauds.'

Oh yes, my Daniel was always smart.

I sat down on one of the high kitchen stools, staring at the images of two different men with matching details, trying to gather my thoughts. Elijah had brought proof that my husband's identity had been pilfered off a redundant computer system. The Daniel de Luc I knew existed only in a crack of bureaucratic oversight. My diligent PI had no way of knowing that I'd almost expected it.

A stranger had tried to warn me – weeks before I went the private investigator route – but I'd relegated her to the category of an eccentric crackpot. Now I could no longer deny the facts. Daniel had been lying to me for years. This meant there was a possibility that everything the Lazzari woman had said was true.

The enigmatic Enid Lazzari had contacted me out of the ether. That's what it had felt like, anyway – her eerie prescient voice on another desolate evening. She caught me in the bath contemplating perdition. It was Day 5 with no Daniel and I was nearly out of my mind with worry.

The incident after he took the dog back *wasn't* when it started. I'd been going through it all in the bath and felt better when I remembered. It started a few days after our wedding lunch. We'd spent the weekend moving into the apartment and I'd gone back to work on the Monday. I came home to a note saying he was doing research for a book and that he'd be back in a day or two. I remembered some part of me registering with relief that he'd finished unpacking the boxes. A couple of nights later, I'd walked in late after a long day to find the apartment lit up, Daniel reading a book on the couch, and dinner in the warmer drawer.

I'd eaten my supper on a tray while he spoke about driving around the countryside, how he'd stopped now and again to talk to people, and how he'd come upon a farmhouse on a stretch of deserted road framed by misshapen, wind-beaten trees where he'd stopped and asked for a room. The room he was offered was spotlessly clean and comfortable and the German farmer was hospitable. The farm had a quaint name: Groot Grafwater. He'd come to it just outside the missionary town of Wuperthal. The meetings of the day still humming in my head, I'd listened with one ear, my attention finally jolted by the realisation of how far he'd travelled over mountain tracks and fords to get to a place he hadn't known existed. He'd mentioned the three children quiet as mice, the woman being pregnant with a fourth and the man reading from a German family Bible at the dinner table.

When the phone rang, I was tallying the numbers in the bath. The longest Daniel had ever been away before was four nights. I sat up straight in the bathtub listening. An image of a hospital reception area flitted through my mind but I immediately discarded it. *Trust him to phone when I'm in the bath.* It was after ten in the evening. Why was Daniel doing this to us? The mutt next door started yapping madly. Officially, dogs weren't allowed in the apartments but Sharon Berger was blind and she'd been there forever so each successive body corporate made an exception.

I stepped out of the bath, naked and dripping wet. I was hyperventilating, I was so furious with Daniel. Husbands were supposed to stay home. Wasn't that one of their functions? That they should be available when you needed them to be?

He'd said I should marry him while we waited to cross at a pedestrian crossing in the city.

'Why?' I'd asked, pumping the red pedestrian button.

'Pourquoi non? I can't think of two people with more reason to get married.'

We had made our way through the middle of the pavement flower sellers. Daniel emerged from the humid, water-misted air, saturated with sweet floral scents and exotically spiced breaths, holding a big bunch of white and orange roses.

'L'amour c'est une folie, n'est pas?'

Weeks later he'd brought up the topic again on top of the mountain, a tablecloth of fog hiding the Mother City and its coastal bays from us. We had climbed up through the forest to the view-site next to the water dams.

'Do you really think it's a good idea?'

'Of course. Otherwise I would not be asking.'

It was peaceful in his arms, surrounded by white, swirling mist.

'Why don't we just live together?'

'Living together is what people do when they are afraid love will fly out the window when they are not looking, as a bird can escape from a cage. Then one day they wake up and look at the person lying next to them and decide the person is fat and ugly and they have been proven right. And so they live in a state of sin against love.'

He held me tighter. 'I am explaining it badly. Marriage is the true test of love. It has the stamp of the eternal. Otherwise what are we to each other? Another amiable liaison? Another change of address? Je me débarasse des autres obligations.'

It was said softly but I'd heard. 'What other obligations?'

'I want the whole shebang with you. I want to risk everything.'

'You don't know enough about me. What if we're not compatible?'

'So tell me.'

'I'm a professional career woman. I don't want any children for a long time. Maybe not ever.'

'I can live with that.'

'I'm not religious at all and I never will be.'

'You see, we are made for each other! I have enough religion for both of us.'

'You do?'

'Oh yes, absolutely. I will say prayers for both of us. The Almighty always listens to a sinner.' His tone was serious but his eyes were smiling at me.

'You're laughing at me.'

'You are very beautiful when you're so serious.'

'If you ever walk out on me I'll hire a hit man at the taxi rank and have you shot in the knees.'

'That seems fair to me.'

'I can't stand people using my towel and I always have my own coffee mug. I also can't stand dirty floors, toilet seats left up, and draughts.' I was finding it difficult to concentrate with his mouth nuzzling my neck through my hair.

'I think we can get past those problems.' His hand reached under my T-shirt and undid my bra with miraculous ease. The lingering caress of his hand across my breasts had the effect of electrical pins plugged into my skin, charging electricity through my veins. I had to gather together the remnants of my willpower to finish what I had to say.

'I hate fuss, so no big wedding or anything like that.'

'It will be just you and me.'

You and me ... You and me ... A buzzard circled overhead, its mewing cries background echoes as Daniel laid his jacket out with the flourish of a musketeer inviting me to lie on his cloak. We made fierce love on a grassy ledge on top of the mountain.

A summer holiday we'd planned to Zanzibar over the Christmas festive season became a honeymoon. In typical style, Daniel had uncovered an excommunicated Catholic priest who agreed to conduct a nuptial mass in exchange for a donation to his ramshackle interdenominational church. For an additional donation, the Portuguese padre would also take many, many photographs of the happy couple. So we are forever captured on film: exchanging gold wedding bands that Daniel produced from his pocket under a bamboo structure on a beach, holding hands, kissing, talking, gesticulating, and walking against a backdrop of cloudless azure sky and full-sailed dhows moving across the distant horizon. After the impromptu ceremony, the white-bearded padre insisted we stay for lunch and meet his family. With a graceful bow of her head and a slight movement of her hand, his young wife invited us to sit at a low table covered with clay bowls of fragrant spicy food. When I picked up the camera, she quickly backed away on her knees, covering her face with her scarf. She crept back after I'd put the camera down. The children giggled as she deftly demonstrated how we should break pieces off two freshly baked flat loaves and dip them into the dishes.

Back home in the new year, we went through a civil ceremony. Monica had booked a lunch table outside at a new restaurant on the promenade in Camps Bay, which held pulsating salsa parties when night fell. My mother and a few family members and university friends joined us, and Helen and Ernesto gave us a box of French vintage champagne as a gift. Daniel, with a large white napkin tied around his neck, tucked into a huge bowl of pasta with mussel and garlic tomato sauce and pronounced it to be excellent. A few days later he departed without warning, leaving me a note. That very first time he was only away two nights.

Now here I was, twenty months later, dripping water everywhere. I breathed out three times in quick succession, giving myself time to control my voice, so that he wouldn't hear the forded fury. I ended up sounding cold-hearted and brisk.

'Hello? Daniel? Is that you? Should I fetch you?'

A woman's voice said, 'I have a message from Gabriel.'

The fury left me. The carpet under my feet felt soggy. The familiar suffocating fear constricted my windpipe.

'You must have the wrong number. There's no Gabriel here.'

'You've done the right thing, not calling the police. You'll never find Gabriel if you involve the police.' She spoke in a soft, oddly tuneless voice.

'I don't know anybody with that name.' I slammed the receiver down.

The phone rang again. I switched on the answering machine and waited until it kicked in. I sat listening, shivering from head to toe.

'You think you're a tough cookie, don't you? I know your husband as Gabriel. You can contact me at this number, day or night.'

I listened to her recorded message again and again, but there was no doubt. She said, 'I know your husband as Gabriel.'

I left the answering machine on after that, but at the last minute I would always answer the phone myself, grabbing at the receiver. There was no sign of Daniel and no word from the mystery caller again. I could smell him in the apartment, more with each day that passed. I left his cupboard open. I buried my face in the thick pile of his bathrobe. The smell of a male. Not the smell of his deodorant or his aftershave, but the smell of human male. It lingered in the air as I fell into a troubled sleep on the goose-down pillow I had given him for his thirty-third birthday, imagining it would help with the insomnia. I didn't change the bed linen or the towels, imbibing his scent through my pores.

When I arrived home from work, I walked on the beach until night came. I went away from the lamplight along the path, into the pitch darkness of wet waves that circumscribed the shoreline. The car guards in their glowing yellow bibs watched me impassively as

I emerged from the tumultuous blackness, and then I walked back to the empty apartment and ordered take-away food. I worked on the laptop in a daze, sometimes falling asleep at the desk. Each morning I considered phoning in sick, but once I managed to brush my teeth and wash my face, I knew I would make it through another day.

I jumped every time my mobile rang, so eventually I put it on silent mode and just listened to messages. In the apartment I took calls on the landline. My mother called to say she was off to Amsterdam to visit a gallery that was interested in Jerico's work. I knew of Jerico Lotter from previous calls. A plumber by trade, he had started painting after a car accident left him paralysed on one side and wheelchair-bound. Jerico would be housesitting for her from now on so I needn't bother. She sounded smug. How can a semi-paraplegic look after a senile dog and a vicious cat? Is it possible that my impossible mother is falling for a pony-tailed plumber who is thirty years her junior?

I'd hardly put the phone down when it rang again. This time it was Annie, my sister-in-law. She leapt right in. 'What's wrong? Are you sick? You don't sound right.'

I tried the age-old excuse women use, even to each other: it was just that time of the month, the usual sore back, cramps and swollen boobs. But I might as well not have bothered.

'The two of you are arguing, aren't you? There's something wrong. I can feel it. Hey, are you pregnant?'

'Oh God, Annie, not you. I'm too young to have kids.'

'How's lover boy?' Annie was the only woman I knew who was impervious to Daniel's charm. She'd never said she didn't like him, but she had a funny habit of keeping her lips firmly pressed together if he was in the room. As if she had to contain herself around him.

'How's Max? How'd the first day go?'

'Oh, great! I took masses of photos. He looks so grown-up in the uniform with those black polished shoes and the blazer. Can you believe it? He wouldn't kiss me goodbye, just turned his cheek and said he was too big for that stuff now. I'll send you some pics.'

73

Max Jnr was a hyperactive brat but in his mother's fond eyes he had grown angel wings the day he was born. I was just congratulating myself on successfully deflecting her suspicions when she came right back.

'You'd tell me, wouldn't you, Paola? If something was wrong? You know how it is with me.'

Annie's full name before she married my brother was Marta Annalena Jacoba van Tonder. Her colourful ancestry included a great-great-grandmother who could foretell the future and was credited with finding natural spring water for Simon van der Stel's grandiose agricultural pursuits before she succumbed to madness, and, more recently, a single-parent mother who supported herself and her three daughters by drawing up astrology charts and telling fortunes as she went. Annie herself had a university degree in forensic medicine and practised as a pathologist, saying she preferred the real dead to the unreal dead. Her sister, Secunda, escaped her fate by relocating to Austria and playing first violin in a Viennese orchestra. It was left to the oldest, Leandra, to take on the career of a practising psychic, race-horse tips being her speciality, although you'd never believe it. She conducted herself with the flamboyance of an A-list socialite.

When Annie was born, her mother gave the names of Marta the mad water-diviner to her youngest daughter. Annie the forensic scientist and I had hit it off straight away. We didn't see each other often but we had agreed that psychic phenomena were all hocus-pocus and mumbo-jumbo, and we said so. In our combined opinion, science was making steady progress in accounting for so-called supernatural and paranormal experiences. Abnormal brain activity caused by electrical disturbances and sounds at frequencies not normally heard (such as an overhead ceiling fan might make) seemed like reasonable explanations to us. Leandra had just shaken her sleek head and proclaimed that Annie was in denial; her powers came directly from great-great-grandmother Marta.

'Paola, the spirits want me to ask if Daniel is there.'

My sister-in-law freaked me out when she talked like that. It all started with Massimo's death – my brother and her husband, the dreamy soccer-mad boy who became a police detective and ended up in a shallow grave.

My scalp prickled. I had to remind myself that Annie's voices were the equivalent of a nervous breakdown. It would take time for her to recover. 'You can tell your spirits to relax, Annie. Everything's fine.' Technically, it wasn't a lie; it was within the realm of possibility. Annie finally let me go. I needed to sit down. I knew I should probably eat something.

On the seventh desolate night, I picked up the receiver and dialled the number.

'What do you know about Daniel? Do you know where he is?'

'Good, that's much better. Meet me tomorrow at Harriet's on Loop Street. You'll find me at the table at the back, next to that lighthouse painting.'

We met the next day. A flaming blue sky and the boom of the noon cannon on Signal Hill accompanied me as I crossed the street. Harriet's Restaurant, an inner-city institution, had a world-weary air about it. I hurried past the greasy pine tables and chairs, through the unlit interior with its thick odour of fried food, ceiling fans turning lazily overhead.

'He said you were tall.' A spiral of cigarette smoke undulated worm-like from the table under the lighthouse painting. The tiny woman sitting in the corner didn't move except to remove the cigarette holder from her mouth and release smoke from bright glossed maroon lips before putting the cigarette out as she waited for me to sit down. She wore a midnight-blue dress encrusted with the outlines of golden creatures. The coiled, plated bodies and whipping tails of embroidered dragons shimmered in the gloom. She was quite possibly a Chinese midget.

A biology lesson memorised: A midget is a perfectly proportioned little person born as the result of a genetic malfunction; dwarfism is most commonly the result of a growth hormone deficiency.

'My name is Enid Lazzari,' she said. I stared at her, rudely I'm sure, nonplussed. Her miniature frame exuded a glow, much like a firefly in a dark forest. Monica's thuggish cat Marmaduke had the same hair colour as her. It hugged the small head like a shining orange helmet. Quid pro quo. Bright inquisitive monkey-eyes inspected me back.

Get a hold of yourself. She's just a crackpot who shops at flea markets.

She took my hand and turned it over before I saw it coming. My hand felt hot and clammy under the overhead light, all beating blood and throbbing veins. I yanked it back.

'Are you a psychic? Is this about money?'

I was fighting an attack of something that felt like motion sickness, as if I was at the railings of a ship going down in an ocean of ten-foot-high waves.

'I have always strived to see beyond science.' She looked at me with that penetrating, insistent gaze of hers. 'These days I concern myself with specific fields of treatment.'

The waitress leaned closer to hear my hoarse request for a cup of tea. A stone glinted in the cartilage above her left nostril. She was probably around my age.

Did piercing the nose cartilage hurt more or less than a soft earlobe?

Daniel and I wander into a jewellery shop in the mall after catching sight of a window display that includes a treasure chest of natural pearls and matching drop earrings. The pearls glow oyster-pink against the deep purple velvet, an effect the jeweller lovingly describes as *pearlescence*. Daniel decides spontaneously that it is a small price to pay, getting one's ears pierced, if such splendour can be had. Our heated exchange is held in front of the astonished jeweller in a store full of customers. Why would I want extra orifices? I have enough of my own. And Daniel's caustic response: What are you afraid of? That someone will mistake you for a woman?

I waited for the waitress to leave. 'So what are you? A psychologist?'

'I prefer to call myself a psychotherapist,' Enid Lazzari replied.

'How do you know my husband?'

'Has Gabriel told you about the night terrors?'

'I'm hungry. I'm going to order a sandwich.'

In desperation, I beckoned the waitress over again. Maybe food would clear my head.

'What can I get you?' Fluffy peroxide-blonde hair framed a pleasant face. The piece of costume jewellery in her nose made the unflappable waitress seem even more human. I had the absurd urge to ask her to stay, to sit next to me on the padded bench opposite the peculiar little woman in her Chinese outfit.

Instead, I asked for a toasted cheese and tomato sandwich.

'White, brown or wholewheat?'

'Wholewheat.'

The waitress asked Enid Lazzari if she wanted anything to eat but she shook her head, asking instead for a glass of tap water.

'Why do you call him Gabriel?'

'My patient's name is Gabriel Montaigne. I have known him a long time. As I was saying, I treat him for a recurring form of nightmare.'

I absorbed this information.

'Where's your office? What kind of treatment are we talking about?'

'My home and my office are close by. We talk mostly. Hypnosis has been partially successful. We have been able to relive the circumstances of his upbringing.'

My heart was jack-knifing with the desperation of a fish caught in a net. 'What circumstances?'

'Gabriel was four years old when his mother joined a religious commune in France. He was a sensitive boy who was fond of birds and animals. His first recollections of that time are of being separated from her.' She paused, for effect maybe. 'He spent much of his childhood running away and avoiding the police. When he was twelve, she made the decision to rejoin the outside world and came to South Africa.'

What does a person do when told something like this about her husband? Something so fundamental and mind-blowing that she knew nothing about. She ploughs on, regardless.

'Daniel is the man I married. That's who's missing from my life right now. I don't care about who he was. We were all somebody else at some stage.'

Her eyes glinted in the darkness. After a moment she returned to her narrative. 'Three years ago he rang my doorbell to say he was back. He'd been in France, he said. There'd been a woman. Later he spoke about other women. You're all different. He has a different reason for going with each of you.'

'What are you saying? That my husband's been married before?'

I sounded breathless and panicky, even to myself. One of those female responses I'd always despised. As a small child I'd demanded to pee like the boys did, facing the bushes. When I turned seven I announced that I was to be addressed only as Paulo. My tomboy leanings had amused my father immensely and he'd gone along with it, introducing me solemnly as Paulo, ignoring my mother's fulminations.

The dark, unblinking pupils bore into me. 'You and I both know *Marriage*, with a capital 'M', is not the only possible close relationship between a man and a woman. There are other relationships.' She consulted a notebook. 'The longest he has ever stayed with one woman is a total of ninety-one days. You have broken all the records.'

She wants to rattle your cage. She is pretending to know everything about him.

'Why are you telling me this?'

'His threshold of reality is quite different, to yours, for instance. For a man like him, the constancy of marriage can be a dead end. Usually it is best to let such a man go.'

Did I imagine the sly challenge in her voice? I wanted to be sick. I thought of Daniel's random gifts while we were dating – a poem, a sea shell, a posy of wild flowers, a meal, a pencil sketch of my bare foot, all delivered with the exact number of days that we had been together. When did he stop counting?

My darling, my darling, my darling, I cannot live without you. This is not possible. This is not happening to us.

I left the table abruptly and hurried to the bathroom. I vomited into the ancient, yellowed toilet bowl, heaving a thin, rancid fluid, and then sat on the cracked seat and rocked backwards and forwards for what seemed like hours but was probably a few minutes, feeling more desolate than I had ever felt in my whole life. And that was saying something. More desolate than when my father blew his brains out in the garden because the notion of a lingering demise was distasteful to him. More desolate than when my brother's beaten body was unearthed from a makeshift grave. More desolate than when my father left me behind, taking Massimo with him. *A boy's place is with his father; you must stay with your mother. It's all decided.* Perfect recall is a curse. Reliving these moments reminded me how I had despised my mother for letting her husband, my father, go without a fight. And the meek shall inherit the Earth. Was that all religion taught one?

Night after night I had boxed my pillow, tears streaming down my cheeks, convinced that if it had been me I would not have given up until he came back home. The tears had dwindled until eventually they dried up altogether.

With my last breath I will love you.

I washed my face with cold water and returned to Enid Lazzari, facing her. I dreaded her pity, but her voice was steely, unsympathetic.

'Are you able to continue?'

The cheese and tomato sandwich had turned cold and rubbery in my absence. I eyed her coldly. 'What if I don't want to forget about him?'

She shrugged, flexing little plump fingers. 'It seems you are the only one he has agreed to marry.' She made my attractions sound mysterious. 'If you were a different woman I'd suggest a child.'

The words were delivered without any intonation of emotion to warn me. Some things never leave you.

What does she know? He's a writer. He writes stories like this. He doesn't live them. Comforting, empty words. I hadn't slept for days. The half-eaten sandwich was the first attempt at solid food in two days. The bleak lighthouse painting gave me the creeps. *Roman Rock, 1986.* I was so confused that I wanted to weep.

'I always ask for the same table. It's a remarkable piece of work.' The mechanical toy voice cut through my reverie.

I wasn't there to discuss morbid paintings. 'Let's pretend for a moment I was this different woman. Why a child?'

Her sigh was a soft hiss in the hot restaurant. 'We are all co-creators with the universe. Call it a hunch based on a lifetime of looking behind the scenes.'

She knows. He must have told her. He really thought I'd come round.

'To accept responsibility for a defenceless child is a logical evolutionary stage,' she continued, sizing me up with every word. 'A privileged step on the journey, if you prefer.'

I leaned forward and looked her straight in the eyes.

'It's a bit like the chicken and the egg situation, isn't it? How am I supposed to have his child if he's not here?'

'It is not necessary for a child to be of one's blood for one to love that child.'

'So, whose child would it be?' I asked, stupefied.

'I cannot help you with that.'

'Perhaps the police can help me.'

The bright eyes darkened. 'I had hoped you would understand. It would not be wise to involve the police.'

'You tell me where he is and I won't have to go to the police.' I was tired of being accommodating. 'Of course I might just go to the police anyway and tell them you have information on my missing husband that you're withholding.'

She tilted her head to one side, eyes glittering.

'I've been out of the country. He left a message on the answering machine saying he was going away.' She picked up the glass of water and drank from it, taking small unhurried sips. 'He also asked that I should tell you there is no cause for concern. That was it, nothing else.'

He's alive.

I sat back, stunned. 'No cause for concern? I'm nearly crazy with worry and that's all he can come up with?'

She was silent, the small hands on the table in front of her.

'Why should I trust you?'

'It's up to you,' she replied neutrally, 'but through the years he has kept in contact with me.'

'He made me marry him. He said he wouldn't live with me in a state of sin.' You don't know everything.

Her eyes flickered in the gloom. I couldn't tell if it was surprise, or something else.

'The theory of unconditional love is different to the practice. As you are discovering.'

I left the woman Enid sitting at her table. On my way out, the waitress and I passed each other. I couldn't leave not knowing one small thing, so I stopped her.

'If you don't mind me asking, what kind of stone is that in your nose?'

'It's a Swarovski crystal. Pretty amazing, huh? My sister-in-law sells them. Do you want one?' I saw she was far younger than I had thought, unabashedly enthusiastic and gracious to the uninitiated.

'Yes, amazing. No, but thank you. I was just curious.' I wouldn't have been curious before. I wouldn't have spent a minute wondering about it. But at that moment, light-headed with hope, I got that it was a new-age crown jewel, born of a mysterious alchemy of earth, water and fire, not just a piece of common glass.

I crossed the road and walked into a quiet stone church next to a park. The inside was as unassuming as the outside, without extra decoration or frills, the bare bones of a church with a shrinking parish. I sat on one of the hard pews and wondered what my father saw in churches.

The meeting with Enid Lazzari had induced a kind of daze. Tons of loneliness pressed in upon me, even as I set my shoulders against its weight. Could it all have been different?

Stone walls dissolve into walls of light. Our first husband-and-wife argument is a humdinger.

Daniel is working at his desk in the sunny corner room. He

calls me to watch the play of autumn leaves swirling in an updraft and then pulls me onto his lap. 'One day this will make a good room pour un petit,' he says serenely.

I swing around to look at him. 'I don't want babies. I told you that.'

'Actually what you said was that you didn't want children yet, and you might never want any. It sounded more like a declaration of independence than a definite no.' That scandalously sensual mouth grins at me with supreme confidence.

'I got over babies a long time ago, Daniel. You were there, remember?'

He holds me tighter, digging his chin into my shoulder. 'I think it will be good for us.'

'So, who's going to look after this cherub while you're wandering around the countryside?'

'I'll stay home more.'

'Oh, give me a break, Daniel. Kids don't have a battery you can remove. What happens if I'm on an out-of-town project? I have a career, you know? Teams of people depend on me. I work the hours, I beat the deadlines so that some day I'll be a partner. Kids are attention junkies.'

'We'll work it out. Remember our first date? How we talked about how great it must be to take your own kids to the circus?'

'If I recall correctly that was a theoretical situation you posited. I was hormonally unstable that night – I had the hots for a sexy Frenchman. I've now remembered that I don't want any. *Ever.* Is that clear enough?'

We are both up on our feet. He runs furious fingers through his long dark hair.

'It's unnatural.'

'Is that in comparison to a bear? Or maybe to a she-wolf? What gives you the right to say something like that? You act like you're Hemingway. At least he actually wrote books.'

'You can be a real bitch. It's probably best. With your level of maturity.'

'Well, thank you for that, kind *sir*!'

'The pleasure is mine.' A half-bow, one arm slammed across the chest in sardonic rage, and then he abruptly leaves the room. A door slams in another room and after that it's quiet except for the trickle of tap water running into a glass. My hand is shaking.

Yesteryear's brilliance dissipates.

Rules of
Engagement

I WENT TO SEE CARRIE FISCHER. She couldn't find anything physically wrong but there was obviously something not right (one glance at me had persuaded her of that) so she wrote a doctor's note giving me a week off and said I should take it easy and avoid all stress. And I had to eat.

I faxed her letter to the office for Piet's attention. Then I disconnected the landline, put my mobile phone on silent, watched TV and followed my GP's instructions by gorging on fast food. I thought I might balloon until I popped. A relatively pleasant way to go. If suicide by expansion wasn't such a messy procedure I might have seriously contemplated it. A slow, lingering death – date and time unknown – by comfort foods that I'd eschewed for years in the quest for physical wellbeing and mental fitness. I no longer cared about preservatives or MSG or artificial flavourings affecting the clarity of my intellectual faculties; the offending substances seemed quite benign when viewed against the bigger scheme of things. I ordered three lots of fried chips, one KFC special 'Going West' chicken and cheese burger, and the family basket of eight chicken portions without blinking an eyelid. But

I hadn't lost it completely. I cleaned up after myself. I was not planning to die by cockroach invasion.

I was having leftover pizza for early supper when I heard a distant approaching clanging and barking in the neighbourhood. My sluggish, toxin-dulled brain worked out it was a Friday, rubbish collection day, and our apartment block was the last stop en route. I felt quite pleased that my deductive reasoning powers were still sufficiently intact to come up with this basic conclusion. As if this was further proof that I hadn't lost it completely. I walked around the house collecting rubbish from the dustbins, emptying them into a black refuse bag with methodical efficiency. It was in this pleased-with-myself-for-the-first-time-in-days mood that I walked into the study and peered into the litter basket stuck away in a concealed corner between the desk and the wall.

A wad of pages lay curled up in the basket, printed face turned away. I recalled *The Shining*: manic Jack Nicholson raising lunacy to a new level. Had Daniel sat at the desk and written the same line over and over again? *Marriage sucks. Marriage sucks. Marriage sucks.* I was so wound up that I fully expected to see words to that effect staring up at me. The study had always been his room. He hadn't objected to the new apartment so badly once he'd seen the study with its big windows. A huge wild fig tree stood outside so the room was always cool, catching a few rays of sunshine in the afternoon. If you were sitting in the study it was easy to imagine you were in a house on stilts because we were the last apartment on the row. On a clear day you could see mountain crags and cobalt sky through the deep green foliage of the branches. He'd brought himself and the rucksack along, together with the shoulder bag and a suit carrier full of clothes, a typewriter, the hand-blown Murano artefact and a crate of books and CDs. The typewriter was soon abandoned. I ended up working on my laptop on the bed while he took over the PC in the study. The desktop computer was an outdated machine I'd saved for in my varsity days; the laptop was provided by work. I was just relieved he'd settled down.

I could picture him in the study, the day he'd first seen the apartment, his physical body diluted by a big patch of sunshine, looking around in that curious but remote way of his, absorbing the room. *Scotty, beam me up.* There was something elusive about Daniel. Sometimes he made me feel as if the man I'd fallen in love with was visiting from another planet.

I lifted the wad of papers out and opened it. The title was done bold and hand-drawn: 'LADY LIMBO'. A lightning sketch of a wasp-waisted vamp in an airways uniform and stilettos served as a cover picture. And, in the bottom right-hand corner, 'Gabriel Kaas', in Daniel's handwriting. *My patient's name is Gabriel.* I flipped to the next page and the next and the next, glancing over the rough penned sketches and occasional paragraphs of dialogue. It looked like I'd found an early working copy of some kind. In typical Daniel style, he'd managed to flummox me once again. Nothing gave him greater satisfaction than hunting down ancient, out-of-date illustrated magazines at second-hand bookshops. Was that my restless husband's métier – the adult comic book genre? Somehow I didn't think so. But right now the municipal refuse collection service was swinging away around the corner.

The men in yellow overalls had already moved past but they retraced their path obligingly after I hollered. One of them doffed his cap politely before taking the trolley bin by the handle and rolling it away.

'Thank you for coming back,' I called out to his back, my tongue a thick wad that had lost its way around the spoken word.

He turned around and bared two pointed teeth with a gap of toothless gum at me, producing a grin with the bloodthirsty charm of one of Buffy the vampire slayer's victims.

'Dis net 'n plesier, mevrou!'

The other day, a male caller to a local radio station had elaborated on the mouth as an erogenous zone more easily and frequently pleased in the absence of sharp front teeth. Another caller had said it made giving blowjobs easier. It seemed inconceivable.

I took *Lady Limbo* into my bed, escaping the nauseating smell of carcinogenic fast food in the lounge, and started reading. I remembered something Daniel had once said: to do a comic you had to have the storyline plotted out up front; that's how books should be written. It was my guess that the intermittent comic style was just an entertaining way of conceptualising a new book.

The title recalled the outrageous Lady Limbo of our student days. In those heady anarchic university days I'd found the whole notion of making an appointment for wild sex with a stranger that culminated in natural conception highly amusing.

Daniel had once explained that a writer is permanently on the lookout for possible protagonists. In *Lady Limbo,* the female protagonist (the femme fatale on the cover) is a sublimely sexy French ground stewardess whose heart belongs to no one. On her off-duty day, Amélie enters an anonymous brick building, declares that she wishes to conceive with '*a real man*' (the reader imagines the 'r' rolling off her Gallic tongue), and cavorts naked on a bed with a muscular partner (a few artfully suggestive sketches). The action skips to nine months later (nurse's speech bubble: '*It's a girl!*'), when she checks out of the hospital with her baby. As far as I can make out, Amélie is our Lady Limbo brought to fictional life. That's the thing about fiction. One doesn't know how much of it is fact. Even when it's illustrated. And especially when the writer's made himself scarce.

Lady Limbo turned out to be a dark mystery thriller set in Paris. He hadn't bothered with changing the name used on the original message – there was no copyright on the World Wide Web – and the enigmatic alias was perfect for his purpose. The body of a woman is found in some vegetation next to a river by two schoolboys on a fishing expedition. In the graphic, the lifeless woman on the riverbank is wearing a corset and suspender belt and one stocking is still neatly clipped into place around her cold but attractive thigh. From the detective's discussion with the pathologist, we find out the cause of death is strangulation by (missing) nylon stocking. Intercourse with penetration had taken place prior to death but it is impossible to say whether the sex had been consensual or not. A tattoo of a snarling tiger on her lower back is checked against police records. Dental records confirm that she is a ground hostess reported missing by her flatmate.

An ex-boyfriend does some digging around in Amélie's affairs.

He comes to know that Amélie had an alter ego: a chatroom addict who went by the name of Lady Limbo. He goes through her files and locates an online chatroom where an organisation called Real Man Inc. advertises its services. It becomes evident that Amélie burnt her fingers playing with fire. He finds correspondence with a mysterious suitor identified only as Albert. Emails fly back and forth – the male character (Albert) is sketched from the back, sitting at a desk computer. The words, '*Ma chère Amélie*' are legible on his screen. Amélie is shown firing off messages from a laptop that she carries everywhere in her shoulder handbag. Flying computer screens frame passages of dialogue – the rough beginnings of a book are starting to materialise.

Ma chère Amélie … I feel I know you better now that we are on first-name terms. I had some time so I came to watch you yesterday. I sat at that little café opposite your counter and could not help but be impressed by how masterfully you handled one troublesome foreign visitor after another. How I admired the light touch with which you organised hotel rooms, lunch vouchers, transport, the overwrought Italian woman whose luggage had been mislaid somewhere between Florence and Paris after her flight was grounded by an electrical storm, and still your gay, frozen smile never slipped. How jealous I was when that tall, handsome American took your slender hand in his and held onto it as if he would never let go. I suffered to see you in his clod's grasp. If I was a warrior of old, I would have taken my sword and beheaded him for such impudence.

Cher Albert … It is you who are impudent. How dare you assume the role of my protector? I have no need of a knight in shining armour. I find they suit me not at all and fit badly to my peculiarly independent constitution. I suggest you find a damsel in distress. You are betting on the wrong woman.

Ma chère Amélie … I am not a betting man. Rest assured my intentions are not those of a gentleman. My interest is purely carnal. There is not a hint of propriety in my thoughts. It is not a lover's tryst I suggest, which I know you will agree leads only to inevitable ennui, but ravishment. I feel sure you are as interested as I am in exploring the limits of sensual gratification. I await your reply with avid interest. You would do me a great honour if you would call me Albie. It is, after all, one letter shorter.

Cher Albert ... I am forced to agree with you on the issue of boredom. In other circumstances I might have found your attention flattering. But can ravishment for its own sake serve more purpose than enslavement to what passes for love? I do like the fact that you can count. Reductio ad absurdum. The precise science of mathematics is a forgotten pleasure in today's capricious world. Still, I think not. Oh, and about your name, calling you Albie would be assuming a familiarity I do not feel.

Ma chère Amélie ... If I had a heart it would be broken. But I am hopeful. Are you wearing those tight little skirts for me? And those new strappy sandals that succeed wonderfully in drawing attention to your exquisitely tiny feet. Am I right in saying you are a size 3? Have they been brought out from the darkest corner of your wardrobe, in preparation for the occasion you sense lies in your future? Have I entered your fantasies yet? Oh, how my blood leaps as you swing around the corner, the fabric stretched as tight as silken bandages against your naked flesh. I'm afraid that boyfriend of yours in security will have to go. Of course you see it, that he treats you like any cheap trollop. By the way, how is our child?

Monsieur ... I see you are, after all, nothing more than a common stalker. Let me remind you that you are breaking the rules of engagement. I have taken the step of reporting your unwelcome intrusion in my private life to the organisation. The rights of paternity are out of the question. I ask you to refrain from further contact or I shall have to file a complaint with the police.

Ma chère Amélie … Your heartless words set fire to my loins. Yet your attitude deeply saddens me. Such threats are ill-advised – you have our precious little daughter's health and happiness to consider now. Any attempt to involve the authorities will only complicate your circumstances. Did you imagine I would let you go once I had found you? Desire is a cruel, fickle mistress. I would have been more patient. But you have angered me now so I must insist on our meeting. Shall we say 11 pm tomorrow night in your bed?

The sinister, cryptic exchange gives me goose flesh. The correspondence raises the insane possibility that Amélie was murdered by a sex predator who is also the hired biological father of her child. Night has descended and a cold, salty wind blowing in from the roaring black ocean has reached our bedroom. I'm shivering but I can't stop reading.

There is something of the voyeur in us all. I could be watching an erotic home video with subtitles. I turn the page and a young woman with heavy eyeliner and smudged shadows under her eyes is sitting on a window ledge, her legs dangling, as the people below her go about their business, not noticing just yet. The perched frozen figure looks huge and tiny at the same time: a wingless bird contemplating its last flight into the void. We are inside her head with her fluttering memories, reliving choices made that cannot be undone.

There she is, a black pen etching of the day fear arrives, pacing her apartment, phone in hand: *'Amélie, C'est Isabelle. Il est fou. J'ai peur.'* It is part of a series – each scene starts with Isabelle's frantic messages. Who is this cold-hearted, unreachable Amélie? we ask ourselves. While Isabelle on the ledge revisits her own undoing.

Yes he was crazy that one. Always reminding her, not letting her forget. After Amélie had set it up, she'd met with him over breakfast months before. 'It's very simple. You meet with a handsome man in a nice hotel room. He orders a nice dinner with escargots and champagne. It's really a five-star holiday! Nine months later you get driven home from the clinic in a chauffeured car and on the seat next to you is an envelope with a large sum of money in cash. Et voilà! Your troubles disappear.' That was what he had said. 'I can start again,' she had thought to herself. 'This time I will stay away from the dealers and the gambling tables.'

There she is, the day panic arrives, pacing the clinic waiting room, phone in hand:

'Amélie, c'est Isabelle. Pourquoi ne me parlez-vous pas?'

When the tension becomes unbearable, Kaas punctuates the dialogue with dashes, the way a French writer would.

How unsettled Isabelle is later that day, still groggy, held down on a clinic bed.

– I want to see the baby.

– That isn't possible.

– I can't go through with it ... I'll pay the money back. I swear I will!

– Give her the injection ...

I feel sick to the stomach. When I reach out for some water my hand is trembling. What kind of animals are these people?

'Amélie, c'est Isabelle. Il vient. C'est fini.'

He is coming. My life is over. The final Isabelle sketch shows her body splayed on the pavement far below, crows circling, a crowd gathering for the sideshow, precisely as it might appear to the killer taking stock out of the window.

Lady Limbo gives no further clues but throws us back headlong into the seduction game between Amélie and Albert. Only now we have a new perspective. Could it be that Amélie is the ultimate temptress, one whose purest emotion is greed?

Ma chère Amélie ... Have you thought about my proposal? It is not every day that one gets the chance to leave one's old life and slip into a new one, the way one clips a newly purchased pair of silk stockings onto a favourite garter. My proposition is purely selfish. Call it a rich man's whim. Think of me as the devil and our little arrangement a devil's pact that cannot be undone. Did you not crave limbo? I offer you limbo. To the others I have offered only death. The terrible ennui they induced! Our little daughter will have her life. I look forward to meeting the other member of my instant little family. I am in my own way sentimental. What is the point of desire if we do not carry it to ridiculous extremes? Do you have an inkling of how far you will go? No matter. We will go there together. I have much to show you. L'amour c'est épouvantable.

Mon cher Albert ... You do yourself no credit to speak of love in such schoolboy terms. I have learnt that there is nothing less reliable and nothing more exaggerated. Love is quite unimportant to me. If you are truly the devil and understand my true nature then prove it and perhaps I shall dance for you one day. I am Lady Limbo, she who dances alone under the rod of fire.

That's where the illustrated draft of *Lady Limbo* ended.

Was it possible that my husband had made all this up? Had he dwelt on Lady Limbo's curious request all these years? Daniel had once said that every story was a metaphor. Was it his way of exorcising ghosts? Albert and Amélie – and tragic Isabelle – seemed real, as if he'd known such people in his life.

Nothing had been resolved. All the intriguing questions were left up in the air. Who is the murderer of Amélie? What was the motive? How is her murder related to Isabelle's suicide? What has become of Amélie's girl child? If super-creepy Albert is not the killer, what can the tough ex-boyfriend do to solve the case and move on with his life? Daniel used to say that the majority of readers want a story to be delivered in a chocolate box with a large red ribbon. The partial story I had in front of me was missing even the smallest red bow.

There were two Daniels. There was the passionate lover and animated comedian who loved making me squeal by sucking my toes, but there was also the other reserved, enigmatic Daniel, who had a disturbing affinity for stories without endings. He might come back from a walk on the beach and say he'd seen a dog with a pineapple in its mouth and a hobo wearing a dinner jacket. I'd say, *Was the dog the hobo's dog? No*, he'd reply, looking puzzled at my question. *Real hobos don't have dogs.*

Then he'd disappear into the study with a sandwich on his plate and a glass of juice. I had come to the conclusion that it was a right-brain creative process. I'd read an interview with a famous writer who claimed that his own creativity was frequently the result of the layering of mundane scenes of daily life, both real and embellished, into new, 'increasingly more desperate and thrilling variations'. What I had in my hands was an incomplete fantasy.

Maybe Patrice could tell me something about the new book. I'd always had the impression that Daniel and Patrice went back a long way; it was something about the easy way they traded insults. After I'd left the message for Patrice to buy time, he'd called back a week later and demanded to speak to Daniel as if I were hiding him under my pencil skirt. I'd said Daniel was ill and couldn't talk to him, but I'd give him the message. 'Merde!' Patrice had muttered before slamming the phone down in my ear. Perhaps that was when Patrice realised Daniel was not ever going to call back. Was *Lady Limbo* the book Patrice had been waiting for? The only way to know would be to ask him, but that would mean telling him I had lost Daniel. I could hear Daniel's voice: *One loses a set of keys, ma chère, not a husband. With a set of keys one is always the agent of loss; with a human being one has no idea.*

The pages I held in my hands must have been discarded the week he left, maybe even the same day. In the month before his disappearance, he'd returned to conducting housekeeping blitzes with boundless energy and enthusiasm. Did the fragments of a story have a bearing upon 'the de Luc case'? Was it what Elijah would call 'hard evidence'? Evidence of what? No crime had been committed as far as anyone knew.

Panic swept over me. I got up to wash my face with cold water and forced myself to breathe slowly and regularly. It was just a story that he'd created around an incident from our youth. Why did I believe the woman Enid that he wasn't dead? Why hadn't I gone to the police? There was nothing to assure me that he hadn't been kidnapped or murdered so what was I waiting for? I phoned her at 2 am from the phone next to our bed.

'Does the name Gabriel Kaas mean anything to you?'

'Should it?' she said after a moment.

'You tell me.'

'Ms Dante, it's dark outside, perhaps you'd like to tell me why you phoned so we can both get back to sleep.'

'I found a plot outline for the new book. There's nothing about children.'

'Nothing?'

'The murder victim has a baby and that's it.'

'Sometimes what is not there is more important than what is.'

You and Elijah would make a great team. How many lacunae to find a missing man?

'Gabriel Kaas is my husband's pseudonym. But I'm sure you knew that.'

'Many authors use a pen name,' Enid Lazzari remarked. And then, after a moment, grudgingly, as if I needed coaching, 'He is a chameleon who changes habitat whenever he chooses to. To a creative mind, a name is nothing but a temporary label.'

'I want to know he's alive and that he's left of his own accord. I must speak to him. If I don't hear from him I'm going to the police.'

'The police will ask why you haven't reported it yet.'

'You can reach him. I know you can. I keep thinking, what if he's Mr Smith in some hospital ward? What if he was involved in an accident and lost his memory?'

She didn't bother to sigh but was merely silent for a moment, as if thinking my words over. I preferred her on the phone where her mannerisms were imbued with a certain sangfroid and did not seem so theatrical. 'Daniel contacts me. I don't have any means of finding him. I will do my best but I wouldn't hold my breath.'

Peculiar little woman, with her way of talking like a retired policewoman.

'I'm not going anywhere.'

I walked into the study with a cup of black coffee so strong it could have been used to tar a road, switched the computer on and checked under My Documents. There it was: a folder called 'Daniel'. It felt as if I was prying, but I shook the feeling off. He was my husband and he'd abandoned me, for God's sake, and I was worried about the niceties! The date of modification showed '2005/09/09 11:47 AM'. The last time he'd accessed the folder was the morning of the day he disappeared. He'd probably made a copy and taken a CD with him. I clicked on 'Daniel' but it was password protected. I spent the rest of that long night in front of the computer trying different combinations of letters and characters and numbers, reaching back into the minutiae of memory, grasping at the straws of dates that once seemed solid and real, considering significances that never seemed very significant at the time, anything that might unlock the secrets of the secured folder, but when the first garden bird called out to the diluted light of a dreary dawn, I was still locked out and seething with frustration.

Patrice, I will keep this simple. I know you understand English. Who is Gabriel Kaas and what is your connection to him? Why can I find no mention of Pocket Policiers on the Internet? I must talk to you. It is a matter of time before someone starts asking questions.

Patrice's number rings and rings. I start to hear an odd hollow quality to the ring, as if it comes from an empty room inhabited by ghosts. He never acknowledges any of my messages. I begin to think Gabriel Kaas is another figment of my husband's fertile imagination.

October 2005:
Twenty-Four Days

THE TWENTY-FOURTH DAY, six days after Elijah Bloom came to our apartment, was the Monday after September's month-end. I dragged myself out of bed. If I stayed home I would only pore over *Lady Limbo* one more time, like a woman possessed. Man-hour time logs for September 2005 had to be approved before midday so that clients could be billed, and monthly project reports had to be finalised. Lying around moping was not going to get the job done.

It was one of the few times when we project managers were together in the company offices. Once the time recons were sent off by the press of a hi-tech button, there was a natural release of tension and time for a break before starting on the monthly project reports, with the numerous glossy graphs designed to mitigate risk by their very existence.

Helen Georgiades-Da Silva came thundering over. For a short person she packed a ton of vooma.

'Somebody remind me why I do this job?'

'The money.'

'That's probably it.' She gave me a wicked grin. 'Let's go get some caffeine.'

Helen wanted to give me the low-down on her overseas holiday. She had booked herself on an under-thirty-five trip to get a fresh perspective on life – 'I won't be under thirty-five for long so I'd better take the opportunity now!' – after she and her husband Ernesto had embarked on a trial separation.

I knew Helen and Ernesto Da Silva, her gynaecologist husband, well. She had been the senior on my first project straight out of university. They'd come to our wedding and when they were still together we'd seen them socially. Helen's mother had left Greece as a fifteen-year-old girl to marry a middle-aged used-car salesman who she'd only ever seen in a black and white photograph standing next to one of his cars. Ernesto's parents were storekeepers who had set off for Kenya from Portugal, lost everything during the Mau Mau rebellion, travelled to Angola, and then to a Portuguese colonial town called Lourenço Marques, and finally arrived in South Africa with a single ebony chest filled with their worldly possessions, and a young son.

Helen and Ernesto had a volatile marriage. The fights were characterised by the hurling of crockery, glass ornaments, soap – their quarrels frequently seemed to reach flashpoint in the bathroom – and foul language. Helen could utter oaths with the fluid proficiency of a pirating sea captain, a seemingly natural talent. She was philosophical about the replacement purchases that had to be made after the destructive bouts. It was the frequency of the fights and Helen's titanic Greek temper that eventually made Ernesto call it a day.

Normally I'd be nervous of Helen's sharp eyes – she'd notice immediately if I wasn't my usual sparkling self – but not today.

'I had mind-blowing, cataclysmic sex in Indonesia,' she announced with staggering honesty as she scanned the menu. She didn't bat an eyelid at my expression. 'Oh, stop being such a Catholic!'

I opened my mouth to protest that I hadn't been a Catholic for a very long time, but she was already telling me what it was like to reach orgasm three times in one night. That's what made her an excellent project manager. *Cut to the chase!* The ability to skip the irrelevant paraphernalia and home in on the important stuff. She had no shame where carnal matters were concerned. I always wondered if it was a Greek thing, like the swearing, and the bald acceptance of biological urges. By contrast, Italians have a tendency to over-sentimentalise.

And the French will play you tinny circus music on a garage-sale record player while they spin you round the room and whisper sweet nothings in your ear.

She told me that the group of travellers she'd gone with had been, to all intents and purposes, single people – she'd removed her own wedding band early on – bent on having no-holds-barred fun. Indonesia had been the highlight of the trip. It had been surprise upon surprise, as their Julio Iglesias lookalike Spanish guide had promised it would be. On one night they had gambled till the early hours in an underground casino, on another they had visited a high-end nightclub in Jakarta – it was mainly frequented by tourists – where they'd danced and drunk till the early hours of the morning. Entertainment included erotically charged stage acts involving male and female performers, lap-dancing and a live sex exhibition. Nothing tasteless like the donkey fellatio that one of the group had seen in Las Vegas. Helen freely admitted that before the trip this would have shocked her.

'Donkey fellatio?'

'No, watching a live sex show.'

But after a month of non-stop partying and inter-group sex it hadn't seemed that remarkable any more, and anyway, they were all pretty smashed by then. The club was also extremely accommodating and well run, providing male and female companions singly or in combo packages, depending on one's predilections.

'So there I was, a sex tourist who hadn't had sex in over a year. With the help of a couple of little white pills – everyone uses ecstasy in the clubs – the inhibitions fell away. It was like being in a candy shop. There were all these divine men dancing in a cage, naked butts gyrating, oozing libido. All I had to do was pick one. It was so easy.'

'How was it?' I asked, in spite of myself. There was interference in my head like records on turntables spinning around. I imagined a dimly lit locale, grime and sleaze and losing control, two writhing bodies on a stage. Another Helen watching.

She looked at me as if I was being particularly dense. 'It was *hot!* As in, Fantastic! Out Of This World! Amazing!' she said.

'What about Ernesto?' I asked weakly.

'I've asked him for a divorce. The big D. This whole separation thing is just putting off the inevitable.'

I stared at her, dumbfounded. This was the woman who couldn't live without Ernesto, the same woman who threatened a very messy suicide in the bathroom of the flat he'd rented when they split up, the same woman who told me breezily she wanted a minimum of five children with Ernesto, and ten would be fine.

'He agreed. We're better off without each other. It's the modern marriage syndrome. We love each other but we're better off apart.'

I was struggling to make sense of it all. We love each other but we're better off apart?

'Anyway, it's all worked out for the best, now that I've been offered the casino project in Dubai.'

Like everybody else at P&P, I was fully informed about the casino project, which was scheduled to start in early 2006 – a two-year project to get a group of Palm Island casinos, jointly owned by the Saudi royal family and the Sheikh of Dubai, onto a new, fully integrated platform using the latest out-of-the-box technology and software. It was a dream project, the prototype for future similar projects in the Middle East. It was best to be footloose and fancy-free to do assignments like that. *Singles preferred* was implicit. Relationships and kids made it difficult to work fourteen-hour days, six or seven days a week. The whole office knew that Piet had tried to move his household to Dubai for the two-year project, but he'd backed down when his paediatrician specialist wife had dug her heels in and threatened divorce. Now he was going alone and commuting between countries. The bets were on as to how long the marriage would last.

Helen was enjoying herself. The expression of disbelief on my face had her on a roll. It was that same impish streak that made her well-liked by clients and colleagues alike. On projects she used a potent mix of charm and hard-nosed intelligence to get her way. She reminded me of the new breed of city-smart car that could be parked in one manoeuvre. Compact and pushy.

'And Indonesia's just a short jet flight away. But, anyway, Dubai's probably got similar *hot* nightclubs.' The way she breathed *hot*, made me feel hot and sweaty. I couldn't stop the mind visuals of Helen in a sleazy nightclub.

'Where did you go?'

She pretended to have moved on to the gold-paved streets of Dubai. 'I haven't checked Dubai out yet.' She grinned when I pulled a face. 'Oh, you mean the sex. There are cubicles at the back of the club. It's clean and comfortable. You can even stay for breakfast if you want, but the coffee's lousy so most of us decided to go back to our air-conditioned hotels.'

Anyone could turn into a sex tourist. Later in the day I saw Helen standing by the tall windows looking out at the city skyline, some documents in her hand and a far-away expression on her face. In a meeting that afternoon she was asked a question about the Dubai project, but she carried on doodling as everybody looked her way expectantly. Piet addressed her by name and she finally looked up. At least she knew where Ernesto was. She could draw a black line through the relationship, chalk it up to experience, and walk away. Even if it hurt like hell.

Helen was so caught up in the new reality that was unfolding for her that she didn't ask me about Daniel, so I didn't have to tell her – or not tell her. Daniel had been gone for over three weeks and as far as my colleagues were concerned nothing had changed. It was the same old world turning on its axis, not letting anybody climb off the spinning roundabout until the ride was over. Nobody knew, except Gregory August, Elijah Bloom and Enid Lazzari, three strangers in the city.

Those long-playing records kept turning round and round on their turntables, and I was spinning with them, but there was no sound coming from me.

Moving On

I LAY ON HIS SIDE OF THE BED that night, but a futon is not as impressionable as other mattresses. I pressed myself into the shape he should have left behind, but snippets of the conversation with Helen kept intruding, arrows shooting off wildly into a pitch-black night, the marksmen invisible. In the background were the whispering voices of Amélie and Albert having wild no-boundaries sex in her bed.

When I could bear it no longer I slung one leg over the bed sheets and blankets, squeezing their hardened form between my legs, riding the dark galloping horse of passionless sex and achieving moist orgasm, like a hormonally charged teenager. Some time later I woke up with a start. Sharon had fallen next door. It happened occasionally when you were blind. Sitting on the toilet a few minutes later, with the residue of lust's dream still drifting in my head like the artificial fog they used for stage shows, a different scene flashed through my head. It was the bump in the night that did it.

My mother on a stopover in Paris, stranded at Charles de Gaulle Airport, her luggage lost. A ground stewardess phoning from the airport to let me know my mother's flight had been one of many incoming flights delayed because of a storm, but the luggage was arriving on a later flight from Florence and everything was très bien.

It made a good travel story.

Always a great admirer of style and class, my mother had been entranced by the flawless complexion and Parisian chic of the petite young woman who had gone out of her way to assist her. She hurried to keep up, clutching meal vouchers for rafraîchissement, sandwich and boisson in her hand. A group of airport security officials wolf-whistled as they passed and one of them came over and spoke briefly to the ground stewardess. As he left, he called out 'Au revoir, ma belle!' When my mother asked what he'd said (she was without shame), the Frenchwoman – who was not so young after all, my mother observed – answered that he had complimented her by telling her she was the sexiest woman he had ever seen. Of course, he might have known her, and it might have been an act of affection, not flirtation, and he might have used other words, like, 'You are the sexiest woman at the airport tonight', but how was my astute mother to know for sure? Her fascination with the sexy stewardess was by then enormous, so she asked the young woman if she had a man in her life.

Daniel had raised an amused eyebrow as he refilled my wine glass.

'Many men!' the lovely stewardess had proclaimed. 'Not one man. I prefer to live my own life. With no one to tell me what to do.'

'And what about children?' Did I mention my mother's second name was Persistenza? I could hear the Frenchwoman laughing by then, an intimate laugh, the way my mother told the story. How she must have laughed!

'But of course!' she exclaimed. 'I will have my own child one day.'

Well, then she would have to get married, my mother replied, ever the pragmatic one. Or at least she would have to have a steady partner. My mother must have realised that the ground stewardess was nothing that the Catholic religion had anticipated. No, not necessarily, was the reply. There are other ways of fathering children. My mother could not let this subject be, not when it had gone so far, become so promising, not when she was engaged in conversation with a truly stylish Frenchwoman. Ah, so it would be a test-tube baby then? But that wasn't very nice, not to know what the father looked like. My mother's bird eyes would have been glinting by now, the prize of the conversation within reach. But she had not expected the answer she got.

'Ah, non!' the younger woman declared, with a delicate shiver of horror. 'Donor insemination ... is so ugly and *Anglo-Saxon*. I will go to a place in Belgium, and I will choose a man to father my child. A real man, you understand, oui?'

The sound of a popping cork made us all jump. Daniel removed the cork from the corkscrew, his expression inscrutable. *I am a 32-year-old single woman ...* Somebody else had once searched for a Real Man. But, with the oblivious self-centredness of youth, we had treated it as a game. My absorbed mother recited on.

'There must be something between a man and a woman, a spark, before one decides to have a child with this man. Oui? N'est-ce pas?' the irrepressible stewardess continued.

'And then?' my mother asked, breathless with admiration and relentless in her pursuit.

How they understood each other, the ground stewardess and my mother at Charles de Gaulle that night!

'And then I will have beautiful sex with him.'

Daniel rose from his chair like a man in a dream.

'She had a pretty name,' my mother pressed on. 'So French! Celestine!'

After that, everything happens in slow motion. My mother's eyes widen preternaturally, dark pools of candlelight frozen in the gloom. I swing my head around. The crash of glass is always shattering. Daniel's shoe has caught on the corner of the carpet, an arc of red wine has marked us, the wine bottle has decomposed into amber shards and splinters. Miraculously, he has landed on the carpet outside the ring of broken glass.

Sharon and the dog had settled down again, their noises dim echoes on the other side of the wall. Another human body slipping to the floor next door has brought me to this moment of crystal recall. In that split second, as he lets the bottle go, I see Daniel's bloodless face, his eyes filled with horror, and then it is done.

The conversation with Helen coming so soon after finding Daniel's manuscript had unsettled me enough to remind me of the incident with my mother. *So French! Celestine!* I headed for Daniel's desk, my heart pounding, as cold as a soldier without boots. I rifled through the drawers with mechanical efficiency. In the second drawer I found an old zip-up black folder that still held the last few yellowed pages of an A4 pad. Something a university student might have used. Inside were articles, pictures cut out of newspapers, a death notice.

Nick, don't be an idiot! Nicky, get down from there!
Look, Paola, look! I'm Thor, god of lightning and thunder!

I shuddered and turned the death notice over. Right now I was looking for something else. My thoughts were scrambled. I was frantic. There was no time but I had no clear idea what I was looking for. The night my mother came for supper and told her Celestine story. What if she was a messenger he hadn't been expecting?

Daniel disappears soon afterwards and I find him sitting on a children's park bench with a stab wound in his arm. Rifling through his drawers, memory kicked in again, how we had both laughed nervously at my mother's travel story, how I had sought his eyes and he had avoided mine, how, later, after she'd left and we'd cleaned up the mess in the dining room, he'd poured himself a tot of whisky, neat with ice, and sat out on the balcony with the whisky bottle at his feet.

'It's just a coincidence, Daniel.' It irritated me that the reminder of our student days should unsettle him so. It was all such a long time ago.

'Nothing is a coincidence, ma chérie.'

Daniel's strained voice in my head.

Perfect recall is agony. Breathe, just breathe. I had blamed my mother for the disastrous evening and promptly forgotten all about it. But the brain remembers everything. I believed I saw it now: Amélie, the wasp-waisted vamp in an airways uniform and stilettos of *Lady Limbo* was a fictional creation based on a living, breathing ground stewardess who worked at Charles de Gaulle Airport. Celestine had told my mother about a place where one could have a baby with a real man. What if my writer husband had set out to find Lady Limbo in the flesh and got more than he bargained for?

Overcome with fresh desperation, I emptied drawers straight out onto the parquet floor: various scraps of paper with notes, boxes of used stiffy disks and CDs, a shoebox filled with stationery, mostly junk. In the fifth drawer I found a large manila envelope. It contained newspaper clippings from French papers. I pulled out a chair and opened the French–English dictionary Daniel kept on the desk. After a couple of hours of painstakingly unravelling headlines and captions, I concluded they were all related to the deaths of women over a period of roughly ten years.

The first death had occurred while we were still at university, and the last after Daniel and I had moved into our new sea-view apartment. The early deaths happened in the vicinity of Paris, the later deaths all over the world. They didn't seem to have anything in common except that in each case someone – a family member or friend or investigative journalist – disputed the verdict of accidental death. Was this source material for one of Daniel's books or something else? A bulky object was stuck at the bottom of the envelope. The musty cover of a diary fell out onto the desktop. At the same time a small square of paper floated down onto the floor, the tell-tale blue and white stripes of the university mainframe printer paper faded by time. I leaned down and turned it over. Lady Limbo's glacial fingers reached out across time and space, settling around my throat.

The message I had shown Daniel and Nicky with such glee in that other carefree dimension had been cut out and pasted onto the inside back cover of the diary. A snail's trail of dried glue was still visible, running from corner to corner. Somebody had stuck it at the back of the diary for safekeeping and there it had stayed, all these years. The diary itself was gutted, all the pages for 1994 ripped out at the binder.

The piece of paper with its printed words – Lady Limbo's unusual request from more than a decade before – could have been nothing more than a youthful keepsake.

I tugged at the sixth and final drawer without success. This had once been my desk; now I was locked out. I tugged and pulled, sitting on the floor and jamming my feet against the legs as I pulled on the handle like a woman deranged. I brought a huge screwdriver out of the toolbox and practically stood on it, trying to wrench the drawer open, but the screwdriver bent.

'Cheap piece of Chinese shit!'

I had to admit it was no good. The drawer wouldn't budge. If I couldn't find the key I'd have to call a locksmith in. Where could he have put it?

At the first meeting in our kitchen, Elijah Bloom had cocked an eyebrow at his notepad. 'You've definitely confirmed that he took nothing with him? His mobile phone charger is still here? All his clothes are in the cupboard except for what he was wearing?'

'That means he didn't plan it, doesn't it?'

'Or he wanted us to think he didn't plan it. In this work one must keep an open mind,' Elijah Bloom had reflected, not one to draw hasty conclusions.

Daniel's clothes were still in the cupboard where I had left them. At night with the dim light it was easy to imagine the jackets were inhabited by the ghosts of men standing in a long row, obedient to some unnatural law, an invisible army lined up like a column of lost lovers. I waded in, flailing my arms left and right, yanking garments off hangers with brutal force, my fingers hunting through pockets, Geiger counters checking for radioactive materials.

When every hanger hung stark naked, all semblance of an army of men destroyed, I was panting. I started on the shelves next, delving in and pulling out every clothing item within reach, touching, patting, searching, moving on. Then I grabbed a stool and a flashlight and peered into the dim recesses of the top shelves, lowering the Nikon camera bag to the ground and then sweeping my arm across the dusty spaces and watching with detached interest as the rest of the paraphernalia rained down: a hairdryer that needed fixing, two promotional sport caps, a water bottle and rucksack, an ancient shiny black box of oil paints, the thirty-six tubes of colour now spread all over the carpet, a few paperbacks in French and various other bits of bric-à-brac that a man might accumulate over two years. I used my big toe to turn over a framed photo of Brutus, tongue lolling happily after a walk, taken in the courtyard at my old garden flat. Now that I thought about it, that was all he had ever used the camera for – pictures of Brutus. With Brutus gone, he'd stuck my birthday gift away on the top shelf and never taken it down again. I'd used my digital camera for the wedding trip. I kicked the unwelcome reminder of the dog under the bed and set about emptying shoeboxes with renewed energy, a heap of men's footwear growing as the shoes thumped down to ground zero. I didn't stop my frenzied search until every cupboard, shelf and drawer he'd used was bare.

Clothes maketh the man. Who said that? Shakespeare probably, twisting words around. Even Shakespeare could be wrong. It was the other way around. Without the man, the clothes were nothing but empty husks that made no sense. If he were right, I'd reduced the essence of a man to a heap of crumpled shop garments on a carpet, the same shaggy carpet that had once inspired love antics.

'This rug has the spirit of a yeti!' Daniel had exclaimed before donning the new rug as the pelt of an abominable snowman and chasing a screaming Paola around the apartment.

I shifted my eyes to the other more meagre pile of miscellany: some coins, a pencil stub, a ticket to *Amadeus* at the Baxter, a folded-up invitation to a poetry reading, four clipped bus tickets, and a green stub – the right half of an entrance ticket – with the stamped letters 'DOUR' still legible, a crumpled Camel packet with two cigarettes and a pocket match holder with a few unused matches. I'd pulled out of going to see *Amadeus* at the last minute because of work so he'd gone alone, coldly fuming at what he'd termed my lack of commitment to our relationship. In retrospect it may have been my lackadaisical attitude to art and culture that so enraged him. The poetry reading had been scheduled to take place at a community theatre a couple of weeks after he disappeared.

The bus tickets were all to Woodstock. The kids' park where I'd gone to fetch him was in Woodstock. Maybe Monica could help with the halved green entrance ticket. There was still no key for the sixth drawer. I picked up the Camel packet and placed a cigarette in my mouth. With a flick of a match the tip smouldered to life. I closed my eyes, savouring a scent I associated with Daniel. He could have been in the other room, or he could have just stepped out to buy a newspaper.

In our student days, when a heady combination of shagging and drugs was practically de rigueur, I had maintained an anachronistic attitude to drugs. I'd never seen the point of artificially enhancing pleasure, besides which I had no intention of ever waking up one morning and having no idea what I'd done the night before. But occasionally, when the three of us chilled on Nicky's emperor bed, I'd taken a drag on Daniel's cigarette while Nicky drew beatifically on a self-rolled zol of marijuana. Daniel refused to smoke pot; he said he'd tried it once and it had addled his brain. I'd always relished that picture of decadence we three had projected so effortlessly.

Puffing away at a cigarette was curiously enjoyable. What would Daniel save if the apartment were burning down? The answer arrived like a silvery fish shooting up from the depths into a pool of clear fresh water, as if it had always been there, waiting for me. The book of French poems his mother left him. His pillow book. I walked to his side of the bed and opened the night table drawer. The book was gone. Wherever he'd gone, he'd taken it with him, but he'd left me something in its place. The missing key to the sixth drawer.

It was after midnight when I phoned the woman Enid. The phone rang for ages and then someone picked it up so softly that it sounded like a moth's wing brushing against a lampshade. There was silence on the other side.

'I need to ask you something.'

'What would you like to know?' her voice replied, a thin metallic echo resonating. She didn't sound sleepy.

'Is it a child or my love that will save him?' I could only ask this because it was nearly pitch dark inside and out, only the greenish haze from the street lamp climbing the walls to keep me company, my second cigarette down to a stump, my spread fingers the ears of a rabbit in the shadows.

Surrounded by an uncanny silence I waited for her reply.

'It will be like putting together the fragments of glass from a shattered goblet, and then still hoping to drink from it. That is all I can tell you.'

Why is she talking about fragments of glass? Tonight of all nights.

'How many other women are there?'

'That is not a question I can answer.'

'Because you don't know or because you don't wish to?'

'It is not information that will help you. He is no longer with those other women. Only you can decide if he is worth fighting for or not. Goodnight, Ms Dante.'

The woman was telling me to move on. A good business lesson. Something that divided the boys from the girls, a man from a woman. How the average woman likes to dwell on things, I had noted to myself so often. I had long ago decided it was to be one of my strengths, something Helen, with her obdurate Greek heritage, and I had in common. The ability to move on. But with Daniel I could not. I was vulnerable again.

As a young child, I liked to believe I had the power to vanish. In a far, run-down corner of our large garden, under a big tree's protection and surrounded by thorny thicket, was a concrete slab, cast by a previous owner, that had special powers. It was circumscribed by invisible walls that stretched right up into the sky. If I stood anywhere on that magic square, within the walls of laser light, I too became invisible. I found this immensely useful in awkward situations. The rest of my family rarely ventured beyond the green verges of the main house. Later on, my mother insisted I join the school theatre group and take ballet lessons, all while war raged in our household. And so I learnt how to project substance. But with Daniel it was different. With him I felt that I truly had substance, that he always saw me exactly as I was.

In my mind I saw the Swan Lake birthday cake my mother extravagantly commissioned an artist friend of hers to make to commemorate my thirteenth year and make amends for being herself: an enchanted lake of powder-blue icing, white long-necked swans gliding across the icy water in languid silence. I did not eat a single slice of that mythical cake myself, but watched in silence as my friends gorged themselves, swooping down on the swans with the glee of predatory birds gulping down frogs. As I carefully observed pieces of perfect beauty being masticated and minced with saliva before they disappeared down my friends' throats, the thought crystallised that I would henceforth avoid all matters of the heart. Indeed 'matters of the heart' was a nonsensical phrase invented by non-scientists. The heart was an organ designed to pump blood around the body. It could not be held responsible for the undisciplined emotions that rendered human beings gross.

* * *

I put the mobile down and reached for the leather-bound journal I kept on my bedside table, the encounter between a love-struck Dante Alighieri and his muse immortalised on the front cover. My father's peace offering brought back from the open-air market in Florence. I'd retrieved it from the back of a drawer after his death. Even in embossed leather Beatrice appeared to float six feet above the ground. It held verses of poems that Daniel had carefully written out in his own hand, bits and pieces of his soul presented as paper gifts that I might keep. I had laughingly called it my very own pillow book and Daniel had gently chided me – mais non, ma chérie, un pillow book c'est quelque chose de votre esprit. He insisted that a pillow book was by its nature something that one had written oneself, an outpouring of one's spirit. It fell to each one of us to create our own souls. He could not be responsible for my soul. Daniel came out with stuff like that sometimes. In the next breath he was pointing out that the original 'pillow books' were used to enlighten nervous young brides, and that the ancient Chinese believed sexual harmony between man and woman led to spiritual enlightenment. Green eyes wide with mischief, he had offered to assist with my tantric education, thereby providing practical material for my pillow book.

I let it fall open gently and closed my eyes, waiting for his footfalls, as if he could talk to me in this way from wherever he had gone and I would hear him.

I opened my eyes to Izumi Shikibu's ode to true love:

As I dig for wild orchids
In the autumn fields,
It is the deeply-bedded root
that I desire,
not the flower.

There was no mistaking Daniel's handwriting: the forest of letters heading face-forward into an oncoming wind.

We've come full circle, to the beginning of everything. I'm showing them both my day's accomplishment, my student lover and his best friend, my head thrown forward, my thick brown hair escaping from the hair slides I employed to control it, my neck vulnerable, my lips parted with excitement, when I turn and meet Daniel's naked gaze. I am a swan caught in the hunter's sights. That is all it takes. Nicky notices nothing. Not that night. He is too entranced with Lady Limbo and Real Man Inc.

Abandonment. What exactly does this word mean? *Desperation.* Another word I am learning to grapple with. *Forlorn.* I am losing hope.

I tucked the Dante journal under my pillow where it now belonged.

That night, I tossed and turned as I grappled with how much I would tell Elijah. How much did Nicky have to do with all of this? Daniel was Nicky's best friend before I came between them.

Cape Times, Friday May 19, 1995

QUESTIONS RAISED OVER DEATH OF VAN DEN BOGEN HEIR

Nikos van den Bogen, 21, only son of wealthy Dutch industrialist and philanthropist Jan van den Bogen has died in hospital. A family spokesman confirmed that he sustained injuries after falling from a tree struck by lightning during a thunderstorm.

It is not clear at this point if van den Bogen's death is linked to the direct lightning strike or to his fall from the tree. It appears that he had climbed the tree to gain entrance to a University of Cape Town women's residence through a window. Emergency rescue services stabilised the injured student on the scene before rushing him to hospital. Van den Bogen, who had achieved SA colours as a member of the UCT fencing team and was also an experienced parachutist, appeared to be making a full recovery in hospital but later died of a suspected brain injury.

Questions have been raised as to the whether the emergency personnel who attended the accident victim were sufficiently trained to handle a severe trauma incident of this nature. A rescue services spokesman acknowledged that budgetary constraints and a spate of resignations from qualified personnel defecting to private companies had put pressure on the unit but assured the public that everything possible had been done and all appropriate procedures had been followed. An emergency worker who asked not to be named claimed that trainee medical personnel were called out because the rescue services were short-staffed on a particularly busy Saturday night. The spokesman denied this. Police have opened an investigation docket.

Jeff Radebe, a spokesman for the ANC government, has extended his condolences to the van den Bogen family.

Ménage
à Trois

In February 1995, I told my boyfriend Nicky that it was over between us. I'd tried several times before. I'd suggested a cooling-off period, I'd told him I needed some space to think about the relationship, I'd told him my university marks were suffering.

That day wasn't too different from any other, except that he annoyed me by driving me back to his place, the ground floor of a double-storey house he shared with Daniel, instead of taking me straight back to res, as we'd agreed when he offered the lift. When we got to the house, Mariella was sitting on the steps, waiting. Mariella was a Dutch girl who had the milk-and-rosebud complexion and strong yellow hair of her tulip-growing ancestors. She immediately apologised for her presence, mumbling desperately about Nicky having said she could come over and borrow a Dutch book. I don't know why that did it, but it did; the sight of the poor girl blushing and apologising when she obviously worshipped the ground Nicky walked on was enough to do it. I waited for her to choose a book and scuttle away; it didn't take long.

'You should ask her out. She's got a major crush on you.'

'You think so? I've never been out with a reborn Christian. Do you think she could convert me?'

'Anything's possible.'

'Maybe I would if I wasn't so crazy about you.'

'Come on, Nicky. It's no good. She's a nice girl. I'm not a nice girl. She'll be good for you.'

They say you have to keep an eye out for the elephant in the room. The spectre of Daniel was the elephant in the room that day.

'It's because of him, isn't it?' he'd said. 'You're in love with him.'

'If you're talking about Daniel, that's nonsense, Nicky. You're imagining things. Our relationship has run its course. It's just one of those things.'

'Sure. Just one of those things,' he said bitterly.

I tried a different tack. Nicky and I had had plenty of good times together. 'Look, Nicky. It's just become too intense. It's over between us. I can't be romantically involved with you any more. I can't live a lie. But I want the three of us to be friends; we can still do things together.'

'The three of us, huh? You're infatuated with him! Why don't you just admit it? You look at him with those doe eyes. It's disgusting!'

Nicky didn't take any of my requests for a cooling-off of our relationship well. That weekend he drove a motorbike up a ramp for a university publicity stunt, the intention being to gain enough momentum to fly over three parked Volkswagen Beetles. *You have to come, Paola. It will be just like Evel Knievel! You bring me luck.* I didn't go, reasoning my absence would send him a message that I was serious about breaking up with him. The bike swerved to one side and he came off mid-air.

I had first bumped into Nicky at an airshow. At just seventeen, in my first year at university, I was hungry for new sensations. He was the only parachutist of a group of six who landed dead centre in the circle on the ground, in spite of strong winds and jumping from an aircraft that looked as if it belonged in a museum. I watched the blond parachutist with the foppish hairstyle put out his hand to high-five kids in the crowd after he had run to a breathless halt. None of the young men in the crowd I was with had that easy confidence, and none of them could parachute. I walked over and introduced myself and asked if he minded my watching while he folded the parachute and packed it away.

'Of course not,' he replied, speaking with a Dutch accent. 'Do you want to learn?' The accented words delivered with an infectious grin had a curious effect on me. I found myself agreeing to the startling suggestion. Physical exertion had never been my idea of fun. That was how I met Nikos van den Bogen, heir apparent to the family's industrial empire. It wasn't that strange that we happened to be students at the same prestigious university: I was super-smart and he was super-rich. The next day, a Sunday, we started our lessons. I took the bus to the address Nicky had given me, where a guy with dark hair opened the door. He seemed surprised to see me so I explained my arrangement with Nicky. Normally I'd have barged right in but there was something about the unusual green eyes that stopped me in my tracks. Finally, he showed me through to the lounge and asked me abruptly to wait. I overheard them arguing. Daniel was telling Nicky that it was crazy taking a girl along, that it was asking for trouble, and Nicky told him to go and read a book and mind his own business.

For weeks, Nicky and I went to the airfield every Sunday, where I enrolled on an Accelerated Free Fall course. When I came to a running halt after my first solo jump from an aircraft door at 10 000 feet, still giddy with excitement and the rush of adrenalin, Nicky van den Bogen grabbed me in his arms, kissed me on the mouth and asked me out. When we arrived back at the house hand-in-hand, Daniel was his usual short-tempered self, withdrawing to his room and shutting the door almost immediately. The only thing Nicky ever said to explain the unfriendly behaviour was that they were boyhood friends, and Daniel, being a couple of years older, was sometimes overprotective. Had I considered those words more carefully, I might have asked more questions.

Nicky was on the university fencing team. He fenced with the lithe, controlled aggression and the speed of a cat. On my eighteenth birthday, Nicky and I did a bungee jump in tandem; for his twentieth birthday, I arranged for him to have a hang-gliding lesson with a professional. He insisted I accompany him so we hired more equipment and booked the trainer for the whole afternoon. The day came when we flew like a pair of birds into the setting sun.

The tingling of my scalp signalled the exhilaration that was my body's response to terror; it was a far cry from feeling nothing at all. After years of mistrusting my body, I was learning to use it. We went for heart-stopping rides on his Kawasaki 1500. I was the one who egged him on to go faster, faster, faster; I was the one who dared him to outrace the traffic officer as I laughed into the wind. It was Daniel who Nicky phoned when we were arrested for dangerous driving and obstruction of justice, and it was Daniel who paid bail of 200 rand to get us out.

In the car I saw another side to the brooding, silent Daniel: Daniel in a towering rage. He told Nicky that he had no right to put my life in danger, even if he was planning to kill himself young. In the face of Daniel's cold fury, Nicky mumbled that it wasn't his fault; I had dared him not to stop. Daniel looked in the rear-view mirror then, and for a moment our eyes met. He was silent for the rest of the trip. I think I realised then that Nicky wasn't as strong as he made out, but it was only a vaguely uneasy feeling in my gut. The new Paola was still having too much fun after years of avoiding physical activity and masculine contact.

After that, Daniel would often come along; we became more and more a threesome. I expected tantrums from Nicky and arguments between them, but the fact was that Daniel was good company and he seemed to fill a gap between Nicky and me. I started to visit them more often. Daniel would cook for us and we'd eat a meal together and watch a film, sharing the big couch. Sometimes I'd wake up to find my head on Daniel's shoulder instead of Nicky's.

When I discovered that Daniel was Nicky's sparring partner, I invited myself along to watch them practise. In spite of myself, I was drawn to applaud the thrust and parry of the pageant. There was something thrilling about two white knights facing each other with shouts of 'En garde!', the air electric with testosterone and the tension of the duel. If the supple, fitter Nicky was tenacious and wickedly fast with his feet, Daniel was ferocious and devilishly quick with the lunge of the epée. When I asked how long they had been fencing together, they looked at each other before Daniel replied, 'A long time'.

Why didn't I ask more questions? I don't know; something held me back. If we went to a club, I'd dance with both of them, but as the evening progressed Daniel would move on to some girl who'd arrived on her own. Sometimes we'd leave in a foursome and in the morning the three of us plus the new girl would have breakfast together. Mostly one-night stands, none of them lasted long. Still, that didn't stop the campus rumour machine. I put up with endless teasing from friends who hardly ever saw me any more. *Want a sandwich, Paola? You know what they say, from man-hater to pussycat! Do you think she even knows what a sandwich is? Un ménage à trois.* I shrugged the comments off and told them they had filthy, perverted minds.

In the hospital after Nicky's mid-air fall during the motorbike stunt, his mother told a story about him as a ten-year-old doing bicycle wheelies around the neighbourhood in the dead of night while everybody else was asleep. He'd always been hyperactive, she informed us proudly as she patted his hand. He'd been riding his own motorbike since he was twelve. All the van den Bogen men were fanatical about motorbikes.

I had rushed to the hospital as soon as I'd heard about Nicky's fall, arriving after Daniel. I was facing the open doorway when Nicky's mother walked in. For a split second I saw the heavily made-up eyes widen and the satin-red mouth twist as she saw Daniel, then she turned to her son, her face recomposed into a maternal expression of concern.

After the bike accident, without any of us speaking about what had happened or about my attempts at breaking up, we all went back to the way it had been. I would kiss Nicky when I arrived at the hospital and he'd kiss me back, the chaste kisses of an old married couple, but he seemed satisfied. Besides some bad grazes, Nicky had dislocated a shoulder and sprained an ankle so it was decided that he should recuperate at the family seaside home in Hermanus. Daniel and I succeeded in avoiding each other during that period. The first Sunday after he came back, Nicky arrived to take me for a spin. He wouldn't take no for an answer, pulling me outside and putting the helmet on my head.

'You're not scared, are you?'

'What kind of a question is that?'

I didn't like the gleam in his eyes.

When the wind started whistling past my ears, I started to pray: *Dear God, please don't let me die on this bike ... I promise to be nicer to my mother ...* In that moment I was afraid, and in a bizarre way the fear felt good. I no longer felt invulnerable. I could be hurt and I didn't want to die just yet. But I had no further time to ponder the exact nature of the elation that coursed through my veins.

The traffic cop who took my statement suggested I change boyfriends. He went off muttering, 'Crazy kids!' The bike had hit a patch of oil and skidded off the highway, throwing us into the bushes on the road island. Nicky ran out across the highway to the mangled Kawasaki, weaving his way among oncoming cars, cursing like a maniac and giving the middle finger to a car that only just managed to avoid the bike. The driver of the car stopped and leapt out, hauling Nicky upright from where he stooped over the wreckage of his bike. The traffic officers broke up the fight. After the van den Bogen lawyers intervened, the driver of the other car agreed not to press charges. According to the statement of his pillion passenger, Mr van den Bogen had been driving at the speed limit and could not have prevented the accident, and since the traffic officer had omitted to do a breathalyser test there was no proof of alcohol consumption over the legal limit. Besides some bad cuts and bruises and a pair of wrecked jeans, I was in one piece; the bushes had broken our fall. Nicky didn't have a scratch that time, but he'd worn his biking suit. The cops gave me a lift home while Nicky waited with the bike. Later that afternoon, Daniel called to say Nicky had gone to make a statement. He wanted to know if I was all right.

'Do me a favour, Paola. Stay away from him for a while.'

That night when Nicky came to fetch me in res, still in the biker's suit, he reeked of alcohol and his eyes were unnaturally bright. I'd dragged my sore body out of bed after Sheona knocked and said he wouldn't stop ringing the night desk bell. I agreed to go with him just to get him out of the vestibule. I could handle Nicky. In the car he talked incessantly about the driver of the car that had nearly collided with the bike, as if he had caused our accident. When I asked where we were going he ignored me. Eventually he turned off the highway onto Ladies Mile and headed towards Tokai. He stopped the car inside the forest and leaned over to kiss me, putting his tongue deep inside my mouth. I pushed him away and told him he stank of booze and piss, and he could at least have had the decency to change out of his filthy clothes. I believed I could manage Nicky in any situation. The next moment he slapped me hard across the face: *Fucking bitch!*

I fought him with every ounce of my strength, clawing and biting like a feral cat in the constrained space, but Nicky was strong and out of control and I didn't stand a chance. As he pulled his leather pants down, he kept repeating that it was time I behaved like his girlfriend, shouting *Fucking bitch!* every time I managed to hurt him. The name-calling gave me strength: I managed to get hold of his scrotum and squeezed. He gave a roar of pain and fell back. I stumbled out of the car and ran. I heard him behind me before he threw me to the ground. My head must have hit a sawn-off stump because the trees became ground and the ground became trees and I tasted grit and pine needles in my mouth as he yanked my jeans off and shoved my head down. Everything went mercifully dark, but pain racked my body. *Don't scream, Paola, don't give him the satisfaction.*

We had always been careful. On safe days I had still insisted on a condom as a double precaution, making it clear that I had no intention of falling pregnant. *It's a red day.* Even now my sense of preservation was strong. I managed to raise my head and get the word *condom* out but it was a soundless whisper swallowed up by the black night before he forced my head down again and lowered himself onto me, ramming into me with rhythmic thrusts.

When he was done, he lay next to me and stroked my naked back, running his fingers along my spine. I asked him quietly if I could get dressed. He brushed his lips against my ear and whispered that I was beautiful. He said he'd drive me back. On the way I told him I needed to clean myself up so he stopped at an all-night garage. I managed to get to the basin in time – I hadn't eaten anything that day so it was a kind of heartbroken, dry retching. My legs were trembling so badly that I sat on the closed toilet seat for five minutes. I found some paper towels and dampened them under a tap, cleaning up the blood and semen that ran down. My breasts were grazed raw from being rubbed against the ground. I did what I could in the circumstances.

When I came out, Nicky was leaning against the car, whistling. He had bought us a Coke and a hamburger each. I forced down some of the cold drink and a few bites of the burger, telling myself to stay calm, not to provoke him. He consumed the rest, making casual conversation as if nothing had happened.

Several weeks later, I called Daniel and asked him to meet me inside the stone church opposite the botanical gardens.

After my father had left, once I was older and independent, he took to inviting me to meet him at different churches in the city. Occasionally we stayed for part of a service if there was a choir or organ music, but more often we were alone in the high-ceilinged temples of faith; we simply sat in the silence of saints and martyrs or walked in the funereal gloom lit only by lamps and candles. I understood it had nothing to do with guilt or religious fervour. My father had always loved churches the way a man is inspired to awe by beauty that is remote and mysterious to his soul. Daniel once mischievously suggested that obsession and love were not so dissimilar, since both were blind to the faults of the loved subject.

Perhaps Daniel had a point: my father's obsession with churches was more lasting than any love of a flesh-and-blood woman. I tackled him once on why churches held such a fascination for him, since he was an atheist who slept late on Sundays. My father, who was known to share his philosophical musings with his dinner guests, replied, 'Here in God's house, everything is so still, so safe.' From his tone I could tell he was quoting the existentialist Kierkegaard, whom he greatly admired and often quoted. It seemed to me that the churches provided us with a different kind of shelter. The silence made it easier on us both; we didn't have to speak.

I found it easier to judge my father in the harsh daylight outside a church so, one day, I refused to meet him there, in the same way my mother, the blood of generations of staunch Roman Catholics coursing through her veins, had flatly refused to divorce him, inadvertently forcing him to live the life of impropriety he craved.

Daniel joined me in the wooden pew. We were alone, the morning light filtering through the stained glass windows.

'In France, many churches are now closed to the public,' Daniel said, looking around curiously. 'Because of vandals. Even in the smallest rural village there's a group of local louts who carry statues and artefacts off to pay for their alcohol and drug habits. They paint walls with graffiti and urinate and defecate inside the building. It's a pity.'

I asked Daniel to listen and not to interrupt. Then I told him what had happened the night after he'd warned me to stay away from Nicky. His face grew as hard as the white marble of the altar, his cheekbones etched as the skin went taut. I told him that I had bought three different pregnancy kits and there was no doubt about it: I was pregnant. He went completely still when I told him I was going to terminate the pregnancy. One of the doctors at the university birth control clinic was a pro-abortionist. Daniel looked like a beautiful, suffering saint as he clenched and unclenched his hands.

'This is what you want?'

'Yes.'

'This is not something you can undo.'

'I don't need a lecture, Daniel.'

'There are people who would take the baby.'

'My mind is made up. I thought you would understand.'

He took my hand and kissed it gently, the way a gallant

121

musketeer might, but he didn't let it go. 'I'll come with you. You can't go alone.'

'The appointment's tomorrow at three.'

That was how Daniel de Luc came to hold my hand in a church and in an abortion doctor's private rooms. That was how I knew the kind of man he was, long before he came back into my life. We all have many sides to us.

A couple of days after the doctor visit, Mariella phoned. I'd heard through the grapevine that Nicky had taken her out a few times. She was hysterical, begging me to come before somebody got hurt. She was that kind of girl: she used euphemisms. Eventually she told me where she was. The Sports Hall. The concrete structure that housed the sport complex was dark except for some light at the far end. I shivered in my jacket; it was a chilly, windless night. The city lay far below, stretching to the horizon, a flickering tundra of burning torches from blue neon and white hot to golden refinery yellow. Highways ran across the tableau, red streaks of traffic melting the view. As I came closer I heard the distinctive clanging sound of metal hurling itself against metal. I entered by the side door. The absurd, comforting thought crossed my mind that the two men in black trousers hitched and rolled up at the waist, darting backwards and forwards as if they were joined at the hips by some invisible cord, were part of a film shoot. But there was no film crew, only Mariella running up and down on tip-toe on the other side, whimpering and invoking the Holy Spirit, by the sound of it.

One part of my brain registered everything in slow motion. The music was playing all wrong as if the LP was on the wrong speed. The other part registered a fuming Daniel lunging and slashing at Nicky with a heavy-bladed weapon. Their bare feet moved backwards and forwards with thunderous power, their movements fast and furious as they parried and thrust, crossed swords and flung each other back. Those large swords looked like the real thing. It hardly surprised me. Nicky's father's collection of antique swords was legendary among the fencing fraternity; his immense wealth allowed such eccentric purchases. Daniel had a trickle of blood oozing down his bicep; Nicky had blood streaming out of a long diagonal cut across his chest. Nobody had noticed me. I could just walk away and leave them to kill each other, or I could switch the lights off and pray they'd both step back and not take a final, ferocious lunge in the dark. I knew where the main electricity control panel was. We res girls sometimes played badminton here when we needed the physical exercise. But there was Mariella the god-fearing one to consider; who knew what she was going to do in her state of semi-hysteria? And the light box was at the other end of the building. I grabbed a megaphone that must have been left there by one of the coaches.

'Stop it! Both of you!' I shouted from the side, my voice booming. The terrible clanging stopped, two startled faces swung in my direction. 'This is childish.' I spoke firmly and calmly, as I imagine one does to little boys who are fighting over an ice lolly. 'The campus police will be here in a few minutes. I suggest you leave.' I didn't wait for anybody to say anything. I just replaced the megaphone, walked away, got into my car and drove off. Later that night I was called to the payphone on our floor. It was Mariella to say she'd taken Nicky to an outpatient clinic. He had needed eleven stitches in his chest. If I hadn't come, Daniel would have killed him. She'd finally ditched the euphemisms.

A couple of days later, Daniel called. I asked him where he was staying. He said Nicky was wild but everybody was, some of the time. That was when I knew for sure Daniel was not planning to kill Nicky. I needn't have bothered the other night. After all, musketeers only ever get wounded, and scuffles over women are short-lived temporary diversions.

The night in the forest was the real end of Nicky and me. The word *rape* slides easily off the tongue in a world where we live and die by the sword of media-hype, where the private is made public, and broken lives are strewn like carrion on a vulture table for the crowds to peck at. In my private arena, I discarded the four-letter R word that would have labelled me the victim of an impersonal act. In my version I was sexually assaulted by someone I once trusted and loved.

Nicky had made it easy for me to finally break it off but I had been unable to face him. Instead, I simply didn't answer his calls and made sure I was never alone, and he hadn't pushed things. It was the sword fight with its symbolic spillage of blood that made me realise I needed to do something clear and unambiguous for myself. I selected a public place: the university cafeteria. As a precaution I asked Sheona to sit at a table a few rows away. She'd raised a shapely eyebrow but left it at that. We acted the parts rehearsed and refined over centuries, the unsuited lovers in a doomed love story: Nicky played the slighted, jealous lover; I played the woman who has fallen out of love. He didn't look back as he stalked off, tossing his blonde hair. I told myself he wouldn't hurt me ever again; his shame was too great. Did I feel a pang over the foetus whose life had been snuffed out? In my version there was no place in my life for a child nobody wanted.

I didn't see Daniel for the next few days. On the Saturday morning I bumped into him doing some grocery shopping. He came up behind me and put his fingers around my neck from behind, whispering, 'You are very pretty.' I turned around slowly, my skin on fire.

'It's all over with Nicky,' I blurted out.

'I know,' he said, smiling at me. 'How are you feeling?'

'He thinks it's because of you.'

'Is it?'

'Of course not.' I looked around the aisles full of soap powder and dog food and all of a sudden I wanted us out of there. 'Are you doing anything right now?'

'You mean right now? I believe I'm shopping.'

'Damn it, Daniel, can't you stop fooling around for once? Oh, forget it.' I walked off in a huff, throwing items into the trolley that I didn't want or need. A rare electrical storm was building up. I returned to res, had a bath and washed my hair, wrapped myself in my gown and sat down to read a book in front of my window with my feet propped up on the sill. Outside the storm had reached uncharacteristic tropical proportions, with lightning racing across the sky and thunder crashing close by. Big, fat drops of rain plopped against the closed windows. After a while I realised I hadn't turned a single page.

In the till queue at the supermarket a baby in a pouch had lost a pink bootie; it had fallen off right in front of me. I'd frozen at the sight of the tiny bared foot with its miniature toenails. *Human embryo 6+ weeks old. The tail is receding and the arm and leg buds are now prominent. Fingers and toes have just begun to form.* The man behind me had retrieved the bootie and given it to the mother.

I got up to make myself a cup of Horlicks. Just then there was a knock at the door. Carrie Fischer, who'd recently moved onto our floor, stuck her head in to tell me there was a hell of a cute guy downstairs for me. He was waiting in the lounge.

I didn't bother changing. We res girls often went down to the vestibule in our gowns: it made for short visits. I turned the corner in my dressing gown, expecting to see Nicky, praying he wasn't drunk. Daniel turned around from where he'd been standing at the window watching the storm.

We looked at each other for a long moment.

'What are you doing here?' Always the perverse Paola.

But by then I'd walked up to him, hypnotised by those eyes.

'Sometimes you talk too much.'

He traced the shape of my face, ran his fingers over my open lips and kissed me. I signed him in with a trembling hand, his arm around my waist. We moved up the stairs clenched in a lip-lock that couldn't be broken, his hands all over me, inside the gown, brushing over my nipples. I saw Carrie's freckled face looking down, her mouth silently forming the exclamation, Wow! We'd fallen backwards onto the bed after Daniel delivered a well-aimed kick to close the door, when through the din of the storm I heard Nicky call my name. I told myself I was imagining things, but Daniel stopped moving over me to listen.

'Don't go, Daniel. He'll see you.' But I was too late. Daniel had leapt up, pulling his jeans up as he rushed to the window and opened it. *Shit, shit, shit.* I put the duvet over my head.

I heard Daniel open the window and shout: 'Nick, don't be an idiot, get down from there!'

And then I heard Nicky shout, 'So it isn't because of him, hey Paola?' *Jesus.* He was as drunk as a skunk.

I pushed Daniel aside. 'Come on, Nicky, get down from there so we can talk. Don't do anything stupid.' I watched helplessly as Nicky played at being a monkey in the giant syringa tree outside my window. When he saw me he shouted, 'Look Paola, no hands!' and let go, hanging from a branch by two legs. It happened as fast as an eye blinking. One second I had him in sight, and the next the gods unleashed the power of the universe upon us. We found Nicky's broken body spread-eagled on the wet concrete pavement at the base of the tree. Around us lightning struck and thunder crashed. Blood was gushing from his head. Somebody was screaming. I stood there in the pelting rain as if I were made of dry ice, my head pounding, my heart bursting, unable to absorb the enormity of what had just happened. Daniel had ripped his shirt off and torn it in half; he tried to staunch the flow of blood but it was too strong. In minutes he was covered in his best friend's blood.

Ever since then, he'd kept Nicky's photo in his wallet – my husband who believed photographs were pointless.

That was the frozen tableau presented to the occupants of the first campus security vehicle on the scene. Carrie must have had the presence of mind to press the panic button. The police arrived soon after. Dumb with horror, I watched as thick, dark blood poured out of Nicky's nose and the policewoman felt for a pulse. That was when I heard someone shouting, 'No, no, no!' I looked over at Carrie, surprised; she hadn't seemed the screaming type. She held my head between her hands and forced me to look at her: 'Paola, listen to me. He's alive.' Carrie was the granddaughter of an Arctic explorer and the daughter of a famous surgeon. After Nicky's accident she changed career direction from mechatronics to medicine.

A policeman made me sit down next to Carrie on the steps.

Somebody handed her an umbrella. The lightning had moved away. A crowd of people had gathered. We watched as other police cars screamed to a halt, arranging themselves in a half-circle facing Nicky's body. Saturday afternoons were busy for the thinly stretched emergency services that shuttled patients to the public city hospitals. The ambulance finally arrived. The ambulance workers' faces were sympathetic but I could imagine what they were really thinking. What was one stupid, drunk white student in the face of the weekly savagery they faced? Shit timing in a storm. They fitted a brace to Nicky's neck and lifted the stretcher into the ambulance. The policewoman in a rain jacket asked, briskly, what had happened, sitting in the car to get out of the rain, notebook in hand. Daniel stood by the open door and did all the talking. Someone had thrown a blanket around him. His face was translucent it was so pale, the long dark hair plastered to his skin, slick and glistening in the gloom.

Carrie found dry towels, made us coffee, put the heater on and then left us alone.

'Did you tell him you were coming to see me?'

'No, I would never have done that. He must have followed me. No one's to blame. It was a freak accident.'

My heart had turned cold as stone against Nicky after his drunken assault on me in the forest. And yet I had screamed without knowing it over his unconscious form and wished him back on the tree playing silly buggers. I wanted to bury my head on Daniel's shoulder and tell him how sorry I was but his face stopped me.

The day after Nicky fell from the tree, Daniel and I visited him in hospital, arriving separately. The specialist came in while we were both there. He said as far as they could tell the patient had – apart from the stitches already in his chest – concussion and two severe fractures to his right leg. They were doing further tests to make sure there was no other damage. He'd have to wear a neck brace for a while but otherwise, with physiotherapy, he'd be good as new in a few weeks. Nicky had some colour in his cheeks and he was hungry; he acted as if the whole situation was a hilarious accident, joking with his visitors about his bandaged head and beaming at us both.

I waited outside in the corridor. 'Daniel, it's unnatural. He knows you were in my room; he saw us both together at the window. It's an act.'

'I guess his brain isn't functioning too well right now,' Daniel said sarcastically, and then caught himself. 'He's my friend, Paola. What do you want me to do?'

I want you to choose me.

Two days later Nicky was dead of an aneurism in the brain. The specialist said they'd done everything they could. It sometimes happened – the body was a sensitive organism. His head must have suffered a direct blow.

After Nicky's funeral I swore never to attend another one in my life. The ceremony was held in Simonstown in an old stone church dedicated to interdenominational services. The coffin was covered by a maroon embroidered cloth with cream corner tassels that hung over the sides. On top of the cloth, a fighting sword and a stabbing dagger had been placed, which had been in the family for many generations, passed from male heir to male heir for safekeeping. In his oration, Nicky's godfather, a retired naval captain, explained in a thin, clinical voice that these implements dated back to Roman times and the fights of gladiators in the Colosseum. I caught sight of the yellow-haired Mariella standing to the side of the body of mourners, her lips working overtime to save Nicky's soul. At the graveside, Nicky's three much older half-sisters from the father's previous marriage to a Greek heiress, who had flown in from various European localities, tried to restrain their stepmother from throwing herself onto the coffin of her son and only child, but the statuesque blonde with the film-star beauty spot threw them off with Amazonian strength. Finally, to everyone's relief, Nicky's father, an imposing older version of the son who lay in the coffin, woke up from his own reverie and moved over to his wife, taking her hand and kneeling on the dug-up ground next to her, his smart suit pants covered in red soil now, speaking so softly that no one besides her could hear.

When I looked again I couldn't see Mariella. Twilight was descending by the time Mrs van den Bogen allowed her husband to lift her up and lead her away with the help of a stout middle-aged woman who had been standing in the wings waiting. I saw him leave his wife with the woman, who held her up by one arm, her sensible shoes planted firmly on the ground as if she were a tree. When Nicky's mother saw me the howls started anew and she hugged me so fiercely I found it difficult to disengage myself. Through her tears she introduced me to Nanny Hoogendoorn, Nicky's nanny when he was a boy. She had come all the way from Holland for the funeral. The plain-faced woman acknowledged me briefly and then turned her attention back to her charge.

Like three black crows, the half-sisters waited, pecking me on both cheeks with cold lips, black grief in their eyes. Did they know I no longer loved their fair-haired, wild half-brother? I'd doused myself in the perfume that Nicky had bought me, out of some obscure desire to mourn a twice-dead lover, but from their faces I saw that I must have reeked of guilt. I'd read somewhere that the subconscious can detect guilt where the conscious mind cannot. It seemed entirely reasonable to me. Perhaps they simply read on my face that my distraught mind was elsewhere. I had watched Daniel give his condolences to the family. I had spoken to him through a slit of frozen lips and asked him not to go. His reply was to lift my hand and kiss it sorrowfully. Daniel was never coming back.

You've won, Nicky, you crazy bastard. You knew he wouldn't stay if you killed yourself.

Nicky's mother made an exhibition of herself that night, tottering around and slopping alcohol over people, telling stories about Nicky, 'my baby', as unchecked tears rolled down her cheeks. At one point she staggered towards Mariella, who stood alone in a quiet corner, the yellow hair a beacon. 'Who are you?' Mrs van den Bogen enquired rudely. 'I didn't invite you.'

I could have gone over and said, 'She's a friend of Nicky's.' But I'd always shied away from mortal female embarrassment. She wasn't my problem. Nanny Hoogendoorn said something in a soothing voice, leading her charge away firmly, but Mrs van den Bogen was still declaring 'I don't know her,' as they passed me.

For a moment I am there again. It's May 1995, and Nanny Hoogendoorn is the Rock of Gibraltar in the midst of a sea of Shakespearian grief, doling out men's tissues from a cavernous black handbag. My eyes are as dry as sin. You don't need one? She questions without smiling. I never cry, I say, even when my heart is breaking. It is better so, she says, talking to no one in particular. I am tipsy and I flirt outrageously with Nicky's cousin, who asks if I need a lift home.

From that day on I arranged funerals when I had no choice, put notices in the paper and attempted to follow to the letter the finer points of the wishes of the dead, but it would be many years before I personally attended a funeral again. I left it to my mother and father to attend the funeral of their son Massimo, my brother, shot dead at the age of twenty-seven by the target of a sting operation. My father's eventual suicide resulted in a quiet memorial service that I avoided by volunteering for a conference in Ireland. The sum total of my funeral experience as an attendee was one ex-lover, and at that point I judged it to be sufficient for a lifetime.

Did that other young Paola once love her madly jealous half-Greek boyfriend? It's true she had thrown herself at his best friend with wanton intentions. But passion is a giddy firefly. She roves the coursing darkness with her glimmering light and alights where she chooses, even if it means immolation. Her girlhood daydreams on the enchanted patch of concrete at the bottom of the garden had anticipated an extraordinary mate, one who would understand instinctively that she was not like other women.

II
BEAUTIFUL SEX

The St Helena Tribune, International Edition, Friday November 22, 2002

FRENCH MINISTER OF INTERIOR HOLIDAYS ON ST HELENA

Helène Depardieu, French Deputy Minister of the Interior, was spotted by this reporter disembarking from the RMS *St Helena* with a male companion yesterday. This rising star in French politics has become well known not only for her political acumen – she is reputed to think and act like a man – but as a style icon in the Coco Chanel mode.

Most of the island was waiting for the ship to dock after the week-long voyage from Cape Town. Her chic French outfit drew plenty of oohs and aahs from the bystanders, who were convinced she must be a famous actress. Ms Depardieu was dressed in an eye-catching all-red ensemble that consisted of an elegant pantsuit, a transfixing fluted pillbox hat in a slightly darker shade and designer leather ankle-high boots. Her luggage was genuine Louis Vuitton.

Perhaps some of her style has already rubbed off, because this reporter noticed a brand new Union Jack blowing on the mast. The grand old dame that has brought so many illustrious visitors to St Helena is in desperate need of a revamp. In its heyday, a passage on the RMS *St Helena*, with its luxury berths and haute cuisine, was a sought-after vacation. But perhaps in today's world it is the promise of a restful holiday out of the public gaze that attracts the famous personages who arrive on our remote island. In Ms Depardieu's case, she is taking a deserved break from affairs of state. A secret liaison with a younger married politician in her own party ended in a blaze of unwelcome publicity earlier this year, after Ms Depardieu told a *Paris Match* interviewer that her greatest wish was to become a mother while there was still time.

A spokesperson for Ms Depardieu declined to comment on the identity of her dark and handsome companion, saying only that she was on holiday with a good friend.

The owners of the RMS *St Helena* and the committee charged with looking at the viability of an airfield to provide new economic opportunities for the island must take heart from this event. It is hoped that Ms Depardieu's visit bears fruit and heralds the start of a new phase in the island's history.

The Party
Network

I<small>T WAS THE WAY SHE SAID</small> 'baby'. Peggy, the Rubenesque receptionist on lunchtime duty at the insemination clinic had grown used to my presence there. Before long, she was telling me her life story over lunch. Two prem babies lost, a third baby dead in his cot. After years of depression and counselling, her marriage had collapsed. Now she was seeking the goddess within by going to belly dancing classes and posing naked for art students.

'Funny, isn't it?' she said without any bitterness. 'I'm scared of having babies; you're here because you want one.'

For a moment I saw her in a rocking chair – long, loose auburn hair and absurdly heavy breasts dripping milk, arms empty. I shut the image down instantly.

I don't want to have a baby. I want to bring Daniel home.

A month had passed and there was no sign of him.

A sexy air stewardess had told my mother about a place where one could conceive a child with *a real man*, her words eerily echoing the Lady Limbo message of our university days. Daniel had reacted to my mother's travel anecdote as if the Devil herself had put in an appearance. The truth was, it had been an odd coincidence; there couldn't be too many of those kinds of organisations. If the *Lady*

Limbo he'd binned was some kind of an early plot outline for the new book, why get so worked up about my mother's story? Wasn't it more grist to the mill?

It made my head spin. And in the back of my mind was the midget woman, Enid, who thought that having a child would help. I couldn't explain it properly to myself just yet but I decided to locate the place the stewardess, Celestine, had mentioned to my mother. It wasn't exactly a lead but it would be a starting point.

My first port of call was the world's largest library and greatest free marketplace of ideas. Presumably things had developed since Lady Limbo's time, when someone had first turned an esoteric need into a promising business venture. I didn't want to take the risk of working on my company laptop. Instead, I worked in the study at Daniel's desk on the computer he'd had 'beefed up'. My Lady Limbo had disappeared into the ethers of time: there were no hits on Real Man Inc. and searches on the name 'Lady Limbo' yielded one porn site after the next. It slammed you full in the face. The longer I searched the worse it got. In cyberspace I had clearly been dubbed a sex maniac and the material came at me from every side; I could no longer go onto normal sites without being bombarded by the sexual antics of the human race. It became apparent that bestiality was not just practised by frustrated goatherds in ancient Greece. Sadomasochism was rampant in middle-class suburbs and not only on the lunatic fringe.

In a moment of cyberspace weakness I discovered that frequent blowjobs could cause cancer. A pop-up screen offered me the opportunity, at a certain price, to view visuals of the particular actions that might cause said dastardly disease. I discovered that there was no limit to the number of sex positions known to man and woman, the permutations restricted only by the imagination. The battlements of infinity had not yet been broached. Huge cocks penetrated and vaginas thrummed; sex was as cheaply available as a burger at McDonalds. There was a strange, horrible thrill-seeking voyeuristic fascination to it all.

I found myself tempted even when I did not want to look. I came upon an erotica site belonging to a collector who described his collection dating back to the Victorian age as necessary to understanding basic human desires. He explained how male doctors in those times cured the condition of female 'hysteria' (whose symptoms are now recognised to correlate to a state of arousal) by inducing an orgasm, using their hand to stimulate the clitoris. One doctor was driven to invent a 'hysteria' machine with different 'attachments' when his hand grew tired of its relieving function. Historically speaking, this then was the first vibrator, a *pomping* machine that looked like something out of a torture chamber. My dreams became orgies, my fantasies out of all control. I would be sitting in a meeting, or writing a report when last night's guilty glimpse would flash before me, maybe of a man humping a young girl, a school skirt raised, the knot of a school tie loosened over an unbuttoned shirt, her white cotton panties on the floor, and I would experience, first-hand, the condition of 'hysteria' as an involuntary ripple of electricity under the skin, accompanied by a restless thrumming of the clitoris. Arousal was always followed by self-disgust.

These porn actresses were frequently no more than children – young girls who knew no better. I began noticing things I had never noticed before. In a shopping centre my newly enlightened eyes spotted a young girl in school uniform wearing moist make-up and a navy pleated skirt so short she must have rolled the waistband up. Then they picked up the tubby middle-aged man who followed a couple of metres behind her, unconsciously licking his lips. I watched them leave the shop and both disappear behind a door leading to the public toilets, the titillating pied piper and her sewer rat.

Orgasmic screams pursued me relentlessly in my waking and sleeping hours. I was going too far. I worried about becoming addicted to the dark no-boundaries world of online pornography but there was no going back. I had to find Daniel before it was too late. After weeks of hunting them down I discovered that the only Limbo Ladies left in the sordid world of smut, sex and sin were women who offered limbo dancing as an erotic precursor to the cherry on top of the sundae.

Eventually, I abandoned Daniel's computer, now saturated with lust, and started frequenting the Internet café around the corner. My experiences had taught me one thing: how to avoid the hard-core porn sites. I tried the medical sites but they turned up nothing useful. After that I started turning my attention to the more serious sites that dealt with women-baby issues. I used heavy nouns like *eugenics, natural conception* and *human reproduction*. I trawled blogs and chatrooms looking for clues. The reality was that Real Man Inc. had disappeared and the Lady Limbo I sought existed only in a place now forever out of my reach. She might as well have fallen through the crack between Heaven and Hell and truly landed in Limbo.

At our next meeting in his office, I quizzed Elijah on whether he had any intention of using the facilities of the information technology highway; I imagined a web of cyber detectives networking online. Elijah expressed some grave reservations on the matter.

'There's a lot of hullabaloo around the Internet. For one thing, it's too big. For another, you can't tell what's real and what's not. Before you know it you've lost yourself in a place like that. It's like trying to find a rare butterfly in a swamp that breeds nasty mosquitoes. I'll work with anyone I know by reputation, but most so-called cyber detectives know nothing about detective work. The Internet makes them lazy. Solving cases is about solid ground work; it's always better to go direct to source. If you can, that is.' Two television-screen eyes radiating pale blue static studied me pensively. 'Was there anything specific you had in mind?'

'Nothing specific,' I said, ultra-casually. 'Just wondering how you work.' I decided not to say anything about my own private investigation just yet.

Elijah was right. Being an arm-chair cyber detective wasn't getting me anywhere. If I was RMI, where would I find a captive audience for my unusual services? Finally something Daniel had said – to my mother's chagrin – came back to me. *These places exist everywhere, not just in Belgium.* I decided to research locally available donor insemination. That took me further. It was a lucrative field with many overseas clients availing themselves of the specialist skills and facilities at a fraction of what they might pay in private clinics back home. I made several appointments, endured the interviews and paid the hefty fees. At the end of each interview I asked if there was a possibility of natural conception. It became easier; I started to enjoy the startled expressions of the medical practitioners. My husband had disappeared (again) and I wanted to have a child to see if that would bring him back and keep him home. But I wanted to know the father of my child face-to-face. I acquired a certain celebrity status that allowed me to sit in their coffee shops and get to know individual staff members, a cup of coffee or a plate of sandwiches the price of a conversation. People wandered over to talk to me. People like Peggy, who had once had everything a woman could want.

'Why don't you just go to a sperm bank?' Peggy had asked, the day she sat down opposite me with her tray. 'It's much simpler.'

'I don't know how I'd feel about my child if I did that. I want to look the father in the eyes.' I surprised myself. Lady Limbo herself could not have been more ready.

She babbled on about a friend of hers, a nurse at the clinic, who acted as an agent for something called The Party Network.

'I went along myself once, but it was pretty much a damp squib. It wasn't that the men weren't interested, I was just too nervous. My therapist calls it associative memory: I link sex to having babies that die.'

The conversation had taken an interesting direction.

'Who runs it?'

'Basically, it's an underground network run on the lines of a by-invitation private club. They stay one step ahead of the sex police by enforcing a strict age limit – over 21s only. Everything that happens at a party is voluntary and between consenting adults.'

'They must be making a packet.'

Peggy guessed the organisers made their money off the bar and the membership fees. If money was exchanged at the party for anything except booze, then it was behind closed doors. Most of the partygoers were regulars with annual membership; others were occasional visitors like herself. She'd heard that the party network had started out as a group of friends swapping partners for sex sessions. They'd rotated the venue each week and used email to invite new people recommended by couples in the in-group. It had started off as heterosexual couples only but things had progressed. They offered something for everyone these days.

'What about violence?'

She shook her head. 'You don't have to worry. They're strict about things like that.'

These days there was one main party house; they'd probably paid off people like police commissioners and judges with lifelong memberships. They were never raided. Peggy was shrewder than she acted.

Some of the guests were older men and women looking for sexual adventure without ties. Others were bored socialites looking to expand their sexual horizons. Most of the partygoers were just there to experience sex with new partners in safe, clean surroundings and occasionally, she had heard, there were high society young women who wanted to procreate with a genetically suitable younger man rather than their mega-wealthy older husbands who lacked libido. Everyone knew they weren't getting any sex from the old goats; otherwise they'd just use artificial insemination. She eyed me speculatively, a question in her eyes.

'I don't know if my husband's ever coming back.' That part at least was true.

'Would you be interested in speaking to my friend, Kim?' I had hit the jackpot.

A young woman in nursing uniform fell into step with me as I left the clinic, swinging along beside me in a go-getter kind of way and chewing gum as if we were family. She'd heard I was asking about the possibility of natural conception. She could introduce me to a few people at the next party as her guest, but of course there was a small referral fee involved. There was this guy she knew, he'd done something like this before; maybe he'd be what I was looking for.

'You want kinky? He's *the* guy. You want the missionary

position – maybe you think that works better – he can do that too.'
She was in the wrong profession, she should have gone into sales;
covering all her bases like that showed natural talent.

'Such versatility. That takes a load off my mind.'

The sarcasm was wasted on her. If that didn't work out, she
continued, maybe Madeleine, one of the organisers, could help. It
was all kept very hush-hush but she'd heard on the grapevine that
Madeleine was in contact with an overseas organisation that set
up introductions for people in South Africa. My heart leapt. I was
happy to pay what she asked; it was not an unreasonable amount
for an unusual service. She'd call me to make arrangements.

She was actually a very kind girl. Her parting shot was, 'If
you want to get laid, you should drop the business suits. Think
nightclub, flashing orbs, sexy men and gorgeous women, plenty
of champagne, cool music. You'll have a ball!' I winced at her
unfortunate choice of words. That woke me up. What the hell was
I doing ordering sex like a club sandwich in a clinic parking lot?
We were probably about the same age but she made me feel 104.

At that moment I felt miserable, deeply and sadly at a loss for
what to do next. When was the last time I'd been to a nightclub? I
had once loved going to late-night party spots – the vibe, the loud
music, the dancing, the smoky atmosphere, getting dressed up for
an evening on the town. Daniel's idea of a perfect night out was
an intimate restaurant with an elegant lounge lit up by jewelled,
stylish women and their discreet perfume. Slowly and surely we'd
stopped going. Nightclubs seemed to make us argue. Everything
I found delightful Daniel found wanting. The final straw was one
of those stupid arguments that only married couples have. By
chance we'd hit a nightclub when a rowdy promotion was on for
a new brand of beer. It had been brasher than usual, the music
awful bubblegum pop and rap, the girls more abandoned and
scantily dressed than ever. Two girls were snogging on the dance
floor right next to us and a couple was doing their best to have
intercourse through their clothes at a nearby pillar, an activity
Daniel contemptuously referred to as 'le frottage'.

'Why is it that women act like sluts in places like that? Is it true there is a slut in every woman?' This was an old argument. We'd even laughed over it sometimes, but not that night.

'Oh come on, Daniel. A certain kind of woman goes to places like that.'

'Ah, so what were we doing there?'

'Are you saying I'm a slut?'

'Logically, that is what I must deduce from what you have just said,' Daniel declared staunchly, never one to back down in an argument.

'What about the men all over women they don't even know? Is it true that every man thinks with his penis?'

'*Quod liset jovi non liset bovi.*' He had a wealth of Latin proverbs garnered from *Asterix and Obelix* that he loved to use. This one advocated that what was okay for Jupiter was not okay for his servant, the bull.

'Do you have to be so patronising? What's wrong with having *fun*? Why can't we be like other people and let our hair down sometimes? I'm sick and tired of staying home and eating your home-cooked extravaganzas.'

'Nothing. If that's the kind of company you want to keep.' One of the most infuriating things about Daniel de Luc was that he rarely took my bait, no matter how poisoned the barb was.

Daniel often slept on the couch because of nightmares that shook his body; that night he slept on the couch because he didn't want to lie next to a slut. The next morning, he flung the curtains wide to let the sun in, nuzzled my neck, hauled me out of bed for American bacon-and-banana-filled pancakes drizzled with syrup, and blew me kisses that flew like homing pigeons over the breakfast table.

When my brother and I were very young, my father's role as roving African trade attaché representing the Italian government had required grand parties where the men arrived in oyster-white dinner jackets with bowties and the women wore extravagant once-off couture gowns, dressed like the socialites they were. As children, Massimo and I were allowed to watch from the landing, our faces squeezed between the bars of the balustrade, our legs hanging down over the landing. Visitors on their way to the upstairs guest bathrooms would find us sitting there in our pyjamas. When the guests moved outside on warm summer evenings or for a spectacular fireworks display, we would move to the gabled window of the upstairs study and look down upon the lantern-lit garden with grown-ups milling about like film stars.

'We women are princesses-in-training, darling, non dimenticare!' In those days my Italian mother was a butterfly in perpetual motion. As we grew older, I used her lipstick and put the same nail varnish on my nails as she had on hers, and Massimo stayed in his room.

'You must learn from these elegant women in their evening dresses how to carry yourself with grace and poise, Paola,' my father advised. 'A woman does not have to be born beautiful, but she must always dress well and pay attention to herself and, most of all, she must be intelligent and a good conversationalist.'

When I thought of those magical parties with the soaring music that my father insisted on, I understood how much my mother had lost when my father left her for an official from the Russian Consulate. Perhaps he had tried to tell her when he went through a phase where he insisted on mournful Eastern European music, overruling her suggestion for something happier and Italian (or at least African!), but she had not listened hard enough. Perhaps he had mentioned the young Russian official who displayed initiative relating to a trade matter that involved a joint venture with Russia, long before she became his secret consort on his frequent business trips out of the country. Perhaps it was her good conversational skills that made up his mind, finally.

So I knew what Daniel yearned for in his soul and why he hated the cheap, glitzy nightspots the rest of the world frequented. Like my father, he had the aristocrat's disdain for an unruly crowd.

My contact phoned during the week.

'Where do you stay? I'll pick you up at 10 pm on Friday.'

'I'll take my car. Just give me directions.'

'I'm afraid not,' she said breezily, sounding as if she was using a toothpick between words. 'You're my invited guest. I take you in. I take you out. We go in my car. That's how it works.'

On Friday night, she drove us out of town in a metallic blue Smart coupé with a turbo engine. Nice car. A girl's got to do what a girl's got to do. Every ten minutes on the badly-lit West Coast road, a car would drive towards us going in the opposite direction, heading for the city lights. She put on a CD. The car was a moving pool of shifting darkness, the evening sky a colander of pinprick lights. I felt like Thelma or Louise, on a road trip into the nether regions of my own black heart.

'Where are we going?' Through my window I gazed upward at the vast expanse of flickering velvet night.

She flashed me a sideways glance. 'Bulldog Beach,' she said before raising the volume on K.D. Lang's pool bar voice.

Bulldog Beach. I was glad of the darkness and the loud music. It wasn't a name you easily forgot. Daniel's deadpan expression, the sparkling green eyes, as he told the story about the cute little bulldogs marching in pairs along the beach. Et voilà! I'd suggested driving out once or twice but it had never happened.

Daniel said he'd come to the city (and me) for diversion; Bulldog Beach was where he worked. It wasn't a particularly scenic part of the coastline or a good place to swim. There were too many jagged rocks and a bad undertow. Dogs had been known to disappear in the surf. The beach itself was mainly frequented by anglers and dog walkers. But when a friend had contacted him in France, saying he was off to the States for an indefinite period and offering his apartment, he'd jumped at the opportunity to return to South Africa. The isolated location suited him for his writing, he had said. It was quiet and private. Most of the people who lived there were professional couples who used their homes on a weekend and holiday-only basis. One of the conditions of the original property developers, registered on all the title deeds, was that no children were allowed.

'This is Manolo. He's Argentinian.' Ms Party-pants introduced the dark-skinned young man who slunk over, lithe as a panther, as soon as we stepped into the high-ceilinged lounge. Manolo's sinewy body was adorned in skin-tight black leather jeans and matching bolero over a white open-necked flamenco-style shirt that framed a silver bolo tie around his neck and emphasised the bronze skin. His gleaming silver-studded boots winked at me so enticingly that I felt nauseous again.

'He's the one I told you about. Manolo settles with me directly. I'll leave you two alone now.' The girl actually winked at me.

'What a splendid idea.' I dripped venom.

Manolo grinned at me with perfectly aligned teeth that could have made him a fortune in toothpaste commercials. 'Can I get you a drink?'

'Look, I'm sorry … This isn't … Oh God, I'm going to be sick.' I escaped past him through French windows into the garden. Luckily it was early so people hadn't moved outside yet. I could puke undisturbed into the bushes.

I managed to find a bathroom and clean myself up before rejoining the party. Damned if I do, damned if I don't. I'd come this far. If I didn't see this thing through tonight I'd never come back.

'Champagne?' Manolo hadn't strayed far.

'Thank you.' I grabbed the gold goblet he held out.

'You are Kim's guest? This is your first time?' He seemed unfazed by my opening-night nerves, his dark eyes glancing over me with the polished sheen of a predator. His Spanish matador accent turned my insides to mush – a kind of mush that started in my pubic area and travelled all the way up to my navel in a tingling rush. My nausea had disappeared. Would it be so terrible to spend a single night with an attentive lover?

'Yes. And yes again,' I acknowledged, taking small panic-stricken sips, feeling a beetroot shade rise to my cheeks.

'Perhaps you would like some fresh air?' he asked solicitously. 'The garden is very nice.'

'Do you know someone called Madeleine?' I blurted out, looking around wildly, a desperate act of cowardice.

'Ah, you are here to see la Châtelaine,' Manolo murmured, 'but the night is still young, yes?' The glistening black eyes locked onto mine. 'She will understand.'

'No, I'm afraid I can't. We have an appointment.' *Chicken*. Just tell him you're not interested. 'Perhaps another time,' I squeaked, before asking brightly, 'Do you like Cape Town?'

'It's an incredible place,' Manolo grinned. 'There are very many beautiful women.'

Manolo took his role of Don Juan seriously. Perhaps that was all that saved me from a serious indiscretion. After a while he excused himself, saying he'd spotted someone across the room he hadn't seen for a while, gave a half-bow, wished me a pleasant evening, expressed a hope that he might see me at a future party (once I knew what I wanted), and moved on to a group on the other side of the room. From a better vantage point, he worked the room with quick appraising glances, between making idle chitchat. Later he glided past with a woman on his arm, her flaxen shining hair piled high on her poised head, her unblemished porcelain skin off-set against a backless midnight blue gown. They disappeared up the stairs, the tip-tapping sound of designer heels and light laughter receding down a corridor. Why did a woman like her need Manolo? I did not see him again that evening.

I grabbed another fluted goblet of champagne from a passing waiter and gulped the bubbling liquid back.

'What happened? Didn't you like him?' Ms Party-pants pouted.

'He's too short.' I said sweetly. 'And he dresses too much like Zorro.'

'You got cold feet, didn't you?' she demanded of me with a certain amount of insight, still chewing gum like cud. 'Manolo's *hot*. He doesn't do the rough stuff. You should see him in a G-string. Women go for him. You want to come again?'

'What about this Madeleine person? Is she here?'

'Sure, she's here.' Ms Party-pants regarded me candidly. 'She's into big-time organised stuff. Have you got the bucks?'

'Just introduce me,' I hissed at her.

'Jeez. Keep your hair on. Wait here.'

About ten minutes later a regal woman in a red and gold sari approached me, a shining black plait draped over one shoulder.

'Good evening, Ms Dante. I'm Madeleine. Shall we move to the balcony? It's quieter out there.'

I silently rehearsed my lines as I hurried to keep up with her. 'Manolo was not to your liking? He is one of the best.' Of course, she would know everything. And then some stuff I couldn't even guess at.

'Yes. I can see that, but he's more of a professional gigolo, isn't he? Perfect for a one-night stand, and even a repeat performance, but maybe not who I'd choose if I wanted to ensure a confidential arrangement. There are too many eyes on him.'

She removed two goblets of champagne from the tray of a passing waiter and handed me one, her serpentine-green eyes assessing me coolly. 'Please continue.'

'I want to conceive a child naturally with a man of appropriate background and an excellent genetic profile. I require absolute privacy and confidentiality. I will back out at any stage if I feel uncomfortable.'

'Of course. We are here to act in your best interests.' She acted as if we were negotiating a bank loan. 'We have a very simple process. The administration fee for the service we offer is 50 000 rand, or equivalent dollars. We require the full amount to be paid up front. Any additional or travelling expenses incurred for an overseas destination are for your account. A further introductory fee of 20 000 rand, or equivalent dollars, is to be paid once you have made your selection and are ready to make a firm booking. Our lawyer will arrange everything. Are you ready to take the number?' She waited while I dug around in my handbag for my mobile and then reeled it off.

'How do I know you'll keep your side of the deal?'

'We are professionals, my dear. We offer an exclusive service to those who are willing to pay for it. The organisation I work for, The Love Bank Foundation, works closely with The Party Network in South Africa. We value our reputation highly.'

'The Love Bank? What kind of a name is that? Why don't you just call it the Love Boat?' I was a bit tipsy by then.

The woman called Madeleine did not digress, carmine lips curving upward in a gracious half-smile, tiger eyes dilated. 'Where would you prefer to conceive? On the Trans-Siberian? On an ocean liner? Paris, Brussels, London? It can all be arranged. The world is your baby's oyster.'

I will go to a place in Belgium. That's what Celestine said.

'Brussels sounds nice, don't you think?' Oh Daniel, where are you? I am stumbling about in the dark, clutching at straws as if they were lampposts.

She nodded. 'A good choice.' The irony of life escaped her. 'Please have a pen and paper handy to take down the contact details when you make the call. The Love Bank Foundation offers a unique service. I trust you will find the experience to your satisfaction.'

'Why don't you people use email?'

'We prefer to keep a low profile and not attract unnecessary attention.'

'Is all of this cloak-and-dagger stuff really necessary?'

'It is for our safety and yours, my dear.' There she went again. 'And eventually even the safety of the unborn child depends on your co-operation in following these simple precautionary measures. Not everybody views our activities in the same way.

'There is one other matter. We provide no guarantees. We conduct extensive screening and we provide a full medical report on each of our practitioners, but understandably, in a field as complex and unpredictable as natural procreation, there can be no guarantees. Your money is non-refundable. Goodnight, Ms Dante.' Madeleine exited in a stately rustle of crimson silk.

That was it. I looked around me. It was a warm evening. Below me scenes of Rabelaisian lechery greeted my eyes. The trees and bushes in the moonlit garden were teeming with raunchy sexual activity and on the lawns and in the lit-up swimming pool human figures cavorted in various states of inebriation and public indecency. A woman was walking around with one breast exposed and her high-heeled shoes in her hand. A group of partygoers jumped into the swimming pool in full evening dress. A soaked woman wrapped herself around another soaked woman with python-like ferocity, giving her a long probing French kiss while at the same time a soaked man lifted Ms Python's long hair and planted kisses all over her exposed nape before tenderly coiling and coiling her tresses around her neck as if he meant to strangle her with his attentions. It struck me that Her Serene Highness might have brought me out to the balcony with a purpose in mind.

'They say the full moon has a way of loosening inhibitions.' A strongly accented voice spoke from behind me on the balcony. I tore my eyes away from the threesome in the water but for a moment I couldn't make out anything in the dark. 'Of course, it could be alcohol, drugs, the illicit factor, or a combo that make the parties such an *orgasmic* success.' A deep-throated laugh followed. 'So, what's your poison?'

A luminous pair of skimpy white hot-pants and a fringed bra top hung suspended in a thick emulsion of darkness. A tall figure with skin like black rain emerged from the darkness at the other end of the balcony railing. The powerfully built sloe-eyed young woman with the Afro hairdo had the muscle tone and limbs of an Amazon.

I'm out of my depth, that's what I think. I'm tired of games. 'No comment.'

She considered my answer. 'You don't approve of orgies?'

'I've got other things on my mind.'

'You are referring to your missing husband,' she said laconically. It was not the reply I'd expected. 'How the hell do you know?'

'I keep my ears open.'

'So much for confidentiality.'

'Have you made any progress?'

'My progress, or lack thereof, is none of your business.'

'I know someone. An ex-policeman. Maybe he can be useful to you.'

'I'm on my way out. Give my regards to the boss.'

'Wait.' She took a pen out of her bag and scribbled something on the back of a card, the tip of her pink tongue running lightly over her top lip as she scribbled. 'Here.' The onyx eyes gleamed in the dark. It would have been churlish to refuse the extended card so I took it.

'My name's Heidi. In case we meet again.'

I wondered if she'd done it on purpose: chosen the most unlikely name possible. The strong francophone accent suggested a central African origin.

'I doubt it. By the way, I love the 007 outfit,' I said.

'Never say never,' she shot back, white teeth flashing.

She was still watching impassively when I left. I walked down the long driveway and out onto the road expecting to find a taxi waiting for a party of this size to finish, but there was just a guard hut and two watch guards patrolling with dogs. I held the card under the light. There wasn't much on it: a name 'Nat' followed by a mobile number.

My party contact phoned the next day, a Saturday.

'What happened to you? I told you guests have to leave with the principal member. Madeleine shat all over me for losing you. Taxis are not encouraged. It's not good for security.'

'I forgot. One of the catering vans gave me a lift.'

'Huh! I bet you never forget anything.'

'Who's the sassy black girl with the Jimmy Hendrix Afro?'

'You mean Heidi? Why?' Her voice was guarded.

'No reason. She seemed eager to strike up a conversation.'

'You'd better stay out of her way. She doesn't like people bothering Madeleine. Madeleine is strict about her privacy.' I'd guessed right. But I couldn't get anything else out of her. That was it.

'What about the woman who went with Manolo? What's her story?'

'You did like him! I knew it. Her husband's some retired international banker. He's got erectile dysfunction problems. Manolo looks after her.'

The girl was so cute, she made me feel ill.

As soon as she let me go I called the mobile number for the Love Bank 'lawyer' I'd been given the night before. On principle

I mistrusted people who indiscriminately called other people 'my dear', but I was going to do exactly as Madeleine had instructed, expecting nothing and hoping for everything. A woman picked up. The conversation was brief. I was to make the payment into a bank account whose details she would now verbally provide. From there on, she would deal with it. I had forty-eight hours before the account and the mobile number I had just called became inoperative.

Next, I called the executor of my father's estate. He sounded pleased that I wanted to invest 70 000 rand of my untouched inheritance in a start-up business venture. Funny the way things turned out. My father and Daniel were both men who found it difficult to stay home.

Two business days later, late on the Tuesday afternoon, a foreign male voice informed me that the payment had been received. The person I was looking for was a Monsieur Bok, le directeur, in Brussels, Belgium. A phone number was provided.

Voilà! The door had opened. After more than a month of searching I was elated, heady with my success as a sleuth in a new world laced with intrigue and carnal desire. I put a bottle of champagne in the rucksack and celebrated alone on the rocks with waves crashing around me. There was no one I could tell. With each sip of champagne I became more convinced that I would find Daniel. What if my suspicions were correct and The Love Bank Foundation was the latest incarnation of Real Man Inc.? Had Daniel's research for the new book led him into deep waters? Could Daniel have gone over the edge? Where was over the edge? *Lady Limbo* flashed through my mind: Isabelle perched on the ledge, out of her mind with terror, dark shadows under her eyes as she looks down, a wingless bird about to plummet. A terrible morbidity settled over me with the creeping chill of a graveyard. Night was falling as I trudged up the walkway to Beach Road.

The last thing I remembered seeing as I stepped into the apartment was a donkey braying on the television screen. In cartoon films the donkey always brays with bared choppers when a cowboy gets pitched into a deep, dark, bottomless well.

Elijah found me passed out on the carpet.

'Can you sit up?'

'My head hurts.'

'You banged it against the table.'

'It was the donkey's fault.'

'The donkey?'

'Donkeys are poor, stupid, dumb creatures.'

I sat up groggily. Elijah swam into focus. He helped me up onto the couch and held a dishcloth filled with ice against my head. 'Amazing what ice can fix.'

'Can it fix a broken heart?'

He smiled. 'You must have a hard head. Most people would need stitches after a fall like that.'

'He thought I was heartless, you know.'

'I don't think it was the donkey's fault.'

'What do you mean?'

'When I came in someone ran out behind me. I had to think about you so I couldn't go after him. He must have been hiding behind the door.'

'I thought it was a drunken hallucination.'

Elijah ran his hand through the red mop, his forehead crumpled with thought. 'You need to check that nothing's missing.'

The last place I looked was in our bedroom. My pillows were flung aside and a drawer stood ajar. The bump on my forehead was throbbing.

When I got back to the lounge Elijah was inspecting the lock on the door.

'Everything's there,' I confirmed.

'If you didn't leave the door open then whoever it was had a key. There's no sign of forced entry.'

My heart lurched. 'Maybe it was Daniel.'

'If Mr de Luc was coming to collect something, he wouldn't have risked finding you at home.'

My heart shrivelled to the size of a pea. 'Yes. I suppose so.' Brutal but true.

Elijah was in deep thought. 'It's unlikely that an opportunistic burglar would have slipped past security, come up two floors and chosen your apartment just on the off-chance ... That leaves us with the possibility that we're dealing with a professional who picked your lock without leaving a trace. Could he have been looking for something?'

'Like what?' I said. Elijah seemed as baffled as I was. We agreed I'd inform the committee about the security breach and get a Yale lock fitted the next day, just in case the intruder came back. And then Elijah came out with the reason for his visit.

'I've been talking to people in the building. The security guard mentioned a woman in a sports car asking for Mr de Luc.'

'Sounds like you've found a new buddy.'

'I let people think I'm an agent for a prospective overseas buyer, and then I make some discrete enquiries about the other tenants. The security guard also mentioned the make and model of the car. A silver Porsche cabriolet.'

'Trust men to talk about cars when Rome is burning.'

'The 911 Carrera is not just any car; it's a top-of-the-range luxury roadster. Do you have any idea who she might be, Mrs de Luc?'

'Why so formal? What happened to Paola?' I didn't like the suspicious tone of his voice. 'Daniel talked to all kinds of people. He has a way with people; they trust him. He has long chats with the postman, and he knows all the names of the security guard's kids, and then there's Sonja and Sarel, the local *bergies* ... Even I know their names because they're always ringing the intercom looking for cardboard and bread. "Dis mos Sonja en Sarel. Is Meneer Daniel daar? Ons soek karton en 'n bietjie brood." Then there are the council rubbish collectors that he knows by name, then there's Frankie the fruit and vegetable guy who rips him off every time with rotten apples at the bottom of the box and seedless naartjies with seeds, but Daniel says it's important to help the small entrepreneur. Do you get the picture?'

Elijah was unshakeable. 'This woman was different. Your husband took her upstairs to the apartment with him. Apparently she came again, and that time went straight up. The security guard was very specific.'

The sixth drawer.

'Maybe she's an estate agent. How the hell should I know?'

'Is the woman known to you?'

I stayed silent. Silence had been my fortress for so long, but now the buttresses were crumbling. Elijah Bloom's kind owl eyes met mine.

'Paola, you will have to trust me if you want me to help you. Has your husband left you for this woman?'

Dear Elijah. If only it was that simple. Enid Lazzari was right: Daniel was an odd candidate for marriage. How could I explain that it wasn't Daniel's style to have a sordid extramarital affair? *There are other relationships.*

'So, that's why you're here.'

My fingers measured the swollen lump on my forehead. There was no gash, no blood. I tried to stand up but my head spun like a windmill.

'Would you mind putting the kettle on to boil? Maybe some coffee will help. I've given up on the green tea. It tastes like rotten seaweed.'

Elijah jumped up. 'Of course.'

'And on your way back, would you bring the brown envelope from the bottom drawer of the desk next door? If you look inside there are three envelopes held together with a white ribbon and some newspaper articles.' I closed my eyes and leaned back, floating away on the tide. Soon somebody else would know. At least part of it. My PI might as well start earning his keep.

'Your coffee, Madame.'

I opened my eyes. Elijah wore a pair of thin white gloves.

'Now you even look the part. All you need is a top hat and some doves.'

Elijah carefully undid the white ribbon of the slender packet that held three airmail-stamped envelopes addressed to a M. Gabriel Montaigne. *Par Avion.*

'May I?'

'Be my guest.'

Elijah extracted a flimsy sheet of paper, holding it by the corners with his gloved fingertips. Somebody had cut newsprint messages out of French newspapers: easily understood words like 'assassin', 'homicide', 'meurtre', 'crime' and 'cause de la mort'. There was no sender's address or note but the ink stamp of origin showed they were posted in Paris.

'Do you have any idea who sent them?'

'None whatsoever.'

Elijah's brows were knitted together in concentration. He seemed more interested in the envelope than the message, occasionally lifting it to his nose and sniffing. He asked if I had a magnifying glass. I sent him back to the study, where I knew he'd find one in the old biscuit tin that came along with my father's stamp collection.

'You knew? That he had this other identity?'

Follow the name.

'No.' I lied fluently, fluidly, without batting an eyelid. Enid Lazzari knew Daniel as Gabriel; she had said no one else could know. I had no intention of losing my tenuous connection to Daniel.

'You think these anonymous letters are somehow linked to the woman?'

'I don't know. It's possible, isn't it? You were the one who said that if you can make links between seemingly unrelated things then you start to get a picture of what happened.'

Elijah eyed me. 'I did?'

'I don't know who she is.'

He turned back to his inspection. 'These are the newspaper articles you mentioned?' I watched him look through the stories on the dead women. 'I'll have to get a translator,' he said, an eyebrow raised. 'They don't come cheap.'

I picked up one of the threatening letters. 'Daniel's not a murderer. He wouldn't even let me buy a fly swatter. He said they had more right to be on this planet than we did. On the other hand, he hated anything ugly, so maybe he just said it to stop me buying the thing, and maybe he's actually a murderer and I never knew it all this time.'

Elijah looked at me. 'Sometimes one doesn't have to be the murderer to feel as though one is. You told me he was here when at least two of those girls died. That rules him out.'

'I know. But why did he collect the clippings?'

'Why indeed,' Elijah said thoughtfully. He turned back to the material spread on the table in front of him. 'I'd like to take these envelopes away to be dusted for fingerprints. We got a partial print off the coffee mug. It might allow us to eliminate Mr de Luc's prints.'

I watched him pack the letters into a clear plastic bag that had silently emerged from a pocket. 'I'm going away for a while. I'll be out of the country for a couple of weeks.'

'I'll continue sending through the weekly reports,' he said imperturbably, standing up. 'Don't forget to get a locksmith tomorrow.'

'Will you see what you can find out about the Porsche?'

'I'm on it,' Elijah said. 'And I'll see what I can dig up on one Gabriel Montaigne. Maybe that post box is still in use, but somehow I doubt it. When you return we should compare notes.'

My PI was pretty sharp.

'By the way,' Elijah continued, 'did you know donkeys originated from wild asses? If you go to the mountainous northern part of India that borders Pakistan you can see them with your own eyes. They have survived against all the odds with a mixture of luck and tenacity; they are considerably more intelligent than their tamer cousins. The domesticated donkey is a poor shadow of its wilder cousin after suffering the indignity of being neutered to calm its naturally rampant sexual drive.'

He closed the door gently behind him. For a moment there I imagined Elijah Bloom's eyes had shone red like the eyes of a timber wolf in the dark.

Later, I go into the study. Just to sit in Daniel's chair, touch his things. I take his sketch pad out of the top drawer and start paging through it, casually, without looking for anything in particular. I turn a page and freeze. After a moment I adjust the desk lamp. A figure in a grey hoodie, torn jeans and tackies, a crumpled rebellious ghost sent to haunt him, has been captured by the carbon markings of my husband's soft 2B pencil. The waiting girl at the bus stop is ringed by a smudged glow.

The Love Bank
Foundation

I MADE AN APPOINTMENT. It was so simple. I imagined I was Celestine. Piet didn't take it very well – the first quarter is a hectic time on projects – but I didn't leave him much choice. I said it was a health emergency. That made his brow furrow, especially as he stared at the bruise on my forehead that had turned a yellow-purplish shade. How long? A week max. Eventually he agreed.

What was it Celestine had said to my mother? There must be *something* between a man and a woman. *A spark? Oui? N'est-ce pas?* The taxi dropped me at an unobtrusive red-brick building on the outskirts of Brussels.

It took longer than expected. I hadn't contemplated any of it: the genetic background tests, the blood tests, the full physical examination.

They just want to make sure some gold-digger doesn't come after them with a law suit. That would blow them out of the water.

A slim brochure in English informed me that factors such as good health, the serenity of the woman and the vigour of the man created favourable circumstances that would enhance the experience and promote fertility. *And then I will have beautiful sex with him*, Celestine had said. Since it was the policy of The Love Bank Foundation to avoid all external interventions and encourage natural ways of conception, the scheduling of the typical twenty-four-hour encounter was left up to the client. Longer encounters could be arranged on request. The Maldives. St Helena. Or Timbuktu. Wherever the client wished.

It's all bollocks, I thought, sitting in the plush waiting room leafing through the glossy booklet. The chances of the average woman falling pregnant in a randomly scheduled twenty-four encounter are statistically low.

I could say this with a reasonable amount of certainty. At an age when the functions of the female body held a ghoulish fascination, I'd uncovered a brochure entitled *Birth Control for the Practising Catholic* in my mother's jewellery drawer. All my mother's attempts at a mother-daughter conversation ended in failure, but through the years updated versions went into the same drawer. By the time Nicky came to a running stop after his impressive dead-centre parachute landing, I had decided he would be my first lover. He was to be my gateway into the sensual world of adulthood. By then I had done my research. As antiquated as the rhythm method was, it had some unique advantages compared to the pill – zero cost, no embarrassing visits to a public clinic and no side effects. I'd followed the guidelines and worked out a calendar that I refined as I went along. It was easy enough to convince Nicky of the merits of the method – it was that or a perpetual condom.

With thoughts of Nicky came the inevitable stinging scent of pine needles: my legs refusing to support me as I struggle to get up off the forest floor, Nicky closing the zip of his bike-suit trousers as he staggers off towards the car headlights, the forest heaving and circling: *It's a red day on the calendar.* It was like wearing a bullet-proof vest and finding a hollow bullet had pierced to the flesh.

I took a certain perverse satisfaction in inflicting the rhythm method on future lovers, never once letting on as I ignored statistically more reliable modern-day methods. In my view, it was natural and within my control. The only downside was that my body wasn't as predictable as I'd have liked. A part of me would always be checking that it wasn't a bright red-letter day; I was strict about those.

The organisation required a confidentiality agreement to be signed up front. After the necessary health checks it would take another forty-eight hours to know if my application to The Love Bank Foundation had been accepted. I would then be able to make a booking. The director noticed my raised eyebrow and explained that it was necessary to ensure that I was sincere in my application, and not a journalist or a person seeking publicity.

What the fuck does sincerity have to do with it?

The organisation prided itself on a high conception success rate. The health and mental attitude of the prospective mother were of primary importance, Monsieur Bok explained further. Also, it was necessary to ensure that the interests of the unborn child were at all times protected and paramount. The financial transaction was secondary – c'est moins important, oui?

Bullshit.

I interrupted his carefully delivered speech to ask about the bronze plaque on the door. Why did it say Research Management Institute, with the letters RMI below, and not The Love Bank Foundation? If he was surprised by my question, he didn't show it.

These were delicate matters that could not be handled without discretion. The Research Management Institute was a legitimate enterprise involved in research related to fertility. They were proud of their success record. All possible avenues were explored to ensure women conceived naturally. There was a time when RMI had been used as an acronym for Real Man Incorporated, and, in fact, many of their clients continued to use this name. In later years, they had created The Love Bank Foundation as a trade name in order to prevent any confusion with the research institute. Did that answer my question satisfactorily?

I had found Real Man Inc.

Lady Limbo had called the tune a long time ago, offering her hand to whoever was ready to take it. Is that what happened to us? Now that I thought about it, that's when things started to change in our blithe threesome. I realised it had started to rain – the outside world had been erased to a fluid-streaked film of running glass. The water dropped so softly and silently; there was something depressing about its natural efficiency. I could hardly see what lay beyond the room.

'Where do I sign?'

On the third day I returned to be told that my application had been successful. It was all very discrete. I never saw another person in the small lounge outside the director's office except a PA. The director slid a folder across the desk from his side to mine. My medical report. A signed letter declared me to be healthy and encouraged natural conception. A second sheet consisted of my ovulation chart. Shit.

I hadn't expected them to be so thorough. RMI gave its female clients free rein to play the game of risk any way they wanted – sex or conception – but first they covered themselves.

A second folder slid across. After careful consideration involving many factors, including a computerised assessment of my personality and physical profile, six excellent potential candidates could be offered. I pushed the folder back without opening it.

'What about a complete set on computer?'

A few murmured words into the intercom and it was organised. He was clearly used to headstrong women.

I was left alone in an adjoining office to search through a digital parade of men. There were no names, only codes like AZN-7658. There were two photographs per male candidate: one clothed and one bare-chested. The black and white studio photographs projected a collective impression of intelligent body-confident masculinity. An independent-minded woman would have to look no further to satisfy her secret desires and sublime wishes. Coloured pictures, nude shots and voice interviews could be requested as a 'special'. It was clear that this world had its own reality filter. The information was skimpy on the personal details and comprehensive on the health and intelligence data. Rigorous medical testing took place to ensure candidates were free of infectious diseases. I would know everything about the father of my future child, from whether he suffered migraines to how many university degrees he held. I would even know something about his hobbies and his likes and dislikes, but I would have no way of ever finding him again.

Daniel was not in the database of candidates on offer for the three-day window I had booked. What now, Ms Smarty Pants? I decided to take it step by step. In the end I brought it down to three possibilities, all dark-haired like Daniel.

'We've wasted enough time,' I said coolly, back in the director's office, as I sent a ring of smoke in his direction. I'd purchased a pack of slim cigarettes at the airport on impulse. The average adversary is easily unnerved. 'So, let's try to speed it up, shall we?'

How far do I go before I skedaddle out of here?

'That is your privilege,' the director assured me solicitously. 'An ashtray, Madame?' A glass ashtray in a shade of molten red with floating wisps of cloud-white that reached the fluted edges appeared in front of me. For a moment I couldn't figure it out. How had our Murano artefact landed up on this suave man's desk? *There are no coincidences, ma chérie.* Later, I could not be sure if the incendiary clarity that made my eyes widen had its origins in shock or rage.

Do you all have complimentary copies? Was it a happy-to-have-you-on-board gift you brought into our home?

It was as I casually flicked ash into that obscene object that I realised I was going to go through with it. There were to be no half-measures. I wanted to know what it felt like to discard inhibitions and leave fear behind. I would march through the ring of fire that guarded the entrance to another dimension. I would throw myself onto the bonfire of murky motives and unredeemed motherhood.

I am the woman ticking a box for a 'live' interview with three possible candidates, suggesting that money is not an issue. I am the woman who makes the call to pre-book a night 'session' with my selected partner. I am finding mystery within myself. It is an aspect I have neglected thus far. I see myself mirrored in Monsieur

Bok's eyes. It's there in my maximally stylish Italian suit with the luxury designer shoes and the immaculate lipstick. It's there in the smouldering cigarette I leave behind in his ashtray, my Gucci shades reflecting the glowing embers. Monsieur Bok will not forget me. A man in his position values dominant femininity.

The interview room was a conversation pit that looked like something out of *A Clockwork Orange*. Lounge music played softly in the background. A chrome and glass drinks cabinet stood against the side wall. The couches were plush and purple, the colour of Roman emperors, with white silk cushions. In the end it was a ridiculous little episode that decided me. I had an argument with the youngest and shortest of the three. In my mind I had dubbed them Ponytail, Shorty and Cocky. Shorty (aka MTX-5545) came to the interview in the same outfit he'd used for the studio shots: blue Levis, white shirt and a dark blazer. He said he'd been told I was from Africa, with a cool, judgemental gaze, his tone implying my privileged status. I said, yes, I was. But what the hell business was that of his anyway? He ignored my outburst.

'Are you looking for a Caucasian European father, to ensure the gene pool, or why are you here? What's wrong with the men at home?' The man was downright rude. He didn't seem to be angling for my favour or care that I might be paying his month's salary. But there was a quickening of my pulse I could not deny. I felt heady with the power of choosing. For an additional sum I could choose how I wanted my child conceived. Chained-to-the-bed bondage sex. Schoolgirl socks and short skirt and schoolmaster kinky, or the nurse–doctor variety. For the more adventurous, lesbian stimulation before heterosexual sex. These were clinical choices on a tick-box form designed to encourage spermatozoa to swim for the life of an unborn child, any one of which I could have ticked for a nominal additional charge. 'The woman was at all times in control, this was what made the foundation unique,' le directeur had murmured. Desperate, confused people are easily fleeced. I'd felt positively prudish refusing optional extras. A phrase I'd read somewhere kept flashing through my head: *The Future is*

Now. What the hell am I doing? Aloud I said, 'No more goddamn foreplay. How do we do this? What shall I call you?'

'Tonight, I shall be Jack.'

That made me laugh. Jack the Ripper came to mind.

He had a remarkable mouth for such a short man. An arrogant mouth. And wonderful strong, brown wrists.

'You can call me Jumping Jack Flash.'

'Jack will do. You're Canadian.'

'Canadian men are popular with European women for some reason. I once lived in North America. Right now it suits me to be here. You're South African.'

'Why do you do this work?' I could not resist the impulse that drove me to self-destruction.

'Didn't they tell you the rules? No personal questions? After all, have I asked you why you're here? Besides the reason that you want to create an orchid-white child with a man who has real sex appeal?'

'Don't flatter yourself. What's orchid-white got to do with anything? You're here because you're nothing like my husband.'

'So what's his problem?'

'No personal questions, remember?'

We argued about everything from nuclear proliferation and the Chinese taking over Africa to whether the Internet should be regulated. I'd found the father of our child. Arguments were a heady potion for sex, I'd long since discovered. Besides, I wanted to hate him, I needed to hate him, if I was going to do this and walk away from it.

After several drinks and slanging matches, I despised the tautly packaged man opposite me with a passion I'd rarely felt about anyone. Part of growing up is learning how to hate properly. Well, here I was, all grown up. My hatred was my fuel. If it was true that hate could obliterate moral terror I was ready to face the Minotaur at that moment. 'Enough bullshit. Where do we go? Let's get this over with.'

He regarded me with a sardonic smile. 'Is that how they do things in Africa? Boom, boom, bang?' He slapped his hands together, sliding the one palm away from the other with force, whispering *bang*, baring tiny sharp irregular fangs, like the teeth of a wild dog. 'Life is not a circuit board. It is not possible to switch people on and off.'

I glared at him.

'Do you dance?'

'No, I don't dance.'

'Of course you dance. You're an African woman, aren't you? All African women can dance. Come!'

It was the command I had crossed the seas to hear and obey. I had found my own Napoleon. I was Josephine that night. We danced, first as adversaries, then as accomplices; that is the power of a dance between a man and a woman. He led, I baulked, he gripped my waist tighter and bared his sharp teeth, compelling me backward towards the dance floor, letting me hang there precariously. My feet, devils in the night, moved of their own accord as my body settled into this new sensuous rhythm, all rational thought reduced to a pinprick of matter on a spinning dance floor, to the thumping beat of my heart, the heat of his hand folded imperiously around mine, the firm pressure of the other hand on the small of my back, his fingers pressed over the invisible skin. Resistance was futile; I was in the hands of a master. Samba, salsa, cha-cha, tango, he showed me how, his strong, stocky body moving with the supreme arrogance of a natural dancer, all his movements subordinated to the command of the song.

'Come.'

The man who is not my husband leads me, holding my hand by intertwining his fingers with mine. No man has ever held my hand like that; my body trills like a little bird whose head is about to be bitten off in an ecstasy of misdirected feeling. In this trance-like state, I tread softly on the plush damask rose carpet walkway that leads to a gilded elevator shaft. The elevator doors open in soundless invitation. It strikes me at this precise far-gone moment that my underwear is too business-like for the woman I am about to become. The hotel is of a genteel era, everything is cushioned and gilded. My feet disappear into the luxurious pile of the woollen carpet, the baroque room has a view over the old quarter; light voices in conversation, music and evening smells of food and geraniums come in the open window. I sink back onto the magnolia-white silk sheets on a bed that can accommodate a multitude of lovers. The stranger's strong hands hold my wrists down as his mouth guzzles at my neck. Miniature versions of unsuitable bras and panties float off into outer space. I have discarded Paola Dante-de Luc, she is the shadow of this other woman.

On my form I'd chosen 'normal' by default so we did it straight with him on top of me. His eyes looked mockingly into mine as he held my wrists, his strong arms a force of nature. After the dance there were no inhibitions between us; he charged into me, a bull into a china shop. I preferred it that way, rough and hard, two creatures mating in a paddock of a bed. I'd seen it in the movies often enough; a man has the hots for one woman and he lands up in bed with another that same night. In real life it happened to women too. I pretended to myself I was with Daniel and it almost worked. Later, Jack let me roll him over onto his back. I looked down into chestnut eyes and asked if the fee was for once only? That depends, he said, on the woman. How good she is at fucking. As if he were hiring me and not the other way round. I spat in his face. He held my hands – and then I turned into someone else: a raving sex lunatic, moving my body over his, taking him with me to a place I hadn't gone for a long, long time. I shrieked his name again and again within my head but I swear I never said it out loud.

Walk for me.
Walk?
Yes, to the door and back.
Can I stop now?
You have nice tits.
I do?
I bet nobody ever told you that before.
No, not quite in those words.

And your ass is great. Not too big, not too small, firm but with a nice wobble.

Could you say that again?

That I like your ass?

Yes, I like the way you say 'ass'.

He asked me to stay till the morning but I said no, it was done. I had planned to track my elusive husband down, but the word 'husband' had seemed unutterably pathetic from the moment I'd entered RMI's portals.

How sad, Napoleon said as he scratched at his hirsute stomach. We may never see each other again. When I came out of the bathroom, he was still lying there propped against the pillows.

'So, one of these days you will have a bambino. A pregnant woman is very sexy. I shall have to look you up.'

'Don't bother.' Maybe it was because I had the feeling he was laughing at me that I stopped with my hand on the door handle and turned around to face him.

'Do you know someone called Gabriel Montaigne? He's one of you.'

'Ah. The old fuck-me-tell-me.' His eyes raked my body with clinical professional detachment. 'The last Gabriel I knew was at primary school. But of course if you were to stay ... I could remember others.'

Of course you could. The old tell-me-fuck-me.

'Let's say someone had left some money to this Gabriel you don't know. How would I find him?'

'That would make you his fairy godmother.' The lazy satisfied smile never slipped. 'If he's "one of us", as you put it, then he checks the classifieds.'

Bye, Shorty.

I went straight back to my hotel room, had a shower and packed. In the hotel elevator on my way down to meet the taxi, I watched with distant interest as the only other occupant lit a cigarette. A tallish woman with shadows under her sunken eyes, lived-in-for-a-week jeans sitting slackly on her hips and a baggy black sweatshirt with a hood that made her look more forlorn than streetwise. The hand with the cigarette gripped the strap of a shabby rucksack slung over her shoulder, the other held onto the handle of a small wheeled suitcase. The woman swayed under my puzzled scrutiny, the hood slipped and I saw my newly cropped black hair. Self-inflicted penance. Hello, Paola, you look terrible. What would George the Genius say if he could see your latest hairstyle? You look like one of those French women who betrayed their country by sleeping with an enemy soldier. La collaboration horizontale. All you need is a tar-and-feather makeover and the look will be complete.

Nothing happened. I paid all that money, had mind-blowing sex with a total stranger, and nothing happened. One particular sketch in the Kaas manuscript kept flashing through my head: Amélie with sunshades and shoulder bag walking out of the clinic, her heels going *klik klak klik klak* as she flagged down a taxi, a small pouched bundle in the crook of her right arm. I wondered how many women had successfully conceived after the prearranged loveless unions. In my case, the gods decreed no baby. Who could blame them for being tetchy? All these humans tampering with the mores of culture and society, experimenting with procreation. And so another six weeks had passed with no sign of Daniel.

I thought about calling Enid, but decided against it. I kept reminding myself she wasn't his mother, just a delusional midget who thought she was psychic and Chinese. Anyway, it wasn't like it would have really been his baby. But it felt like it was, like I'd lost our baby. So I phoned her anyway and left a message on the answering machine. I wanted her to stew on something too.

'It's me. It didn't work. I'm not pregnant. For future reference, the organisation my husband works for is called Real Man Incorporated. But I'm betting you knew that all along. Why didn't you just give me their calling card? If I don't talk to him, I'm going to the police.'

Mares of
the Night

ENID LAZZARI WOKE ME UP the next morning. I was still asleep when
the phone rang.

'He will call you tomorrow on this line, at midday exactly.
That is the best I can do.'

'Tomorrow?' I said, half-asleep and dazed by the sudden turn
of events. 'So you *can* contact him.'

'Your husband is my patient,' the tinny voice chanted.

From the bedroom window I could see the vast ocean in
shadow, the horizon a shimmering silver line.

'I have been out of town,' she continued, smoothly, plausibly,
'so I only picked up his message yesterday, together with yours.'

I'd had it with her cloak-and-dagger games. It was time to tell
Elijah about Enid Lazzari and her shady relationship with Daniel.
It wouldn't be easy but it had to be done. I'd leave out the parts
about the other women, the child that was supposed to bring my
husband back, and his other identities. It all seemed beyond belief,
the fevered delusions of a deranged woman.

I found Elijah busy cataloguing some books. He led the way
upstairs to the dusty, light-filled office. He sat sideways with his

legs on the desk, as if he had all the time in the world to hear me out, watching the pigeons scuffle, as was his habit.

I launched straight into my edited story, starting with Enid's original phone call. He turned to look at me, interrupting the flow of my words.

'You did say ... *Enid Lazzari*?'

'I did.'

'A very small woman with russet hair?'

'Yes. A midget with orange hair,' I agreed impatiently.

'She met with you at Harriet's coffee shop?'

'Yes, yes, yes. Why is this so interesting?'

'You don't find it interesting that someone like Enid Lazzari calls you to say she knows your husband's whereabouts?'

'She says he contacts her; she's adamant that she doesn't know his whereabouts.'

After that he listened quietly as I told him about meeting my husband's psychotherapist under the lighthouse picture.

'And this all happened how long ago?' he asked meaningfully.

'We don't have a lot of time, Elijah.'

He let the point go. There were other more interesting things on his mind. 'It's an odd story, isn't it? It brings another whole aspect to the case.'

'I want to have the call traced,' I said. 'Can we concentrate on that for now?'

'I know who can do it,' he said, coming out of the reverie that Enid Lazzari's name had induced. His fingers were on the phone keys before I'd quite finished.

He talked fast. Listened. Talked some more. In the background, a bolshie rock pigeon pushed others into flight off the precarious ledge as he advanced, wings akimbo, Muhammad-Ali style.

'I've left a message,' Elijah said. 'This man's a crack SE.' And then, seeing my blank look, 'A surveillance expert.'

I'd never seen Elijah excited. He was excited now. His blue eyes bulging and the curly red hair almost alight with joy.

'What about the police?'

'What about them?'

'What about all that good advice you gave me about going to the police?'

Elijah stopped levitating and crossed his arms.

'You're thinking of going to the police?'

'I just want to find him, Elijah!' I snapped at him, almost losing control. I wanted to wail and keen like a she-wolf at full moon.

Elijah smiled at me benignly. 'Actually, this man is an ex-cop. He works with some cops who do surveillance work as a sideline.'

'Crooked cops, you mean.'

'It helps to think of it as effective use of public resources. They belong to a specialist unit that has access to underutilised electronic equipment. This may be our only chance to find your husband. If we do it right, we get the prize. We don't have much time. They'll need access to your apartment. These guys are boffins in their field.'

'Fine. I'll leave the keys in an envelope with the security guard downstairs. We don't even know for sure that he'll phone.'

'Oh, he'll phone. If Enid Lazzari says he'll phone then he'll phone, you can be sure of that.'

'How do you know her so well?'

Elijah sighed as if he wished he didn't. 'If someone sees a flying saucer, or they think their cat's behaving like an alien in disguise, they call Intergalactic Detectives. Sometimes an experienced psychologist like Enid Lazzari comes in useful.'

'Their *cat*? Does she do animal psychology?'

'No, it's the human beings we need help with. In professional hands, hypnosis therapy and vibrational alchemy can tell you quite a bit about a person. Unfortunately, human imagination knows no bounds when it encounters encouragement.'

'My point exactly. Quacks like her feed off other people's emotional issues.'

He considered my objection. 'The realm of religion and spirituality is complicated, Paola. If you go with the school of thinking that says something is true until it can be disproved ...'

'Come on, Elijah, that's just pseudoscience babble and you know it. The position of real science is totally clear.'

'Is it?' my PI asked mildly.

'Take reincarnation,' I said. 'So what if the Buddhists and the Hindus have believed it for thousands of years? There's still zip-all proof. So long as it's an untestable hypothesis, it's just gobbledygook.'

Quel mot particulier! Come, Oh Queen of numbers, spell gobbledygook for your love slave ...

My love slave should not be making fun of his Queen!

Ah, but he will reward her amply.

'And? What's the possible rational explanation?'

The echoes of the past faded away. My PI's preternatural perspicacity no longer surprised me.

'Cellular memory is a possibility. Maybe, just maybe – but it's a *huge* maybe – residues of ancestral memories reside in our DNA and that's what people interpret as past lives.'

'Maybe it's one of those things that requires some revelatory first-hand experience before you believe it,' Elijah responded, a gleam of mischief in his eyes.

'Like faith?'

'Yup. Or love.'

He had me there.

Women in general, even the very young ones, like to analyse dreams. They believe dreams are significant in some way, that they are highways to the psyche. At university, my female friends used to say that a foolproof way of telling a gay man from a heterosexual one was to gauge his response to any talk about dreams: gay men got involved in dream talk, heterosexual men always changed the subject. Then there's Paola, my friends would say, pulling their mouths at me in lemony smiles.

It's hard to believe in dreams if you're a cynic. Did the child who sat with her legs dangling over the landing as society's rich and beautiful were entertained in her troubled family home believe in dreams? It was one more thing that was blanked out in my childhood. Daniel's tortured sleep had put me in a quandary: should I do something anti-reason and ask about them, or should

I simply wait for the dreams to pass? In the end, I chose to do nothing. Talking about it would only make the dreams seem more important than they were. The nightmares continued unabated and he never raised the subject. Occasionally, he'd shout and thrash around and wake up shuddering and sweating. Then I'd be awake for his departure kiss on my forehead, *C'est un cauchemar, ma chère*, before he slipped out of bed. More often I'd wake to find him gone. I made sure the couch in the study had cushions and blankets. We colluded to ignore the horrors that came in the stealth of night to terrorise him. Now the mares of the night haunted me. I, who had never dreamed much, was being bombarded by frenetic multimedia shows on a nightly basis. I started wondering if dreams were delivered through valves. Perhaps in my case the valves had become blocked with years of disuse and Daniel's departure had loosened the logjam in my psyche.

What kind of voices did you hear, my love? Tonight I hear police voices at the outer perimeters of my sleep. It is the very beginning of the dream but I cannot change anything.

In my dream they make me listen to the tape they have made. I insist it is his voice, I know it is his voice, there is no one else who speaks like he does, I explain patiently, it is the sound of rolling thunder that brings rain, it is the voice that whispers in the rain, it is the rain that fills the river, but they make me listen to it again and again. Who else would know it was his voice? Someone in his family? I am his family, I reply. What of his agent in France? Or the neighbours in the other apartments? The police officers know somebody has phoned me but they can't be sure who it is. Only I can be sure.

Elijah called first thing in the morning. I'd just made myself a cup of coffee.

'I think Nat Behr will do it,' Elijah said without preamble.

'Nat Behr?' I asked faintly.

'The SE. There's a condition. He likes to meet his clients up front.'

'No.'

'Surveillance is tricky, Paola. He has his own way of doing things.'

'It's not necessary for the job he has to do. If he won't do it, find somebody else. I've had it with meeting people. Do whatever it takes. But I'm not meeting any SE.'

'I'll see what I can do,' Elijah said, for once not arguing. Fifteen minutes later he called back to say it was on. It hadn't been easy but Nat Behr had finally agreed to do it. Normally the fee would have gone up because of the added risk. Nat Behr didn't like dealing with faceless clients, but he was doing it at the original quote because he knew Elijah.

'Good egg,' I said drily.

'Yes, everything's hunky-dory now,' Elijah replied, apparently blithely unconcerned about my attitude.

Mid-morning, I was drying my hands in the company bathroom when the team leader came in. I told her I had important personal business to attend to, could she handle the weekly project meeting? She gave me one of those pursed lips are-you-the-project-manager-or-am-I-the-project-manager looks. No problem, she replied as she dried her hands expertly and efficiently. A project is a very fragile ecosystem. Frog eats insect. Bird eats frog. Human being eats bird. Human being eats human being. *Have you never had a personal crisis in your life?* I wanted to shout after Ms Smug-Face, but the question never left my lips. Events were spiralling out of my control; it felt as if I'd agreed to take a ride on a high-speed bullet train on one of those mind-bending tracks that span über-modern cities like Tokyo.

'Tell me how it works.'

'They use electronic equipment to bug your phone. They have access to police tracing systems. He calls. They try to trace the call. They have someone on standby ready to go. The call could be coming from anywhere in the city. There's a good chance you'll have spent all this money and you won't know anything more than you knew before. Are you ready for that possibility?'

'Are they going to sit in a van outside and listen to the conversation? Like in the movies?'

Elijah gives a snorting hee-haw laugh.

'Something like that. It's just less glamorous in real life; it's like a sauna in there.' I try to imagine Elijah in a sauna but fail.

'How long do they need to trace the call?'

'A couple of minutes. The reality is he'll probably use a callbox.'

'What do I have to do?'

'Keep him talking.'

Elijah's parting words ring in my ears throughout the morning, as if someone is beating empty buckets in a well. *Keep him talking*.

I rushed home from the client office. I could hear waves of traffic crossing behind him. He didn't even bother to find a quiet place.

'Paola, listen to me, I won't call again. I'm okay. This has nothing to do with you. Don't look for me. I won't be back. Oubliez-moi. Carry on with your life.'

Click.

He'd hung up. I didn't get a chance to say anything. I couldn't keep him talking. It was beyond me.

They traced the call to a payphone booth on Bree Street, right in the city centre. Elijah said it was unbelievable, such a short call, Nat's a wizard. His guys are on their way right now.

It was Elijah who went to open the door after the loud official knock. Two uniformed policemen filled the doorway. Their talk was a distant mumble. When Elijah returned, he met my watchful gaze with woeful eyes. 'He was already gone when they got there. There wasn't enough time.' He showed me a slim CD in a cover marked with the date and time: 'Dante, 19/03/2006, 12.00'. I'd expected a huge tape, like in my dreams. Later that evening, Elijah played the audio recording again and again, asking me to listen carefully each time. Was I sure it was his voice? Could it have been someone else?

'It's enough, Elijah. It's his voice. He has a very distinctive voice.'

'Is there anything about his voice that's different?'

His voice was cold, unfeeling. He hates me.

'He sounds flat, uninterested. The way he was sometimes in the last few weeks before he disappeared.'

Elijah eyed me in a puzzled way.

'Could it be medication-induced? Could he have been taking medication for some condition – maybe depression – without you knowing?'

'Daniel hates medication. He mocks people who have bathroom cupboards full of pills and vitamins. He won't even take a Disprin.'

He played it again. 'This time, try and listen to the background sounds. Anything that might help.'

'I can't do this, Elijah.'

'Yes you can. Empty your mind. Concentrate on the background. Listen to the traffic. Isolate the cars. Put yourself in the city next to that phone booth. Is there anything else? Something we've missed.'

'Why's it so scratchy? Is that normal? Surely they wouldn't have used an old CD?'

Elijah said nothing for a while, listening attentively, then he finally looked up. 'No, they wouldn't have, but maybe somebody else did.'

Elijah started pacing up and down, his hands behind his back, his face a whirr of emotions.

'What are you getting at?'

'What if what you heard was a pre-recorded message?'

'Why would he do that?'

'Why would he call you from the city centre where he'd know the call could most easily be traced?'

'Maybe he thought I wouldn't go that far, maybe he thought a short call couldn't be traced. There are all kinds of possible reasons.'

Elijah played the track again. 'Listen carefully. What happens in the city every day at noon?'

I heard the distant boom in the background. I wondered how I'd missed it before. 'The noon gun ...'

'Why does he choose to call at precisely midday – it's hot, it's busy – just as the noon gun is firing on Signal Hill? Isn't it possible you are being led to believe he is still in the city?'

'But why?'

'I don't know yet.'

'You're thinking someone else had the tape made.'

Elijah smiled at me with dreamy satisfaction. 'We must talk about a partnership someday, Doctor Watson. Who organised the call? Enid Lazzari. I think I'll work on that tack for a while and see where it takes me.'

I tried to call Enid but the number just rang.

Click. Click. Click. The recording played over and over in my head. Paola. Click. *Why do you hate me so much?* Click. My nightmares continued to be populated by thuggish policemen who made me listen again and again, their lunging shadows thrown against a wall-mounted tape-recording apparatus as a giant tape whirred around. Maybe you killed him and that's just a friend of yours on the line, a detective insinuated, pacing behind me, invisible, but I knew who he was. Bad Cop. Who could corroborate your story, another invisible detective asked. Good Cop. *It was his voice! No one!* Some nights my anguished cries woke me up and the nightmare detectives vaporised into thin night air. Sometimes Napoleon, aka Jack the Ripper, materialised in my sleep, promising to visit me when I was pregnant – *Go away. Go away. He won't come if you're here* – but when I woke up I was always alone, drenched in a cold sweat and struggling for air. The dream-police hung around for weeks but they couldn't find anything, not a trace of Daniel. They moved on to other more desperate cases. People who actually existed.

The Piano's
Love Lament

It was nearly eight months since Daniel had disappeared. I was no longer surprised not to find him in bed next to me when I woke up. I continued to hear the vestiges of his indifferent taped voice in my dreams. Sunday afternoons were the loneliest time; a girl could go insane in a big, empty apartment. I started listening to R.E.M. with the headphones, the way he used to do after I complained that it was all he ever played, lying on the couch with his bare feet up and eyes peacefully closed. *Nightswimming* ...

* * *

'Ciao.'

'Paola, what a surprise. Can you call back tonight? I'm going out to a gallery opening.'

'Can I have the piano?'

'You want the piano? I was going to give it to Romina for Storm. She wants him to play violin. I keep telling her piano is a good basic instrument. From there you can go on to other instruments.'

Romy is my cousin, the family's believer. We grew up together, sitting in the same pew at church every Sunday and attending catechism classes together. She had hardly spoken to me since I refused to attend Massimo's funeral.

'Storm is only two years old. I think he's got time to make decisions like that.'

'Well, it is your piano, I suppose,' my mother said grudgingly. She sometimes had a short memory. Perhaps it was better so.

'I'll let you know when I've arranged the transport.'

My old baby grand piano, the objectification of my mother's excesses, now sat in the far corner of our Camps Bay lounge. Its arrival by crane via the balcony had been undignified.

The transporters I'd hired were no more prepared for its impressive one-and-a-half metre width and length than I was. The goods lift was big enough but the front door wasn't, so the only other way was the balcony. Timing is everything. A tall crane was being used to lift concrete slabs for a new luxury apartment block going up next door. Money may not be able to buy love, but it can buy time. The building site manager scratched his head in amazement. I conceded that it was a foolhardy idea, an impossible task, and that the only thing to do was give up and send the piano back. I took a gamble it was a challenge no qualified project manager could resist. His eyes narrowed to slits as he considered the large balcony I was proposing as a landing site for the 250 kilogram instrument. Good thing it's roofless, was his brisk assessment. In the end he convinced me it was in fact possible, even organising a special rate and throwing his best crane driver into the deal. Building came to a temporary stop while builders in hard hats and bystanders watched slack-jawed as the blanketed piano hung suspended twelve metres above the ground before being manoeuvred up and over the balcony railing, where helping hands waited to grab the attached rope and assist with the painstaking landing. Finally the piano stood shakily on its four feet again. The crowd below cheered and whistled. Reality TV was happening in the neighbourhood. Six strong men carried it through the sliding door opening and carefully placed it against the waiting lounge wall.

I lifted the heavy shining lid and ran my fingers over the dusty keys. Elijah knows that I have perfect recall. Perfect recall is a curse.

Is September a running-away month? On 17 September 1989 my father collects his personal belongings, together with his son, and leaves a daughter, who now understands she is his less favourite child, behind with a wife, their mother, who is no longer in his favour at all. Later that day, twelve years old and engorged with rage, I slam the heavy, shining lid closed. I have decided to decide I shall never play again.

It is the beginning of the War of the Piano, in which neither I nor my mother will give an inch. Liberties are removed, pocket money withheld, minor transgressions punished. There are nights when I go to bed with nothing but a glass of milk sloshing about in my stomach, but surrender is unthinkable.

The tension in our reduced household kick-starts my child's body into early puberty. I grow like a beanpole and suffer from a weakened spine and aching joints. Like a puppet with stiff wooden hinges, I command my legs to obey, sometimes holding onto walls and banisters for support. I have to wear ugly reinforced shoes and sport and ballet are forbidden. Schoolwork is a mental diversion, the order of mathematics and science a relief. I eat only as a biological necessity and hardly leave the house, devoting myself to learning the sparse, unfeeling language of computers. I know my mother has conceded defeat when she flings a cloth over the piano. For the dust, she says.

At fourteen, my body slows down and I acquire breasts. I am taken for sixteen or seventeen. With the pain gone, I practise walking on my mother's high heels with a pile of books on my head. I take to looking at myself in the mirror again, considering my dark Italian eyes and high breasts with large, pale areolas to be my best features. I become part of the mainstream of school life again, attend proper parties with music and dancing, and other girls ask where they can buy awesome reading glasses like mine.

So I move on. And one day, at the age of thirty, I find myself touching a familiar shining piano lid. A spirit voice emanates from the polished wood: *What do you want from me now? After all these years you want to make music? It's because he played me, isn't it?*

I'd gone to see my mother at the gallery to tell her we were getting married. 'Oh Paola,' was all she'd said at first, looking tired.

'Aren't you pleased? You're the one who was always saying I'd end up an old maid.'

'I never said that.'

'Of course you did. You said I was married to my work. That's just another way of saying the same thing.'

'Where did you meet him?'

'Here. But he's French.'

'French?' My mother said faintly, hope stirring in her voice. 'Why didn't you bring him home?'

'Home? What home? Your home? I haven't had a proper home for years.' All the acrimony I'd felt since I was twelve years old was threatening to boil over and burn us both like a corrosive bath of acid. 'I'm going. You know now. This conversation isn't going anywhere useful. Consider yourself informed.' You see how cruel I was. As if she could ever have changed anything.

'Wait, Paola. Don't go. Of course I'm happy for you. I'm your mother. I should meet your fiancé, that's all I'm saying. There's nothing wrong with that, is there?'

'No, I don't suppose so.'

'You must both come for dinner. This Friday.'

I don't know why I agreed, but I did. I wasn't accustomed to performing acts of pity. They'd both dressed up for the occasion, my mother in a flowing gypsy dress with swirling panels and flashing crystal rings, looking very much the part of flamboyant Italian gallery owner hosting her son-in-law-to-be, who wore navy trousers, open-necked white shirt and tailored jacket, looking very suave and Gallic. I wore jeans and a casual top. On the way down in the apartment lift Daniel had hooked his hand into my jeans pocket and whistled softly.

The years of grand soirées now long behind her, my mother still knew how to set a resplendent candlelit dinner table. She brought a bottle of Pinot Noir through that was so deep and dark it was almost black and decanted the contents into a crystal jug while we waited for dinner. Daniel judged it to be an excellent wine, proposing an exuberant toast to Bacchus that had my mother giggling like a schoolgirl. Finally, an assortment of ceramic bowls of Aegean hues emerged on an enormous wooden tray, in each bowl a different vegetal concoction. We were eating vegetarian Turkish tonight. Daniel seemed unfazed by the oddly spiced food, meat nowhere in sight, tasting everything and declaring it delicious.

The two of them conversed animatedly while I struggled to suppress my yawns and irritation. They discovered a shared love of opera music. My mother told him about her trips to organise international exhibitions and he regaled her with stories of his culinary experiences in the French countryside. After dinner, we moved to the lounge for coffee. In one of the frequent reorganisations that my mother's art collection necessitated, the piano had emerged from obscurity. The sombre corner where it had stood ever since I could remember was now lit up by a rail of spotlights. It stood centre stage in front of a large canvas composed of body outlines in bold oil colours against a matt black background. The contorted bodies shimmered and shimmied from afar like a group of madcap street dancers. Daniel walked over and lifted the shining lid with its reflections of gaiety, gently removing the strip of felt with faded gold letters: *STEINWAY*.

'Do you play?' my mother asked coyly. As a reply, he hitched his trousers up and sat on the stool, fingers running over the ivory and ebony keys and a foot moving on the pedal before he'd quite settled. A haunting melody filled the room, a merry polka from a distant forgotten time and place that evoked dancing pairs in a glittering ballroom. It sounded Russian, or Polish perhaps. With the last few notes lingering in the air, he took his fingers off slowly, almost regretfully, replaced the felt, and closed the lid gently.

'Bravo!' my mother shouted, clapping so hard that her rings must have hurt.

When she asked him where he'd learnt to play like that, he smiled at her and said, 'I had a good teacher.' That was enough to send my mother off on the saga of my abandoned music studies. The *best* piano teacher in the city, an Austrian woman of Jewish descent whose students appeared with the *best* orchestras all over the world, had said Paola had *natural* talent. All art was a gift from the gods. Art made men and women complete. But Paola always had her own mind. Like her father. Now the piano was a black elephant. *Ha. Ha.* It's a Steinway, you know.

I said we'd skip the coffee, it was late; I had to go in to work tomorrow.

'Other people in your office work on a Saturday?'

'You go in to work on a Saturday. What's different?' I hated myself for participating in these futile circular discussions but I couldn't stop myself.

'I look at beautiful pieces all day. It's not work, it's pleasure. You don't have a balanced perspective on life.'

On the way home, Daniel asked why I'd stopped with my piano lessons. I told him I played because my father enjoyed it and when my father left it didn't make sense to carry on playing. Anyway, where had he learnt to play like that?

'My mother,' he said briefly. 'Your mamma is quite a lady. That was some dinner she put on for us.'

'The food was awful,' I said. 'Why can't she just cook Italian? Was your mother a musician?'

'Different,' he replied. 'Not awful. No, she taught piano.'

'Did she play well?'

'Comme un ange.'

* * *

The arrival of the piano caused consternation among the members of the body corporate. It was pointed out to me by an irate Mrs Shimansky that I had to obtain my two immediate neighbours' consent for any musical instrument that might disturb 'the communal peace' of Sandkasteel residents. Since we had the corner apartment, it would be the two closest neighbours. I duly approached my next-door neighbour about the piano. Sharon and Miss Potter both had their heads cocked as they considered my request. The mutt let off a series of barks, looked up at glassy-eyed Sharon and barked again, in a different pitch this time. It was unnerving how the dog seemed to translate for her. Sharon shook her head spasmodically as she listened in.

'I don't think there's a problem. You're not going to play the same ditty all night though, are you? You'll be more like *Not* the Midnight Mass, I hope?' She gave a high-pitched giggle and the dog let off a tremendous fart of satisfaction now that its job was done. I told Sharon to bang on the wall if I lost track of time. As for the other neighbour, one apartment along, I'd occasionally seen her sprinting out of the building – a slim, well-endowed young woman with dark, smooth skin and a lioness mane of blonde Rasta hair. One morning, she'd dropped a gold platform sandal out of her kit bag as she charged out the front doors, and I'd picked it up and left it in front of her door. Occasionally, going up in the evening, I'd share the lift with a businessman carrying a briefcase, who'd bolt out on our floor and head for her closed door as if he were being chased. He'd always knock loudly like an insurance salesman making a marketing call. I left a note in her post box and the next day she knocked while I was having breakfast.

'Hey. I'm Katinka. From number 33. Everybody calls me Kiki.' Her handshake was firm and cool. Close-up, her eyes were an unusual jade-green that harked back to her Malay ancestry. She couldn't have been much over twenty years old. 'Piano music rocks.' She sounded more enthusiastic about the piano than I was. 'I work most nights anyway. I'm a dancer. You know, pole dancing, cage dancing, stuff like that. Maybe you've seen me at Xanadu? That's my steady lunchtime gig. We get a lot of businesspeople coming in.'

That explained the irregular hours and the glitter shoe.

I shook my head. 'I know where it is. But I've never been inside.'

She waved a hand as if it didn't really matter. 'I've been dancing there for over a year now. They don't expect us to sleep with the customers like some other places.'

183

Kiki peered around me. 'I dig the white leather couch. *Jisslike*, it's a real concert piano!'

'Thanks.' The ponytailed piano tuner had recommended a spot against the inside wall where there was no sunlight or humidity. 'Luckily these old apartments have a lot of space.'

'You're telling me. You should have seen the dump I was in before. Anyway, like I said, it's no problem.'

Watching her bounce down the corridor back to her apartment, I decided she was probably more like twenty-three going on thirty and that her boisterous unapologetic manner was oddly appealing.

I was about to close the door when Sharon's front door opened. She materialised with Miss Potter's lead in one hand and a butcher-striped laundry bag in the other. Laundromat day.

'Good morning, Paola,' she said, before I could greet her.

'Good morning, Sharon. It's uncanny how you do that.'

'Oh, not really. I've had years of practise, you know. Are you staying home again today?'

'No, I'm not.' I didn't want to be abrupt to a blind person but her nosy question annoyed me.

'You can tell me it's none of my business, you know, but "The bridge is love, the only survival, the only meaning".'

'You're right, it's none of your business, but since you raise it, what do you know about love?' Now I was being rude, and I didn't care.

'You mean because I'm a blind person? That makes me without feelings? Without the possibility of loving? Or maybe you think that you can't love someone if you can't see them?'

I was surprised at her spunk. It was a fair question. But I was running late with a long day ahead of me.

'I have to go, I'm afraid. But no, I don't think that.'

'Will you be at home on Friday night?' she asked quickly, holding me back with her hand. 'Kiki and I do a pizza evening occasionally. Would you like to join us? You have that wonderful balcony with a view of the sea.'

View? What view? She's blind. It was outrageous. She had just invited herself and Kiki to supper. I tried to think of something to say that wouldn't be totally impolite but couldn't.

'I know Kiki's off this Friday,' she said hopefully, the milky eyes looking straight past me.

Maybe I wanted to apologise for being rude. Or maybe I had new insight into what it was like to spend one long Friday after another alone.

'Fine. Why not?' I said, conceding defeat. 'Shall we say Friday, 7.30 pm, at my place?'

Miss Potter barked. 'Bring the dog if you want.'

Sharon inclined her head. 'Thank you. We would like that very much. We don't go out much, do we Miss Potter? I'll let Kiki know. She's a good friend of ours.' Miss Potter did a series of excited barks that accompanied me all the way to the lift.

It's just the two of us now. *Strangers in the night ... da da da daa daaa ...* I lift my hand to the keys. The little tune I produce sounds silly and wilful, the simple childish notes echoing against the empty walls. My stiff fingers slowly limber up, warming to the task at hand. The music begins to wax and wane; I am a desert dune shifting light and form as the wind stirs and drops. In the glacial cold of deepest night, frost forms on the leeward side, a radiant evening blue under the creamy luminosity of the moon; in the searing heat of daylight the fine sand is the colour of disintegrated bone gone to salt. As the air currents blow and billow, I swoon within the shifting silk – this desert wraps me inside itself. Outside, a great fiery globe holds night at bay and a distant faraway tune interweaves with the undulating sounds of sheltering sands. On a distant shore of memory, Daniel plays his mother's merry mad polka, notes sink and rise and sigh, dancing on red sand, twirling, swirling shadows move together and part. I play and I play and I play until Miss Potter's yelping barks penetrate and I realise Sharon is banging on the wall.

In the morning, I wake up on the couch. What strange urges and surges I have become subject to. I make myself a cup of coffee and then open the laptop and search for the piano sheet music to R.E.M.'s *Nightswimming*.

The pizza evening turned out to be more fun than I'd expected. Kiki and Sharon made me laugh. I learnt that Kiki had a four-year-old son, Brad (*Brad Pitt is the sexiest man in the world!*), christened Bradley, who lived with an aunt in Wellington and suffered asthma attacks. I told them about my rambunctious nephew, Max, who had broken a leg and an arm and nearly drowned twice before the age of four and was a carbon copy of my brother. Sharon told us that Miss Potter was the second dog she'd named after the small-town spinster headmistress who had accepted a sight-impaired child into her school, ignoring all naysayers and critics.

Sharon said it felt like we were old friends. 'Perhaps we met in a previous life!' she tittered. I responded by raising my wine glass to toast a convivial evening and Kiki automatically guided Sharon's hand. Later on, Kiki started to yawn. She apologised immediately, saying she'd only come off duty at six so she needed some sleep. The next day she wanted to work on her costume for a new routine. She told us proudly that she'd been selected from a group of girls to work at another club. It was an evening job that paid double her daytime job. Maybe now she could send Brad to a better school. The choreographer had worked out a new solo act around her hair; from now on she was Queen of the Jungle. Sharon teased her, saying it was the youngsters who always faded first. She'd offer to help but she didn't think her fingers knew how to thread a needle any more.

I saw Kiki out. Before leaving she stepped back into the apartment to tell Sharon they could go shopping on Saturday for a toaster if she wanted. They arranged a time and then she was gone.

'She's a good girl, Kiki.'

'I didn't know you could make a decent living from pole dancing.'

'She has someone.'

'Someone?'

'A married man. He pays for the flat. She just has to pay expenses.'

'Oh.' That explained the pinstriped caller.

Sharon and I went out onto the balcony for fresh air. She sniffed at the salty air and said it was wonderful to be able to hear the sea properly. The dog arranged itself with its muzzle on Sharon's foot and promptly fell asleep. Sharon and I talked softly while the dog snored and made noises as if it was chasing imaginary cats into the boughs of tall trees. It was a warm, windless evening. When we were dating, on evenings like this Daniel would pack a picnic basket and a bottle of wine. We'd sit on the great round rocks at the beach and watch the lingering spectacle of the sun setting the sky on slow fire. We'd have to pour surreptitiously, keeping an eye out for beach patrol officers. We invented names for the shifting tinted sky. *Mellow Yellow. Papaya-whip. Tangerine Dream.* When did we stop doing those things?

'Does she do it for the money or is she in love with him?'

'Kiki? Well, she's been seeing him for over a year now and he's kind to her. So she probably imagines herself to be in love with him.'

I won't be back ... Carry on with your life. How could you dare say that?

'What was it you said the other day about love being a bridge?'

'The bridge is love, the only survival, the only meaning?'

'Yes, that was it.'

'It's from *The Bridge of San Luis Rey* by Thornton Wilder.'

'How do you know that?'

'I come from a family of readers. My father taught English for forty years before he died.'

'I meant ... do you get books like that on cassette?'

'Sometimes tapes, mostly books written in Braille.'

Can one put love together again? Or is love like Humpty Dumpty?

'Can it be that simple? Is love the answer to all questions? That's what he implies, isn't it?'

'Wilder? I don't think he implies it's simple, just out of our control perhaps.'

'Have you ever loved somebody like that?'

Sharon rubbed her arms. The dog groaned in its sleep. 'There was someone once. But I couldn't give him the life he wanted. Robert became the captain of a boat carrying medical supplies along the African coast and married a nurse, an English girl, who worked for Médecins Sans Frontières.'

Oubliez-moi. No, no, no. You couldn't have meant it. Voices drifted along the sea breeze with its fragrance of seaweed. Out at sea lights twinkled. On the surface everything was the same, but my life had gone from Heaven to Hades and I didn't even know why. I stood up.

She let go the hand under each elbow and rubbed her thin liver-spotted arms. 'It's become quite chilly, hasn't it? I think we'll be off now, but thank you for a wonderful evening.' She leaned down to stroke Miss Potter. 'Don't give up,' she said. 'Go and find him.' For a moment I thought she was addressing the dog. 'Daniel needs you.'

'You know.'

'Oh, yes. He told me. We were in the middle of *The Unbearable Lightness of Being.*'

I cleared my throat. That's why she'd talked about love.

'Daniel read to me every Monday. Did he never tell you that?'

'No, actually he didn't tell me.'

'He popped his head in on the Friday to say he wouldn't be reading to me the following week. I understood he was going away and not coming back any time soon.'

Don't look for me. If you weren't in the city centre then where were you?

'Did he say anything about where he was going?'

'He said he'd be travelling around, here, there and everywhere – he used the French word "partout" – and then he was gone.'

'Gone' is such a final word. The banality of Gone terrifies me. It has the brutality that words like 'vanish' and 'disappear' lack, with their smoke-and-mirrors aspect.

'We're biological creatures,' I raged. In the background, waves crashed on the dark shoreline mingling with the distant pulse of salsa music. 'Love is just a mental fixation that promotes the long-term survival of the species. In a biological sense, it doesn't exist; it's a figment of the imagination.'

Sharon smiled a little and lifted her head in that funny way she had as if she was beaming into the upper atmosphere. 'Daniel said you were a cynic.'

'Really? How did that come up? While he was reading to you?'

'I asked him if you enjoyed reading and he said you didn't read fiction much, that you usually read non-fiction, and then it usually had something to do with your work. He said it was probably because you were a cynic.'

'Funny. And I always thought it had something to do with not having time for such pleasant diversions.'

She ignored my sarcasm. 'Did you know that in Ancient Greece a Cynic was a member of a school of philosophers who held wealth and pleasure in contempt? That's so interesting, isn't it?'

I glared at her. The impudence of the woman was astounding. She seemed oblivious to my irritation as she patted Miss Potter's head gently to wake her up.

We said goodbye at the door. I ran a steaming foam bath and mulled over our conversation, a slippery fish that eluded me, while my skin slowly crimped.

I am the woman in the hot bath considering my toenails that badly need a pedicure. I let cold water out and add more scalding water. How does one explain RMI to someone who hasn't been there? I'm a failed cynic. I don't believe I'll ever get over you, Daniel.

Trust
No One

I TRIED TO CALL THE WOMAN ENID. A call centre operator confirmed the number had not been disconnected. So she wasn't picking up. I'd broken the rules. Her rules. No policemen. Somehow she'd found out. The walls had eyes. It didn't matter if they were maverick policemen whose only loyalty was to their own pockets.

Nothing made sense any more. Elijah's suspicions about the telephone call being pre-recorded played havoc with my mental and emotional state.

I found myself driving around suburbs that I had no idea existed. Overtaking taxis with slogans like LOVE THEM ALL, TRUST NO ONE on blind rises. On weekends I haunted neighbourhood coffee bars and laundromats, and more than once ended up stalking strange men on foot or following them by car, driving through amber robots and narrowly missing pedestrians to avoid losing them, mistakenly believing them to be Daniel from afar. It was a game that gave me a temporary purpose. I grew more and more convinced that Daniel was not in the city any more.

Most mornings I put my running shoes on and left the apartment block. I ran longer and longer distances with other joggers and insomniacs. I started to recognise the regulars. Like the retired gent with a cane who walked the concrete pathway, a live yellow cockatoo clinging to his jacket shoulder. Or the North African woman who ran, come rain, wind or sunshine, a long burnt-sienna scarf knotted at the back of her neck, fringed tassels bobbing against her strong back as she left me behind.

Saturdays were different. I always ran in the late afternoon, otherwise the weekend stretched on forever. A blonde leapt out of a metallic blue Smart coupé she'd parked sideways with its nose on the pavement just ahead of me. Talking into a mobile as she ignored zebra crossings and evaded hooting taxis she crossed the promenade heading for a male figure waiting on the other side. They disappeared inside The Grand so I carried on running my normal route. On my way back, he was waiting at an outdoor table.

I was coated with a sheen of perspiration and rivulets of sweat were running down my back, but I slowed down anyway.

'Hola, muchacha. You live around here?'

'Hello, Manolo. You buying coffee?'

The blue coupé that had carried me to the party at Bulldog Beach was nowhere in sight. A waiter materialised at my elbow.

'A single espresso. And an orange juice.'

Innate confidence is always sexy. This time he was casually dressed in jeans and a tight, long-sleeved T-shirt, hands loosely clasped on his lap, long silver-spur-booted legs stretched out in front of him in a pose of relaxation, but I sensed the dark eyes behind the shades were watching me, alert, shining. Even in broad daylight he made me think of a sleek jungle cat, muscles gleaming as it slinks its way through the city, following some primordial scent.

'Where'd Miss Party Girl go? Is she really a nurse?'

'Kim? She is the best kind of nurse. One who will see to your every need.'

He asked about the jogging. We talked about the rain that was coming. And then it happened, smoothly, while I was drinking my fresh orange juice and the sundowner crowd were starting to arrive, just as I had known it would from the moment I saw him.

'Do you want to fuck?'

The curiously melodious proposition made my stomach flip-flop as if I was on the Congo Queen galleon at Ratanga Junction theme park. How does one respond to something like that? 'Don't you have to check in with Miss Party Girl first?' My voice sounded faint.

He smiled, not insulted. His teeth shone. 'We can call it a freebie.'

'No. I would want to pay.' If love is commerce then I must understand it. This man with perfect teeth lounging in the restaurant chair was hypothetically as good a place as any to continue my education.

Manolo shrugged. 'Maybe 1 000 rand.'

If he'd removed his shades or set a lower price I'd have stopped it right there.

'So cheap, really. A bargain,' I murmured sweetly.

The smile never slipped an inch.

'Where would we go?' I heard myself ask, out of revulsion, out of fascination.

'I have a place we can use,' he grinned, a carefree ruffian looking around for a waiter so he can pay the bill and we can leave together.

There are forces that move the world that cannot be neatly catalogued. The last few months have taught me that. Desire is a dream. Fantasy is reality. We're in a seedy flat in a seedy Sea Point building. It's the kind of place I imagine for a gigolo.

'Where is your husband that he allows such a chica to be alone?' I can hear Manolo ask, glinting brown eyes focused in the forest gloom, as he runs slender fingers along my bare arm.

Mesmerised by lust's vision I watch him use his leather belt to tie my wrists to the bed. Then he sits next to me on the bed and applies freshly whipped cream to my naked skin in slow circular movements. '*Los senos,*' I hear him whisper when he reaches my breasts. He licks it all off, flicking lightly, backing off each time my body quickens.

I am in the hands of a masterful predator whose virtuoso fingers know ways of stroking neglected, sad bodies to life. Time and time again we teeter on the brink.

As the sun sets through the nylon curtains we still lie in those stained sheets. He runs his hands over the contours of my back before covering the length of me with his taut body, his lithe maleness pressing into me with stiff urgency, his sweat mingling with mine. In the mirror, a tawny-skinned human male, perfectly toned muscles rippling, fingers interlocked with mine, slides over me, his movements coming faster and faster. Just when it seems he is going to come without me, he rolls off and lifts me up against him, joining us. The universe trembles, the stars go out and the moon drowns. That other Paola's coital screams mingle with Manolo's rasping cries.

'No.' I stood up carefully, holding onto the chair for dear life. The world around me tilted dangerously, a hall of distorting mirrors.

'No? Why?' He sounded unsure of himself.

He could be Daniel. I could be any other woman except myself.

'I need a shower. No, just no, that's all.' Wimp. Why don't you just say it: I'm a married woman.

He lifted the shades onto his head as if to see me better. 'Come on! So many rules. Spontaneous lovemaking is very important for the circulation.' The tone of disbelief was almost funny. I'd obviously spoilt his plans. I supposed it was boring to be a full-time lover unless you had someone to practise on.

Before letting me go, Manolo grabbed my hands with cat-like grace and gazed deep into my eyes: a real pro.

'Not so quick, muchacha. Will I see you at the next party?'

'No. They're too public.'

'Kim will know how to find me.'

I left him sitting there, staring after me in puzzled amazement as I ran off, my back cold with sweat, my legs unsteady, my breath coming in gasps. I could have been a suicide bomber who'd changed her mind.

Back in the apartment, I faced the pale woman in the bathroom mirror.

Freshly whipped cream? Where the hell did that come from?

That's how easily it can happen.

Is love fled?

I no longer knew myself. Jack was a necessary step to achieving my objective. Even Sun Tzu would have acknowledged that. But Manolo? Manolo was something different.

It wasn't really one thing that made me decide to go; it just felt as if I was careering down a hill without any brakes.

The same night after I rejected Manolo's overtures, I decided to go through to the office and fetch a file I'd forgotten. Most Saturday nights were spent in front of the laptop with my supper and a glass of wine next to me. Work had become a life-preserver; it was the one constant that made sense.

Driving back home an hour later, a cop car screamed past me. Seconds later an ambulance followed. I was a block away from our apartment. I watched them tear around the corner. When I got to the apartment block, pandemonium reigned. Mrs Shimansky was talking to a cop. Residents were milling around talking in small groups. People were looking over the railings. A stretcher was being loaded into the ambulance.

'What happened?'

Mrs Shimansky fixed her beady gaze on me. 'Sharon was attacked with a knife. She heard somebody in *your* apartment and went to investigate.' The policeman's gaze moved in my direction. The ambulance drove past us through the gates with the siren on.

I ignored him. 'Is she alright?'

'She's alive, isn't she? No thanks to you,' Mrs Shimansky said, muttering to herself as she walked away, dragging Miss Potter behind her.

'I'll need to take a statement from you,' the policeman said.

Later I called the hospital. They said Sharon had a knife wound on her arm but no main arteries had been affected and she'd recovered consciousness. They'd given her a sedative. All very cut and dried. Patient in tiptop condition.

The apartment looked as if a whirlwind had ripped through it.

Amazing how one's living space can change personality. My home had turned into a movie set. A hulled futon lay sideways on the base. Someone had taken a knife to it. Wads of cotton filling lay all over the place, between books and clothes. Every shelf had been cleared, every cupboard emptied. The shaggy rug resembled an intimidated pelt kicked into a corner. The piano looked subdued, its lid lifted. An exhaustive, destructive search had been conducted.

So that's why Manolo propositioned me. To keep me out of the way.

Visiting hours started at 3 pm. Sharon managed a skew grin. 'Pretty stupid, huh?'

'I'm so sorry,' I blurted out.

'Don't be,' Sharon patted my hand. 'It's not your fault. Sometimes things just happen.' Her hand tightened. 'Did you see Miss Potter?'

Things don't just happen.

'Mrs Shimansky has her.'

She sighed with relief and lay back again. 'I was having terrible thoughts that the police might have taken her to an animal shelter. She couldn't stand that, you know.' Tears filled the milky, sightless eyes. 'Not after what she went through as a puppy.' She blew her nose hard and then told me what had happened the night before.

She'd heard someone moving around in our apartment and instantly known it wasn't me – it was a much heavier, bigger person who was bumping into things. She'd closed Miss Potter in her apartment and, armed with her cane, she had tried the door handle to our flat. Someone had come shooting out past her. She'd instinctively grabbed in the direction of the fleeing body and shouted out. That's when she'd felt the pain in her arm. She remembered hearing Miss Potter barking madly behind the closed door. The next thing she knew, she woke up in hospital.

I shuddered to think what might have happened to Sharon. They hadn't held back this time round. For one thing, they'd practically destroyed the door to get past the fancy new lock. I told myself RMI was looking for Daniel, too. If he was still in the city, they would have found him by now.

Eventually I cornered Piet. I told him I needed a tough overseas project or I'd go mad. He looked startled, as if I hadn't been out of it for months, as if it wasn't alright for me to say I was going mad, as if that was a bad sign that he should take particular note of. I'd phoned around: our Italian office had a project in Rome that needed a project manager yesterday – one of their own PMs had inconsiderately fallen ill – so I'd have to be subcontracted out to them. Andrew had agreed to step in till someone else took over my workload. I could start on the Italian project in a week's time. Piet looked more perturbed and muttered something about running away from my personal problems, and Andrew was stretched as it was. What about the evening classes I'd wanted to attend at the business school? I didn't rise to the bait. 'Not this year, Piet. Thanks. You're a sweetie.'

I almost knocked Andrew over on my way out. He steered me to the cafeteria. 'You look like you need a sandwich.'

'He says you're overextended.'

'Bring it on! I'm on my way to the top. Why's it so important to you, anyway?'

'I need a change.' It's not that difficult to lie about the small things. But he didn't seem to be listening anyway. He was watching someone over my shoulder.

'That's the Portuguese contractor they want off the team.'

I turned around and saw a youngish, black-haired woman getting coffee. I knew the story. It was one of those awkward situations. She had a bad case of BO. The team leader of the predominantly female team didn't want her contract extended.

'She's got a photo of her kid on her desk. He's the only thing she ever opens up about besides work. You know the type: gluttons for punishment, the lifeblood of a project.'

'What are you going to do?'

'I thought I'd send her an anonymous email from professionals.net suggesting she starts using deodorant. That way she'll never know it was me,' Andrew replied through a mouthful of ham sandwich.

'You're a bottom feeder, Andrew. When are you going to be straight with people?'

'I can see you doing that,' Andrew grinned. 'Telling someone to their face they've got a body odour problem.'

'Assign her to another team. Maybe they don't give her such a hard time and the BO goes away.'

'That's quite an insight.' He put the sandwich down. 'It's like target practice. They're total bitches.'

It wasn't worth mentioning he'd once called me a super-bitch. It didn't seem important any more.

'My bill's on its way.'

'Forget it. If I curate your project all debts are cancelled.'

'Big if.'

And then, casually, as if there'd been no office gossip after Daniel hadn't pitched for the last office function, as an afterthought, he asked. 'So, how's your man?'

My man is a mirage in a white-hot desert. I can't even find his bones.

'Daniel? Fine. Great. Okay. The research is taking longer than expected.'

Andrew wiped his mouth and stood up.

'I'll put her onto the casino project. That'll give them something to chew on.'

In the end, Piet came through. He found a new hotshot male graduate who impressed the client with his grasp of techno jargon to take some of the load off Andrew, and he arranged my temporary assignment.

There were never enough apartments in Camps Bay, so the agency came back to me within twenty-four hours to say that they'd let the apartment fully furnished for six months. Daniel's books and everything else went into storage. All I kept were the clothes I could carry in a cabin-size wheeled suitcase and the rucksack. For some reason, the whole mess reminded me of Brutus walking away from me with his tail between his legs, the dumb look on his big, square face reminding me of the trucks on the highway with the calves going to slaughter. Daniel's eyes meeting mine, pools of dark-green accusation.

The only thing I kept was the old PC with the password-protected folder, 'Daniel'. I went over to Monica and asked her to hold onto it for me: I was going away on an overseas project and I didn't know when I'd be back. She could use it in the meanwhile if she wanted. She waved me through to the airy high-ceilinged room with open sash windows and some sagging bookshelves and a trestle table she used as a study. I set it up while she made us some coffee. Over a strong cup of Kenyan dark roast, I told her I didn't know if Daniel was ever coming back.

She tapped away on the keyboard with long, tapered fingernails. *Dear Monica. I love you. I love you not. I love you. I love you not. I love you. I love you not!* She asked why the PC was important and I told her, more or less. Monica eyed me quizzically, not taken in by my blasé attitude.

'How come you can't get into that folder yourself?'

'I've tried every password combination I can think of. It needs someone who can get into the program code. Security software is a specialised field. The actual files might even be encrypted. I can't believe he even knew this stuff.'

Why didn't she get her friend Igor to take a look? If anyone could crack password-protected folders he could. He nearly went to jail for hacking into various government computers but, luckily for him, they realised he was a genius so he'd been working for the government on a freelance basis ever since.

I shrugged and said, 'Sure, it can't hurt. So, why are you writing love letters to yourself?'

She'd reached a decision: she was going to kick that Jezebel out once and for all. It wasn't working. She gave me a tremulous smile. Female pulchritude was the problem, Monica said morosely. Why did the woman have to be so goddamn drop-dead gorgeous? That reminded me. I pulled the green stub out of my purse. Did this mean anything to her? It was with Daniel's stuff. Maybe it was a clue. She laughed. I sounded like Nancy Drew.

'Who's Nancy Drew?'

'Oh boy, what planet did you grow up on?' Eyes rolling, she took the ticket I held out. 'Mmm, jeez, Paola, it's time you had some fun. It's from Pompadour. It's *the* club, really high class, one of those places with a lounge atmosphere and designer lighting. The best pole dancers in the city perform at Pompadour. Everything's very upmarket and the girls are top-drawer babes. I chatted up one of the hostesses once. Mind you, it's not easy to have a conversation when the music is that loud, but she said most of them were models. You should see it: stunning masked women working the party floor on glittering stilettos. The masks are a Pompadour thing; they get sold at the door. They're all in Louis XV style, you know, like at the masked balls where the nobles were prone to indiscretion and excess. It also means that the patrons get to stay anonymous in public if they choose. The private lounges are upstairs. The story goes that that's where the Russian and Chinese mafia bosses hang out and the best girls get sent upstairs, where they walk around starkers but still in masks.'

Monica frowned.

'They take those masks seriously. I was there once with a group when a guy tried to pull the mask off a hostess. Those bouncers were all over him in a flash. A few days later, there was a report in the paper that the guy's body ended up in the Liesbeek River. The club produced witnesses to say they'd seen him walk away after he was kicked out and that was it.'

'Daniel doesn't like places like that.'

'Maybe Daniel's looking for pointers for his next book. He writes thrillers, doesn't he?'

All of which was accompanied by a wicked, comforting grin. Monica was city savvy. She said it came from starting young. Her mom had held down three jobs to support the two of them and keep the family estate from getting taken over by the bank, so she was never there. Monica herself, never low on self-confidence even as a teenager, had found herself a casting agent to do television and film work. A year after Monica left school, her mother was diagnosed with emphysema. Monica's earnings were sufficient for the two of them to live on but not enough to properly maintain the rambling property and cover rising medical costs. That was when she decided to take in tenants. The big, old pink house had seen people come and go, always singles, always unsettled rolling stones. I had answered an advert for a garden flat with access from the garage, which opened onto a courtyard, and became Monica Stavros's first tenant.

We had become friends on the night the ancient geyser gave up its ghost in an explosive finale. The two of us had spent backbreaking hours mopping up water with the ruptured ceiling over our heads and the geyser lying perilously on its side. As the sun rose, we'd sat in the courtyard with mugs of coffee, the ginger cat at Monica's feet, surrounded by threadbare carpets drying in the sun. 'What about insurance?' I'd asked. 'It was too expensive,' she'd replied, 'so I cancelled it.' Moved by my exhaustion and Monica's obvious distress to make the kind of suggestion I normally avoided at all costs, I mentioned my mother's lifelong friend, Francesca Goldman, who owned a property agency, and offered to give her a call to see if they were taking in trainees. 'They want you to write an exam,' Monica had said doubtfully. 'You can make several times what you're making now,' I'd pointed out. 'This pink museum is a money trap.' In the end, I'd convinced her to at least meet with Francesca. Monica turned out to be a natural. She'd passed the board exam after her internship, and her low, soothing voice and ability to read people's unfathomable desires had helped her to close deals other estate agents only dreamed of. After living and medical expenses, all her commission payouts went into renovating the pink house.

I didn't sleep that night. It was time to analyse the enemy. In the words of Sun Tzu: 'When your objective is nearby, make it appear distant; when distant, create the illusion of being nearby.'

The next morning, I stopped by Monica's on my way to work.

'I need someone to come with me.'

'Where?'

'That club.'

'You mean Pompadour?' she said in awed disbelief. '*Jeez*, Paola. You shouldn't be playing detective in places like that. Daniel will come back.'

'Come on, Monica. When was the last time you did something really interesting? You know I'll go anyway. I'm leaving in a week's time so we have to do it on Saturday.'

'You've gone loco,' Monica said, shaking her head in amazement. 'Didn't I tell you what kind of place it is? It's where Russian mobsters and Chinese gangsters hang out.'

'*You* went. Anyway, wasn't it you who said it was time I had some fun?'

'I'd follow a nubile young thing with taut thighs into the jaws of hell. You don't just *walk* into places like that. You have to dress like the crowd and do the moves.'

She did a kind of Indian dance movement thing and raised her stencilled brows in mock scepticism.

I could see her point. 'You can be wardrobe and deportment mistress. Besides, they wear masks, don't they?'

Monica's eyes narrowed. The idea was starting to work on her. 'Why, exactly?'

'Somebody stabbed a blind woman to look for something in my apartment. I can't just sit back and hope Daniel's going to come back. I have to do something.'

Monica insisted I practise walking on high heels with a bum wiggle. 'You have to look like you belong, otherwise you'll attract attention.' I knew I had it right when I caught her gawping. One of Monica's reckless strappy numbers, teetering silver sandals, some skilfully applied make-up and the use of curling tongs, and a hot floozy gazed back at us from the mirror.

'Oh my gawd!' Monica muttered. 'Am I good or what?'

On our way out, she put a long-nailed hand on my arm. 'Are you sure you know what you're getting yourself into, Paola? Is he worth it?'

I tried to grin nonchalantly but my lipstick stuck to my teeth. 'You worry too much.'

I had no real idea what I expected to find at Pompadour. Was it simple curiosity that drove me? To know part of how my husband had amused himself during those vanishing periods?

We rolled up in Monica's heirloom yellow Merc, which she gleefully referred to as old-school vintage. Just two friends having a night out on the town.

From the moment that door swung shut behind us and we handed over our coats, we entered a different world. Everything was bathed in a soft blue light that gave it a kind of extraplanetary underwater feel. Monica slung her arm casually around my waist. Female bouncers frisked us professionally before permitting us to pass. A sign on the wall advised that weapons and drugs were prohibited in the club.

We sauntered in like old hands. I quickly cottoned on to the unique advantages of a mask. I could stare unabashedly. Astonishingly long-limbed, masked hostesses on clear-heeled platform sandals floated past in transparent shades of chiffon, the club floor a catwalk for a different kind of fashion item. We followed a masked hostess in emerald green. She crossed slim feet and limbs as if she was on a spot-lit ramp that led to a table against the back wall. The fabric was so thin I could see the cleft of her bottom above the gold G-string and the sculpted ribs of her slender back beneath the gold knotted bikini top string. Monica indicated a different table further along with a better view of the room and she moved on. It was curiously empowering to swing my hips and have eyes follow me. In a place like this, a clothed woman attracted attention. I'd left women's rights and political correctness at home. In this place those kinds of ideas died stillborn, irrelevant to the commercial activity around the female form. The cat-eyed girl who came over to take our drink order purred in a Slavic accent that her name was Tatiana. Her blonde hair formed a fine platinum veil that brushed back and forth over milk chocolate areolas, the thin fabric creating friction over her bare breasts.

We had booked in the dinner and cabaret section. That was where the gambling gents started their evening. At about 11 pm, a compactly built man in a silver jacket arrived, flanked by two bodyguards. He moved among the front tables and then sat down at one. The guards took up position at the bar. The floorshow started promptly at midnight. I was new to pole dancing, but years of forced attendance at ballet premiers had taught me to recognise the dedicated professionals. These lissom double-jointed girls with the superb inner-thigh control made swinging around poles look easy. But it was the closing act that brought a frisson to the room. There she was. My neighbour, Kiki, of the temptress jade-green eyes. Queen of the Jungle. She hadn't mentioned the albino python that shared her act. Or that her sultry dance involved wrapping her pouting lips cheekily around the creature's nose and losing her G-string.

With the show over, the men sitting at tables closest to the stage started to leave the room through a doorway at the far end. I waited and when the moment was right I stood up and whispered, 'Nature calls,' in Monica's ear. She gripped my hand hard. 'I'll be back in a flash, babe,' I said sweetly, extricating my hand. The curtained doorway was momentarily unguarded. If anyone stopped me, I'd say I was looking for the ladies' room. I slipped through and found myself in front of a lift. Next to the lift was a staircase. I took my heeled sandals off and crept on bare feet up the stairs. On the landing I heard voices. I tiptoed onto the wooden floor, staying close to the wall and praying it wouldn't creak. A light under a door.

'He wants to see her again.' A man's voice. Soft. Controlled. French accent.

'She is afraid of him.' A woman's voice. Husky. Calm. East European accent.

'You can handle her. He's running out of patience. He's tired of photos. He wants to see the real thing.'

'Can you control him?'

'The auction will take place as agreed. But we need him in the game. Will you come upstairs later? Volkov asked after you.'

'Perhaps.'

I stepped back into a dark doorway just in time. The door opened. The stocky man in the silver jacket passed right by my hiding place. A few paces on, he stopped. I stopped breathing. After a full minute he carried on walking. I heard the lift doors open and close. The darkness was a physical force pressing into me. It was a good thing I had a sensitive nose. Monica had generously offered one of her perfumes but I'd refused. Something told me the man who'd just walked past had an excellent nose for the fragrance of a woman. I stepped out of the doorway without thinking. A loose plank groaned with an ear-splitting crack in that oppressive silence. I hot-footed it down the corridor on bare feet and made it to the staircase just in time. A light went on in the corridor. I heard the woman ask, 'Who's there?'

A burly shape rocked back against the heavy fabric. The bouncer in front of the curtains was back from his pee break. I tapped on the massive shoulder with regal insouciance. He moved aside obediently and retreated into position behind me. I was careful not to look back as I did the walk. That fun female walk to a different kind of destination. I felt his eyes linger on my backside and I knew he wasn't going to stop me. *Walk for me.*

Monica's whole body relaxed when I sat down. We moved to the bar. The silver jacket was acting like he owned the place. I pointed him out to Monica. 'That guy was upstairs talking to a woman. Something about an auction.' I shuddered. 'It sounded like they were grooming somebody to be a call-girl.'

Monica shook her head. 'These people are big-league players in the crime underworld, Paola. Why are we here?'

'I thought maybe Daniel hung out here.'

'What would Daniel be doing with people like this?'

It was a reasonable question. 'I don't know. Maybe he got in over his head.'

'You can't take responsibility for other people's bad judgement calls,' Monica said.

I had that funny gut feeling one sometimes gets when one is being watched. When I looked up, the head honcho in the silver jacket was talking to the barman at the far end of the bar counter; they were looking our way.

Act natural. Keep the conversation going.

'So, why are you hanging on to that pink museum?' I asked. 'It's practically bankrupted your family.'

She shrugged. 'I like it.'

Did I imagine that eyes were upon us? Where we'd struggled to get the barman's attention previously, he now plied us with drinks and clever chitchat. The sultry hostess in a state of emerald green undress who'd showed us to our table earlier in the evening drifted over and flirted with Monica. I could see Monica going cross-eyed every time the chiffon shifted. It was time to leave.

My mobile showed 4.18 am when Monica dropped me off. We sat there a moment looking at each other.

'So, did you give her your number?'

Monica grinned wickedly. 'She gave me hers. Her name's Paloma.'

Back in the apartment I swabbed off the thick make-up with baby oil and cotton pads, congratulating myself that we'd got out of there alive, and then pulled the duvet up over myself on the couch.

When I went over a few days later to say goodbye, Monica gave me a hug like a big sister and told me to take care. She's taller than I am and with heels on she towers over me. I let my head rest where it was for a few moments, warm and comforted against her breast. I confessed to myself that I was envious of her in some way I couldn't define. At almost exactly the same moment, I realised she was the closest thing I had to a real friend. I wanted to tell her about Celestine. I wanted to say out loud, 'I'm going to find Celestine. She will tell me what's going on.' I had convinced myself that the stewardess at Charles de Gaulle was Lady Limbo. I just didn't know whether Lady Limbo existed only in my vanished husband's fertile imagination or whether she lived and breathed. The online searches had led me up the garden path and back. I'd come up with Lady Limbos that were short stories and others that were ocean-going yachts, and many more sexually active Limbo Ladies and Limbo Lays, but I'd found no trace of the online bulletin board that lured women who wanted to have children by natural conception. I was convinced it existed but I had no idea how to find it. Celestine would know.

I tried Enid Lazzari one last time. To my surprise, the soft tuneless voice came on the line almost immediately.

'It's Paola Dante. I'm going away for a while. Why haven't you been answering your phone?'

'Perhaps I've been out.'

'What does he dream about?'

'You never asked him?'

'He never wanted to talk about it.'

'The nature of night terrors is that, often, the sufferer has no recollection of the details of the dream. It is a nameless terror that presents as life-threatening.' I recognised the smooth, professional tone that glossed over all edges. It was the tone of generality that denied the individual and specific.

'And with Daniel?' I insisted.

My words echoed as if somebody was tapping on hollow limbs. The silence deepened as she considered whether or not she would reply.

Eventually she said, 'He experiences the sensation of drowning.'

'What does it come from?'

'Feelings of guilt, helplessness, vulnerability. Similar emotions to anybody else. Perhaps a chemical imbalance. Who can be sure?' I could see the eloquent shrug of small shoulders. 'Some might say water is symbolic of the feminine principle. But that is a simplistic view. Gabriel is a man of the world.'

'Do you know where he is?' Please tell me I'm off on a wild goose chase.

'He has put himself out of reach. You chose to ignore my advice about the police.'

'They weren't ... Oh, forget it. What do you expect me to do?'

'We are all free to do whatever we want. But to ignore the obvious is foolish.'

'Could you try to be a little clearer? I'm struggling to see anything *obvious* about the current situation.'

'Soul, mind, heart. All things seek balance,' she chanted, sounding like an eerie clockwork bird in a faraway tree. 'I have an early appointment tomorrow.'

Click.

La Tour

AU REVOIR. A BIENTÔT. In three days I was out of the emptied hull of an apartment that strangers would infuse with their foreign odours. The piano stood in the corner with a brown throw over it. I'd made it a condition of the lease that the piano should stay.

I allowed time for a stopover in Paris on my way to the Rome project. The Paris Airport Holiday Inn made an ideal base for someone who wanted to hang around Charles de Gaulle for a couple of days, trudging from one information desk to the next.

Finally I found her. She stood out because most of the ground crew weren't very attractive and she made walking on six-inch heels look easy. I wondered why she wasn't in the air. I went over and introduced myself. I explained that, over a year ago, she had helped my mother, a Mrs Dante, trace her luggage after the plane she was booked on was grounded in a bad storm in Florence and the passengers were bussed to Charles de Gaulle. I said my mother had asked her to call me. To my surprise, she remembered the whole incident immediately.

'Mais oui! Your maman was très agréable!' Perhaps I could invite her out to lunch by way of thanks? She asked where I was staying. Early supper was easier for her; lunchtime was busy. We agreed to meet at 6.30 pm at a restaurant in the airport terminal open to the public. Satisfied with the progress, I went back to the air-conditioned hotel room but found no rest in that artificial cocoon. Eventually, I opened the window and let the sounds of airport traffic in. That must have lulled me to sleep because I woke up to the electronic beep of the mobile alarm. It was time.

I watched the petite Frenchwoman I had pinned my hopes on make her entrance. She had that rare ability to stop human traffic and make jaws drop. Every man within a fifty-metre radius swung around to watch her. And if he had a woman with him, the woman gaped too, before she yanked him back to attention. Celestine's assets were displayed to devastating effect: dainty feet arched until they were almost vertical, a perfectly proportioned body with a wasp waist, legs that seemed outrageously long and slender in their proportions, and high perky breasts. She made the standard issue airways uniform and neck scarf look chic and feminine. I could see why Daniel would want to sketch this woman. We finished supper and I feared it was almost too late. Perhaps she sensed my panic because in a deliciously husky voice she asked me why I was really there. Nobody hung around the airport just to say thank you.

I told her about my husband's disappearance and the *Lady Limbo* novel he was writing. He'd heard my mother relate their conversation about a place in Belgium.

She gave an expressive shrug, accompanied by an elegant flick of a slender, manicured hand and a loud definitive, 'Mais oui! Where a woman can make a baby with a real man.' I sneaked a quick look around, checking out behind the pillars and even the woman in cleaner's uniform emptying the dustbin, but she looked as if she had troubles of her own. Celestine noticed my discomfort.

'Allez. You do not need to worry. We are in France, where mistresses are de rigueur and acts of passion are admired. You don't smoke?' She lit up while she waited for me to enlighten her. 'It is different in South Africa?'

'I'm not sure,' I told her frankly. 'Take the cigarette ... My country is going through a phase of reinvention. Cigarettes in public places and 4x4 vehicles on the beach have been outlawed, but excessive alcohol consumption, the primary cause of sexual abuse and criminal acts against women and children, is tolerated, and young girls have free abortions and take morning-after pills but men still don't wear condoms.' It felt good to let go after days of pent-up anxiety traipsing the concourses of Charles de Gaulle, so I continued. 'AIDS has become a sexy cause – excuse the pun – but nobody talks about how many people are killed by TB.' None of these issues intruded much upon my day-to-day life and I had never felt compelled to resort to any action on their behalf. Under Celestine's amused gaze they emerged from the latent area of my brain that dealt with irony. Her joie de vivre and European background made me want to confide in her. 'So I really have no idea,' I concluded, 'what South African law or public consensus would have to say about the idea of having sex by appointment in order to conceive a child.' I could have added that in general I agree with Spinoza: it is my opinion that human beings tend to chaos.

She seemed to understand. 'Ah, oui, the ways of Africa are complicated for people like us. It is understandable – you are nervous, you do not know if it is the right thing that you plan to do.' That explained her willingness to talk to me. In her mind I'd come for directions to RMI.

'I want to introduce you to some très chères amies – very dear friends, yes? – of mine. I am sure you will find them interesting.' She smiled radiantly at me. 'Do you have time? My car is not far. But first I must call them.'

Charles de Gaulle was still buzzing with activity. Celestine explained that there was no metro running directly from the airport so she preferred to use her own car. We made our way to the underground parking area, jumped into a white Fiat and headed for the motorway, French rock music blasting away. Celestine turned the music down and explained that she had known Gi most of her life. They were high school friends. It was Gi who had first gone to Real Man Inc. in a desperate attempt to save a previous childless marriage, after trying everything else. Her assigned partner was a Belgian student who worked for RMI to make money for his studies. To make the story short, Gi and Peter fell in love. Gi went home pregnant but when the child was born it had health problems, and tests revealed that Gi's husband, a dentist, was not the father. He committed suicide. Celestine mentioned a television programme she had seen about dentists having one of the highest rates of suicide among all the professions. It must be something to do with looking into people's mouths every day. She would find it impossible. A twenty-eight-year-old man. Gi was devastated. All this time, Peter had not stopped thinking about her. Then, just when her life was at its lowest point, he arrived on her doorstep. When he learnt what had transpired, Peter did not hesitate. He was that kind of a man. A man in a billion. A man in a hundred billion. They have been married now for eight years and they have another child, a daughter, who is perfect.

'Here we are. Viens. They are expecting us.'

We parked in a quiet street and I followed Celestine's six-inch heels up a stairway to a first-floor apartment. 'So, out of strange beginnings and all this tragedy,' she said, turning to look back at me, 'a great love was born and has survived.'

Gi was in the kitchen when we arrived – a thin, gamine woman with a boyish haircut and pretty dangling earrings. Peter was a soft-spoken man with an amiable baby face and a rosy complexion. I was introduced as a friend from South Africa who wanted to know about RMI. No mention was made of a missing husband. The son, Stefan, who looked about ten years old, greeted us with the boisterous enthusiasm of an untrained puppy, shaking hands vigorously and speaking too loudly, dribble running down both sides of his mouth. He obediently said good night and dispensed heartfelt hugs to everyone before carrying away a huge bowl of freshly fried potato chips. I watched him shamble off after a young girl who lived next door, to watch television. It was the children who bore the scars of the progenitors' guilt. In *Lady Limbo*, the reader was not told what happened to Amélie's baby girl. Each time I went over that peculiar omission I heard the echo of Enid Lazzari's voice reminding me that sometimes what is *not* said is more important than what is.

'Stefan loves people,' Peter smiled, bringing me back to the present as he bounced his two-year-old daughter on his knee and nuzzled her with his nose. The little girl shrieked with pleasure. Gi chain-smoked and the rest of us ate hot chips with warm Belgian beer while we talked.

It wasn't long before Peter took the angelic Hana off to bed, warning that a bedtime story could take a long time. 'Especially when the father falls asleep!' Gi laughed in a cloud of smoke.

'So, what do you think?' Celestine asked on the way back to my airport hotel. I'd offered to take a taxi but she'd insisted, saying she passed there anyway.

'They're not what I expected. They're normal people,' I admitted.

She rested her eyes on me for a moment before looking back at the road. 'I cannot think of them as normal. They are superheroes to me. They have not slept together in the same bed a single night since they have been together. Tonight, Peter will fall asleep next to Stefan. It is his turn.' She was silent for the rest of the trip, keeping her eyes on the wet, slippery tarmac.

Before we left, Gi had invited me to visit the next day, when her daughter would be occupied at crèche. Stefan was at a remedial school during the week. This was the first year he was old enough to go.

The next day, I waited for her at a coffee shop in downtown Paris where she dropped her daughter off. I watched her cross the road, a slender, good-looking broad, as they say in American movies.

Gi told me she had worked as a nurse in obstetrics before her son's birth. That was how she had come to hear about Real Man Inc. She talked freely. At first it was strange even for her, who had seen many naked men but, in the end, it was not as difficult as some people might think to go with a strange man. Everything was done in a hygienic way. One felt safe, Gi said. Most of what she told me I already knew from Monsieur Bok and his glossy brochures. But she had inside information gleaned from Langstrom (as she still sometimes called her husband, Peter) as well.

Contrary to what one might expect, preference was given to men who were established in their fields, professionals, men whose past, and even their future in some cases, was an open book to RMI. This increased the chances that the attributes of success would be passed on to any offspring. Every precaution was taken. The bookings per practitioner were limited to reduce the odds of half-sisters and half-brothers later marrying. Women who were known to be related or acquainted were not given the same partners. Addresses were scanned to reduce the likelihood of several women in the same area using the same partner. Contracts were signed prohibiting the men from associating with clients after coupling. Women's identities were protected as far as possible, although this was obviously difficult, 'since what man would forget the scent of a woman who had slept with him like an animal does?' Gi asked as though she knew what she was talking about. She looked thoughtful for a moment and then told me she had not chosen Peter as a partner the first time, and nothing had happened. She had gone home barren.

The *first* time? She had gone back more than once? It had never occurred to me that one might consider a second visit. I had regarded it as a form of once-in-a-lifetime Russian roulette.

A client was never given the same man twice, Gi explained. She had chosen Langstrom on an impulse. She had seen the possibility of kindness in his eyes. The mind is very strong; she had known that she was pregnant by the time they left each other that night. It was fate. She herself was une jolie-laide, one who was pretty and ugly at once, otherwise she could not explain it. She did not deserve Peter. Gi told me that she was very ashamed of what she had done, but it was stronger than her. She could not look her previous husband in the face when the results proved he was not the father, and he hanged himself from the beams in their bedroom to punish her forever.

'God gives and God takes away,' Gi said. 'Celestine told us about your husband. If you want a child enough it will work, you will see.'

We exchanged calling cards as we said our goodbyes. 'Wait,' Gi said as I stood up, taking Peter's card from me again and scribbling a telephone number on the back. 'This is for RMI in Brussels.'

Celestine and I had supper one more time, at a Thai restaurant owned by a friend of hers. It was packed with Parisian and Asian customers sitting at small tables. At the table next to us, three men in suits shovelled long noodles from decorative red china bowls into their mouths between an animated business discussion.

'Alors ... have you found what you came for?' my new friend asked innocently while signalling for a menu. I waited for the waiter to leave.

'Celestine, do you recognise this man?' Daniel cooking pasta while singing an aria from *La Traviata* in our kitchen at home. An unguarded moment captured with my mobile. Why had I chosen that intimate picture and not something more formal? It required superhuman strength to control my voice. It was the ghost of my husband I was holding out to her. I watched her closely, ready for the smallest sign that might give her away.

She took the mobile from me. 'Ah, this is your amour? He is très beau – very handsome. Non. I do not know this man.' She handed it back to me – smiling, casual, her eyes skating away – and suggested the Thai green chicken curry dish. 'C'est délicieux. The dish of the house. What London does Paris must always do better, so now Parisians adore spicy food.'

I decided to play it her way for now. I told her Gi had provided me with all the information I needed.

She clinked her wine glass to mine. 'A tes amours!' Outside the restaurant, she kissed me the habitual twice and wished me well, saying I shouldn't disappear, as people do. I should stay in contact.

'Don't worry, I'm like the proverbial bad penny,' I replied. She was momentarily puzzled, so I explained. Nobody wanted a bad penny around, they kept on giving it away, but it always found its way back.

Walking away from her that night, her sexy laugh still ringing in my ears, I decided she was hiding something. It made me feel less bad about not telling her and Gi and Peter that I already knew all about Real Man Inc., including how to get there. Celestine knew that my showing her the photograph was significant, and yet she had displayed no curiosity as to why she should have known him. By putting me in contact with the Langstroms, she intimated that she herself had no direct experience of RMI. I knew that in France bad manners were despised more than a murderer's foul deed so I'd held my peace. It was the last time I saw Celestine.

I was sitting at the airport waiting for my flight to Rome when an SMS from Monica came through on my mobile: 'Folder mt. 2bad. Monica'. It took me a moment to work out that the folder on the old PC was empty. Another dead end. I took out the little maroon notebook, and wrote: 'Friday 4/5/2006. Certain C recognised him in the photo. Lady Limbo???'

What was the probability of a man bumping into the same woman who'd caught his attention with an online advert in his student days, a continent away and several years later? Not high. If I was a bookie I'd have said the odds were 1 000 000:1. I did a calculation on my palm pilot. Friday to Friday he'd been away for exactly thirty-four weeks, which totalled 238 days or 5 712 hours, which equalled 342 720 minutes or 20 563 200 seconds, which was a long time for anyone to be away without explanation.

When I become nervous I turn to numbers. My dominant left brain naturally processes information in a logical, sequential fashion. Numbers do not lie. People are lying, devious skunks but numbers do not lie. I repeated this mantra to myself as I put the stylus back. It was one of those small arguments I couldn't win with Daniel. His view was that numbers did lie. He showed me how he saw it. He wrote the number '100' on a sheet of paper and asked me to tell him the significance of that number. I replied that it could mean anything. How could I know what he meant it to represent?

'That's exactly it,' he pointed out, with a satisfied smirk. 'A human being had to interpret that number, and that was when the trouble started.' I pointed out that 100% of something was still 100%. And he lifted an eyebrow at me and said, 'What if it was 99.9%? Did it make a difference?' I accused him of being a shades-of-grey person and he accused me of being a black-and-white person.

Okay, Daniel, I wanted to shout. *You're right.* What does it mean to be 100% disappeared? Does it mean you're dead or just absconded? Does it mean I'll never see you again, or I will if I do the right thing? What is the right thing? Did I cause you to leave me or was it a question of time? Did I never stand a chance? Did it boil down to the simple numbers that you kept tabs on, like 'Days lived as a different person'?

For some reason the amiable Peter popped into my mind, bouncing his daughter on his knee in another man's house. A dead man's house. We'd never really got the chance to talk. He'd know about living another man's life, about walking in another man's shoes. Did Peter ever think about it? Did he agree with Gi that it was fate? That he could not have changed anything even if he had seen it coming?

The concourse was humming with activity. Next to me a couple catnapped while their son immersed himself in a PlayStation game, thumbs flicking expertly. It struck me that I'd assumed Daniel had never worked on a computer because he'd arrived with a typewriter. I'd never even bothered to ask before I'd set it all up and launched into my training routine. I'd done it a thousand times: getting client users on board, overcoming their resistance to the new technology by confronting them with the implacable object of their fear: a desktop computer. He'd smiled at me, that dreamy smile of Daniel's that turned me on. I told him sternly to listen, and he said, 'How many Kama Sutra positions are there, oh Queen of Numbers?' My first and last computer lesson to my new husband ended in us attempting the eleventh Sutra position and collapsing in a heap of undignified giggles.

But Daniel had known enough to secure his files. And he'd had the computer 'beefed up'.

I sat up straight.

Nancy Pebasco. Shit. I don't believe it.

Some time after the abandoned computer lesson, Paola the good wife asks her husband how it's going with the PC while he prepares to dice an onion. To watch Daniel chop anything is to watch a maestro at work. 'C'est lent, très lent,' he grimaces. 'It can't be slower than the typewriter,' I say. 'It needs beefing up,' Daniel continues drolly. That gets me going.

'What's up with everybody? Did you have breakfast with Nancy Pebasco?' It's a rhetorical question. Nancy Pebasco is our demanding tough-as-nails CEO who has flown in from New York and left a trail of exhausted pepped-up consultants in her wake. 'The whole office is "beefing up" now! It's like one of those sales routines where you copy your customers' body language so they'll feel comfortable with you.' I mimic the voices. 'Can we beef up those resumes? Can we beef up that PowerPoint presentation?'

The sharp blade is paused mid-air. Daniel has an odd look on his face. 'I must have picked it up from you then,' he says lightly and starts chopping again. A bad feeling is tramping all over the kitchen. I know for sure it's an American phrase I don't use. 'Daniel, where did you learn to cook?' I ask in a demi-trance.

'What is this, ma chérie, Twenty Questions?'

'Just for once can you answer my question?' What am I pleading to know?

'Alors. C'est comme ça. A writer must eat and pay the rent like everybody else. In Paris there are many restaurants and many sous chefs; from waiter to assistant chef, it's quick if food interests you. In the daytime, I sat at my typewriter and at night I became a sous chef. I, Daniel de Luc, was personally responsible for concocting some of the most delicious dishes in the whole of Paris!'

Daniel always knows how to make me laugh, so the bad feeling traipses out of sight, but in retrospect I see its forked tongue. *I'll be back,* it seems to say. The tightness in my chest starts that night and it never quite goes away ever again.

Nancy Pebasco paid my husband to fuck her. Years later the thought was a disembowelling fish-knife.

An olive-skinned woman a few years older than me walked past, with a heavy bosom and soft, dark curls falling to her shoulders. I watched her distractedly as she paused at the magazine stand and acknowledged silently to myself that I was a pitiful fool. Of course there were other women before me, I'd always known that. Wasn't sex just another commodity and marriage a convenience? So why was I finding numbers greater than one so difficult to take? My mind slipped away from me beneath the electric perimeter of love's fear. I let myself wonder about his past lives. How had he supported himself with those other women between the RMI appointments? If he'd married the curvaceous brunette who'd now selected a magazine, what kind of a man would he have been with her? The French magazine seller made no effort to keep his eyes off the deep cleft of the woman's décolletage. She walked away, swinging broad hips to let him know what he was missing.

Enid Lazzari said he changed habitat like a chameleon. Did that mean professions too? He'd paid his share of everything. When we bought the apartment we'd needed to pay deposit and transfer fees up front so he'd asked his agent for an advance on the new book.

I'd checked with the bank: he'd closed his accounts. They wouldn't tell me anything else, like when or what balance he'd withdrawn, except to say he'd also taken care of the balance owing on the HP agreement for my car. So he'd done the decent thing. Paid off my car to offset the monthly payments on the apartment that came off my account. Daniel must have reckoned that I could go back to living as I'd done before. Life Before Daniel. LBD my life was empty. I didn't want to go back to LBD. The time before I opened my door and let love in.

* * *

I was in the Rome office when Monica called and left a message on the voicemail. 'Give me a call, honey bunch. I know something you don't know!'

I could hear the excitement in her voice. It was typical of her to draw out the suspense. Except for getting her own way, there was nothing that made Monica happier than having a secret or three up her sleeve. I finally managed to reach her. The big news was that Igor had continued fiddling with the PC hard drive and found some files that were technically deleted but not removed. Files in limbo, so-to-speak. She was disgruntled because he'd refused to tell her what was in them.

'He says it's private. For your eyes only. Can you believe that? Do you know how much work I've sent his way? He won't even tell me the names of the files!'

I'd known Monica long enough to know a heart of pure platinum beat under the conniving exterior. I calmed her down and managed to get Igor's contact details out of her. Then I called Piet and told him I was available to do that financial audit he'd been pestering me about for a project back in South Africa.

A week later I was banging a brass knocker on a door in Observatory. Igor lived with his mother. He came to the door barefoot and wearing a T-shirt that looked as if it had survived a barbed wire fence.

'My mom's a cat freak,' he explained artlessly as we waded through a reception committee of cats lying around on worn furniture and threadbare Persian rugs. He switched a light on so I could see where I was going. 'She rescues them and brings them home. She says they talk to her.' He shrugged placidly as if anything was possible. No big deal.

In the study, Igor invited me to sit down after tilting a resident cat off the chair and turning the cushion. Standing next to me, he navigated around the seventeen-inch touchscreen monitor with supreme casualness, his fingers moving in a blur. The high-tech system provided all the light in that dark room. Computer equipment filled the shelves. A pair of expensive-looking headphones lay on the desk. When I looked again, a folder icon named 'Daniel' blinked on the screen.

'Looks like some kind of a shredder program got rid of the rest of the files in the folder but these files were separately encrypted. I had to play around a bit.' He scratched his head. 'Maybe the oke didn't want to delete them.'

I gave the 'Daniel' folder a hesitant tap. Seven files fanned out across the screen. *Grace. Hela. Isabelle. Jasmine. Rita. Tamara. Veronique.* When I looked again, wondering what he must be thinking, Igor had slipped away.

The names made it real. These women meant something to my husband. I would soon know something of what was going on inside his head – why he stayed with us, why he left us. *Us.* I said the word aloud. It was at that moment that I fully acknowledged the presence of other individual flesh-and-blood women in the equation of my relationship with Daniel. I had skirted around the idea, but now I was here. With the vocalisation of 'us' came the realisation that he would henceforth be a stranger to me, just as he had been – still was – my husband, my soul mate, the only lover I'd ever felt kinship with. It was the green-eyed monster that had awoken from its slumbers, breathing fire. All the stomach crunches in the world could not have made me feel the way I felt; a year of constant period pain could not have equalled the terror-induced agony of curiosity laced with the acid poison of jealousy and sorrow.

In the twilight room that smelt like a cat latrine, I opened the files of the seven graces. The truth is always both more and less than we expect. When I was finished I had no idea what kind of truth I was dealing with. Which of us can decipher another's truth, no matter how beloved the other is?

Each woman's file followed a format reminiscent of the files I'd seen at RMI. There was background information, statistical and descriptive information, dates for major life events as well as brief notes of dental and medical visits. A category called 'Assignment date' provided a record of each woman's assignations. Most of them had several. Generally only a date was given but in some cases the letter 'X' had also been inserted. Only Rita had a single assignation and it was marked 'X'. In addition, it was highlighted in red, as was the last assignation for each of the other women. Rita was the oldest. She was born in 1950. She could cook sublimely but she lived her life as timid as a house mouse on the edge of a canyon. Jasmine's eyes were described as violet-blue. There was a comment about the effortless sinuous grace of her movement. Profession was given as 'Dancer'. And inserted just below: 'Her unusual beauty is incomparable; it is as distinguished as it is strange.' That didn't sound very dispassionate. In typical Daniel style, he hadn't resisted the impulse to romantic subjectivity. Of Grace he said that she did not talk very much but she did not have to: 'Her low silver-toned voice haunts the mind'. Isabelle – could it be the same Isabelle? – he described as lazy: 'At night she is a moth in the moon's garden, prone to self-destruction'. Tamara was 'the long-limbed warlike daughter of a Cossack.' Veronique had the ability to make the dullest man laugh. Hela's grey eyes under the thick black eyebrows were 'as pure and startling in their intelligence as wild geese flying over a vast ocean.'

Were these exploratory character sketches, or were they the précis notes of an RMI practitioner? I came to the conclusion that they were probably both. It was possible that Isabelle had a cameo role in *Lady Limbo*, but it could just as easily have been another Isabelle. None of the other names rang a bell.

I was a distant observer of these mercurial women who fiercely asserted their right to be independent. I even allowed myself to imagine their various meetings with X: how they took place, the cities where they met, the season and its time: the initial encounter, the subsequent rendezvous, the lingering fragrances the perfume of transient ecstasy. There was no reference in the files to children. X was always the last person to have had an assignation with each of the women. There were others before him, but never any after him.

In the end I suffered less than I'd expected. Celestine was not among them.

The International Weekly Telegraph, August 21, 2006

FRENCH STEWARDESS'S BODY FOUND IN PARIS FOREST

The body found by a pheasant hunter and his dog near Villegny, on the outskirts of Paris, has been positively identified as that of Celestine Nothomb, 36, a ground stewardess at Paris Charles de Gaulle Airport.

Senior Detective Marcel Olmi, a member of the regional specialist sex crimes unit, told a media conference that the young woman was buried in a shallow grave covered with branches and leaves in a deserted, overgrown part of the forest a few kilometres out of town. Nothomb's identity was established after a police search recovered her handbag in bushes close to where the killer is believed to have parked his car. A postmortem is still to be conducted.

The Nothomb family history has been marked by tragedy. In 1978, a head-on collision claimed the lives of Nothomb's parents. Celestine Nothomb and her younger sister became orphans overnight. In 2001, Nothomb's sister, Jasmine Nothomb, was killed in a hit-and-run accident. The 29-year-old single mother died instantly. The case made national headlines after police delayed interviewing eyewitnesses. Despite extensive investigations spurred on by an outpouring of public sympathy for her young daughter left orphaned by the act of a reckless criminal, the speeding vehicle was never traced.

Nothomb's surviving niece is reported to be staying with friends until arrangements can be made to house her in a suitable place of safety.

Murder
Most Foul

I ALMOST MISSED IT. The announcement of her death. In its fourth month the Rome project was ratcheting along, and I was working long hours together with three other project managers to meet the tight delivery schedule. Project Hadrian's brief was to computerise the antiquated systems of the Agenzia del Demanio, an agency for state-owned property whose interests ranged from army barracks and forts to palazzos and villas rated as having particular historic and artistic value. In time, every relic and artefact contained in thousands of rooms would be catalogued using state-of-the-art software.

I sat with *The International Weekly Telegraph* in front of me, my lunchtime panino forgotten, reading the article again and again. Celestine was dead. Another shallow grave. I remembered bumping into my cousin Romina some time after Massimo's funeral. Sunglasses firmly in place, she'd carried on walking as if she didn't know me, but when I'd called out 'Romina, can we talk about it?' she'd turned around and come back. 'Fine, let's talk,' she'd said. 'Tell me, Paola, would you go to Daniel's funeral?'

'There wouldn't be a funeral,' I'd replied, ever sure of myself.

'I'd just scatter his ashes. That's the way he'd want it.' She'd sighed, a deep profound sigh, as if I was lost on a small boat in the middle of the ocean, out of reach of search-and-rescue operations. 'A funeral is just saying goodbye with everybody that cared about that person, Paola. You always act as if you're so special but some day you'll realise it's not about you all the time.' And then she'd spun round and marched off again.

Would you go to Daniel's funeral?

Two days later, I was back in Paris to attend my first funeral since Nicky was buried. I even had this berserk thought that Daniel might pitch up at Celestine's funeral. Daniel adored newspapers. He bought a local newspaper every day and often an international one as well. Maybe I'd glance over and a tall, dark stranger would smile at me. That's how deluded I was.

I contacted Gi, who wept openly and said Celestine did not deserve it. Whatever this person thought she had done, she had not deserved such a death. It was an odd choice of words that stayed with me.

The funeral was held in one of the oldest cemeteries in Paris, where members of the Nothomb family had been buried for generations. Celestine would lie with them, not with her adoptive parents. Later that day in the Langstrom kitchen, as we cleaned up after the last of the mourners had left, Gi told me the story, as she had it from Celestine. After the car accident that claimed their parents' lives, Celestine and her sister had been taken to an orphanage. Only Celestine had been adopted. When the sister, Jasmine, was run over years later as she used a pedestrian crossing on her way back from work, Celestine had taken her niece Dominique in and looked after her as if she were her own daughter. It was then that she became a ground hostess.

At Celestine's funeral, I'd noticed an elegantly dressed woman standing in the background next to a nearby grave while I waited for Gi, who was talking to the chaplain. As we left, the woman came towards us on the path and stumbled into our way as if her heel had caught on something. Gi and I both put out an arm to steady her and then we stooped to help her recover the scattered contents of her handbag. As we scrabbled around, she spoke to us in a low, urgent whisper, excusing herself. She gave her name and said she was a friend of Jasmine's, and had once met Celestine. She very much regretted this terrible thing that had happened to Celestine. She wished to offer her condolences. Please to continue as if nothing had happened, as if our encounter were an accident; please not to look back after her. And then she was gone. It happened so quickly that Gi and I were astonished, but we had heard the fear in her voice so we didn't look back.

In the car, sitting next to Stefan and Dominique on the back seat, I opened my notebook. Where I'd recently scribbled 'Detective Marcel Olmi', I now added the name 'Eveline Kaas', drawing a black line underneath the surname with a thudding heart. Was it just a coincidence that she shared a surname with Gabriel Kaas, my husband's authorial alter ego? I was reasonably sure she wasn't one of the women in the Limbo Files but that didn't mean much.

At the graveside, Dominique, a thin, dark-haired child, had stood next to Stefan and kept her eyes down. I'd seen the child's lips tremble as the spades of earth were shovelled in but she had managed to maintain her composure by slipping her hand into Stefan's. She did not leave his side for the rest of the day, eventually falling asleep on the couch beside him. Occasionally, Stefan would stir and mumble, and she would adjust her position to his. Peter had given one of the funeral guests a lift, so Gi and I sat there talking while she rocked her baby daughter to sleep in her arms.

'What will happen to her now?'

Gi spoke quietly, her face pinched with tiredness. 'I cannot take her in permanently. We have enough just to take care of our own two. It is not easy. I cannot work because Stefan needs me and sometimes I worry that I neglect Hana. Peter has enough on his plate.'

'She seems very attached to Stefan.'

Gi hesitated and then said, 'They have known each other since she was born. He tells people he is going to marry her. I worry about their relationship as Stefan gets older. That's another reason why she can't stay.'

It seemed a good moment to ask about Daniel. I showed her

a photograph taken at our wedding celebration lunch. 'You have still not heard from him?' She asked me to hold it again while she put her reading glasses on.

'I'm sorry. I do not remember ever having seen your husband, but if you like, I will ask Langstrom. Sometimes he knows things.'

I told her she could keep the photo to show Langstrom. She put it face up on the side table and we talked about other things. She asked me what it is like to live in South Africa. Last year she had bought some pretty earrings made of feathers and beads at the South African stand of a travel fair Peter had helped to organise. I told her it was a spectacularly scenic country full of irony and contradictions. Destruction and construction were in constant opposition. After good rains everything smelt new and untried again. Her face was pinched with tiredness. I thought to myself that I might as well be talking about the planet Mars. She was a European born after the Second World War. Africa was the hellhole of famine and war she saw on television.

When Peter came home, he untangled the two youngsters gently and lifted Stefan, a big, strong boy, up against him, his hands making a sling for his son's bottom. He carried him off to bed that way, saying goodnight over his shoulder with a bone-tired smile. Gi showed me where the bedding was. Would I mind sleeping on the sleeper couch with Dominique? She was still rocking the baby girl who was now barely awake, the soft honey-brown eyes half shut. I groaned inwardly. After taking days off at such a critical stage of the project I was in for a heavy week.

The child Dominique had woken instantly when Stefan was lifted off the couch, and now she watched me anxiously, her mint-blue eyes startling against the dark, tousled hair. When I switched off the lamp she cried out in such alarm that I immediately switched it back on. I explained that we would both be sleeping on the couch so she needn't be afraid and then I flicked the light switch again. There was a slim chance I might get a few hours' sleep if I turned sideways with my back to her so that we each had our own space. But I'd hardly climbed in next to her when she started to whimper like a small lost animal. I couldn't sleep with the light on, and I

225

wouldn't sleep if she carried on with that piteous noise, so I rolled over and pulled her against me, her thin back – it was all bones – against my stomach. The whimpers became softer and softer as the stiff little body relaxed and gave itself over to sleep. I hardly slept that long night, holding her. I recalled the feeling and smell of her for months afterwards, as if a warm nocturnal creature had crept in beside me, the small body curled against mine.

I once read that if one wants to gain the trust of a young wild animal, one should sleep next to it at night; a bond of trust is established in the nocturnal hours. But it was something that had to be repeated and constant. I couldn't give Dominique that and she knew it. The next morning, the sleepy child dropped a coffee cup and saucer when she was told to help with breakfast. I saw Gi's mouth tighten a split second before she slapped the child hard across her face. Peter looked at his wife in horror and drew a sobbing Dominique into his arms. I was the only one who saw the smirk cross the child's face. I realised that Gi and Dominique were mortal enemies vying for Peter's attention. I understood why Dominique could not stay in their house.

Gi came to the door with me, chubby Hana on her hip. 'I have the keys to Celestine's flat,' she said. 'The police have finished their work and I have to sort out her personal effects tomorrow. The landlord wants to let it.' Hana squirmed and gurgled. Her mother held a tissue to her snotty nose and told her to blow hard before depositing her on the ground. We watched her scamper off and then I held my hand out and thanked her. She ignored my stiff gesture and hugged me. Through the light jersey I could feel ribs as she pressed her skinny frame against mine.

In France there is a police station in each suburb, responsible for its own cases, including homicide. The best detectives are assigned to investigative teams with wider jurisdiction. Detective Olmi of the Villegny commissariat was out when I phoned so I left my name and number. I'd read his name in the news report with a shock of recognition – it was the same name mentioned in some of the clippings Daniel had kept. Olmi had investigated the deaths of several women who had died in suspicious circumstances in the vicinity of Paris. But in the end, foul play could never be proven. When he phoned back later in the afternoon, I travelled to Villegny on the metro, wondering how Celestine had landed up there, so far from her home in Orly, which was north of Paris.

The Hotel De Police was an imposing building of an earlier era. Le tricolor flapped in the breeze above a corner doorway that announced itself to be the point of welcome in electric blue. Detective Olmi was on his way, a young policeman informed me in good English after making a call. He asked me to sit and wait.

Detective Olmi was a well-dressed, trim man in his forties. I'd googled him. Divorced with two daughters, he'd had an illustrious career – solving some high-profile crime cases – but had elected to remain a detective over a more political career path, and he belonged to an archery club. I told him I was a friend of Celestine Nothomb, the woman who'd been murdered. He looked disappointed when I said I'd only recently met Celestine but considered her a friend. He was courteous but stressed that the investigation was at an early stage. The full pathology report was still not available. Only then would they know how she had died. I knew what it was like to be pursued in a forest, how the darkness disoriented one, how the trees blocked every terrified movement, how savage night closed in without pity. I hoped that death had come quickly for Celestine.

The detective's voice brought me back to his office. Did I have information that might be of assistance to the investigation? In his experience that was usually the reason why people bothered to come and see him personally. In general, people preferred to stay away from police stations. Unfortunately, they had no similar aversion to crime scenes. He was leaning back in his chair, his hands clasped behind his head, shrewd eyes fixed on my face. I didn't know how to respond. I wanted to tell him the truth. I was so tired of keeping all my secrets. I told him I found it difficult to believe she was dead. I was hoping she could help me – give me information that would assist me in finding my husband. Now I was on slippery ground, and there was no way back.

'Your *hosband* is missing?' He leaned forward, his two index fingers together, staring at me with new interest.

I asked if I could talk to him in confidence, told him that I believed my husband's life would be in danger if his disappearance were made public. He undertook to handle the matter avec discrétion. I told him what I knew about Daniel's disappearance. I didn't know why I was reporting Daniel as a missing person to a policeman one continent away from home, but it felt right; there was something studiously honest about his eyes so I went along with it. He listened without interrupting, asking an occasional question here and there. It was a relief to talk about Daniel. I showed him a wedding photograph taken by the padre in Zanzibar, the two of us smiling for the camera, a dhow in the background, to prove I wasn't fantasising about that at least.

He looked at the photo intently, as if he was burning Daniel de Luc's image into his brain. Then he said, 'Your friend Celestine went missing a few weeks ago. The child phones her aunt's friend that night, a Mrs de Villeneuve, to say her aunt hasn't come home. Mrs de Villeneuve collects the child. She contacts us when the aunt isn't home by the next morning. We put out a missing persons broadcast and posters in the neighbourhood where the woman Celestine lives and on the way to the underground, following the route that she uses to drop the child at school and get to work at the airport. We receive a few calls but when we investigate it turns out to be somebody else, or she's gone. Nothing conclusive turns up. Five days later she arrives to collect the child from Mrs de Villeneuve and claims she was knocked over by a motorbike and lost her memory temporarily. She has some broken ribs and is badly bruised but there is no way to corroborate her story. So I file a report together with her written statement, and in the back of my mind I make a mental note that she is lying. A young, attractive woman disappears. She cannot tell us where the accident happened in her own neighbourhood? She cannot tell us where she was for five days, but she remembers everything else? The facts do not tie up.'

From the window I see modern city office blocks reaching into the sky, interspersed with the spires and domes of stately buildings steeped in French history. Celestine will never walk the streets of France again. Another unexplained death for Daniel to keep in his drawer.

'Why do you think there is a connection between your *hosband* going missing, and this woman's death?'

'I did not say there was a connection to her death,' I said. 'I found his plot outline for a crime novel. He's a writer.' I told him that Daniel had used the same story my mother told us on her return from Charles de Gaulle Airport, so I was hoping he'd gone to see Celestine as part of the research for his book. He'd done that before, and then phoned me afterwards to tell me where he'd gone. It was close enough to the truth to sound believable.

He looked thoughtful. 'Perhaps it is a coincidence – a Frenchman missing in South Africa – and this woman missing in Paris. And now a murder victim. And the only link a plot outline for a novel that is not yet written. But sometimes a coincidence is a clue – a path of crumbs leading us to the murderer. A detective on a murder case without suspects is grateful for crumbs.'

I thought about the French newspaper clippings Daniel had collected. Because of those other deaths I had come to find Olmi in his office. Were they all crumbs?

'I'd like to keep this for now.' He held out the photo.

'Go ahead,' I said. 'I have others.'

'Where can I reach you? To return it?'

As we exchanged business cards, he said, 'Your friend had courage. She refused to go to the hospital. Eventually our own doctor strapped her up, and the next day she phoned me from work, broken ribs and all, to thank me.' He shook his head. I see Celestine the day I first saw her at Charles de Gaulle, head held high, the sexy laugh as she swung her hips and wowed every onlooker in sight. I heard Detective Olmi's voice coming from afar. 'She was killed in a part of the forest that is not frequented by many people because of its remoteness. If it was not for the strong nose of the dog ...'

The murderer had not intended her to be found. It was only chance that had defeated him. This was a cold-blooded killer,

229

perhaps one who intended to eliminate a problem.

'Madame, you must give me your word that you will not play the detective yourself. These are dangerous matters to become involved in. I do not wish to dig your body out of a hole in a forest. Is this clear?'

'But of course,' I said. 'I would not dream of interfering.'

'Madame, this matter of your *hosband's* disappearance will have to be reported to your police in South Africa, but I will contact someone I know, an inspector I have worked with once before, and see what we can do to keep it out of the newspapers, since it may influence our murder investigation.'

'I understand.' I had handed Daniel over to the world, and I felt curiously dispassionate about the consequences.

'Les amateurs!' he muttered softly, my signed statement in his hands.

When I arrived back in Paris, there was a message on my mobile from Peter. 'This is Langstrom …' I called him at work. He asked if we could meet at a nearby bar before I returned to Rome.

Peter ordered me a dry martini and a beer for himself. We sat there looking at each other while the waiter cleaned the table top. 'Why did you really come to find Celestine?' His question was not unkind. The masculine tone of his voice made me want to hear him talk. He knew I had already been to the clinic in Belgium. A friend of his worked in the office there. He should not be here talking to me as his contract prohibited him from making contact with a client of the clinic.

I told him about the plot outline I had found. How I was convinced there was some link between Celestine and my missing husband. He gave me a long look before commenting that I should heed the truism that only the living lie.

'Gi showed me the picture of your husband. She has a kind heart; she wants everybody to be happy. I wasn't going to tell you but Gi insisted. I met him once.'

The clockwork orange lounge flashed through my mind.

'He was with Celestine.'

It took a moment to register. I'd guessed right. Still, it didn't seem possible.

'You're sure?'

He nodded. 'He is a striking man, your husband. It was last year in November. I was on my way to a conference in Berlin. By chance I saw Celestine at a coffee shop in the transit lounge so I went over. It seemed I had arrived at an awkward moment. She made a light-hearted comment about him changing his name so often she had lost track, so he introduced himself, an unusual name for a man. Virgil. This thing with Celestine has upset Gi badly, so I agreed to tell you.'

Virgilio. Nothing wrong with that if you were an absconded writer. I even found it comforting, the reference to Dante hidden in his temporary name. Perhaps he thought of me that day.

'Celestine had her own life,' Peter continued. 'We did not see her very often. But something happened.'

Had Daniel decided to reply in person to a message Celestine had sent via my mother? A message I had yet to decipher. I forced myself to concentrate on what Peter was saying.

'It was last year, before I saw her at Charles de Gaulle, long before all of this. I have not told the police.'

'What was it?'

'Celestine phoned me one day to say she was afraid, that she was certain she was being followed. I told her she should report it to the police.'

'Why did she phone you?'

'She seemed to think it was somebody from RMI. That I might know something about it.'

'Celestine went to RMI?' *I will choose a real man to father my child.* I should have guessed. In the comic Amélie wears dark sunglasses as she enters the clinic. 'I don't understand,' I stammered. 'So Celestine had a child? I thought there was only Dominique.'

'There is only Dominique. Perhaps she accompanied a friend, perhaps it didn't work for her. Who knows?'

He fiddled with his glass. Neither of us said anything for a while, then he broke the silence.

'What is the title of the comic book?'

'*Lady Limbo.*'

Peter bumped his glass over in surprise. As he fumbled for a serviette, I knew that this was the real reason we were sitting here: whatever he was about to say.

'This changes everything. Have you considered that you are suspecting the wrong woman? Perhaps it is not Celestine but her sister, Jasmine. Celestine was sexy, perhaps too sexy for her own good, but Jasmine was – how shall I say it? – magnifique.'

Langstrom was in his own world. 'She had the kind of untamed beauty that can drive a man mad, like a thirst that cannot be quenched.' His voice was subdued. He and I knew all about sadness and regret.

'The kind of beauty that will make a man kill?' I asked.

'Who knows?' he replied, squinting down the nearly empty glass into the last bit of ale and froth as if he could obtain answers there. 'But what I do know is that Jasmine was a striptease dancer. She specialised in dancing the limbo.'

It was under my nose all the time and I'd missed it. *I am Lady Limbo, she who dances alone under the rod of fire.* All those times I'd hunted for 'Lady Limbo' and ended up with the search result 'Limbo (dance) …'

'It was her signature show,' Peter Langstrom was saying. 'The limbo dance. The place was always packed when Jasmine danced. You could almost think it was a trick; no woman with breasts could do it. They came to see her oiled body catch alight under the pole of fire.' He shuddered as if it was happening before him.

Lady Limbo. My head reeled. Stick to the plot. I told him how Daniel's fictional killer contacted Lady Limbo via an online chat site. But I never spoke a word about the seed I had planted in our youth and how it had grown into a carnivorous plant that was snapping its jaws and consuming everything that came within its reach. Peter didn't appear surprised.

'She was like that, Jasmine. More intelligent than people knew. I once asked her why she danced in those clubs when she could have studied further, become successful in a high-profile career with her fearless ways, and she replied that it was only when she danced that she felt alive. It was typical of her to say something like that. The other girls made comments about her frequenting the refectory of the American University in Paris. They thought she picked up clients there, but she told me she went for the open-access computer room and to learn English. So, it's possible.'

A couple had come into the bar with their young daughter, the way families seemed to do all over Europe. I asked Langstrom about Dominique's whereabouts and he looked uncomfortable.

'The social workers came to fetch her today. She is in a good orphanage run by the Sisters of Mercy where there are only girls. We are just hanging by a string in our household. Sometimes I fear that a small push will send us over the edge.' I could hear the apologetic tone in his voice, but I could not properly meet his eyes. There were too many questions between us now.

When we took leave of each other, Peter said, 'Gi does not know about Jasmine. Please say nothing.'

'Of course,' I replied. I had no wish to hurt Gi.

The next morning I was having breakfast before setting off to the airport when Gi called on my mobile. She sounded harassed, distressed.

'Can we meet somewhere? I have something for you.'

I told the taxi driver where to go. It was a bright spring day in Paris. The wide boulevards were thronged with tourists; everywhere I looked I saw lovers hand-in-hand. When was it that I'd last held someone's hand? What a peculiar ritual of love that physical action was. Gi was waiting at the same coffee shop in front of the crèche.

'She left an envelope for me in her apartment,' Gi said. 'I found it when I went to get clothes for her to be dressed in in the coffin. But I couldn't bring myself to open it. When Peter came back last night I was so sad that he couldn't help you, that there were so many secrets without answers. This morning I opened the envelope. There was a note that if anything was to happen to her I was to take her and Jasmine's jewellery and keep it for Hana and Dominique when they were older. Here.' She held out a slim white envelope, her hand shaking with the effort. 'This is for you. It was inside my envelope. I have also brought you a photo of Dominique taken a few months ago at school. She is all that is left of her mother and her aunt. Perhaps it will help.'

'For me?' The envelope was strangely light. 'She expected to be killed then.' It seemed impossible.

'C'est incroyable,' Gi agreed in a small tremulous voice.

I kissed her on the forehead when I left, like one might kiss a child to show affection and reassure all at once.

'Peter loves you.'

'I know he does. But it's possible to love in different ways. All I ever wanted was to be the great love of his life. How is it possible to be jealous of a dead woman and her child?' She stared at me out of hollow, bloodshot eyes.

'You're asking the wrong person.'

Back in the taxi, now racing for the airport, I held the envelope to my nose before opening it. For a moment I imagined Celestine sitting next to me, one leg folded over the other with a peep-toe shoe dangling, her eyes sparkling with anticipation. The taxi driver braked and cursed. Merde! The envelope slipped to the floor, spilling two photographs. I hesitated, watching Paris fly by, my vision blurred by the speed at which my life was moving. Eventually I retrieved them because it had to be done. The first photo was a black-and-white one of a group of young girls in school uniform. The photographer had zoomed in on one child's face: her light-coloured hair tied up in a thick ponytail, her school shirt askew as if it had been buttoned incorrectly and her eyes narrowed as she looked straight into the lens. I turned the photo over. *Simone Sarrazin, Cape Town 2005.*

The second was a faded instant holiday snap of three figures against an illuminated Eiffel Tower in the background. Holding it up to the overhead light, I felt my heart almost stop.

A young woman with abundant shining curls stands between a young student Daniel on her left and a grinning, dishevelled Nicky on her right. Nicky has a possessive arm around her waist and he's holding an open bottle of champagne up for the camera. Whoever she is she looks sensational in a revealing red-sequinned halter top and she's posing in a sensual showgirl kind of way, as if she's on a stage and the world's her audience. She has that supernova-of-hotness look that can't be faked. I turn the photo over. The black ink writing is faint and smudged. *Jasmine avec Nicky et Gabriel.* Celestine's sister, Jasmine. *Jasmine was – how shall I say it? – magnifique.* Of all the things I've considered, Nicky as Jasmine's lover is not one of them. I can hardly take it in.

Breathe, Paola, breathe …

Nicky and Daniel had sometimes gone away without me during varsity holidays; the van den Bogen family had several overseas homes. It's easy enough to leap to conclusions and make deductions, but I know better than most that the devil lies in the details. I look hard at the handsome threesome: Nicky, who even on a bad polaroid day has that light-blond knightly look, in an aqua-blue, open-necked silk shirt; debonair Daniel with hands in pockets and a sardonic half smile revealing his discomfort at being caught in the glare of photographic headlights; and the provocative Lady Limbo whose shimmering eyes give nothing away.

There is no date on the photograph. From the way they are dressed it's a warm Parisian evening after an endless sun-soaked day, but to me it seems that they are covered in a light coating of snow. Lady Limbo's glacial fingers are already tightening their grip.

I put the photos in my bag with the one of Dominique and turned my attention to the envelope.

A faint fragrance of carnations and lily of the valley came from the envelope on my lap. A quick glance at my watch confirmed I had run out of time. I would read Celestine's letter on the plane.

The Letter

'NOUS SOMMES ARRIVÉS.' The taxi driver's voice broke into my thoughts.

I stuffed the envelope into my handbag. 'C'est Air France departures?'

'Oui. C'est cela.'

'Merci.'

I checked in with barely five minutes to spare. When a voice eerily similar to Celestine's announced that flight AF 9840 for Rome was boarding, I rose in a panic and rushed to the gate.

Once we were airborne, I removed the envelope from my handbag and with unsteady hands drew out a few thin folded sheets.

Courage! Daniel whispered in my ear.

I began to read.

Ma chère Paola
3 août 2006

If Gi has given you this letter, it means we will not meet again. I feel I owe you an explanation. You must not be too angry with me. Sometimes a life explains a death.

You have heard of Jasmine by now – my little sister. When I was nine years old and she just six, our parents died in a car accident. A strange new life began for us then in a state orphanage run by nuns, but we were soon separated when I was adopted. I begged and pleaded to be left with her but it was not to be. Jasmine was a solitary, unusual child, ungainly and prone to attacks of imagination. This perhaps explains why she was never able to find a loving adoptive family. Twice she was taken and then returned as one returns a painting that does not entirely fit in with the ambience of one's home. Naturally, I was tormented by guilt, by what I saw as my good and her ill fortune. In the beginning, she came on holidays to my new home, but it was hard to pretend that we were sisters again and soon these visits fell away. Now I wonder at myself, at how I allowed that to happen. I wrote to her through all the years of separation, and occasionally I would receive a few lines back, always saying she was well.

After more than ten years we met at last again, in Paris, when she was twenty and I was twenty-three. I could not believe it was her. She had turned into a young woman of extraordinary beauty. As had always been her way, she waited for me to make the first move, a handbag nonchalantly slung over her shoulder, a small, secretive smile on her lips, as if she saw in an instant that she'd outgrown me. Then we rushed into each other's arms; or did I rush into hers? We spent the day walking around the city, popping into a museum here, an art gallery there, two cosmopolitan women, and all I wanted to do was touch her to see if she was real, this startling young woman who was my sister. Everywhere we went men fell over themselves. At the pavement café where we had lunch a man came over to light her cigarette. Another sent champagne over. Jasmine took it all in her stride. There was something d'une femme fatale to her already.

I concluded that Jasmine's lonely childhood had left her unharmed and I was glad for her. But quite by chance I assisted a woman who had been at the same orphanage. She told me of the torment one

237

*of the nuns had inflicted on my sister. Jasmine's rebellious spirit
and nascent beauty, which this nun considered unholy, seemed
to make Jasmine particularly the target of her twisted wrath. I
cannot tell you how I felt on hearing this story. We talked through
the night, this woman and I, watching the early morning planes
arrive, great silver-white birds born out of the sunrise. She told me
how my sister had been beaten for bedwetting, humiliated in front
of the other children, forced to sleep on the cold floor. There was
no end to the cruelty. This woman herself had been a sleepwalker
and had been tied to her bed to break her habit. My sister sang
songs to her to soothe her panic. In that faceless airport building,
surrounded by unwashed, dazed travellers trying to catch a few
hours' sleep in transit to other distant airport lounges, the woman
sang one of those songs softly to me to relieve my distress. It was
a simple childhood tune my mother used to sing to help my baby
sister Jasmine sleep. Do you know it? Frère Jacques, Dormez-
vous?*

*So you see, Paola, my sister led a troubled existence as a child,
and as a young woman she intended to be free of all constraints.
Jasmine was twenty-two years old when she met the man you call
Daniel.*

*I came to know him as Gabriel Montaigne so I shall continue
to call him so. By then she had been dancing professionally for
many years and had known many men. She was the queen honey
bee. She lured them and discarded them at will, using many
seductive means. Even the Internet she made sexy. Gabriel and
his rich young friend were enticed by her message. You guessed
correctly – you knew in some way, deep in your bones, that I
knew everything. Jasmine was Lady Limbo and she lived to make
men suffer. Less than a year after this photo he was back, alone
this time. He did not speak of his young friend. They became
lovers and this time Jasmine fell in love. But Gabriel did not stay
long. Like her, he could love and let go. After he had left, she
discovered she was pregnant. She experienced deep depression,*

even attempting to take her own life. A friend of hers called me. Dominique was born prematurely; for weeks that infant's life hung in the balance.

Four years later, Jasmine was killed in a hit-and-run accident in the middle of a normal day. She had stepped out to buy a sandwich for lunch. The driver was never found. Jasmine was dead at the age of twenty-nine, her life hardly lived. I blamed Gabriel for everything that had happened to her. But he was a man who came and went like smoke, with no fixed abode or name. How would I find him?

At Jasmine's funeral, a woman came up to me and expressed her condolences. She said that she knew Jasmine from the organisation known as Real Man Inc. Jasmine had been of great assistance to her. My blood quickened. Did she know someone called Gabriel Montaigne, one of the men who worked for RMI? I gestured to Dominique to come over and introduce herself. Mme Kaas was polite but said she was only a receptionist at RMI and had no access to any of the files. Also, she had taken an oath of confidentiality. 'She was lying,' Dominique said fiercely, as we watched Mme Kaas walk towards a waiting car with dark tinted windows. The back door opened and she stepped inside.

Some weeks later I received a note asking me to call a certain number. Mme Kaas said she had changed her mind. Jasmine's daughter had made a deep impression on her. A cell of Real Man Inc. was operating successfully in South Africa. Gabriel Montaigne had requested a transfer to that country.

I knew the address of RMI well. Many of we professional women had it in our diaries, in readiness for the day when our ovaries would awake. I decided to go to Brussels and enquire about South Africa, an exotic destination for a Frenchwoman who wanted a genetically superior breeding mate to act as inseminator.

*An excellent South African private detective, a surveillance
expert, tracked Gabriel to an apartment on a private beach near
the city where you live. Bulldog Beach. How apt the name! Mr
Khan bugged his apartment and I tortured myself listening to
his calls with his women clients. And I waited. I waited for him
to have something to lose. When I heard about his impending
marriage, I opened a bottle of fine red wine and I celebrated. I
guessed that the pulp thrillers he wrote had started to bring in a
regular income and that he naively believed he would be allowed
to ease himself out of RMI.*

*What your Gabriel did not know was that RMI had no intention
of losing – is it the duck, oui? – that lays the golden egg. I knew
this from his file.*

*I told you Nathan Khan was a fine detective. The RMI file he
put in my hands was a clinical document covering Gabriel's
background, medical history and psychological profile for
the nine years he had been with the organisation. It was also a
shocking document, a man's life reduced to a calculation of profit.
Gabriel was an unusually perfect specimen of manhood. This I
need not tell you. You and Jasmine. Put simply, he was the man
every woman would select as the father of her child if she were
given a choice in the matter.*

*But one small detail in his file caught my attention. Only one
psychologist out of three – a woman – expressed reservations
about him. A master of dissimulation, she called him, a high-risk
employee. Her report was tucked in the back of his file, relegated,
ignored. But not by me. If Gabriel Montaigne had a flaw, I would
find a way to exploit it. I slept with that report under my pillow,
reading every detail, until I had a plan.*

*I knew about you long before your mother and I met. Yes, I
planned that meeting, after Nathan alerted me to her business
trip. I wanted to let Gabriel know I was coming for him, that I*

could reach him even within his marriage, that he would never find contentment while I was alive. I plagued him with anonymous letters. I phoned him pretending to be Jasmine. Once, when I was in South Africa training airline staff, I followed him, wearing her perfume and red coat. Nathan reported that Gabriel was becoming unsettled. Sometimes he left the city after one of my calls.

I knew I would not be the only one monitoring Gabriel's movements. So I had Nathan watch him to ensure he came to no real harm. The cat does not like to share the mouse. I was right. Nathan rescued him a few times, once from knife-wielding thugs who had followed him to a park, another time from some sailors at the dock who made an act of taking his wallet.

And so my vengeful purpose was being achieved. Slowly Gabriel's carefully constructed life was unravelling before his eyes. At what point did he become disgusted with himself? At what point did he choose to disappear out of your life?

Then Nathan surprised me by reporting that he had seen Gabriel meeting with a child, talking with her. Sometimes Nathan saw her hanging around near your apartment. At first we were puzzled but it seems possible, ma chère Paola, that through a twist of fate ... Ah, but how can we be sure? The names of the women and children are not included in RMI files. This information is unobtainable.

I have no answer for you on Gabriel's whereabouts. He began to recognise Nathan and became clever at evading him. On the day he disappeared I believe the hunted outwitted the hunter.

A few months after that, I instructed Nathan to close the file. I no longer knew at whom I should direct my waning rage, and then you came to find me. You puzzled me. I assumed you knew everything but were keeping your cards, how do you say, close to your bosom, oui? Later I realised you felt things you feared to put into words. And I saw that I had punished you more than him.

Nathan continues to search for Gabriel. He feels responsible. It is a strangely ambivalent relationship that the tracker has with the animal he has stalked and come to know almost better than he knows himself. Perhaps only l'assassin knows his victim better. Nathan called me from a bar in your home city intoxicated and dispirited. There were no corners left to look in in South Africa; this Gabriel Montaigne was better than Carlos the Jackal at covering his tracks. I myself believe Gabriel has returned to France, his country of birth.

That is all the comfort I can offer – and the fact that the last entry in Gabriel's RMI file stated that he refused to participate in annual testing procedures and that the matter had been referred to a higher level. You will find Nathan Khan in the phonebook.

I have the feeling I am being followed. Last week our small apartment was ransacked while I was at work and Dominique was at school. Nothing was taken. On the bathroom mirror, somebody had written in lipstick: LES PUTAINS SONT MORTES! VOUS ETES LA PROCHAINE! So now I am a whore and I will be next. I have not called the police but I have spoken to Gi and Peter, who have promised to look after Dominique if anything should happen to me. I believe she will be safe there because he has friends in the organisation that will protect him and his family. I can do nothing more now. I wait.

I have included a picture of the Cape Town child. Perhaps she has an idea what happened to Gabriel. If she, like Dominique and all the children who have experienced too much too young, is old beyond her years, then she sees things others do not see.

You will be wondering about the origins of the other photograph. Jasmine kept a framed photo of herself and Dominique beside her bed. I found this photo beneath it when I cleaned the glass. My sister knew many men but she was not in the habit of keeping photos of them. Perhaps it will mean something to you.

I did not expect to like you. I wish you well. Do not blame yourself.
   Celestine

I raised my eyes and looked around the darkened aircraft cabin. The seatbelt light was on. We were flying through a patch of atmospheric turbulence but a peculiar calm had settled over me. Jasmine of the violet-blue eyes, she whose unusual beauty was incomparable, had once loved my husband. Dominique – the same child who had slept in my awkward embrace two nights ago on the Langstroms' sleeper couch – was the result of that union.

As an RMI employee – what was it Lady Limbo had called them so long ago? 'Candidates for copulation' – Daniel must have spawned progeny all over the world. *Where would you prefer to conceive? On the Trans-Siberian? On an ocean liner? Paris, Brussels, London? It can all be arranged.* Who knew where they all were now? The southern hemisphere could be crawling with them. And if Celestine's hunch was right, at least one of them was in Cape Town.

Oh Daniel, no wonder you had nightmares. These are real live children you've produced.

My Italian neighbour was dozing, his earphones in his ears. Next to him his partner was engrossed in Oriana Fallaci's *La Rabbia e l'Orgoglio*.

Against whom shall I direct rage and pride? A ghost?

I looked past the reading woman in her pool of light. Through the porthole window I could see streaks of lightning zigzag their white-hot way across the faraway blackness. A storm was building in the troposphere.

Arid
Landscapes

EVEN IN DEATH CELESTINE ENJOYED MYSTERY. There was no way of knowing how much she had left out of the story, no way of determining how far a desire for vengeance might travel. She had deliberately poisoned our marriage in memory of her sister. The nightmare was for real. There was no easy way to get him back.

Do you still love me? Impossible question with no answer.

Back in Rome, I found Elijah's latest progress report in my inbox. He had completed his check of impounded car records, rail and air travel computer data and had contacted all the bus companies but there was nothing. If Daniel de Luc had left the country he had done so with another passport. How easy it was to be faceless and nameless if one wanted to be. Later that night, walking around the Piazza del Popolo in the midst of crowds of foreign visitors, a babble of languages carried by a light sea breeze that had replaced the stifling Roman heat of the day, I pondered uneasily how it might be to live in a world of shadows, waltzing adroitly around white market rules and avoiding all attempts to regulate a non-conformist lifestyle. Ever since I could remember, I'd considered myself an independent spirit, but in reality I'd opted for the security of a labelled drawer where I could be easily found and pointed out. So many girls in drawers, waiting for collectors to pick them out.

The only item of interest in Elijah's report was that a toothless crone among the homeless people who lived under the bridge near the Woodstock children's park claimed she remembered a tall, dark-haired white man asking questions about a white girl. When Elijah asked if a white girl had lived with them under the bridge, she suddenly lost her memory and muttered they didn't want any police coming around like last time. Apart from that, Elijah's litany of futile activities reached the depressing conclusion of previous reports: the missing person in my life was still 100% missing.

Elijah's conversation with the old bridge woman made no immediate sense, but it seemed propitious. I decided we needed to follow the trail Celestine had suggested and find out more about the child. I emailed Elijah that same night and attached scanned copies of the photographs, one of the slight, dark Dominique and the other of the fair-haired Cape Town schoolgirl. I called the next morning and asked him to show just the picture of Dominique to the security guard at our block of flats. The two girls were very different but about the same age and it might just jog his memory. Elijah was to ask if he'd noticed a teenage girl sitting at the bus stop shelter occasionally, perhaps even sleeping there overnight. Only if the girl he described was anything like the one in the black and white close-up, was Elijah to show him the second photograph. We wanted to be absolutely sure it was her. Elijah was silent for a moment but when I didn't elaborate he just said, okay, he'd do it and get back to me.

Not surprisingly, the security guard had not recognised anything about Dominique in her French clothes and chic page-boy hairstyle, but a hundred bucks had got him talking about another girl he had seen near the apartment block.

'It worked,' Elijah reported on the phone that night. 'You're a natural. If you ever think of changing professions, give me a call. We'll go into partnership.'

'Mmm. From IT workaholic to PI Jane in one easy lesson.'

'I guess it was a silly idea.'

Elijah sounded as if I'd just taken his saucer of milk away.

'Thanks, Elijah. Really. I'll keep it in mind. The way things are going at the moment, who knows?'

The security guard had been adamant that the other girl was taller than Dominique, more filled out (demonstrating with his hands that she already had breasts), and she had lighter, thicker hair pulled up in a long ponytail.

'What about this one?' Elijah had then asked, showing him the other photograph.

'That's her,' he'd said, jabbing at the picture. 'That's the one.' Apparently she sometimes sat at the bus stop in her school uniform. He'd noticed because it wasn't dark green like the local school, it was brown.

Elijah reminded me that the city was full of schools with brown uniforms, before he cleared his throat. 'He said she looked like one of those schoolgirls who pick up older men. He was scared to mention it earlier in case he got into trouble for not chasing her away. He also mentioned having seen your husband give her a lift once.'

'There's no law against giving schoolgirls a lift.'

'He asked me where Daniel was, Paola.'

'What did you say?' My heart stuttered like a jackhammer. How long could I continue pretending everything was normal?

'There's a simple rule when people ask awkward questions. Be very specific. Don't give out any more than you have to.'

'Thanks. I'll remember that. For when we become partners.' I could picture Elijah with that sweet, trustful smile of his. For a one-second moment I wished I'd told him everything, kept nothing back.

'I said he was overseas writing a book. Then I handed over the hundred rand and that was it. Or I thought it was. But as I walked away he called out he had more information that he was prepared to divulge for another hundred.'

'And?'

There was a pause while Elijah consulted his notes. 'Mr de Luc drove away alone on the day he disappeared – it was late

246

afternoon, the security guard couldn't say for sure when – but he came back to the apartment an hour later. He stopped the car on the other side of the road – the security guard said he was putting a book into his jacket pocket when he came back out.'

His pillow book. The book with poems that his father had given to his mother. He's never going to come back.

'There's more. He saw a woman in the car as they drove off past him. He hadn't noticed her before.'

Everything spun around me. Chairs, tables, ornaments, shoes, jacket, apple, orange, pantyhose, laptop, pillow. The world was entirely silent as it unravelled around me.

'Paola, are you there?'

'Did he recognise her?' I asked at last. 'Was she the same woman?'

There was a pause while he checked his notes. '"The woman was wearing a big hat, like women wear on the beach, and she had sunglasses on." Not conclusive, I'm afraid.'

'Do you think he's a reliable witness?'

'It's pretty dull being a security guard outside a block of flats; I guess he spends his day watching what's happening around him. He rattled off the colour and make of your car and Daniel's as if he was a car salesman. I think he's telling the truth.'

I stayed silent. Silence was my refuge.

'Paola, why don't you tell me what's going on? Who is she – the schoolgirl in the picture? Who's the other girl for that matter? Why in Sherlock's name are we swimming in photographs of teenage girls?'

I just want him to walk in the door, is that so much to ask?

Elijah tried again. 'Paola, if this girl at the bus stop knows something that can help us to locate your husband … you have to tell me who she is. Withholding information is prejudicial to the case.'

'I can't. I don't know anything. Do you think I'd have hired you if I knew what was going on? You're the PI. You haven't found a trace of the missing person,' I reminded him bitterly.

'I don't know what more I can do,' Elijah said quietly from

a continent away. 'We need a different course of action. When you're ready to talk, call me.'

For three months I led two lives. During the week and on alternate weekends I remained in Rome, working seventy- to eighty-hour weeks on the Hadrian project. At night, I returned to the Hilton and ordered food up to the room and then later, after a couple of hours on the laptop, I went for an evening walk through dimly lit viales and vias past the glorious remains and extravagant edifices of the ancient empire, treading briskly over subterranean galleries in the company of ghostly emperors and mighty men who prowled the city streets when darkness presided.

I clung to what Celestine had said in her letter. If he had returned to the country of his birth then it was to Paris, city of the free spirit, that he would have gone. Every other weekend I boarded a budget flight to Paris and combed the streets of the French capital looking for him. I always booked into the same cheap hotel and asked for the same corner room from which the steel girders of the Eiffel Tower were partially visible between buildings. Armed with a street map of Paris I'd set out early each morning and traverse the city from one side to the other, using every form of public transport from the metro to buses, trams, and taxis and even boats on the Seine. In time, I fell into the habit of choosing someone to follow, moving on from Daniel lookalikes to any man who presented himself to my attention by his dress, or the way he stepped off a train. Before long, he would disappear behind a revolving glass door or an ornate entrance portal or into a building with access control and I'd be left outside, unsure of where I was. How did I imagine I would find him in a city of two million people?

Sometimes I was a seductive assassin whose job it was to kill him in cold blood. Other times I was a high-class call girl out shopping for a new patron. The pretence prevented me from cracking under the strain of not finding the one man I truly sought. I watched him buy flowers and jewellery and perfume, aching to rend the objects from his hands. Once my hand brushed his as I hurried out of a shop, and my skin felt inflamed by that brief touch of strange male skin. I saw him enter a parking garage in a city building with lifts and levers and revolving floors that shuffled vehicles as if they were Lego cars in Toyland. I watched him get into a car parked in the street and drive off, leaving me bereft. One day, enraged by the idea of him driving to a house in a village with a picturesque church in the French countryside where a sophisticated, slender French wife awaited him, and little French children who called him *Papa*, and tall lavender bushes and windows with open shutters and garden furniture with peeling blue paint, I stepped into the path of a grey Citroën as it exited the parking bay. The man braked violently. His dilated, disbelieving eyes watched me walk away as if an apparition from his nightmares had crossed his path.

Only once did a man realise I was following him. Perhaps he was a police detective, or a professional criminal, or even a spy – someone trained to watch his back. He waited for me at a pavement café and when I walked past his table he asked me courteously in French if I wouldn't join him, gripping my wrist with an iron hand that didn't allow refusal. I believe he thought I was a hooker paid to tail him. I was not afraid at all. He asked why I was following him. I explained it was a random choice, merely a way to explore the city on one's own without feeling entirely alone. He laughed mirthlessly and said I was lucky he was Parisian. When he asked if I was free that evening, I felt my actions to be fully vindicated by the predictability of it all. It was the way of things in a Darwinian world. I refused him.

It was an exhilarating feeling to stalk all those men and deny them any claim over me. It made the blood course more quickly through my veins.

One Monday morning in Rome, I opened an office email congratulating Andrew Morton on his promotion to associate principal, and Emma Patterson on her promotion to strategic account manager, and all I did was close it, without rancour or regret. There was nothing I could do to change anything.

I might have continued in this way forever, wandering through Paris on a hopeless quest every second weekend, if I had not received a call from Detective Olmi of the Villegny commissariat, who was working late. A white man had been found living in a cave on Table Mountain in my home city of Cape Town, but he had eluded the park guides. Olmi happened to see the report filed by Interpol on the International Reports that morning.

'It is perhaps your *hosband*, n'est pas?'

I spent my last weekend in Paris weaving among the tombs of the dead and the 5 300 trees in the Père-Lachaise necropolis established by the Emperor Bonaparte on the Rue de Repos. I stumbled upon Édith Piaf's final resting place and stood in front of Oscar Wilde's lipstick-kissed art deco angel, while I tried to recall Daniel's face.

I know you're not dead. Come back to me.

At last, sitting on a gleaming slab of engraved black marble looking over part of the city, I made my decision. Olmi's news had precipitated the obvious; it was time to go home. Paris had tormented me long enough. In Rome I would recommend a one-week period for handover to the agency project manager. It was what the Italians wanted anyway.

At night, I waited for dusk and walked beneath the Eiffel Tower. I was almost able to see them: Jasmine arm-in-arm with Nicky and Daniel, a careless and photogenic threesome, late on a simmering summer evening in 1994. It was the closest I would come to finding Daniel in Paris.

III

INTO THE MOUTH
OF THE WOLF

The
Mountain Man

AFTER MONTHS OF COMMUTING between Rome and Paris I had almost given up hope of ever finding Daniel when I received Detective Olmi's call about the mountain man in my home city. Part of me wanted desperately to believe that it was him while the other part rejected the possibility that my husband, who loved double espressos and crisp linen shirts, could have turned into a cave-dwelling mountain-hopping hermit.

Maybe he's had a spiritual epiphany.

Detective Marcel Olmi had fulfilled his part of our deal. The de Luc Disparition Inquiétante folder with my signed statement had been handed over to the commander of a special unit of the South African police that dealt with internationally sensitive investigations.

It was another two weeks before they managed to capture the mountain man and bring him in. The press gave the story front-page coverage, with pictures of mountain guides and a helicopter netting a running man against the background of Platteklip Gorge. I was asked to go to the state's psychiatric evaluation centre at Valkenberg.

It was my first visit to the stark buildings on the outskirts of the city, where political prisoners were routinely sent by the apartheid government and conveniently forgotten. More recently, the modernised asylum had been bedevilled by media reports of manic sex offenders allowed to run amok and patients undergoing coerced psychiatric interventions.

I had been told to ask for a Doctor Sparks. I was given directions to the Wing E waiting room and told to wait there until I was collected. There was plenty of time to consider what it would be like to visit a loved one and sit in this gloomy room week after week, waiting to be 'collected'. The magazine on top of the untidy pile was a threadbare copy of *You* dating back to August 2002, the month when Daniel and I began meeting at the laundromat. My hands shook as I flipped through the well-fingered pages. Did the synchronicity of dates mean something? Beads of sweat lined my brow and upper lip.

What if it's him? What will I say to him? What if he doesn't want to come home? What if he does? Will they give him medication?

'Mrs de Luc, I'm Detective Klaus Knappman. Are you okay?'

I looked up to find the detective that had been assigned to Daniel's case. The motionless fans over his head looked like still white moths clinging to the ceiling.

'Yes. No. Could you get me a glass of water? It must be the heat.'

He waited with me, looking around with an inquisitive air as if this was his first visit too, until a black man in a white uniform called out my name in a baritone voice. We were taken to a small viewing room with a windowpane of one-way glass and I was asked if I could identify the man sitting in the room beyond. The mountain man was sitting on a chair, confined in a straitjacket, with dark, limp head bowed, but I knew straight away it wasn't Daniel.

'It's not him.'

'Are you sure?' The nice detective was nonplussed, but after taking one look at my face he didn't persist. 'So, wie die duiwel is hy?'

Good question, Detective. Who the devil is he?

'It's not so unusual,' a voice spoke behind us. 'People who have forsaken civilisation.' Dr Sparks introduced himself. He and the young detective talked as they watched the unmoving man under the harsh light. 'It's our job to determine the degree of psychic disintegration, what some might call insanity, whether it warrants keeping them here or not.' Dribble ran down the furrows on each side of the unknown man's mouth. 'I'd like to go home now,' I interrupted them, 'if that's alright with you.' They both jumped and apologised. Dr Sparks accompanied us to the front entrance. He would let us know if anyone was brought in answering to Daniel's description. They had the police flyer on file.

I felt as if I'd been asked to identify a corpse at the morgue and found that it wasn't the person I'd feared it would be. Identifying corpses was something I'd had some experience with. They had always been exactly who I had known they would be: my father and my brother. I was the official identifier of bodies in our family.

For a moment there it had felt as if 'dead body' were not that much different from 'insane body'. In the weeks after the park incident, I'd wondered if my husband was having a nervous breakdown. In the back of my mind the possibility of some kind of mental illness had terrified me. But, of course, 'dead body' was very different. As far as I could tell at that moment, Daniel was still alive and not deranged. It was at this point, as I rationalised myself into a corner, that my legs gave way, on the main stairway leading out of Valkenberg. The detective had me in a grip around the waist before I could fall. He was a strapping young man with a calming presence. I imagined he'd be just as good with runaway oxen as he was with a fainting IT executive. He offered to drive me home.

'Daniel doesn't enjoy driving,' I said as he started the car and accelerated away. 'He prefers public transport. He'll use the minibus taxis rather than take the car out, if he can.' The words formed themselves out of nowhere. I told him Daniel liked jazz and R.E.M., so he tuned in to Fine Music Radio, but it was something orchestral, not jazz. He left it on anyway. At the apartment, he politely declined my offer of a drink, saying his partner was waiting downstairs, maybe another time.

When he'd left, I had a long, hot bath, then I tried watching TV but there was nothing worth watching. Eventually, I took a bottle of wine and a bag of potatoes over to Sharon's.

'It wasn't him.'

'Of course it wasn't. Daniel's not mad,' Sharon pointed out with irrefutable logic. 'He's a Gemini. It's an air sign.'

'I can't imagine why I didn't think of that. He's a *Gemini*? Aren't they the heartless ones? That explains everything.'

'Oh, you don't mean that. You're just pulling my leg.'

She showed me where everything was and I deep-fried a pile of crispy potato chips.

'So, has that private investigator of yours made any progress?' she asked. 'Are you following up clues?' She wiped her mouth demurely with a paper serviette.

'There's a teenage girl who waits for Daniel at the bus stop. I think she might be his daughter. You have some tomato sauce on your chin.'

'Thank you. It's difficult to see one's own chin.' She smiled at her little joke. 'Why do you think she's his daughter?'

'The security guard says he saw them together. And she watches our flat.'

'So, I suppose you have to talk to her.'

'I suppose so.'

Later on, once I'd cleared everything away and made us a cup of coffee, Sharon made one of her outrageous suggestions. 'I was thinking, maybe you could finish reading *The Unbearable Lightness of Being* to me.' A sharp retort died on my tongue as she impishly added, 'After all, Daniel promised, so as his family you have to stand in for him now.'

'Give me the damn book,' I found myself saying meekly. 'What page were you on?'

'Just open it at the bookmark. He always read a chapter.' Sharon patted the couch for Miss Potter to jump up next to her and then settled back, her fingers entwined in Miss Potter's silky neck hair, an expression of child-like expectation on the glowing sightless face. I turned the lounge lamp away from her onto the printed page.

'Part five. Lightness and Weight.'

A Simple Law of Cause
and Effect

On the 424TH day of my husband's absence, I hired Nathan Khan, the investigator Celestine had used, to follow the unknown schoolgirl Simone and find out everything he could about her.

A female voice answered his phone. Later she called back to say Mr Khan would meet me in the Company's Garden on Wednesday at 10 am. There was a bench on the main walkway next to the garden restaurant near a big tree. Mr Khan would be riding a bicycle and wearing a black shirt. The youthful Bollywood India voice sounded bored.

'Doesn't he have an office?' I asked.

'Nathan always meets people in the park.'

It was a warm, windless spring day with Devil's Peak and Lion's Head clearly visible above the city. There were more people around on a weekday than I'd expected. A man in a motorised wheelchair shunted past me as I entered the park through the main entrance.

I found the bench next to a restaurant with tables under a huge, twisted tree and watched the park visitors walk by. There were women with babies and toddlers in prams, couples locked

258

in conversation, dog walkers, business people and office workers taking shortcuts through the park, and overseas visitors with cameras, everybody enjoying the mild sunshine. A tall, powerfully built man crumpled up an empty packet of pigeon corn and sat down on the other end of the bench. The whole bench tipped slightly back with his weight.

'*Eucalyptus grandis*' the trespasser said. 'Otherwise commonly referred to as a saligna gum tree.' I barely nodded. How important was it for a PI to be punctual? How important was it for a PI to own a car?

The big man interrupted my thoughts again. 'I believe you've been waiting for me. My name is Nathan Khan.'

I turned slowly and looked at the big man holding out his hand. I had just expected someone different.

'Pudmilla didn't say I was a black guy? Sorry about that.' He didn't sound sorry. FBI bodyguard shades hid the eyes. 'She claims she forgets to mention it.' The voice was amused.

Pudmilla's 'black shirt' had made him sound like a pastor, but a Levi label was visible on the bicep-hugging T-shirt. The man was an uptown dresser and younger than I'd expected.

'You don't look like a private investigator. You look more like a salesman for expensive hi-fis.' Or a Zimbabwean politician in exile.

He cracked a half-smile. 'I can live with that. Sometimes it helps to be black. People don't expect you to be in the surveillance business.' So that bit was out in the sunshine.

'Khan is an Indian surname.'

'I grew up in an Indian family.' Which could have meant anything. 'So. You asked for a meeting?' he reminded me, cutting my questions short. All the time he spoke he was turning his head in a slow 180-degree arc, scanning the park.

'Does the name Celestine Nothomb mean anything to you?'

The shoes stopped tapping. 'Should it?' he asked after a moment.

'She hired you to follow my husband Daniel and make his life hell.'

'Is that what he told you?'

The note of irony in his voice was unmistakable. We both knew Daniel never told me anything.

'No. It's what she told me,' I said coolly. 'In a letter she wrote. Before she was murdered.'

The park shuddered involuntarily. A diagonal scar on Nathan Khan's cheek twitched under my gaze.

'Then it must be true.'

A large group of schoolchildren with two female teachers up ahead came traipsing along the path, a gaggle of goslings led by two geese. He waited for the parade of giggling, squirming youngsters to pass.

'Why are you here, Mrs de Luc?'

'My husband is missing, Mr Khan. Do you have any idea what happened to him?'

'Mrs de Luc,' he paused, 'ideas are nothing but suppositions. It can be very hard to find a man who does not want to be found.'

'You are assuming he does not want to be found. What if he was kidnapped or killed?'

'The law of probability tells us that his body would have turned up. It is a very specific type of killer who enjoys the hide-and-seek of concealing the body of his victim from the police. Your husband does not fit into the category of likely victim for such a killer.'

'What if they are holding him somewhere? They could be brainwashing him, changing his identity so that he's no longer a threat to them.' Did I really say that?

Nathan Khan sighed. 'In my experience there is a simple law of cause and effect. Sometimes we conduct our lives as if they are a long, drawn-out audition for a specific event; usually the actions of outside forces are a reaction to our own activities. Then we call this a predestined event. Do you know what I mean?'

The long speech was impressive. 'Yes,' I admitted. 'That's what I felt when Daniel disappeared. As if that day had been waiting in the wings most of my life.'

I realised I was squeezing one hand so tightly within the other that I had stopped the blood flow. I flexed my fingers until the numbness wore off. He called a cold-drink vendor over, asked if I

wanted anything, and then drank from a bottle of mineral water
before continuing.

'You get to see all types in the surveillance game. Your husband
was the clowning type. He was a quick learner. He found ways to
shake me off. He acted as if it were all a big game. Once he waved
at me from the top of a disappearing bus, another time he came
into a coffee shop and sat a few seats away from me and I didn't
recognise him. I sat there for a couple of hours waiting for him to
come out of the building across the road; I went into the men's and
found a yellow sticky note on the mirror that said 'Daniel de Luc
was here'. Sometimes he'd walk past the surveillance vehicle and
fix a sticky note to the windscreen right in front of my nose telling
me where he was going next.'

'Daniel never mentioned any of this. Not once. Isn't that
weird? You live with somebody and you think you know them
but meanwhile they're living their own lives, being followed,
leading PIs a merry dance around town, leaving yellow sticky
notes.'

'I only ever talked to him once, when I found him waiting in
a doorway around a corner, no raincoat, rain pouring down. Do
you know what he said?'

'What?'

'He said, "You can't change anything, you know, you might
as well give up. Go home. You'll catch a cold if you stay out in
this weather." And then he walked off, bare head down into the
driving rain. The day he disappeared he called me up on my mobile
pretending to be the hospital calling about my girlfriend. I'm still
trying to work out how he even knew about her. One thing's for
certain: he wasn't taking any chances on me being there to see
what was going down.'

'You think he planned his own disappearance, don't you?'

'Maybe. Maybe he didn't want to put me in a situation where I
knew too much.'

'Celestine said you obtained a copy of his file. You know people
on the inside. Somebody must know where Daniel is.'

He reached inside the back pocket of his jeans and took out a wallet. He removed a photograph and handed it to me sideways between two fingers.

I know someone. A little white card pushed into my hand. The Amazon on the balcony.

'That's the girl at the party house, Madeleine's bodyguard.' I stared at the picture. The young woman with the Afro glowering at the camera had an unmistakable penchant for the dramatic; this time she was wearing a drop-dead trench coat and taking aim at a target board with a revolver cradled in her hands.

'That's my girlfriend, Heidi.'

'Is that what you two do for a romantic evening? Go to the shooting range?'

His reply was to reach down, remove his shoes and stuff the socks into the shoes, as if it were the most natural thing to do in a public park.

'She came here from the DRC. Her village was attacked and destroyed by neighbouring villagers who wanted their farmland. She had been sent to fetch water. From her hiding place in the fields, she watched her mother and sisters being raped next to the bodies of her brothers, before they were also killed with machetes.'

Perhaps his bare feet sought some faint trapped vibrations of that distant agony, while I saw it all through the ochre-tinted lens of a photographer looking down from a helicopter: women framed by swirls of colourful cloth lying motionless in the village dust with legs spread-eagled, intestines spilling out of once-smooth berry-brown bellies; the incessant swarms of feeding flies in that febrile silence; hacked-off limbs strewn far and wide between huts reduced to smouldering ruins, carrion left by predators; red stains soaked up by the brown earth, a newly drawn map of blood.

'When the celebrations began she ran for her life. Eventually she made her way here, getting lifts on trucks that were coming down.'

The noise of the park had receded to some vigilant border of time and space. From the corner of my eye I watched his lips move and found myself thinking he had a sexy voice.

'I'm telling you this so you know she's trustworthy.'

Trustworthy. The word trembled before it rose into the scintillating dark green canopy. Are you trustworthy? Am I trustworthy? Is that what love boils down to? Then we are none of us deserving of love. A young woman's torso trudged past on sensible shoes, a thick waistline of bare Jik-white skin exposed, her head burrowed under the hood of a twin-baby pram.

Nathan Khan continued. 'Your husband's employers seem to think he's lying low after getting into trouble with some criminal elements. I gather it hasn't gone down well. They don't like losing one of their best operatives and they're nervous about what he knows and what he might do with that information.' The implication of his words hung in the air like a severed limb. It was weird to hear Daniel being spoken of as an operative. From a man's perspective it was probably something like being a spy. You seduced beautiful women and learnt their secrets.

I leapt up and started pacing. My breathing compromised my thoughts.

'What criminal elements?' I asked, stopping in front of him, the question a block of ice sliding down a slope. All around me the park thrummed with normality.

Oh Daniel, why couldn't you be like other people?

His face was composed, impassive as granite. 'Could be he was involved in some heavy betting beyond his means.'

'But you don't think so?'

He paused before continuing. 'The people he worked for have their fingers in many pies. It could be a clever story to cover their tracks if they had something to do with his disappearance. I told Heidi to get out of there, it's too dangerous, but she's got her own mind; she's still working for them. She recognised you when she saw you at the house from pictures in my dark room.'

A half-formed question vanished. 'You've got pictures of me?'

'Surveillance is my business. Celestine was my client; she wanted to know everything about your husband. Naturally ...'

'That included me. I get it. Don't you get tired of poking your nose into other people's lives? Doesn't it make you feel like you want to take a long, cold shower the whole time?'

'Like most things in life it depends what side of the fence you're on,' he said slowly. 'Sometimes principles are a luxury that has to be jettisoned. For instance, I am certain you want to know about the people your husband met with.'

He was undeniably right. My principles were in disarray. Who was I trying to fool?

'What people?'

'Shall we have a look at that exhibition?' He took a sock out of a shoe, and shook it hard before putting it back on. 'Those young ladies are eying our bench; they look like they need somewhere to sit.'

The old ladies in question were watching his sock antics in amazement.

'A real culture vulture.' I sounded dazed.

'Oh no, no, on the contrary, I was hoping you knew something about contemporary South African painting so you could enlighten me.'

That woke me up. He knows about the Dante Art Gallery.

'Some people think of porn as art,' Khan continued in front of a row of paintings. He asked if I had any knowledge of the porn film industry, craning his head sideways at a surreal landscape with a grouping of dusty ewes succumbing to suckling lambs. He said it was a multibillion-dollar industry worldwide with strong links to the child-trafficking rings run by the Russian and Chinese mafia – the same people who organised betting syndicates.

'There was someone your husband met up with occasionally. They call him the Ice-cream King. The story goes he eats ice-cream while he's directing underage starlets in his porn movies. He also owns the nightclub Pompadour.'

The ticket stub in Daniel's pocket. I shivered, remembering the conversation I'd overheard from my hiding place on the Pompadour landing. *He's tired of photos. He wants to see the real thing.*

We moved on to a ramshackle windmill and farm dam set against a pan-flat horizon under a cloudless, impossibly blue sky. I resented the casual implication of Nathan Khan's words. Daniel was nothing like the man in the silver jacket.

'I don't care about any of that.'

'You don't care about young, vulnerable women being exploited or you don't care that your husband might be involved?' His voice was very quiet.

I wanted to shake him. 'Look, we both know I'm no bleeding-heart Mother Teresa. If your girlfriend's got issues to work through, that's understandable, but the only reason I'm here is because I want to find Daniel.'

When he spoke again it was in a gentler voice but the tone was final.

'I don't know if anyone can find your husband. I've already looked just about everywhere. Sarrazin is where I'd look if I was a fool. Goodbye, Mrs de Luc.'

My head was reeling. *Simone Sarrazin.* 'Wait,' I pleaded, the park melting and coagulating like a surreal landscape around us. 'Celestine sent me a photograph of a girl with that surname, a letter – I don't know what's going on but I know my husband is alive...' I heard my voice crack.

He sighed and turned back. 'Why don't you tell me exactly what Celestine said?'

The letter's story didn't seem to surprise him. I guessed that in his line of work plotlines tended to repeat themselves.

'You have the photo of the girl on you?'

It was in a side pocket of my handbag.

'That's her,' he nodded. 'She used to wait for him at the bus stop.'

'The bus stop in front of our flat? She's definitely the same girl?'

'I saw him pick her up twice. Both times he took her back to school in Wynberg. That's when I got the shot. Full-time surveillance needs a whole team. I had to keep changing cars. He had a key to the locked pedestrian gate at the back of your block; sometimes he'd avoid me that way.'

I stared at him, aghast at my husband's daytime adventures.

'What are her circumstances? Is she loved at home?'

'She is a babe in the woods,' he said sombrely.

'There must be some connection. We need to talk to the girl. You have to help me.'

'What were you thinking of? Kidnapping her?'

He made me feel foolish. 'I just want to find my husband, Mr Khan.'

'I'll keep an eye on the girl. That's as far as I go. If you try any bullshit on me, our agreement automatically terminates. No tricks, no secrets, or I walk. Is that clear?'

'Crystal clear.' He loosened his grip on the photo so I could put it back in my handbag.

But he didn't seem ready to go.

'What was Celestine to you?'

'I hardly knew her, but she didn't deserve to die like that.'

'Nobody deserves to die from fifty-four stab wounds,' he replied quietly. Why had I used Gi's words and not my own? Nathan Khan's finely tuned antennae had picked up the ambivalence I felt towards Celestine, now that I knew she had tampered in our lives.

I opened my briefcase. 'Here. I nearly forgot.' I held out Celestine's letter. A light floral fragrance floated on the breeze.

'You could tell when she was coming from a block away. There are some women whose scent you never forget. Keep it for now.' The square-jawed gaze swept the park one more time then Khan said, 'You shouldn't handle it too much – in case you want it dusted for prints.'

I watched him walk away with long, unhurried steps towards a bicycle leaning against an oak tree. Nice butt. My car was parked in front of the court buildings so I walked back through the gardens till I came out at the main thoroughfare lined with tourist wares that led directly to the city centre.

Back at work, I googled 'Babe in the woods'. 'The abandoned children of Wailing Wood ... These pretty babes, with hand in hand, went wandering up and down. In one another's arms they died.' It was 'babes', not 'babe'.

In the parking lot behind the client's office, every bone in my feet aching and my dried-out eyes blinking at the mobile phone plasma screen – 'you have 31 new messages' – it came back to me: why Nathan Khan was wearing the dark shades.

In the week before I'd left to join the Hadrian team in Rome, I'd rushed out from these same offices to purchase foreign currency. It was a blistering hot day and the shopping centre was undergoing modifications. Outside the bank I'd had to wait impatiently while an athletic black man in a Puma windbreaker and jeans replied in deep bass tones to the security guard's questions about the excitable white ball of fur he had on a lead. When Yoshi the Maltese poodle and his master moved on, the security guard finally wielded his metal detector to check my handbag. Back at the car, a flat tyre had greeted me. I'd kicked the rubber with my expensive work shoe and cursed construction workers and their nails.

The car had been hot as a furnace. I'd left the door open as I made a call to the project office. When I looked up again, the man in the windbreaker was standing waiting, his miniature hound running rings around his feet. He had to stoop right down to ask if he could be of assistance. He'd given me the pup's lead to hold while he changed the tyre in record time. I'd handed him back his frenetic dog, thanked him inadequately and reversed hurriedly. In my rear-view mirror, I'd seen him pick up his dog and watch me accelerate away.

There'd been other occasions, too. A figure with an iPod outside the restaurant I jogged past most mornings. A colossal shadow climbing the wall as a man rose from a table behind me in the local library. Catlike footsteps behind me in an alley taking a shortcut back from an evening walk to the beach. He knew about the Dante Art Gallery. Was it possible he'd been keeping an eye on me all these months? Was he the shadow in dark corners and alleys that I always sensed with a prickle behind my neck but never quite saw?

He'd shaven his head since then and made sure I couldn't see his eyes, but the impressive physique and that voice, together with the brand clothing, were unmistakeable. I started putting two and two together and finally got four. Then I put four and four together and got eight. Soon, I'd unravelled a whole skein of double-dealings. Elijah's surveillance expert Nat Behr, Heidi's Nat, and Celestine's Nathan Khan were one and the same person. The world was full of duplicity.

'You know him!' I accused Elijah after bursting into his office. 'How could you? It's a conflict of interest. You promised me total confidentiality. You knew he was following me. You've been telling him everything.'

'Hello, Paola. I heard you were back from Italy. I see you haven't changed.' The pointed allusion to the fact that I hadn't contacted him just made me madder. And to think I'd been wondering how to break the news to Elijah about a new sleuth on the case.

In the end, Elijah denied nothing, his eyes troubled and solemn behind the thick glass. 'I tried to get you to meet him when he taped Daniel's phone call but you refused. I wanted to tell you, but it went too far. I swear I didn't know he was going to follow you. I just couldn't stop it. Nathan took it personally when Daniel disappeared on his beat. When he heard you hired me he called me up.'

'Khan is an Indian name. You called him Nat Behr.'

He smiled at me, a tentative half-smile. 'Ah, I see, you imagined a swish Jewish detective named "Behr". Khan is his adopted name. I believe an Indian family found him as a hungry waif sleeping under a bush in the park in front of their home.'

'Get to the point, Elijah.'

Elijah sank back into the chair, cracked his knuckles, and sighed. 'Nat Bear – b-e-a-r – is just what I call him. It's shorter than Nat the Bear.'

'Why Nat the Bear?' I was interrogator and interlocutor. I had no intention of letting my slippery PI off the hook.

'Nat's a private person. Maybe it's because he's so big. Maybe it's because he sleeps a lot.' Elijah avoided my question desperately.

'I don't care how private he is. If you don't tell me how you know him, I'll report you both to the professional investigators' consumer protection body.'

'You would?' Elijah sounded impressed. 'I had no idea such a body existed. You can't tell him I told you.'

'Cross my heart and hope to die.' My sarcasm was immense. 'I won't tell him.'

'We were at boarding school together,' Elijah blurted out, still rifling through his hair. 'There were a few Indian boys but he was the only black boy in those days. The funny thing was, nobody gave him any trouble. Everybody liked him. Maybe it helped that he was so much bigger than everybody else. When I arrived he was one of the seniors, but he made sure nobody gave us younger boys any trouble. In winter, Nat would go right under the covers so you couldn't see him, then he wouldn't hear the wake-up gong. We'd have to wake him up so he wouldn't have to do detention, and he'd just turn over and carry on snoring. Somebody – it was probably me – said he was like a hibernating bear and that's where it started. Soon, he was Nat the Bear. He had a funny habit of sleepwalking too. So sometimes you'd come back from taking a pee and you'd find Nat in your warm bed.'

'I don't believe this. You and Nathan Khan were buddies at boarding school? No wait, let me get this exactly right – Nathan slept in your bed at boarding school?'

'I'm afraid so. Yes. I'm really afraid so. But of course I simply moved over into his bed then because he was so fast asleep you couldn't hope to wake him up.'

'I don't care about where you slept. My head hurts trying to figure this all out. I thought you were on my side. How did you both end up becoming PIs? Just coincidence?'

Elijah laid both his hands down on the desk as if he needed the horizontal support, staring at his stubby nails as he spoke, avoiding my baleful glare.

'Strictly speaking, Nat Bear is a surveillance expert and I'm an old-fashioned sleuth. There is a difference, you know. The Muslim family that took him in owned a company that installed alarms and security gates, that kind of thing, so Nathan grew up around electronic equipment. But his dream was to become a policeman – something to do with his background. He was top of his class at the police academy. He ended up on the surveillance squad working with a narcotics team, but things went wrong. An undercover agent Nathan fitted with a new long-range wire was found floating in the harbour.

'There was a big stink and Nathan was put on deskwork so he handed in his badge. He went loco for a while, did odd jobs, mainly working as a bouncer. He was picked up for being drunk and disorderly a couple of times and then he nearly killed a guy with his bare knuckles in a bar fight and, before he knew it, he was in jail for assault.'

I sighed loudly. Ex-policeman, ex-con. I hadn't been so far wrong after all.

Elijah continued. 'By the time he got out I'd started on my own so I offered to show him the ropes, but he had contacts through the family business. He started doing undercover surveillance for a high-powered businessman and he hasn't looked back. We move in different worlds. He does the high-tech assignments for big corporations and government bodies – the hush-hush stuff that pays big bucks – and I do the private badly-paid jobs like looking for missing people. You know the type – the ones even the police don't know about.'

There was some latent irony slipping through, but now wasn't the time to remark on it.

'Why did he agree to work for Celestine if he only does big corporate jobs?'

The words were out before I could take them back. He met my eyes.

'Who's Celestine, Mrs de Luc?'

He'd been waiting for that moment, I saw it then. Of course there was a double game going on.

'You know who Celestine is,' I spat out, furious with him for leading me into a trap.

'Yes, I do, but only because my good friend Nat Bear filled in some of the gaps. Things like you visiting that organisation in Belgium. Things like you going over to meet her. Things like her getting murdered soon afterwards. Things like a letter. Small details like that.'

'Okay, okay. I withheld information from you. I didn't want

to confuse matters. I still have a private life, you know. You were hired to find Daniel, that's all.'

The bookshop doorbell rang downstairs. Muffled voices came up through the wooden floorboards: Uriah of the red lips in conversation with a customer.

'This isn't working, Mrs de Luc,' Elijah finally broke the uncomfortable silence. 'When you feel like you can trust me, call me. Until then, consider me off the case.'

'Elijah, you're being ridiculous.'

But Elijah was resolved. 'Nathan and I can't protect you if you don't tell us what's going on. We can't be responsible for your safety. Both of us have gone down that road before. Nathan says I should remind you of your discussion with him in the park. He says unless you fulfil your obligation and divulge everything you know, as well as what you've been doing on your own, your agreement with him is null and void. Sorry, Mrs de Luc, but that's the only way it can work.'

Having delivered his ultimatum, Elijah looked almost sad. I had no choice but to leave and rethink my options.

* * *

A few days later, I'm woken up by a late-night call from a bar. I can hear the background sounds of loud voices and clinking glass. My mobile shows it's nearly 1 am.

'Is that Mrs Pa-ol-a de *Luck*?' a slurred voice asks.

'Elijah, is that you? What's going on?'

'Yes, ma-am, it's Elijah Bloom. I'm drun*k*, ve*rrry*, ve*rrry* drun*k*. It feels wonderful! I'm calling to thank you for helping me break my two-year abstention record. I'm sick and tired of missing persons. Do you know what I mean?'

'I absolutely know exactly what you mean. They are enough to drive anyone to drink. Where are you, Elijah? I'm coming to fetch you.'

'I thought you were my friend, Paola. You lied to me. You lied to Elijah. I can't do my job if you lie to me.' Short silence. 'I don't know where I am.'

'Hand your phone to the barman.'

'No. I won't.'

'Come on, Elijah. I'll make you a nightcap,' I wheedle. 'You can sleep on the couch.'

'Now you want to be nice to me, just because you want me back on the case. I can't remember the last time I had *sex*.'

I can't think of a single cheering-up thing to say.

'*Sex, glorious sex*,' Elijah sings sadly into the telephone. 'Paola de *Luck*'s husband is still missing. That's all she cares about.'

For the rest of that night and into the following morning I reread the reports that Elijah had diligently sent through every week; he'd been meticulous about detailing his activities on a daily basis using a sad- or smiley-face system. Most of the reports made depressing reading with a pox of sad faces, but sporadically a smiley face would burst through the thick fog of gloom, with three smiley faces indicating a promising development.

I called him every half hour but he wasn't answering his phone. Eventually I got hold of him in the late afternoon.

'I thought you were dead. I don't know where you live.'

'What do you care?' he said in a morose, slurred voice. 'Leave me alone, Paola.'

'The booze isn't going to solve anything. Come for supper tomorrow and I'll tell you everything you want to know.'

The next day, I gave him Celestine's letter to read while I cooked supper. He handled it with the usual conjurer's white gloves, raising it to his nose and murmuring, 'Interesting.'

When we eventually sat down at the table he said very primly, his blood-shot eyes looking down at his plate, 'I need to hear everything you've left out. Nondisclosure by people close to the missing person is the main reason for cases not being solved.'

I told him almost everything. At least the stuff that was pertinent to RMI. The hardest was telling him about Jack. How does one explain infidelity, even when it comes from some dark loveless part, even when one can't be sure of one's own motives?

'Enid Lazzari told me that a child could bring Daniel back. When we were all young I found this message on the Internet about an organisation called Real Man Incorporated. So I went there to see if I could find Daniel, but I didn't want to have a child. Only, events kind of got a momentum of their own – and I went all the way. It seemed to be what was always meant to happen. I know it sounds as if I've short-circuited but that's the truth. Cross my heart and hope to die. Really.'

'How do I know you mean it?'

'Croix de bois, croix de fer. Si je mens, je vais en enfer.' I did the cross on my chest, to show I meant it. 'It's Daniel's musketeer oath.'

He smiled grimly.

'It's a matter of trust. Anything material to the case I need to know about. If this is going to work we need new rules. Nathan keeps an eye on the girl. I work on the rest, including Enid Lazzari and the two other identities, Gabriel Montaigne and Gabriel Kaas.' He shook his head as if he could hardly take it all in. 'You have a copy of the letter?' I nodded. 'I'll return it when I've dusted it for prints.' Elijah's pale blue eyes met mine. 'No more secrets, Paola. Shall we shake on that?'

I shook his hand.

'So, now we're partners again, why did Nathan agree to do detective work for Celestine?'

'I think they had a thing going for a while. He was introduced to her by the owner of a French company that he buys surveillance equipment from.'

'And Heidi?' I asked.

Elijah looked embarrassed and ran his hand through the fiery mop. 'Heidi's a great girl,' he muttered. 'I suppose these things just happen sometimes.' He sounded acutely uncomfortable about the situation but I wasn't going to let him off the hook.

'So he was just after the girl,' I remarked.

'He's the best detective I know,' Elijah replied solemnly, rubbing his bloodshot eyes. 'But he's a maverick. We don't always agree on the modus operandi, but I wouldn't trust anybody else to watch my back. Nathan doesn't back off, not for anyone.'

'Is that a warning or a recommendation?'

'Both.'

Nat the Bear and Celestine must have made a sensational coupling. That is what I had learnt thus far. No ulterior motive was more underestimated than lust.

They made an unlikely team: Elijah Bloom, the red-haired mostly sober Little Prince keen on interplanetary affairs and Nathan Khan, ex-policeman, ex-con surveillance expert and Maltese poodle lover.

In my dreams that night, Nat the Bear fed Yoshi sausages on my couch. They turned into writhing eels faster than the dog could gulp them down, slithering away beneath cushions as I lunged at them. Soon my couch was covered in a disgusting slimy tangle of slippery mud-brown eels. I phoned Elijah and told him about the nightmare, my heart still pumping.

'That's a good omen,' Elijah said sleepily. 'Eels are considered good luck in dream symbology. Go to sleep now. Sleep tight and don't let the bedbugs bite!'

Funny little man.

The Daniel I know is deeply troubled by philosophical questions that he shares with me. I hear his voice as he feeds me sinfully dark-red cherries. *Lucre or love, ma chérie, this is a philosophical question that has teased philosophers through the ages. I ask you, is it possible to have both?* Was this the question laced with poison that Jasmine had faced? Was this the reason she was with Nikos, heir apparent to the van den Bogen empire, in the Paris photograph? And then with Nicky dead, she looked for love in Daniel de Luc's arms?

Sleeping with
the Enemy

I WAS NEGOTIATING MY WAY PAST an accident scene opposite the Mouille Point lighthouse, the glaring early morning haze of sunlight a sure sign that another unbearably hot late November day was upon us, when my mobile rang. Joggers and walkers were out in force. A traffic cop was directing the early morning traffic around a fallen motorbike and a teal BMW with its bonnet crushed in. A man loosened his tie as he talked on his mobile, eying his wrecked car morosely while a pale girl in black leather knelt over a motorcyclist lying flat on his back on the tar. For a second I was back on a distant highway: the stench of burnt rubber rising off the tarmac, getting slowly to my feet, amazed to be alive, Nicky in his riding suit stooped over the mangled bike.

Seagulls dive-bombed each other for scraps from a greasy polystyrene container discarded on the sidewalk. I accelerated away. Later, I checked my missed calls but it was one of those no-number calls that make it impossible to get back to the caller. My mobile stayed in my handbag most of the morning while I attended meetings so there were other missed no-number calls before he finally reached me.

'Paola Dante speaking.'

'Hello, Paola. It's Jack.'

Napoleon was in Cape Town. My bowels turned to ice slush. 'What are you doing here?' I whispered in a mortal funk, as if I had no knowledge of transport systems and global travel, as if he'd arrived on a spaceship from a planet in a distant galaxy. My horror could not have been greater.

Jack chuckled, a dangerous laugh. 'Did you think I would forget you so soon? I never forget the good ones. Sometimes I look them up. Nobody else needs to know. It's between us. Come, let me take you out to supper. You have nothing better to do, cooped up in that apartment of yours. I'll be there at 7.30 pm. Dress is cocktail.' Speechless, I stared at the phone in my hands. It wasn't supposed to work like that. The details of my life were confidential. He wasn't supposed to know where I lived or what my number was or that I was cooped up in an apartment.

My head reeled, but I found myself powerless to disobey.

The woman who stares back at me as she applies mascara to dark lashes is beyond stopping. Recklessness has entered the picture. Her body will be present without her mind; she will be her own avatar. I want to warn her that avatars slip beyond our reach, live beyond the call of our voice, but my avatar has a mind of her own. Love has let her down. She can hardly believe in it any more. The terrible mystery of passion must be brought to an end.

She daubs scent from a pink glass Jean Paul Gautier bottle onto her neck and walks into a spray of fragrance, remembering from a magazine that perfume lasts longer in the hair. Her mouth in the mirror is a gash of vermilion.

His hand was as strong as ever. His eyes lingered.

'You've cut your hair. I like it.'

Does he know I cut it off in the hotel? Does RMI know everything?

'It's easier to handle.'

276

We drove out of the sunset city in a white convertible, hood down.

'Is it yours?'

'For tonight.'

'Where are we going?'

'Big Bay. Do you eat Asian food? I know a very good place.'

'Asian's fine.'

The restaurant was Chinese, on the undeveloped side of the seafront with a red lantern hanging at the entrance. From the outside it looked unprepossessing, the windows blocked out and encrusted with salt, but the inside was decorated with lacquered Chinese furniture and authentic-looking Ming vases. Chinese patrons at packed tables stared unabashedly as we walked past, their laughter following us. The manager, a Chinese woman who stood as straight as a ramrod, spoke impeccable English.

'Mr Hidalgo. We are honoured to have you with us again.' She conferred briefly with her son in Mandarin, before he led us to an alcove behind some curtains, bowing slightly as he backed out.

'Hidalgo?'

'I like horses. It's a great movie. I've got it on DVD. I've probably watched it about twenty times.'

'That explains the way you dress.'

'You noticed? I like to think Viggo and I have similar styles.' He grinned irrepressibly, his sharp teeth bared, as if I'd just paid him a great compliment. He probably had a poster of Viggo Mortensen wearing nothing but jeans at home. It seemed funny. We had something in common after all. I thought Viggo was sexy, too. Maybe Jack was bisexual. It was probably an advantage if you had a heightened libido.

'Why didn't you tell me you knew Cape Town?'

'I am a citizen of the world. For my work, I travel. But right now I am taking a summer holiday in your beautiful city.'

'I don't believe you. I travelled all the way to Belgium to ensure total confidentiality, and now you follow me here. It's not supposed to work like that. It's not what I paid all that money for,' I hissed.

I was interrupted by the reappearance of the pocked young

man who had shown us to our table. He laid a clean red cloth and placed chopsticks and bowls on the table.

'May I recommend the specials of the house?' In the dim red lantern light of the cubicle, his round face swung over us like a cratered moon.

'It's always very good,' Jack murmured solicitously, and to the young man, 'Bring us a flask of your house wine.' The young man slipped away, wraith-like, through the brocade curtains. The thin strapped-in wire felt hot against my skin. After a glass of rice wine I excused myself.

It was Elijah's idea. I'd told myself there was no reason to inform him about the planned rendezvous with Jack but a sense of self-preservation had kicked in at the last minute. Something didn't feel right about Jack looking me up. Besides, I didn't want Elijah getting all hot under the collar again because I hadn't 'divulged'. He'd said it wasn't safe for me to go, but I'd insisted – it was my only chance to find out what RMI's intentions were regarding Daniel – so he'd put his foot down.

'This man is your enemy, Paola. If you were Captain Kirk, he would be a Klingon. There's a name for this – it's like Stockholm syndrome, where hostages become attached to their kidnappers. You get him to talk and then say you've got a stomach bug so you can get out of there. It's the wire or the police.'

He was pacing up and down, running his hand through the fiery hair so that it stood out in all directions.

'Elijah, this is not your decision to make, its mine. But I'll put the wire on if that makes you happy.'

'I'll call Nathan,' Elijah said quietly.

Nathan only agreed to the plan when he realised he couldn't stop me.

The device was nifty and small. Heidi and I went into the bedroom while the two of them waited outside. She was going to teach me how to strap it on so no one could see it. At some point I would have to take it off; I shouldn't leave it too late. Nathan and her would be within a fifty-metre range of me at all times – I should scream if I was in trouble. *Three easy steps to undercover agent for the blues.*

A languid eyebrow raised above a sloe eye told me what she thought of my planned outfit: an understatedly elegant evening pantsuit.

'What? We can't all be dressed to kill.' *Shit.* 'I'm not the seductress type. Besides, don't we need to hide that gadget?'

She snorted softly like a highly strung warrior horse. 'You planning to find out what he knows or not? This isn't Businesswoman of the Year.'

I resigned myself to the inevitable. 'Go ahead, be my guest.'

'Here!'

She insisted on a ruffled royal blue organza top with a low neckline and little pearly buttons that had always seemed entirely too feminine in my wardrobe, together with a forgotten pair of black satin harem pants and some wedge-heeled gold sandals I'd shoved into a far corner because they were uncomfortable.

I stared at my reflection. 'Have you ever thought of becoming a fashion stylist?'

'You'll have to choose your moment,' was her only reply.

'You mean not while we're in flagrante delicto?'

She grinned, showing a little gap between her teeth. 'Something like that. And be careful about leaving him alone with your bag. Men like him search women's bags. Do you want a knife?' Before the question had properly registered, she'd unzipped a boot and extracted a short-bladed knife from a scabbard fitted below her knee. She flipped it over and offered it to me, handle first.

'No. Jack's not dangerous.'

'He's not a man?'

'It's my call.'

'Okay.' The knife slid soundlessly back into hiding.

Now I was locked in the ladies room of a Chinese restaurant. I hoisted the organza top up and checked in the mirror, rotating my torso the way they do in the movies. It was firmly in place under a carefully chosen bra. All that was left to do was follow the advice I'd been given. *Be cool.* I took some deep breaths, reapplied my lipstick and sailed out past the bright inquisitive eyes that had followed me in.

Jack was right. The ambience was perfect and the food excellent. Before long, I was feeling pleasantly lightheaded and frivolous.

On our way out, Jack took the coast road, taking curves at high speed and turning the volume up on the radio, occasionally resting his hand on my leg as if we were long-time lovers reunited. The speeding darkness had a curiously disorientating effect so that when he finally cruised up to within metres of elaborate wrought iron gates and a security guard in a booth, it took me a moment to trust my eyes. It was the gateway to the party house. The bending driveway and a hedge of tall trees served to hide the mansion from prying eyes. All that could be seen of it was a deep amber glow in the sky.

He put his arm across the seat behind my back. 'This is where you met Madeleine.'

'What are we doing here Jack?'

He shrugged in the darkness, his sharp chin turned to the house. 'Did you think you were the only one? Do you have any idea how many relationships have started with a meeting in this house? It is not as easy as one might imagine to switch from one relationship to the next. It is the mystery that entraps us. Consider Lauren Bacall, Grace Kelly, Sophia Loren, Audrey Hepburn, even Marilyn Monroe – to become an erotic icon one must cultivate an air of elusiveness. There is nothing more seductive, more alluring to a man. It is easy to find an available cunt, but when you look at such a woman she promises only delusion. It is not so easy to find a genuinely passionate woman, a woman whose nature is wild and free.'

As he talks, his hand slips lower, a thief scaling castle walls in the darkness. I am the lonely female heart beating a thousand times faster, sending blood coursing through hapless veins, as I wait on the ramparts.

'There is an inevitable desire to find out more, to experience more, to learn about this other person you are not permitted to pursue. Do you know the kind of … power I am talking about?' He breathed the words against my tingling skin, his mouth brushing over my defenceless ear and bared neck, a sibilant wind in the black night. 'That is a question I have often asked myself.'

The fingers of the man who is not my husband wander over my upper breast as if outlining a mysterious continent, then they surround my erect nipple and squeeze. My body, which has disobeyed all instructions to repel the intruder, is a burning plain. Lust's brushfire has broken through flimsy defences, spreading unchecked through a thirsty epidermal covering to a soft, hungry belly. He squeezes a little harder, imposing his male will.

I can still leave, open the car door and find a taxi, and the rest of the evening will never happen.

I pushed his hand away and started to laugh, trying to control my nervous hysteria in the enclosed space. I'd forgotten all about the wire. His hand had been so close – I improvised desperately.

'This is the last thing I expected. You going existential on me. Reality check: your apparatus didn't work ...'

'Now, I am deeply offended,' Jack said, sounding very hurt indeed. 'I shall have to try harder.'

'In a biological sense, that is,' I added hastily.

'Ah, biology! Of course,' Jack said gravely.

'What the hell, I took my chances. So, now I think of it as Napoleon and Josephine having a one-night stand.'

He seemed impressed. 'I was General Bonaparte? Epic love is made in the aftermath of victory. Why did you not tell me?'

'We were otherwise occupied,' I reminded him sternly. 'In any case, Bonaparte left Josephine because she couldn't have children. That was a game, Jack. We both know it was a game. Maybe tonight I want to be Mata Hari and sell your secrets to the enemy. I don't like you pitching up on my doorstep. It makes me feel unsafe.'

He removed his arm from the seat and started up the car. 'You laugh at me, but you have no idea. You have no idea.' I was discovering that Jack was mercurial; his mood shifted gear. 'And if you are Mata Hari, then who am I?'

'Whoever you choose to be.'

'Very well, Mata Hari. I am yours for the remainder of the evening,' he said sardonically as he took my hand and kissed it. 'But is it not true that Mata Hari was executed for her indiscretions?' He leaned over, the car still running, and kissed me full on the mouth, a hard, rough kiss that left my lips feeling bruised.

'I've been wanting to do that all evening. Now, if it is Mata Hari you wish to be, you shall be her.'

I felt shaky. 'She was innocent, of course,' I said, touching my fingers to my lips. 'It's important to remember that.'

'Of course.'

The security guard in front of the booth lowered his crackling radio as Jack engaged gears and slowly pulled away.

Something very strange happened to me that night. I found Mata Hari within myself.

Jack phoned 'someone I know', who ran a business hiring out costumes from a 'spooky Victorian cottage' on Station Road.

He rang the doorbell and spoke into the intercom. A burly Slavic-looking man with a mass of grey hair and a full beard let us in without giving me a second glance. He led us through the front cottage to a second building at the back, unlocked a door, flipped a light switch, and then abruptly left us, fading into the shadows in much the same way he'd appeared. The walls of each room were taken up by ceiling-high open cupboards. The light was provided by chandeliers, the wooden floors were covered with rugs and the costumes glittered and shone. As I fingered the exquisite fabrics and wondered at the many games of love they had been used for, a night train thundered by, shaking the house and wooden pillars to its foundations.

Jack the Ripper knew his way round the rooms. He selected silver bells for my ankles and wrists, he found me a veil of a diaphanous beaded fabric that he swore came straight from the harem of the Turkish Sultan's seraglio, a present from his first wife to the wife of a Western diplomat. He selected a pair of silk bloomers and pointed toe-slippers that belonged to a handpicked concubine. 'All authentic,' he said, flashing small pointed white teeth.

I could smell the perfumes of other women, a musky amalgamation of scents. Another night train thundered by, the enemy's horses running in the moonlight. I was losing my bearings.

Almost as an afterthought, Jack removed a longhaired wig from one of the dummies and added it to the soft carry bag he'd located in a cupboard. When we left, he pulled the door hard till it clicked and locked, then he led me round the side of the main cottage to the front gate, holding me by the hand as he stepped surefooted through the darkness.

We did not talk on the way back to town. I fingered the black wig on my lap; the smooth strands felt natural, like stroking a real woman's hair.

You bastard, Daniel. Where the hell are you?

Jack took me to a rooftop suite in a trendy industrial-style block of flats in the city commercial centre, all double volume glass and industrial polished steel. That night, Mata Hari danced for Jack the Ripper in a designer loft apartment, her wire safely stored away. In that huge impersonal space, everything became possible. If I flew into the rafters he would come after me, pull me down, plunder me. I had not imagined I could dance like a siren, or wiggle my belly like a belly dancer, or jingle my foot bells like Samson's Delilah. He plied me with exquisite red wine, and played the sinuous music of a snake charmer as he adorned me with silken veils, showing me a side of myself that was as exhilarating as it was terrifying.

My body became a sinuous, undulating serpent. I discovered muscles and sinews and breaths that had been strangers to me my entire life. He sat on a white flokati rug in the midst of enormous cushions, watching me intently, occasionally leaning over to pour more wine, his arrogant mouth twisting, his eyes glinting hard as hailstones tap-dancing on a tin roof. I seduced a man by dancing for him. There was a moment when I caught a glimpse of myself in my new racy underwear in one of the many mirrors. I stopped, gazing at this apparition in bare feet and sensual pose, her hand on her stomach, a small triangle of black lace starkly inviting against her white skin. Mysteriously, I had lately gone shopping for black satin and lace underwear – Paola the seductress had planned this all unbeknown to Paola the wife.

Afterwards, I sank onto the rug and he put the glass of wine to my mouth. I drank slowly, looking into his eyes. His will possessed me. When the red wine ran out of my mouth and down my chin and onto my breasts he licked it off; when a few drops spilt onto the flokati he laughed, and I laughed, the crimson stains fantastic gems that glistened on the snow. Soon, I rose once more to dance, my whirling shadow a dervish on the walls, my feet twirling me round and round, my temporary long hair a sheet of jewelled black rain that I swung back and forth. I'd always wondered what it felt like to let go like that. Jack whooped encouragement.

In this mood of feverish abandon, I fall through the curtain of jewelled black rain and find myself naked in front of a familiar mirror.

Daniel has his mouth against my ear, my hair coiled around both our hands. He has walked unannounced into our bathroom, smelling of booze and tobacco and stale breath.

'You have Scheherazade's hair,' he says, slowly uncoiling the length of it as he watches me intently in the mirror.

'Do I know her?'

'You don't know *Tales from a Thousand and One Nights?*'

'What about the days? Can we leave the story for another time? I'm cold. Where have you been, Daniel?'

'The days come later. It's a story you'll appreciate. A beautiful and ambitious young woman uses a sizzling combination of intelligence and guts to climb to the top.'

'Well, I couldn't miss that, could I? You know me …'

'Each night, the Sultan takes a different virgin into his bed and then he has her killed to avenge his first wife's betrayal.' His hand is stroking my neck. It's an effort to gather my wits and speak.

'I bet a man wrote this fairy tale.'

'When Scheherazade offers herself to him, the Sultan has already had over 3 000 women killed. She tricks him into listening to a story and after that he's hooked.'

'Is there more?'

'For the next thousand and one nights, she entertains him with a different story every night and finally he forgets the disappointment of his first wife. Scheherazade becomes Queen of the Sultan's empire and the most powerful woman in the world. Isn't that what all women aspire to?'

'I didn't sleep with him, Daniel.'

'Of course you didn't. C'est un bouffon.'

'Flirting with a client is not a sin.'

'Not one of the Ten Commandments or one of the Seven Deadly Sins? Then it should be,' my husband says, handing me a towel.

Scheherazade wasn't just a cold-hearted, ambitious bitch, I know that now. But I can't prove it.

The past calls, coalesces, coagulates while the man who is not my husband waits, his mouth a scimitar.

The next morning, I woke up groggily to the sounds of activity in the kitchen. *The wire.* I bolted for the bathroom. It was still there. Wrapped in some tissues in the pocket of the five-star hotel towelling gown with the pink satin finish clearly intended for female visitors. I had to steady myself against the basin. *Be cool.* My face was a mess. I put the gown on with shaky hands and headed for the shower on the rooftop.

The buttresses and spires that presided over all human affairs in the city loomed over the glass-walled shower, crushing me in the embrace of perfect recall: I am face-to-face on a doorsill with my boyfriend's housemate and best friend startled by an emotion I cannot fathom; I am driving to the laundromat on a Saturday morning, praying to whichever gods might be in attendance that he'll be there one more time; I am sitting on my husband's lap contemplating the change of seasons through the study windows; I am lying in the desolation of a king-size futon that has become a desert. The hot water ran over me as if I were an obelisk.

On the way back to the bedroom, I paused in front of the open French windows. Jack was doing a martial arts routine in a pair of white drawstring trousers. The smooth, calibrated movements of the taut, bronzed torso and compact limbs flowed like water over silky pebbles in the early morning light, the body movements precise and delicate as he turned towards the mountain and the city skyline that stretched around in an arc. The noise of Sunday traffic was a muffled chant rising from below. I could have been in a Buddhist inner-city retreat for my spiritual wellbeing and awakening, considering the photogenic Zen-like calm of the scene before me. I walked away before he could notice me watching.

By the time I emerged, the innocuous wire with its cool snake's head once again against my skin, a breakfast spread had been prepared on the terrace: filter coffee in a plunger, fresh rolls and steaming croissants with jams and orange juice. He'd changed into boxer shorts and T-shirt and wore dark shades against the sun that had risen higher in the sky.

'Good morning. Did you sleep well?'

'Very well, thank you. The little sleep I got.'

His mouth curved upwards. This morning in the bright sunlight it was a blurred, sensual mouth. 'Coffee?'

The night before I had abandoned thought and surrendered myself to temporary insanity. Now I felt oddly removed from myself, as if I'd stepped outside my body, as if my skin had become too tight. It was Daniel's fault that I was in this mind-bending situation, so what could I do but go through with it. *Keep it real. It's important to stay in the role. Otherwise he'll guess.* Jack made light conversation over sliced melon and two-minute eggs. It is surprising how easily one can make conversation without reference to family, friends, the past or the future. We spoke only about the present: this apartment, architects and interior designers, this city, the inhabitants of the city, the country and its problems, the people who come to make their fortunes under the African sun.

But it couldn't last. As I bit into a chocolate croissant, the warm chocolate slipping into my mouth, he said, 'You know Langstrom,' without preamble.

I half choked and had to wash the croissant down with orange juice. He ignored my distress, continuing, 'It is not easy to leave.

Once you start. I did not know your husband ...'

I held up a hand. Just as I'd seen traffic controllers do with their stop sign outside schoolyards. 'Don't *ever* talk about my husband,' I spluttered. '*Ever*. At all.' This was not easy to say with little bits of buttery croissant still stuck in my windpipe.

'Stop looking for him, Paola. It is a futile quest.'

My heart thudded, shuddered, as if it would grind to a stop. The skyline tilted and then righted itself.

'What are you saying? How do you know about him?'

'Langstrom told me. They know everything. There is nothing that is hidden from them. Langstrom was worried about you. He asked me to speak to you.'

'Langstrom asked *you* to speak to me? You fucked me the whole night, you sanctimonious prick! The least you can do is tell the truth!' I leaped up, knocking my coffee over as I did so. I stared down at the bath gown. It was no longer virginally white; now it sported a brown, ugly stain that was hot against my skin.

'Sit down, Paola. Calm down. You said yourself it was a game. Do you want to know about your husband or don't you?'

I sat down. 'Tell me.' It came out in a hoarse whisper.

'Let us start with the facts. Your husband worked for RMI, the same company I work for. We offer a very special, unique service.'

I sipped orange juice to show him that nothing he could tell me would change anything.

'He was paid a retainer as well as a substantial fee for each encounter, although not a sum of money sufficient to live a life of luxury without pursuing other work. Over a period of nine years, he provided his live sperm to a maximum of ten carefully selected women each year, never more but sometimes less. You can do the sums.'

'Mathematics is overrated.'

'According to company records, he has fathered more than forty known children. RMI is not merely a business; it is an organisation with cells in every major country in the world. Think of it as a secret society, a society that offers exclusive membership to those willing to pay for its services as well as to those who offer the services. There is a degree of danger attached to any endeavour that goes contrary to society's mores. We are no different. You are no different. Your arrival was a complication.'

His facts had the relentless brutality of a hobnail boot coming down, the heel scrunching into the most vulnerable internal organs. I hardly had the breath left to attach myself to the infinitesimal pause. 'A complication?'

'Yes. You were married to a practitioner. This was a unique situation, that the wife of a practitioner should request another practitioner. Sometimes the one hand does not speak to the other hand. Because you used your maiden name, the problem was not picked up until Langstrom filed a report.'

'He filed a report? The two-faced, dick-headed worm.'

'He sought only to protect his family. He was granted special dispensation to marry his wife, a previous client, due to the unfortunate circumstances of the child's birth but, in reality, poor results on the annual tests made it an easy decision for the company. Nevertheless, he makes sure he stays on the right side of the company. Of course, marriage per se is not a problem. It's even encouraged because it allows the older practitioners to be integrated into normal society and gives them a solid alias. It also ensures that they have something to lose.'

It will be just you and me. That's what you said.

'Do the wives know?'

'Sometimes. Sometimes not. It's left up to the individual. But if she knows, then she is bound to take an oath of secrecy.'

'Does all the cloak and dagger stuff really work?'

'It's surprisingly effective.'

'Does Langstrom's wife know he filed a report?'

'I don't know.'

'What else about my husband?'

'The women who used his services include a cabinet minister, an Oscar winner, a golf champion and a businesswoman who featured in the Forbes list of the 100 most influential people in the world, and then, of course, there are the women who act as consorts to some of the most powerful men in the world.'

'Oversexed alpha females can be a real problem. So what went wrong?'

'You're quite something,' Jack shook his head. 'He decided he wanted out after you made plans to get married.'

Je me débarasse des autres obligations.

'I can understand why,' Jack continued, the arrogant mouth mocking me. 'But it didn't go down well with management. There is a small elite group of practitioners who are in high demand. Your husband was one of them.'

'Do you know where Daniel is?'

'No.'

'Where do you think he is?'

'I believe he disappeared to protect you. Once he realised they wouldn't let him go. That's what I would have done.'

'To protect me?' I stared at him, stunned, bemused, my head spinning, trying to take it all in. 'Wait. Those dead girls in the newspaper articles ... And Jasmine, Celestine, all those so-called "accidental" deaths from drug overdoses and falls out of windows. What did they know? Jack, take off those sunglasses and look at me.'

He took them off. His jaw was set, his gaze unflinching.

'They made waves. A company like The Love Bank Foundation is not isolated. It is part of a vast organisation of business dealings that are sometimes conducted within the parameters of the law and sometimes not. This kind of business requires a certain rigorous inflexibility. You have been the bull in the china shop, trying to find your husband. Hiring Nathan Khan has made them nervous. Mr Khan has earned quite a reputation. His surveillance skills have made him invaluable to some very important people who hold high public positions.'

You are not the only one who can play games.

'Ah. I see now what brought you here. And I imagined it was my charm.'

He ignored my facetiousness. 'The problem as I see it is that your husband, the man you apparently remain devoted to, has fathered the children of some of the most important women in the

289

world. So you can understand why the organisation cannot afford to let you make this public.'

The Limbo Files. *Grace. Hela. Isabelle. Jasmine. Rita. Tamara. Veronique.* Daniel's other women. Jack's explanation had given me an idea.

'Paola, are you listening to anything I'm saying? You will die before you find him if you carry on this way.'

I forced myself to concentrate on Jack. What else might he know?

'Is that a threat? Is that what happened to those girls?'

'They will not touch you if you play this the sensible way.'

'Instead of the hysterical my-husband-is-missing way? Come on, Jack.'

'It is not in their interest to attract negative publicity.'

'Negative publicity? You're calling a girl's death negative publicity? You really are a bastard. So who's "They"? If you're so concerned about me, tell me who "They" are.'

'Let it rest, Paola. He will come out eventually. And the Sarrazin girl will be taken care of.'

They know about Simone. Why did he mention her?

'There is something you should understand, Jack ...' I said.

Listening to the recording later, I was amazed at myself; it's true that impending danger focuses the mind. When I'd said everything it was necessary to say I stood up, brushing imaginary crumbs off my clothes.

'Tell that to your bosses.'

I walked away, placing my bare feet carefully down onto the cold paving, determined not to let the tilting skyline overpower me. As I reached the enormous industrial-style doors with their metal frames and windowpanes, I put out a hand and held on, letting the sound of breaking glass wash over me like a wave of benediction.

I made it to the bedroom. Then I did something that seemed necessary at the time, though less necessary in retrospect. I took his penknife and slashed Mata Hari's costume, directly descended from the harem of a Turkish sultan, stabbing at the exquisite hand-beaded fabric until deep gashes ran through every item, shredding centuries-old beauty in minutes. Then I washed my face with ice-cold water until everything appeared real again.

'Paola,' he called after me as I hurtled out past him, 'it doesn't have to end in this ugly way!'

'Yes, it does. Hang loose, Jack!' It was a curse of sorts.

An immaculately groomed woman came into the lift a floor down, carrying a red ostrich-skin briefcase. Another workaholic who worked Sundays. She reached into her handbag and offered me a tissue and a hand mirror, politely indicating my eyes.

'He's alive,' I said, by way of explanation as I cleaned myself up.

She nodded her white-gold head sympathetically as if it all made perfect sense. We rode down the rest of the way in companionable silence.

He's alive. He's alive. He still loves me.

Back in the apartment, I struggled to remove the wiretapping device. My hands were trembling so badly I could barely drink from the glass of water Heidi handed me.

'So, you're a woman who likes playing games after all,' she commented, the Afro hairdo a black halo, watching me sip.

'Depends who I'm playing with,' I responded shakily.

She laughed out loud. It was the most appealing sound I'd heard in a long time.

'Here, let me do it.'

'Did you and Nathan stay awake the whole night?'

'We got a few hours' sleep in the surveillance van.'

'Thank you.'

'Mrs de Luc, you should know something about me,' Heidi said as she gently removed the wire. 'We're not necessarily going to always be on the same side. I hope you understand.'

It was my turn to laugh. She was telling me survival came before friendship.

Nathan and Elijah listened on my laptop to the audio recording Nathan had brought with him while I took my second shower that day. This time I washed my hair, massaging shampoo in again and again until the last vestiges of Mata Hari's perfume were running down the sinkhole.

I was in time to hear the last part. Listening to that recording in the apartment I once shared with Daniel took my breath away with fear; this was not a dream that would disappear in the morning.

– Let it rest, Paola. He will come out eventually. And the Sarrazin girl will be taken care of.

– There is something you should understand, Jack … If you come near me again or you try to harm the Sarrazin girl, I'll go to the police.

– Don't you see, Paola? There's nothing you can do for her. One of these days they'll put her on a private plane and in some faraway country a chauffeur will open the car door for her. Virginity is a rare commodity.

– Stay away from us, Jack. If anything should happen to either of us, the police will receive a CD with files detailing the activities of RMI. I don't think those very important people you mentioned would care for that kind of embarrassment, do you?'

– Nobody will believe you. Just walk away from this, Paola. You'll get your life back and one day it will be nothing.

– Remember those rendezvous you mentioned with all those very important women? Daniel left his memoirs in computer files. There are names and dates. Right now the CD is in a safe place, and that's where it will stay so long as nothing happens to us. Oh, and if Daniel should wind up dead, that CD will bring your precious RMI crashing down like somebody exploded a ten-ton bomb in its grotesque belly. Tell that …

The last few words were drowned out by the shattering echo of breaking glass and porcelain. Jack had kicked the breakfast table over, but he let me go. When it came to the exchange in the lift, Elijah stopped the recording.

'Wowza, you go for it, girl!' Heidi exclaimed into the sudden silence. Her knuckles gently touched mine. 'Now we've got proof that they exist. You're warlike, girl!'

'Do you really have his memoirs?' Elijah interrupted, a perturbed frown creasing his freckled brow.

Only I knew what was really in those files. Not enough to incriminate anybody. That was not Daniel's way. Those women were written up as if they were fascinating candidates for a literary character. Whether there were enough real-life particulars to identify them was doubtful. Even their Christian names could have been experimental pseudonyms. But those files were all we had. For a bluff to work the illusion had to be maintained by sticking as closely as possible to the truth.

'Daniel left some protected files about the women he met through RMI on the PC at home. I thought it was background material for a book but it makes sense that he kept them as an insurance policy. My guess is he had to leave in a hurry and the files were left behind.'

Elijah sighed. 'I suppose you're not going to tell us where the files are now.'

'No. They're safe where they are.'

Elijah and Nathan exchanged looks.

'Paola, these guys play for keeps.' Elijah's face was crinkled with worry. 'There's too much at stake here. What if they pick you up and get it out of you?'

'You mean like that dentist scene in *The Marathon Man*?'

'Speak to her, Nathan.'

'These people are serious about protecting their interests, Mrs de Luc. Those women in France ended up dead.' *Madame, I do not wish to dig your body out of a hole in a forest.* It was the only time Nathan had opened his mouth the whole evening. He looked as if he needed a good night's sleep.

I relented. 'Relax, both of you. I have a backup plan. And another backup plan if that one goes wrong. And, finally, you should both know that if anything happens to me, an email will be triggered from my P&P workspace a week after the scheduler picks up no activity from me. It will give you the detailed location of a set of files stored in the firewalled work area of the new server for project Hadrian. I have access from our server here.'

I was making it all up as I went along but it was entirely plausible and it was beginning to sound like a damn fine idea. I'd been asked to conduct regular audits on the project from afar, so I had full security clearance. Project Hadrian was the ideal Trojan horse.

'Smart plan,' Heidi said approvingly.

'I still don't like it,' Elijah muttered. 'These people have no scruples. Those files are trouble.'

'Come on, Elijah. It's brilliant. You know it.'

Nathan stood up, bike helmet in hand.

'Hey, you can't go yet. We haven't talked about the Sarrazin girl.'

'I'm working on it,' Nathan said, not looking at me as he handed Heidi her helmet. 'I'll call you when I know something.'

In the quiet of a windless night I heard the motorbike roar off.

'What's his problem?' I mused to myself, since Elijah had the headphones on again.

'You never know when that might come in useful,' he said soberly when he eventually took the CD out. 'I'll make sure this is put in a safe place. Did he suspect anything?'

'No, not a thing. Enid was right about not going to the police, I can see that now. RMI can't figure me out so they sent Jack to give me a message, to make sure I don't get ideas. Jack just works for them. If he wasn't doing this he'd be a toy boy kept in champagne and caviar by some ultra-rich heiress who breeds race horses.'

'Let's hope so,' Elijah said doubtfully. 'These people don't kid around.'

A good night's sleep seemed out of the question. All the elation had seeped out of my faithless body.

'There's nothing to be done, Elijah. We still have no idea where Daniel is and there's no sign he's planning on being back any time soon.'

'We'll see,' Elijah said thoughtfully. 'We'll see. Do you remember our first meeting when I told you the number-one Law of Detectives?'

'Yes: follow the name.'

'Mmm. Did I say that?' The blue eyes twinkled. 'That's actually the corollary of the Detective's First Law. The first and most important rule of all detective work is always: *Follow the money!* Yesterday we got lucky. A contact at a bank called – not from your bank, another bank – picked up a regular foreign transaction for a Daniel de Luc, with the same box number as the threatening letters. Now we've got proof he's not a ghost. A sum of money was transferred to the local account from a French bank every month. Any guesses what the French account holder's name is?'

'Brigitte Bardot?' I suggested wearily.

'Gabriel Kaas. Any guesses who paid the money into the Kaas account?'

'No.'

'My contact asked a colleague in a French bank to do a trace on the debit order. A certain Monsieur Patrice Musso!' Elijah announced triumphantly.

'So, there really were royalty payments,' I said in wonder. 'He really wrote books.'

Elijah gave me a funny look out of those gentle flat-screen eyes. 'Well, we know he was getting paid for something. We're still not quite sure what for.'

I sat down on the couch. 'I think I want to be alone now, Elijah.'

Elijah leapt up apologetically. 'We're getting closer, Paola, I can feel it in my bones. The payments continued for four months after he went missing and then they stopped. Why would they have stopped? I'm going to carry on with this line of investigation.'

'Into the mouth of the wolf,' I said wryly. Elijah looked mystified. 'That's how they say good luck in Italian.'

'There's something else.' He ran his fingers through his hair; it practically crackled with nervousness.

What more can there be?

'I'm not sure if I should tell you with all of this going on, but that luxury roadster? The Porsche Carrera? The Sarrazin woman owns one, same colour. We don't have the registration so it's not a positive identification, but as things stand it all fits. I'm almost certain the woman who visited your husband was Nada Sarrazin,

Simone Sarrazin's adoptive mother.'

'Way to go. Elijah.' My voice was a resigned murmur.

'I'll let myself out.'

The next morning, 3 am, found me sitting on the balcony chewing a large yellow apple. Far out at sea, ships glided serenely through the blackness. I made a mental note to buy a packet of prunes and go for a longer jog. Months of erratic eating habits and oily takeaways had finally caught up with me. It seemed to me that digestive problems caused by irregular bowel movements were seriously underrated as factors affecting the history of the world. What legendary general could strategise while suffering from constipation?

Daylight is beginning to break like an army on the march. Three ships lie as if becalmed in the glassy aquamarine sea. There aren't many sights more spectacular than Camps Bay first thing in the morning. I hear the veneration in Daniel's voice one morning on the balcony. Mon Dieu! C'est très joli, n'est pas?

Somewhere out of view a vast golden sphere rises on the eastern horizon of the planet we inhabit. As it rises higher and higher in the firmament, it lengthens its inexorable gaze over the planet.

With my last breath I will love you. You are out there somewhere.

Unspeakable Things

ANOTHER WEEK DRAGGED ON. Friday night found me at Dizzys, staring at the ice in the bottom of my glass. There'd always been a night bar on the corner but it had changed names through the years. These days, the trees on the pavement sported fairy lights and there was live music most weekends. A tall black dude with a diamond earring and a sharp haircut sat down on the bar stool next to me.

'You shouldn't be out alone, Mrs de Luc,' he said once he'd ordered.

'Don't you think it's time you stopped stalking me?'

'I was in the neighbourhood. You weren't at the flat.'

'Stop bullshitting me, Nathan. I'm a big girl. You never called. When are you going to tell me what's going on?'

The whisky loosened his tongue.

'They auction the kids, Paola. The gigolo thought you knew.' It was his turn to stare into his glass.

He means Jack.

'A few weeks ago we picked up unusual activity on one of the sites we routinely monitor.'

'Who's "we"?' Stick to the facts. Evaluate. Stay in control.

'Just listen, Paola.' It was Nathan Judge-and-Jury talking – the one who thought I was a spoilt white woman who lived in Cloud Cuckoo Land. 'A couple of days later a new entry came on – blonde, blue-eyed Caucasian female, twelve, unspoilt goods – and straight away that's where all the traffic was going. Everything pointed to a high-value special package that could lead us to the racketeers running the show. Then, last night, the site shut down. Now we're back to square one.'

'Are you saying it's her?' My voice was too loud in Dizzys' gloom.

'I'm saying maybe. The shoe fits. It's all speculation – no one's prepared to stick their neck out on this one.'

'But there must be a photo?'

'They use random-number-generating software to scramble the images. We're talking about a highly sophisticated child-trafficking operation.'

'What happens now?'

'If it's a done deal, the girl disappears. Just like the gigolo said. They get her out the country.'

They'll put her on a private plane ... a chauffeur will open the car door for her. I saw it now – Jack was only the preamble.

I gritted my teeth. 'When, Nathan?'

'How long is a piece of string? Maybe they've moved the auction to another site. This is Tom and Jerry time.'

'But you can watch the house and stop them, can't you?'

'It's not that simple. We pass information on to the child protection units that have the muscle and the firepower. They need a warrant. This girl's the daughter. Sarrazin has friends in very high places. He's strictly off limits unless somebody can prove he's doing something illegal.'

'And you're fine with that?'

'They'll get the sicko eventually, but for some kids it will be too late. You get used to it. With missing kids you're always working with the tip of the iceberg.'

She's not missing. Not yet.

'What's the URL of the auction site?'

'Who's asking? It's gone offline.'

'Come on, Nathan. I want to take a look.'

He eventually gave it to me, rattling it off out of his head: a long string of alphanumeric characters separated by dots that had no meaning besides the sequence itself. I made him repeat it to make sure I had it down correctly.

Nathan invited himself for coffee at the flat. He didn't hear me come in on stockinged feet with the tray. I caught him scrutinising the base of a lamp.

'Don't you think if they were going to put in bugs, they'd have done it by now? You're acting paranoid.'

After they tore the apartment apart, Nathan had run a full surveillance check and, after that, he kept checking every opportunity he got. His usual response was, 'Vigilance is the price of safety'. This time he looked sombre.

'You piss on somebody's parade and they're going to come after you, Mrs de Luc,' was his parting shot.

I am the woman who opens a picture file on her laptop. The girl in the photograph gazes scornfully back at me. As if we know each other.

You knew, Daniel. You knew and you left her there. What do you expect me to do?

I know perfectly well that in the bigger picture the girl is expendable. Girls are brutally deflowered every day. Sacrifices are inevitable on a battlefield. These are universal truths. My mind flits back to a small, soaked wire-haired dog cowering against a wall, the pavement coloured red.

'Can we go, Daniel? It's freezing. You can't do anything. It's just a stray.'

The murmurs stop. My husband looks up at me and for a moment I see something in his eyes that is almost hate. But it's just a flash and then his glance is the same measured gaze I know so well.

'I am talking to the dog. It's been in a fight. You go on. I'll catch up.'

When he comes in I ask him what he did with the dog.

He washes his hands methodically with the medicated soap I insist we use, his back to me, his hair slick and wet.

'It's not a life, to live like that on the street. He had a terrible anal wound. I did what had to be done.'

I almost cut myself slicing the hard-boiled egg for a quick tuna salad. I must have heard wrong but when I go looking for him he's in the shower. His clothes are in a heap outside the door. They are full of blood.

I am the woman who can't bring herself to ask the question. Instead I ask if he wants seconds. My husband shakes his head and smiles at me, the way one smiles at a child to protect it, and says the salad is nearly as good as his own, but he doesn't have much of an appetite.

The answer comes to me unexpectedly. Sun Tzu says: 'Go forth where they will not expect it.'

I am the woman who starts typing. The situation requires something unorthodox. Then I shut the laptop down and leave our apartment, hurrying because it's late and the person I want to see lives a good thirty minutes away.

There are times in one's life when the totality of what one knows seems singularly inadequate. All the book study, experiential learning and brilliant tactical advice from sage generals who practise the art of competitive advantage do not quite cover the here and now.

When the doorbell rang the next morning, I almost ran to answer it: the police had come to tell me that everything would be fine, they were onto it. It's odd how we put so much store in the forces of law and order when we really should know better.

I opened the door to find my sister-in-law, Annie, standing there, ashen-faced and pole-thin with an overnight bag slung over her shoulder.

'I phoned your work and they said you called in sick. I flew down this morning on Express Air. Luckily somebody didn't pitch. I can't eat plane breakfasts. Let's go and get some coffee and something to eat, then we can talk. Not here. Are you really sick?'

She was firing away so fast, a nervous rat-a-tat, I couldn't get a word in edgewise so I interrupted.

'Annie, what are you doing here? Where's Max?'

'He's staying with friends. You wanted me to come, didn't you? Something's going on. I've been seeing things. The spirits are talking non-stop in my head. You know what happened last time.'

I hugged her and felt her whole bony body tremble. I was responsible for putting her under this pressure but there was nothing I could do to protect her; the gift that so terrified her was in her genes. We walked to a restaurant on the promenade. Earlier that morning, I'd stood on the balcony drinking my coffee and the day had glowered with a renegade brilliance. But it had turned into a blustery, miserable day and we were the only customers as they cleaned up around us.

'What are you seeing?'

She stared past me at the grey tumbling waves. She could see Daniel in a room somewhere far away. It had large windows with a view of a lake but there was something wrong. It looked like an old European villa; there was a large patio with wrought iron railings where he went to stand. She didn't think he was being held against his will because the doors and windows were always open. She could see pyjamas and slippers. He was tormented by horrible dreams. She could see into his dreams. It was strange, his dreams were more like memories than dreams. They had the narrative structure of reality with none of the irrationality of dreams. There was killing, violence. A terrible fury enveloped him, like a thick, heavy blanket that was suffocating him. She saw images of the girl as well, but these were less clear. People under a bridge, men and women without teeth, a luxury house all chrome and glass. The girl was scared, more scared at the house than at the bridge. There were closed doors. Annie's mind stopped at the closed doors. Unspeakable things happened behind the closed doors.

She'd come back late from book club. They'd had wine to celebrate a birthday – the babysitter had fallen asleep on the couch – and when she'd opened my attachment she'd had this overwhelming feeling that she had to come and see me immediately. There was no time to be lost because the girl in the photo was in danger. She could see a black SUV with dark-tinted windows; somebody inside was banging at windows; the number plate started with CA 777. She was talking so fast she made my head spin. I told her to slow down.

'I can't slow down, Paola,' she said almost in a whisper, her arms folded around her stomach as if she had a gut ache. 'This is how it is, it's a multimedia show, and images come thick and fast. Sometimes I feel like the assistant in the knife thrower's act at the circus, but it's all inverted, a sick joke. As if someone is throwing daggers at me in the pitch dark and I have to catch them, and every time I miss, somebody gets to die. I'm seeing the body of a young woman in a forest ... someone watching ... A car from nowhere ... so much blood ... Find the girl find the killer, find the girl find the killer ...'

Annie stopped mid-flow, imploring me with sunken, dark eyes. 'Does any of this make any sense to you?'

I told her as much as she needed to know. I couldn't have burdened her with the whole story. But I told her about Enid Lazzari. Out of curiosity, I suppose.

'Enid Lazzari is the key,' Annie said in a hoarse masculine voice that made me jump. It sounded as if another being had escaped from a prison deep in her bowels while her body rocked backwards and forwards.

'Enid Lazzari is a quack,' I retorted sharply. I grabbed her hands and held them tight. 'Annie, you've got to get a hold of yourself. This is getting way out of control.'

Slowly the rocking eased up. 'Poor clever Paola,' Annie said finally, staring at the ocean through the salt-crusted window, as if I wasn't there, as if she was talking to someone else about me. 'Determined to face up to this all alone. Tackling life on her terms.' Her normal voice was back but it sounded distant, almost sardonic.

'Annie, are you okay?'

'I'm fine,' she said, giving herself a little shake before she looked at me again. 'I should have told you, but it wouldn't have changed anything.'

'Should have told me what, Annie?'

'Do you have a cigarette?' She looked around with a desperate look in her eyes.

'You don't smoke, Annie.'

She stared at me as if I had just said something stupid. 'I could start again. I only stopped because Massimo didn't want me to, with Max on the way. My sisters say it interferes with their readings if they smoke, that the channels get plugged. Is that why you don't want me to smoke, in case my channels get plugged?'

'If you really want a cigarette, I'll ask the manager; he smokes,' I said steadily, uncertain of this other belligerent Annie who spoke with a stranger's paranoia.

She rubbed a hand across her forehead. 'Forget it.'

'Annie, I need to know about Daniel.'

'About Daniel – what should I tell you? There are always the other Daniels with him, they never leave him alone, always following, following, wherever he goes, awake or asleep, a burden to bear. This lifetime overlaid on other lifetimes. Some cannot see it, but he dreams it. Many women floating, attached to him. Like long-dead ribbons on a tree that cannot be shaken off. I was afraid for you but I sensed he loved you deeply, confusing. I hoped the others were in the past.'

As Annie talked, the air grew icicles around her. She shrank away within herself, her blue lips moving mechanically. Her face was as whitely set as the gesso my mother used to sculpt, only the eyes burning and huge, bonfires encircled with yellow-purple shadows.

I shuddered. 'Annie, let's go. You've told me enough.'

But Annie could be stubborn. 'The spirits are saying that Enid Lazzari is the key. She stayed out of sight in the shadows, too clever for us.'

'Annie, you need to rest.'

'Yes, I must sleep. And you can switch that thing off now. I'm done.' Annie had learnt to rely on a digital recorder whenever she felt one of her attacks coming on, because she had so little recall of what she saw. She had shoved the device into my hand the minute

I'd opened the door and found her trembling on my doorstep.

Her willow frame staggered against me as she stood up. I gave her my arm and she held onto me all the way back to the flat, her breathing laboured, each step an effort of will.

She asked me to call her after an hour and fell asleep almost immediately under the duvet on my bed. When I woke her up an hour later, I asked if she wouldn't mind telling Nathan what she'd told me. I warmed up some Heinz soup and buttered thick slices of bread to eat with it. The sleep had done her good. 'I'm famished,' Annie announced, munching bread while she waited for the hot soup to cool down. When she'd wiped the bowl clean she said she was still hungry for something sweet. After a quick look at what was in my fridge, Nathan offered to make baked apples in the oven with fresh custard – it wouldn't take long – if I could find us a lemon somewhere. I managed to get one from Sharon.

Annie couldn't get over it.

'These are yummy,' she said, staring at a spoonful of baked apple with lemon-yellow custard dripping off. 'Really good. My husband couldn't cook to save his life.' She laughed bitterly. 'Boy, bad choice of words. He's dead, in case Paola hasn't had the chance to brief you yet.'

'I bet you cook so well he didn't have to learn,' Nathan said gallantly into the awkward silence.

'I cook in the Afrikaans way,' Annie said slowly, eying him thoughtfully. 'Rys, vleis en aartappels. Massimo never liked my cooking. He preferred to eat Italian takeaway at work with the other detectives.'

I waded in. 'Annie, is there anything else about the girl? We don't have much time.' She shook her head. It was all on the recording. She would go to bed now, if we didn't mind.

Nathan joined me on the balcony after he'd finished listening. 'Is that sister-in-law of yours for real? How much did you tell her?'

'It was late. I just emailed the photo and said she should call me. Annie comes from a family of psychics. That's why Daniel was hanging around the park, Nathan. Simone must have run away.'

The speaking aloud of a child's name is a serious matter. It cannot be retracted. The woman I have become catches her breath as a girlish shadow slips through a crack and crosses to my world; a logjam has been loosened. Now it is a question of time.

I could feel Nathan's eyes on me.

'Well, she's safe at home at the moment,' he said laconically.

'That's not what you said last night.'

'That was whisky talk. Sometimes it gets to you, all the smoke and mirrors. We blink and some kid disappears. The whole thing's probably another red herring. They dig to give us the run-around.'

'You don't really believe that.'

'I kept an eye on her like you asked; the kid's been going to school every day. She gets driven there and back by a security guard who doubles as a driver, the same times every day. It's not a good environment for a kid but everything looks normal on the surface.

'I haven't seen her this week but I've spoken to the pharmacy delivery guy who dropped some medicines off. He said they were for the kid, who was sick. He also happened to mention she wouldn't be missing much because it's the last week of school before the December holidays.'

'You've told me what kind of people these are. In the Company's Garden you said she was a babe in the woods. The babes in the story *died,* Nathan. You've got to get her out. Annie says there are closed doors in the house and unspeakable things happen there.'

I told him about my brother's death. How Annie was spot-on but way too late. How she didn't think she'd be able to go on if that happened again.

'You're asking me to break the law.'

'I know what I'm asking, Nathan. There's no one else to do it. You know your way around the property and the security setup. Annie says Simone's in serious danger.' I was gripped by the same panic that had brought Annie to my doorstep. 'What if Annie's right and we sit back and let it happen? Besides, they won't be expecting you.'

Nathan considered the far horizon.

'They'll put me behind bars and keep me there this time,' he said. 'It's one thing to walk around the perimeter; it's another thing to get in past a high-tech surveillance system.'

Out at sea, glowing ships loaded with cargo waited to come into harbour. The seductive night-time sounds of human voices and music from the restaurants, interlaced with the energetic roar of traffic, reached us high up on the balcony. What was one adolescent girl in such a big, busy world?

'Remember that story you told me about Heidi and her village? What if somebody could have changed things?'

He clasped his hands on top of his head and stuck his long, brand-attired legs out in a contemplative pose. For a moment he reminded me of the Daniel I'd married. That curious way he had of being relaxed and alert at the same time. I wasn't even sure who this man was, but it hardly mattered. I looked away.

'There are thirteen ships waiting,' I said. 'The harbour must be full. Daniel counted them every night.'

Murmuring voices and laughter filtered up through the salt-impregnated air, against the ever-present backdrop of soughing palm-leaf fronds and crashing waves. The balcony floated above the street. We could have been in a dream.

Nathan stood up abruptly. 'I'll check it out.'

An hour later he was back.

'There's a black Mercedes SUV registered in Sarrazin's name.' His excitement was palpable. 'The licence number starts with CA 777 just like she said. It's not one of the cars they normally use. It's too much of a coincidence to be a lucky guess.'

'Does that mean you'll do it?'

'You wait here with your sister-in-law,' Nathan said. 'If you don't hear from me by 7 am, call that detective friend of yours in France. Tell him what's happened.'

'Are you going in alone?'

'It's best you know nothing in case it doesn't come off. At the worst, I'll be a housebreaker. They won't trace it back to you.'

'What about Elijah?'

'I can't be worrying about Elijah. It's less risky if I go alone.'

'Is there anyone else I should call? What about your girlfriend?'

For a moment he looked blank, then he said, 'You keep my phone. Once a week, Heidi calls to tell me she's okay. After she calls, throw the phone into the sea. Got that?'

'Got it.'

'If something happens to me, you take Yoshi. Don't give her to Heidi. She'll forget to feed her.'

'*Me*? What's going to happen to you?'

'She likes chicken with rice and a little bit of boiled egg, no fish or meat, no sauce, no titbits. Maltese don't look good fat.'

'Dogs and I don't get along, Nathan.'

'You'll get along, trust me. The two of you are similar, both real sassy and smart.'

'Is that a compliment?'

'She's way cuter than you.' He gave me a crooked grin. 'That husband of yours is a fool. If I don't make it and he ever finds his way back, tell him that from me. Here's a key for my flat, I've got a spare.'

A half hour later the phone rang.

'You have to fill up her water bowl with fresh water every day. Maltese get kidney problems.'

'Nathan, she's a princess.'

'Now you're talking!' The line went dead.

At 6.27 am, an exhausted Nathan called from a public phone. 'I couldn't get her out, Paola, they were onto me. I just managed to get away.'

'Nathan, are you okay? Where are you?'

'I've seen her. I woke up the housekeeper and with a bit of persuasion she showed me where the girl was. Your sister-in-law was right. She's been sedated. My guess is she ran away again and they're not taking any chances this time. There's a whole living area under the garages but there's some weird shit down there. Maybe they use it for the films. I tried, Paola. The housekeeper said she was supposed to bath her and get her ready. I disabled the surveillance cameras but she must have pressed a panic button while my eyes were on the girl because next thing I know Sarrazin is charging down the stairs waving a firearm around.'

'Nathan! Are you hurt?'

'Hey, don't worry about me. I'm practically immortal. I even managed to get some footage.'

'Nathan, where are you? Are you losing blood? I'll come and get you.' I could hear myself babbling hysterically, unable to absorb the fact that I'd nearly got Nathan killed.

'Paola, listen to me. I'm in good hands. Elijah's driving me to a doctor who gets paid to keep things quiet. Tell that French detective what your sister-in-law said, that the girl is somehow connected to the killing of all those women. And somebody needs to feed Yoshi.'

'Should I tell him about Jack and the wire?' I felt sick asking it.

There was a short silence. 'No, not yet. Not unless we have to. The footage of the girl should be enough for them to act.'

I sat staring at the phone. I had naively believed we wouldn't need the police. What had I been thinking? If Nathan had brought her to me, what would I have done? Kept her prisoner in the apartment and delivered food to her with a stocking over my head? Blindfolded her and deposited her on the steps of the Department of Social Affairs? I risked losing Daniel forever. The ball of string had escaped from the basket and now it was speeding downhill, unravelling faster than I could ever hope to run.

I phoned Detective Olmi on his private number, my fingers trembling so hard I had to redial twice. Annie was standing next to me, wrapping the cord of her dressing gown around her clenched fist as if it was packing tape.

I told Olmi the girl Simone Sarrazin, adopted daughter of Albert and Nada Sarrazin of Cape Town, South Africa could lead the police to the murderer or murderers of Celestine and the other Paris women, and probably many missing girls as well, and that she was in mortal danger. I told him that the PI Celestine had once paid to follow my husband went to the Sarrazin house to get the girl out after my psychic sister-in-law said there was no time to be wasted if we were to save the girl's life.

'Maybe she's already dead!' I wailed. She can't be dead.

'Merde!' Olmi cursed all the amateur detectives of the world with Gallic fury. He told me the story was *bizarre* and *blobbering* wasn't going to help anybody. I pulled myself together. After asking some pointed questions he asked to speak to my sister-in-law. To my relief, Annie told him calmly about the black SUV and the tinted glass and the number plate starting with the letters CA 777. He asked to speak to me again.

'What is this girl to you?'

'She is my husband's daughter.'

There, I've said it. Another thing that cannot be undone.

'The *hosband* who has *disappeared*?' His incredulous French accent made it sound like an exotic malady.

'The same one.'

'Diable!' After a moment's pause, he said I should stay next to the phone. And I should tell that foolish PI who risked his licence to have a copy of that video ready to be delivered to an address he would give me. He would set up a conference call to the inspector in the South African Police Service who already knew my case. He would call me back. We would get the girl out.

Annie said she'd catch a Rikkis taxi to Nathan's flat and feed Yoshi. She might stay for a couple of days; Nathan would need somebody to change his bandages. I could reach her at Nathan's. I gaped open-mouthed at my sister-in-law.

'Annie, he has a girlfriend. They've been together for years.'

She stood in the doorway, a faraway expression on her face. 'No one can change what they are to each other.'

And then she was gone, head ducked into the cold wind that howled down the corridor.

Olmi was as good as his word. An unmarked police car was immediately despatched to watch the house while the necessary paperwork was done to authorise the removal of the girl from the property. The child protection unit was called in to assist Klaus Knappman and his team. A day later, the Special Crimes police stopped a black SUV with tinted glass and a number plate starting with the letters CA 777 leaving the property. Just after 9 am South

African time on 14 December 2006, Albert and Nada Sarrazin were arrested and an unconscious Simone Sarrazin was removed from her adoptive parents' care. The area was cordoned off with yellow tape and the police searched the house. Various articles pertinent to the case were removed, including ten boxes of video tapes that the Sarrazins had kept catalogued in a walk-in safe. Simone was taken straight to hospital where she was examined by a doctor before being bathed and put on a rehydration drip. I was free to visit her. Detective Olmi had informed the South African authorities the rescued child was a relative of mine.

Simone

I SAT NEXT TO THE BED WAITING for her to come round, preparing my first careful words to the girl who might very well be my husband's daughter. I had several hours to gaze at her. Her face was framed by shoulder-length strawberry blonde hair with light freckles dotted across pale plump cheeks. She slept with her mouth slightly open. Physically, she was taller and bigger than the elfin Dominique, the only girl around her age I could make comparisons with. Her limbs seemed disproportionately long and ungainly, in the way of young shoots that grow in unexpected spurts. Somehow I knew that her feet, hidden from view under sheets, would be bigger than mine. Even though she was unconscious, with a shroud of youthful vulnerability over her, it was impossible not to be aware of the pubescent breasts and rosy lips. The child's hands, with the fingertips ending in chewed-off schoolgirl nails, were immensely reassuring.

It was to my advantage that Simone Sarrazin did not exist in the files of the French welfare authorities. There was no record of her adoption or even her birth. Effectively, she did not exist in the eyes of France. A birth certificate copy obtained from the school had proved to be fake. Since she was found on South African soil, the South African welfare authorities had jurisdiction over her case.

She opened her eyes when I wasn't looking.

'Who are you? Where am I?' She sounded woozy.

I took a big breath. I had no idea what Daniel had told her; he could have said he was her uncle for all I knew. Stick to the facts.

'You're in hospital. I'm Paola. I'm married to Daniel. You're safe now.' I sounded like a character from a hackneyed Hollywood script.

Her blue eyes were flecked with worry. They seemed enormous in her young, pale face, fringed by thick, dark eyelashes and eyebrows that were in unusual contrast to the shining fair hair. What was I thinking when I looked into those bottomless eyes as they focused on me? I saw the folder names fanned on the screen. *Grace. Hela. Isabelle. Jasmine. Rita. Tamara. Veronique.* How many more of you are there? I struggled to maintain my composure.

'Where's my mother?'

Her question took me by surprise but I did my best in the circumstances. 'The police have both your adoptive parents in custody. They were taking you away. We had to stop them.' I searched desperately for the right thing to say.

She struggled to raise herself, looking around the white room with dazed, wide eyes. 'Then I want Sarie.'

I'd read the servants' statements to the police – Sarie was the elderly housekeeper. She had stuck to the terms of her employment, not giving anything away and refusing to implicate her powerful employers.

'I believe she's gone to her son in Swellendam.'

She sank back into her pillow, her teeth clamped onto her lip.

'Can you talk about what happened? Why you were locked up in that room? There are some people who would like to ask you some questions.'

She flipped onto her side away from me, facing the window. That was our first conversation. I asked for more time for her before the questions started, and Esmeralda, the welfare official appointed to her case, agreed with me, saying there was no point in going too fast. We would have to gain her trust. 'But we'll probably only get a few days' grace. They can't hold the parents indefinitely without charging them,' Esmeralda said. 'They'll be expecting my report. Her statement is crucial if we're going to keep them behind bars.'

At my first meeting with Esmeralda, she'd given me a long appraising look and asked if I knew that the little mademoiselle in the hospital bed had a rap sheet longer than her own arm, and she had a long arm and she'd seen some fancy rap sheets but nothing like this one for an eleven-year-old girl. She must have seen my panic-stricken look because she relented. It wasn't so much a rap sheet as reported incidents. Every single time the person reporting the incident had declined to lay charges. That took some important friends in high places and mucho moolah. Still, there were some who'd call her a juvenile delinquent and they'd be those who knew what they were talking about. But experience had taught her every one of these kids had a soft side; you just had to find a way to get to them. And kids were more resilient than we sometimes thought. Did I have any idea what I was letting myself in for?

'No. Not really. It's just something I have to do.'

'Mmm. I didn't think so. So, a piece of advice if you want to make this work. When in doubt, resort to the truth. These kids need to know the absolute truth from the people who care for them. It's the number-one rule to getting them rehabilitated. They're like drunken sailors; the only thing they know is a shifting deck and stormy seas and bad times. You make sure you give her the truth from day one and you've got a small chance of reaching her; you lie to her, you haven't got a hope in hell. She can handle it, believe me. You're the one who's going to battle with the truth, not her.'

'How do I get through to her? She's closing me out.'

'Patience is the key. You're going to need it in bucketsful. I'm guessing patience is something that doesn't come naturally to you, from the way you keep looking at your watch.' There was a meaningful pause before she continued. 'You're going to have to leave your work at work when you come to the hospital, and concentrate on her. Talk to her. Make sure it's about her and not about you. Give her good reasons to act like any other normal teenager. When she tells you she hates you, don't overreact, make her laugh. If she pushes you away, stay close to her; that means making time for you and her to get to know each other. Don't let her drift away into her own world. Above all, don't ever let her down. If you say you'll be somewhere at a certain time, make sure you're there, drop everything else. If you get it right, you'll be the first adult in her life that she can trust. After that, love's easy.'

I stared at her nonplussed. 'That's a long list.'

'Who said parenting was easy?' Esmeralda asked.

I went back to work and rearranged my schedule for the week so I could visit her twice a day, once in the morning and once in the evening. It wasn't a good time; it's never a good time on projects. Time equals money. It was hard to concentrate and take any of it seriously. I found myself harbouring heretic thoughts. So what if a key project milestone is missed? It's not going to change the history of the world.

I sat next to Simone in hospital for three consecutive days – a total of six visits. Pushed into a blind corner, I found myself talking about Daniel nonstop. Perhaps it was more cathartic for me than for her. I told her about his daily routine, how he loved pasta, what a great chef he was, what kind of books he read, how he was always talking to people, how he loved walking to the beach and drawing people.

One day I arrived early and she was sitting on a chair staring vacantly into space while the nurses put clean sheets on her bed. I was right: her long feet were at least a size bigger than mine. But they lacked my hard ridges and bony arch. They were the narrow, gently sloped feet of an adolescent child. A perfectly formed miniature dragon with wings was tattooed on the outside of her right ankle. She refused to acknowledge my presence, climbing back onto the freshly made bed and turning away as soon as she could, folding herself back into her cocoon. I tried moving the chair to the other side of the bed but she simply rolled over again like a mute rock rolling out of my reach. Esmeralda sent in a trauma centre psychologist who had experience with abused children but she had no more luck than I had. Simone refused to reply to any of the questions.

Meanwhile, we'd had a break. According to Detective Knappman, the videos removed from the house, together with the footage Nathan had handed over, were enough to keep the Sarrazins behind bars for a very long time. The French had formally requested access to the DVDs. If they could spot anything related to one of the dead women, then Sarrazin could be linked to the murders. In my calls to Olmi he had never questioned that there might be a connection. Annie had told all of us what we needed to hear.

When I asked about the other girls at risk, he said they were investigating the Sarrazins' link to the online auctions. The Internet was the same as every great modern city: beneath the world of skyscrapers and highways was a giant underground sewer. It was easier for the rats in this underworld than for the cat.

After three days of talking to Simone's rigid back I decided to try something different. Klaus arranged for me to get inside the house accompanied by one of his detectives. Simone's room looked like I imagined any teenager's room would look, just emptier. There were no soft toys on the bed or study books on the desk. The only decoration was a poster of Britney Spears with a pierced navel and belly ring above the bed and a radio on the bedside table. Someone had left a photograph lying next to an empty frame on a shelf next to the bed. It was a photo of Simone with Nada Sarrazin, the two of them leaning head to head and laughing straight at the camera, looking more like two precocious sisters than adoptive mother and child. I had to remind myself that the heavily made-up teenager in the photo was in fact a not-quite-twelve-year-old child, now lying in a hospital bed until her fate was decided. The police who searched the house must have judged it to be unimportant. I slipped it into my handbag when the policeman turned away.

I phoned Annie on my mobile. She'd left after a couple of days, saying Max needed her now. Nathan had brought her to say goodbye on the way to the airport. While she used the bathroom he showed me his bandaged calf. I found it hard to ask what had transpired between her and Nathan, as if that would make me an accomplice.

'What must I look for? I don't even know what I'm doing here.'

'You followed your instincts, Paola. Trust yourself. You've come a long way since you married Daniel.'

'And look where that's got me.'

She laughed. 'Look for Smarties.'

'Look for *Smarties*? Are you serious?'

A faint sigh came down the line. 'I can't give you an explanation, Paola, you asked me a question, and that's what I saw.'

'I don't know if she knows, Annie. That he's her father.'

'You need more time.'

The young black policeman stuck his head around the door.

'I need more time.'

'No problem. I'll wait downstairs.'

They'd told me that the crime scene had been dusted for prints and all evidence removed so I was free to look around. After half an hour, the young policeman was back. He found me standing in the middle of the room no wiser than when I'd walked in. I'd searched every drawer, every cupboard, and nothing. I must have looked desperate.

'What are you looking for?'

'Smarties.'

He didn't seem to think I'd gone mad. Instead he said, 'Have you looked under the bed?'

'It's solid,' I pointed at the wood peeping out from under the duvet cover.

'It looks solid, but it isn't,' he said, reaching down and pulling out a second bed that fitted underneath. 'I used to have one of these. My dad built it himself. That what you looking for?'

The previous searchers had overlooked her treasure trove. There they were, a hidden stash of a thousand Smarties boxes, or thereabouts. I wasn't counting for once. Somebody loved Smarties, that's all I knew. I sat down on the wall-to-wall carpet and felt something moist slip slowly down my cheek. I put a hand up and touched it. At the age of thirty, after what seemed like a lifetime of abstention, Paola Dante-de Luc was brushing away tears for something as mundane as relief.

The next day, they did blood tests to find out what drugs she'd been given because they were worried about her sleeping too much. I'd learnt to come when the nurses were busy with her so she'd be awake. As soon as Simone saw me in the doorway she did her usual trick of turning away to face the window, this time with a thermometer in her mouth. I took my place on the chair next to the bed. When the flurry of bed checks was over and the nurses had moved on, I shook some Smarties from the box. As the multicoloured sweets rattled their signature click-clack tune she swung around, her eyes skating over the candy-coated chocolates in my hand. I popped a few into my mouth.

'Would you like a Smartie?' I asked innocently, holding the big box up. 'I like the purple ones best.'

She eyed me warily. 'Smarties are for little kids.'

I acted nonchalant. 'Everybody's a little kid some of the time. I won't tell if you don't.'

She held out her hand. 'Okay.'

Her hands shut around the Smarties like a squirrel hoarding nuts for a long, cold winter. She turned away again, but it seemed different this time. It was more like she was eating her Smarties in private.

Instead of the pondered carefully weighed words I'd prepared the night before, I found myself telling her about my first proper 'date' with Daniel; how he took me to see a circus act with twenty performing cats and one cat that could talk. She rolled around to face me and looked me in the eyes.

'You don't hate me?'

'Why should I hate you?'

'You're not my mother.'

'No, I'm not your mother.' Did she know Nada Sarrazin was not her mother either?

She sat up in bed with her hair all tousled. 'You don't need to worry. I know I'm adopted. Nada told me.'

Silently I thanked all the gods I didn't believe in. But not a word about her real mother. It was entirely possible, even probable, that Daniel had no idea who her biological mother was.

The clear blue eyes watched me. 'Is Daniel okay?'

'I don't know. I haven't seen him for over a year. One day he left our apartment and didn't come back.'

She flopped back onto the pillows and closed her eyes. I stood up to leave but she opened her eyes again.

'Could the cat really talk?'

'I don't know. Daniel and the cat master became friends. He told me a story about the talking cat's grandmother: the first talking cat. I'll tell it to you some time if you like.'

'Whatever.' She licked at the colourful stains on her palm.

'I'm leaving the Smarties here for you.' I put the box on the side table. 'Try not to eat them all at once or you won't have space for supper.' Did I actually say that?

'What*ever*. Can you go now?'

That night I hummed *Take a Chance on Me!*, an Abba song I'd heard on the radio coming home, as I cooked a meal for myself, Elijah and Nathan. The roast chicken was a touch overdone and the grilled vegetables were a bit charred but they were edible.

'The kid has an addictive personality,' Elijah said gloomily. 'All the signs are there.'

'What kid doesn't like Smarties?' Nathan shrugged as he fed Yoshi small pieces of tender chicken flesh off the thigh.

'A stash of Smarties boxes hidden under the bed isn't normal. The kid's got a problem, just like any other addiction,' Elijah said stubbornly.

'Come on, Elijah. She actually stopped ignoring me and talked to me today. That's a step forward isn't it? What child in her circumstances wouldn't be confused? *I'm* confused for God's sake! She doesn't know who to trust any more.'

Nathan raised an eyebrow at Elijah.

'I saw that! You're wondering if I can do this. I know it's weird but after all the effort we've put into finding her and getting her away from them I feel as if I'm responsible for her, at least until Daniel comes back. I'm not going to give up on her. Isn't that amazing?'

Nathan poured me more wine and looked over at Elijah, holding the bottle up enquiringly. Elijah shook his head. 'Where's your laptop, Paola? And the earphones? I'll listen in peace while you two finish off the bottle, since Nathan's heard it already.' I ignored the petulant tone and handed him the recording we'd made in the restaurant on the promenade. Annie had been spot-on with Simone. If only we could decipher what she saw about Daniel.

Elijah sat on a stool at the kitchen bar counter with his back to us and listened intently, scribbling notes feverishly. Nathan left soon after. Twenty minutes later, Elijah stood up and said he would be going as he wanted to send off some emails. There was some interesting stuff on the recording. He ran his hands furiously through his hair as he talked. The static made it stand up straight in the air as if he'd just had shock treatment. At the door, Elijah stopped and came back, a resolute expression on his pale face.

'I have a confession to make,' he said.

'You do?'

'The day you let me check the study I found something under Mr de Luc's desk pad.' He reached inside the houndstooth jacket. 'I've been carrying it with me for luck.'

I unfolded the sheet of paper. It was a sketch of a teenage girl in school uniform. *The girl at the bus stop*. I looked at him open-mouthed. 'You knew all along.'

Elijah nodded, his eyes moist, rubbing his forehead. 'My sister was a runaway. We never found her.' And then he was off, doing that funny trot-shuffle of his and forgetting to shut the door behind him.

The next day I was once again given the silent treatment. But I had reached Simone the previous day. I would reach her again. I would not give up. I remembered her first question, the confusion in her eyes.

'Shall we speak about your adoptive mother?'

She swung around to face me, her eyes flame-blue with accumulated rage and her nostrils flaring.

'Nada hasn't done anything. It's him. Now because of you

she's in prison. It's all *your* fault. She was going to take me away with her. I don't want to live with you. You think just because my father's gone I'll live with you and then everything will be fine, but that's stupid. If he's gone he's just gone. *You're not my mother!'* She screamed the most hurtful words she could muster into my shocked face. A nurse hurried in and said it would be best if I left. Her tone didn't brook argument.

I drove home on autopilot, my head spinning like one of those plastic windmills on a stick that children blow at with relentless glee. *You think just because my father's gone I'll live with you.* At least we could stop pretending on that score. Simone believed Daniel was her father. But there was still no real proof. At least she was talking, getting things out of her system. That had to be a good thing.

The next day I was back. The nurse in attendance eyed me doubtfully. I settled myself down in the same hard chair and waited for her to leave.

'I just have one thing to say. If Nada was going to get you away, why wasn't she alone in the car with you?' I didn't mention the private jet to Frankfurt waiting at the airport or the substantial sum transferred from a Swiss bank into Albert Sarrazin's Paris bank account the same day the black SUV was stopped, a sum of money for which he had no explanation except that he was a businessman involved in big deals all over the world.

Detective Olmi informed me unofficially that we, Nathan, Elijah and I, like the proverbial fools who rush in, had walked into a hornet's nest. For the past five years, global intelligence agencies had co-operated in the search for the kingpin of an international porn ring that auctioned children on the Internet. Simone's future had been decided in such an auction. If Sarrazin was not the kingpin, he was certainly very high up. They were getting closer to the shadowy crime king who had eluded them for so long.

A small, muffled noise came from the hunched-up figure. I walked around the bed and stood watching her. Without thinking about it, I reached out and moved her wheat-field hair away from her eyes.

'*Go away*!' Her shrill scream brought the nurse hurrying back. But this time I held up a commanding hand and after a moment of hesitation she left us alone. I stayed where I was, looking into the comically scrunched up face.

'I can't go away. There's nowhere for me to go. I'm going to keep coming every day. I'm never going to give up on you. You'd better get used to the idea. Your father wanted me to bring you home. I don't know why he couldn't do it himself, but it doesn't matter any more.

'I don't want to take anyone else's place. If Nada's innocent the police will let her go.' Her eyes remained stubbornly closed. 'Could we try just being friends? I know I need a friend right now.'

'Friends like each other. I don't like you,' the muttered response came.

'Well, we both like Smarties. That's a starting point,' I said weakly. 'And we both like Daniel,' I added in a burst of inspiration.

She opened one eye and surveyed me carefully.

'Just friends,' I repeated. Don't blow it.

'Can I have a tissue?'

She sat up and blew her nose like a trombone. I held my hand out. She stared uncertainly at it for a moment and then at me, and then she slowly reached out and took it. I felt her warm long fingers rest within my hand, as soft as feathers roosting against my palm. We shook very formally and ceremonially. I felt like a woman drowning in quicksand who had been saved by a hand that pulled her to the surface just when her lungs were about to burst.

A week before Christmas, Simone was released from hospital and put into a safe house. Esmeralda warned me it could take months to sort out the paperwork and more months before it came before the children's court. The case was unusual and there were no valid documents for the child. With Esmeralda's help I obtained permission to take Simone out for Christmas and then at weekends. If the forms I completed and signed had not made it abundantly clear who would be held responsible if she misbehaved or should go missing, then my interview with the steely-eyed matron left me in no doubt.

The main building where I collected her was within a gated complex. It was more of a reformatory than a safe house, with burglar bars on all the windows. A heavy door with a padlock led to the uninviting dormitory with rough bunk beds and scrubbed concrete floors she shared with nineteen other girls of mixed ages, cultures and religions. On Christmas day, I had to sidestep my mother's invitation to a big family lunch. I'd been fobbing her off with excuses for a while. This time I told her Daniel and I were going somewhere on our own because he'd been away so much lately, and he had to go away again to see his agent in France. I had become a glib liar.

Simone and I went on like this for a couple of months. Perhaps it worked in my favour, her drab surroundings and the reformatory conditions, because to my surprise she never refused to come. She seemed to be coping with the conditions and the other girls.

'Do the other girls ever bother you?'

'Why should they bother me?' Puzzled, over-innocent voice mimics my concern.

'Some of them look a lot older than you.' Some of them look like hardened criminals.

'You're so over-the-top. You can relax, they leave me alone.' Words accompanied by shaking of head and superior teenage tone.

Some of our excursions were more successful than others. I was determined not to act as her keeper, so I let her go off on her own if she asked, on condition that we met up again at a designated place and time.

Mostly our outings together went off without incident, with her taking what she needed from my time and purse. Often she was silent all the way back to the safe house, the popping of bubblegum the only sound coming from her as I held inane one-sided conversations. Occasionally I was forced to go looking for her. It was a game of hide and seek intended to test my patience to the limit rather than a serious attempt to run away, but each time it happened I entered a zone of terror alternating with helpless rage. When I found her, my relief was so enormous that it was astonishingly difficult to decide whether I wanted to yell at her or hug her. I learnt to act nonchalant.

She set out to provoke me in whatever way she could. When I gave her some money to spend as she liked, she came back with an item of clothing labelled Toxic Candy that seemed more appropriate for a punk rock groupie than an eleven-year-old. The following Saturday, she turned herself into a walking noxious cloud of cheap and nasty fragrances. I had no idea how to handle these situations except to hang in there.

One Saturday, I was told the matron would like to see me. I'd hardly sat down on the straight-backed visitor's chair when she reached into a drawer and held up a black bra top resplendent with shiny silver safety pins. She pointed out that if Simone continued to flout rules and exert a bad influence on the other girls, her 'out visits' privilege would be revoked. She meant every word of it. I only had one Simone to worry about. She had a whole flock of them eying freedom.

Emotionally pistol-whipped and ashamed of my own impotence in the face of adolescent provocation, I crept out to the car. Five minutes later, Simone flung the door open and plonked herself down into the passenger seat. She gave me a quick sideways glance, before looking straight ahead and chewing her thumbnail. I put the offending top, now back in its shop bag, on her lap and gloomily suggested changing it for something that fitted the dress code. The alternative was to give it away to a needy prostitute and cut our losses. Her lips twitched but she was giving nothing away without a struggle.

'Whatever.'

We eventually changed the inappropriate garment for a T-shirt both Simone and I could live with.

She had weekly sessions with a psychologist. I was not a psychologist. I suspected I wanted to be something like a mother. I read everything I could find on teenagers and the art of being a stepmother – that title seemed the closest fit to our unorthodox situation.

Once, in a midnight call to Annie, I must have been feeling sorry for myself, dumped in the deep end, because she asked what my motives were. Had I really considered my options? After all, the girl was safe now.

'If I stopped to think about it, I wouldn't do it,' I snapped at her morosely. 'You're the one who's always telling me I'm too rational in my thinking, now you're telling me I'm not rational enough!' She was right, I wasn't certain of my motives but I knew if I thought about it too hard I might give up.

Each time I tracked Simone down with bloodhound zeal after she'd ignored my specific instructions as to where and when we should meet, it felt as if I deserved a reward of some sort, maybe a chunk of iron-rich raw meat. One Saturday in the mall I came around the corner and found her pouting in a restaurant chair, long legs swinging over the armrest.

'You're late!' she burst out.

'Am I?' I said calmly. 'Now you know what it feels like.' I picked up the menu. 'I'm starving. What shall we eat? Have they got fried banana flapjacks?'

A thought had started to crystallise. I paid a visit to Esmeralda, the fairy godmother of forgotten children who didn't mince words.

'You're sure about this?' She looked doubtful, a frown of concern marring the normally serene features. 'You know you can't disappoint her? These children grow a hard skin over each disappointment and each time it happens it becomes harder to reach them.'

'She's a rebellious teenage girl with a history of bad behaviour. No family wanting to adopt will take her. She'll be kept in that awful place until she's eighteen and then she'll do something stupid and end up in prison and I won't be able to live with myself.'

'The first step is to apply to become her foster parent. That will mean you can take her home with you. After that, it's a long, difficult bureaucratic process if you want to legally adopt her,' Esmeralda warned. 'And it will probably end up being expensive. Not just in money – it'll take up your time,' she said pointedly. 'The foster route means the state remains responsible for her if it doesn't work out.'

'It'll work out. It has to. I'll organise things at work. Let's get the foster application going.'

* * *

In the midst of all of this, something came up at the office: an international IT conference in Amsterdam I was expected to attend. Amsterdam, city of tulips, Nicky's birth city. After two nights of not sleeping, I phoned Elijah.

'Elijah, I want to tell you about Nicky.'

'Nicky? Now? It's 2.30 in the morning, Paola. Some of us need a decent night's sleep so that we can face another shitty day. Tomorrow ...'

'Please, Elijah. Tomorrow I might change my mind. Some things are better told at dawn after you haven't slept for two days.'

'Did you say "please"?'

'Yes.'

'I've never once heard you say please. Are you sick? Do you need a doctor?'

'No, I'm not sick. You said "shitty". You've never been so unprofessional. So we're square. I'll make us some percolated coffee and I've got some biscotti my mom made. I think she just uses them as an excuse to come around and snoop. They're hard as rocks but you can dunk them. I know you're a secret dunker.'

There was silence for a moment.

'I give up. Just for you, Paola.'

'Thanks, Elijah. You're the PI every girl should have.'

'Compliments, compliments, flattery gets you everywhere.'

By the time he arrived he was fully awake.

'What happened to full disclosure?' Elijah demanded to know. 'That musketeer oath was quite something.'

'Don't scold, Elijah. I'm telling you now.'

I told him nearly everything about Nicky. I didn't tell him about the termination of pregnancy blip because that wouldn't assist the investigation.

Sipping a cup of strong coffee he listened, leaning forward, occasionally rubbing his unshaven chin but otherwise hardly moving. The sun was coming up as I finished, the first dilute light slipping through glass panes and curtains. Elijah straightened. 'Remember the private investigator rule "Follow the name"?'

'I remember.'

'You have to go and talk to this woman that was Nicky's nanny. Is Daniel running away from something in his past? Why the false documents? There's nobody else.'

Enid Lazzari, but she won't tell me anything. She wants me to find out for myself. As an act of eternal love.

'Nanny Hoogendoorn?' I recalled the dour, stout woman who'd shown no interest in my presence at the funeral. 'Why should she talk to me? Why don't *you* go and see her?'

Elijah eyed me reproachfully.

'How often do we get to tell the story of our life to someone who really wants to hear it? There are plenty of reasons why people eventually talk to you. You had a romantic relationship with her charge. This one's yours. Sometimes the PI goes in and sometimes the client goes. Whatever makes the most sense.

'I've spoken to my lawyer contact, who works in the copyright field,' he changed tack. 'He confirmed a Gabriel Kaas who writes thrillers under the Pocket Policiers label – it's a small niche publisher that doesn't advertise on the Internet – but nothing on Daniel de Luc, not even on the international computer systems police forces have access to. And that's the man you married. We're not getting anywhere in the Gabriel Montaigne direction either. Do you have any idea how many Montaignes there are in France? We need to know more about his background.' He rubbed his face hard with his hand and then turned his sleep-deprived bloodhound eyes on me. 'Do you know the difference between Limbo and Hell?'

'No.'

'In Limbo everyone's still got a fighting chance. They're coming up with redemptive acts the angels have forgotten. It could go either way. In Hell they've given up.'

Elijah had no idea what he was proposing. Or maybe he knew exactly. Maybe my PI was as in touch with his sixth clairvoyant sense as he claimed. What if Nanny Hoogendoorn knew more than I could bear?

Nella bocca del lupo. Into the mouth of the wolf. The rallying call of my ancestors.

The next day I will call Nicky's glamorous mother and invite her to have lunch with me. I will tell her I found a photo of Nicky after all these years. I will find the right moment to tell her I married Daniel, Nicky's best friend. But she is a woman of the world who has the reputation of having had several lovers herself so she will not be too surprised. I recall the veiled antagonism towards Daniel and wonder what it was all about. Once we have overcome our initial awkwardness, I will ask her casually about Nanny Hoogendoorn. I will say that I promised to look her up and now I have the opportunity to visit Amsterdam for work, could she let me have Nanny Hoogendoorn's contact details? She will look at me with a perfectly plucked raised eyebrow but I will give nothing away, and she will give me the address.

'You're a project manager, aren't you?' Elijah had said. 'You'll find a way.'

I saw that Elijah was right. I was tired of being in Limbo.

After all the initial fuss, it was surprisingly easy to get permission for Monica to visit Simone and take her out at the weekends for the time I was away. I warned Monica that Simone liked shopping and that she slipped off to music shops and clothes shops, especially YDE, and lost track of time. And she wasn't to go anywhere near a tattoo parlour. There was something I had to do. When I got back we would start making plans for Simone's twelfth birthday in March.

'She sounds like a girl after my own heart. I know exactly where I'm going to take her,' Monica said in her most lascivious voice. When I protested that she couldn't do anything that would jeopardise the fragile arrangement we had for the out visits, Monica winked suggestively with long, fluttery false eyelashes. 'Don't worry about a thing, honey bunch. I wouldn't take her anywhere I wouldn't take my own kid sister. If I had one, of course.'

When the Sun Comes Out, Snow Melts

THE NARROW BRONZE NAME PLAQUE on the door of the ground-floor apartment read 'Carolien Hoogendoorn'. I'd phoned her from South Africa as soon as the flight booking was confirmed. I'd allowed for three days before the conference. I explained who I was in Afrikaans, but she found the unfamiliar accent difficult to understand and asked me to speak in English. Yes, she remembered me. Why did I want to see her? Her direct manner, which had impressed itself on my memory, had not faded with time. I explained that my husband and Nicky used to be good friends, and my husband had been missing for some time. I was hoping she could help me with some information.

'What is your husband's name?'

'Daniel de Luc.' She remained utterly silent. I wondered if I'd lost her.

'Mevrouw Hoogendoorn, are you still there?'

'Yes, I am still here. You can come, but only you, no one else.'

Nanny Hoogendoorn was still a vigorous woman, although her hair was now snow-white. Later that morning, she used a walking stick to make her way to the bathroom, explaining that she suffered from gout occasionally.

'You have a specific purpose in being here?'

'Your English is excellent. I did not realise. We spoke so little at the funeral.'

'My English is excellent thanks to Daniel's mother.'

'Daniel's mother?' She had thrown salt over her shoulder and I was turned to stone. I had been led here by a potent concoction of memory and curiosity and shame, armed with a faded photograph.

She looked pityingly at me. 'Is it such a big thing for a man to have a mother? You don't know much about him, do you? And your kind wouldn't ask. What the eyes don't see the heart doesn't know about. She taught me that proverb. Marie. That was her name. She was my friend. I will make us some coffee and then I will tell you what I know. You can ask your questions after that. Do you have enough time?'

'I have all the time in the world.'

'Good,' she said simply. 'Then you have already learnt a lot from your troubles. Make yourself comfortable. There are some slippers belonging to my daughter Astrid in the bathroom, and clean socks in the basket. She won't mind. Your shoes are no good for listening to a long story.'

That night, I dreamt about Nicky's funeral. In my dream the black handbag from which Nanny Hoogendoorn had so efficiently dispensed tissues for the outpourings of grief had developed carnivorous tendencies. When I reached into the dark opening, pain ripped through my body, every nerve riveted to bone and sinew, my hand's flesh devoured by the subterranean creatures of a deep, deep black well to which her handbag was only an entrance. As I yanked my skeletal hand out, shreds of ligament and gore hanging, Nanny Hoogendoorn cackled with insane glee. I woke up in a state of abject terror, the spectres of total darkness baying for my blood on the fringes of consciousness. Gradually, I became aware that night light from the city of Amsterdam was filtering in through the heavy hotel curtains, separating the darkness like a black skin that could be rolled back. The night city pulsed with a remote ebb and flow of its own. A long-ago science lesson on a concept known as black box emissivity came back to me. An absolutely black box has a theoretical emissivity value of zero. In simple terms, zero heat is emitted. In reality, zero is never reached, but in a mathematical equation these ultimate confines are necessary to make the theory work. The pondering of science is a soothing exercise. A measure of calm restored, I switched the clock-radio on, turning the dials until I found a late-night music station. *I Shot the Sheriff* was playing.

She had met Marie at the Sea Point church. The pastor of their congregation, a big-hearted, generous man, had spoken to his gathered congregation about this talented young woman who spoke English, French and German, played the piano like an angel and was in urgent need of employment to support herself and her twelve-year-old son. If anyone was interested in her services as a language teacher – 'I know there are world travellers among you who would be keen to learn a new language!' – or as a tutor for their children – 'All the piano players have a seat reserved right next to God!' – he would like to talk to them after the service. He would himself vouch for her as a good human being. Let us pray.

Nanny Hoogendoorn was in the congregation that Sunday. She spoke to Daniel's mother and suggested that she should come to her employer's house with her son and give English lessons to her charge, a young Dutch boy just turned ten whose family had recently come to South Africa. They had spoken in French, a language Nanny Hoogendoorn knew adequately from her school days. A new life began for Marie and her son.

She did not know the whole story but she told me the parts she knew. Her knowledge of the early period of Marie's life was sketchy – Marie did not like to discuss it. Rien ne dure, she would say. Nothing lasts. But sometimes she made remarks. Nanny Hoogendoorn had worked out for herself that she had escaped from the clutches of a religious cult of some kind in Europe. The issue of her son's name had come up early, because of the discrepancy.

I pricked up my ears. Discrepancy?

Her full name was Marie-France Montaigne. She was the

daughter of a government official. When she fell pregnant with the love child of a musician and poet who went by the name of Antoine de Luc, she was sent away from Paris to live with an uncle, the harbour master of La Rochelle, a port town. Of her family, only Mirabelle, her middle sister, wrote to Marie in secret and sent money with postal orders. As far as Nanny knew, Mirabelle continued with this until Marie's death.

This had all come up when a residency permit had to be obtained. Marie had explained that her uncle had registered her baby as a Montaigne, against her express wishes. Later she had paid a priest to baptise him with the name she had chosen, Daniel, because she had always liked the story of Daniel in the Bible, and de Luc because she wanted him to know that his father was a good man. She had been very firm that her son should be known as Daniel de Luc.

Did she remember the son's name on the passport? Was it Gabriel?

Nanny Hoogendoorn shook her head. It was so long ago. She could not say any more.

How did they end up in South Africa? I asked.

Marie had taken all her meagre savings, mainly the money Mirabelle had sent, and bought a sea passage for herself and her boy to South Africa, determined to make a new start. For the rest, she had no knowledge of what had transpired in Marie's life to bring her to the good pastor's doorstep. Marie had taught her English sayings like 'It is no good crying over spilt milk' and 'It is all water under the bridge', and it was understood between them that Marie had no desire to speak of the past.

At first the two boys were cool towards one another but after watching the untutored boy engage in a mock match with his son, Mr van den Bogen suggested that he join the fencing class. Jan van den Bogen was a Dutch Olympic fencing champion in his time. His collection of ancient swords was displayed all over the house.

After that, Daniel was there nearly every day. If they were not being taught by Mr van den Bogen, then they were holding practise bouts, or diving into the swimming pool to cool off.

Cecilia van den Bogen, Nicky's mother and once small-time actress, had married Jan van den Bogen a year after the death of his first wife. Jan van den Bogen had insisted on the Greek name Nikos for his only son, in memory of his deceased wife who was of Greek origin. In Nanny Hoogendoorn's view, the young woman had been terminally bored. To the outside world she was always the fascinating and impeccably groomed Cecilia van den Bogen but in her own home she drank heavily and was prone to depression. Nicky was more comfortable with placid Nanny Hoogendoorn than with his highly strung mother who demanded extravagant shows of affection from him. There were frequent arguments over Daniel's presence in the house. Mrs van den Bogen accused her husband of being overly generous with the boy. But Mr van den Bogen would have none of her nonsense.

On the surface, things seemed to have settled down. Marie had enough work to support them and Daniel had adapted with remarkable ease to his new environment, the way the young often do. But Daniel gave his mother many problems. The boy – who, Marie said, even as a small child had had bad dreams and crept into his mother's bed – suffered from nightmares. He had a habit of wandering off – one could not call it running away, really, because he often returned on his own. But it was hard on Marie. She grew used to a loud knock on the door. The old pastor convinced a certain senior policeman, who was a member of his parish, to see to it that Daniel was not fingerprinted and classified as a teenage runaway in police archives.

In the meantime, Carolien Hoogendoorn and Marie Montaigne had become unlikely friends. After Nanny Hoogendoorn's husband developed a degenerative eye condition, she had become the sole breadwinner while her husband saw to the children. For twelve years she lived away from her family for ten months of the year as part of the van den Bogen household in South Africa, first as nanny to Nicky and then as chief housekeeper. She gave notice a year before Nicky's death, after her husband had passed away. Marie had been the one to suggest the English lessons to pass the time while they waited for the boys. She took her teaching work very seriously, and soon the English lessons became a pleasurable pastime for them both. And then Marie fell ill, a grave illness of the liver from which she would not recover.

Nanny Hoogendoorn sat without moving, her head bowed.

Can you tell me what happened to Daniel? I asked finally.

Marie Montaigne was rescued from a pauper's grave by the benevolence of Mr van den Bogen. He offered the boy a home but Daniel refused.

As soon as Marie had felt her illness, long before the fatal diagnosis, she had spoken to the old pastor about a place where Daniel could stay. Perhaps some sort of commune, but not too strict, she insisted. Somewhere in the open air without too many walls. A place was found in a small self-sufficient community of organic farmers near Hermanus. He attended school during the week and did farm work at weekends in exchange for board and lodging. Marie extracted a promise from her son that he would stay with them and abide by their rules until he was eighteen. And she asked Carolien Hoogendoorn to keep in touch with Daniel.

He might stop existing if nobody cared about him, he might disappear into the sewers and become a ghost among the living! And what if they came to take him back? Who would protect him from them!

That was how Marie talked on her deathbed, a terrible fever consuming her mind.

Nanny Hoogendoorn had tried to keep her promise by writing letters to Daniel, but he never replied. Meanwhile, the precocious Nicky was falling foul of the rules at his elite school in the Kwazulu-Natal midlands, where the only thing he excelled at was sport. He was caught drinking in school uniform and accused of selling dagga to other boys. I recalled the feverish eyes and the nervous irritability that had marked the last few months of my relationship with Nicky. I'd never considered that he might have been dependent on marijuana, or even something stronger. It had all seemed so harmless back then.

For about two years, the van den Bogens saw nothing of

Daniel. Then, one day, Marie's boy knocked at their front door again. Nanny Hoogendoorn could not believe the change in him. The slight fifteen-year-old with the reticent eyes was gone. In his place was a broad-shouldered young man with thick, shining hair and bold green eyes. It was obvious that the farming life, with its physical work and fresh air, had suited him well.

Mrs van den Bogen noticed it, too. The remark hung for a moment in the small kitchen before Nanny Hoogendoorn continued.

With the reappearance of Daniel, the holiday fencing bouts started up again and the strained relations between Nicky and his father improved. Delighted by his protégé's return, Mr van den Bogen arranged for the two boys to have private lessons with a professional fencing coach. Daniel had a way of calming madcap Nicky down. It was Daniel who broached the subject with Mr van den Bogen of Nicky moving back home and going to a school in the city.

And so the friends were reunited. Their relationship was something more like brothers than friends. Nicky would object when Daniel told him what to do, then they would pummel each other on the floor as brothers do, or he would accuse Daniel of cheating with the sword and storm out of the house but it never lasted long.

When the university term started, Nicky and Daniel both enrolled as students and moved into the ground floor of a house near the university. Nanny Hoogendoorn was relieved that Daniel was there to look after Nicky. She only left the van den Bogens when her own two younger girls, Margit and Astrid, needed her after their father's death. By then, the van den Bogens had no more need of her service.

'Nicky was my charge from the day he was born,' Nanny Hoogendoorn said. 'I thought I had brought him safely through.'

I recalled her composure at the funeral, her pragmatic dispensing of tissues from her black bag, and wondered how far down her own grief must have been stuffed on that occasion.

We were startled back to the present by the arrival of Astrid, who was doing her apprenticeship to become a dental nurse. Exhausted by our day, we greeted her as one might welcome an adjudicating angel, the young fair-haired girl with her cheeks mottled red from the cold outside and the soothing fresh air she brought with her. Astrid apologised for the interruption and invited me to stay for dinner. Her mother looked over at me and nodded grudgingly, yes, I should stay. We should have supper together. After all, every visit now could be the last time.

'Shame on you, Mams! Saying such things. And you so healthy always! Come, let's do a jig, that always makes you feel better!'

And, to my astonishment, Astrid lifted her mother up, as if a dancing flock of snow had entered the small apartment from the wintry evening outside, and led her on a jig all the way around the kitchen table, down the dark, narrow passage and up again, until finally Astrid stopped, depositing her mother gently back onto the kitchen chair. Nanny Hoogendoorn was clutching her chest, breathless with laughter, her gout forgotten. 'Ah, Astrid, Astrid!' With the gloom dissipated, we settled down to an evening together. But Nanny Hoogendoorn grew irritable again during the meal.

'Tomorrow morning we start early,' she declared on her way to bed, as I helped Astrid wash up. 'Every story must reach its end.'

Astrid glanced at me. 'She doesn't mean to sound inhospitable. This story is something she has kept locked away inside herself for many years. I do not think she expected to ever talk of it. Now she is tired. But it is good that you came.'

'She never talked to you of her life with the van den Bogens?'

'Only a little. Each year she brought a new picture of Nicky and replaced the old one in the frame. It stayed on our mantelpiece for that year until she came home the next year, but that was all. Wait, I will show you.'

She disappeared down the dimly lit passage and through a doorway. When she came back, she had a photo album with her, one of those heavy old-fashioned albums with a fake leather embossed cover and black pages, and pictures kept in place with photo corners. Years in the Hoogendoorn family were measured from sunny August to sunny August.

Each August there was a spate of family pictures in the park, at the zoo, at the swimming pool, with tulips, with windmills, on a boat on a lake, Nanny Hoogendoorn with her daughters in almost every frame. Then there were the snow pictures: three sisters sledding, ice-skating, singing carols, opening Christmas presents, photos meant for the absent mother. 'When the sun comes out, snow melts,' Astrid pointed out as she turned a page and left the snow behind.

At the end of each group of winter pictures, just after the daughters who grew up before my eyes, was a photo of blonde, shining Nicky, also one year older, on a page to himself.

'She adored him, I think,' Astrid said dreamily. 'She couldn't help herself. Each summer she came home and brought us pictures of him as if he were our sibling. It was very hard for her to leave him.' She closed the album on the last photo of Nicky. 'But he came to visit her once, you know. I was surprised about that. I thought we would never meet him. After all, my mother was just a servant in his house.'

'Did he come alone?' Where did that arrive from? I am like someone walking through a haunted house, her skin prickling.

She stood up abruptly. 'You must ask my mother. It is her story.'

I took a taxi back to my hotel. It gave me time to reflect on what I had been told. I judged Nanny Hoogendoorn to be a reliable storyteller; she was not the type to embellish the plain, simple facts that spoke for themselves. I phoned Elijah and repeated what I had learnt during the day. I could sense his excitement a continent away.

'Now it's all coming together,' he crowed. 'This is what we were missing – Marie-France Montaigne, you say? Mirabelle with two l's? And could you spell that name, "La Rochelle"?'

'Does she have any idea where he is now?' Elijah finally asked.

'I don't think so. I get the idea she lost touch with him.'

'That husband of yours is as slippery as an eel.'

336

The next day, Nanny Hoogendoorn and I sat opposite each other at the table, with a huge café latte and an amsterdammer on a saucer in front of each of us. Astrid was studying upstairs.

'I love amsterdammers,' I said, as I bit into the sweet buttery texture.

'What's there not to love?' Nanny Hoogendoorn replied. It struck me that perhaps she had her own purpose in agreeing to see me. Her soft white hair was full of static this morning and her eyes had an unsettled look.

'Nicky should not have died.'

'Nicky's death was a freak accident, Mevrouw Hoogendoorn,' I replied with all the kindness I could muster. 'I'm here because Daniel, my husband, is missing.'

'And the fiancée that was betraying him with his best friend?' she retaliated bitterly, refusing to be deflected. 'Was that another girl then? All the years he was away from home he wrote to me. What mother could have asked for more?'

But you were not his mother. You were the reason his own mother could never get close to him. And when did I become the fiancée?

'I never agreed to marry him and I never meant to come between them. Nobody was to blame.' In that instant I knew why I had come. As if a conjuror had removed a silken blindfold that had hidden me from myself. I had come to find out more about Lady Limbo. I would have to get Nanny Hoogendoorn on my side or she would tell me nothing more. I could hear Astrid moving about upstairs.

'Daniel and Nicky knew a girl in France, Nanny Hoogendoorn, who might have more information. I think they were in some kind of trouble that perhaps contributed to Nicky's death. Now Daniel has gone missing. Do you know this woman?' I put the faded flash-lit photograph with the Eiffel Tower in the background on the table so she could see it.

I saw the involuntary movement of her hand to her throat, but she left the photo where it was. 'He brought a French woman here once,' she said at last. 'From Paris. Daniel was with them. She was very attractive but not of his class. I told him that in the kitchen and he just laughed. He said he was just having some fun with her and that I was too straitlaced.' She glanced at the photo. 'It could be her.'

My bone marrow had turned to permafrost. 'Do you remember the year?'

'It was late June 1994, six months after I returned to Holland. The tulips had already bloomed.'

I bit my lip to stop myself making a sound. That meant the photo was taken in the June–July vac of my first year.

Nicky had presented me with a still dripping bouquet of flowers borrowed from a vase in the res lounge and begged me to go with him and Daniel on an overseas trip. We'd stay in his family homes in Holland and France. I couldn't afford it, I'd said, enchanted by the flamboyant gesture, miserable that I had to refuse him. He'd arrange a free airline ticket, he'd persisted; his father had shares in the Dutch airline. My heart bursting, I had still refused him, saying I couldn't accept. Sitting in Nanny Hoogendoorn's kitchen I silently acknowledged that in some way I would always love that other Nicky, the one who went down on his knees to give me borrowed flowers.

I'd already made the calculation but it was what a court would call circumstantial evidence. In a few weeks' time we would be celebrating Simone's birthday. It all roughly tied up. If Celestine's suspicions were correct, then Daniel fathered a daughter in Paris that student vacation July when the photo was taken. Ten years later, she would sit at the bus stop outside our block of flats and wait for Daniel.

I forced my attention back to what Nanny Hoogendoorn was saying.

'I was so pleased to see him I didn't want to argue but the young woman disturbed me. When I asked him what her occupation was his face changed colour, like when he was a small boy telling not quite the truth. He said she was a dancer in a supper club. Away from the others, Daniel said I shouldn't worry, Nicky had a regular girlfriend at university, a beautiful, intelligent girl. This was just a holiday fling.'

You said that about me? My love, where are you? We were so young.

'Do you remember her name?'

'Yes. It was Jasmine.' My scalp prickled at the sound of that name. The ghost of Jasmine seemed to be everywhere. 'Nicky repeated her name often – he said it with a soft 'J' like the French do. He was all over her, kissing her and pulling her to him. It embarrassed me.'

'Did you see them again after that?'

'They had supper with Astrid and me, as you did last night, and then they left. That was the last time I saw Nicky.'

Something in the intonation of her words bothered me. 'What about Daniel? Did you ever see him again?'

She held my gaze, a glint of sadness in her eyes. 'You mean besides the funeral?'

'Yes, I mean besides the funeral.' I would not lower my eyes. The stakes were too high. Daniel's past. I dared the gods with my willpower.

'I saw your Daniel once more, some time after the funeral,' she finally said. 'He was with that same woman who came to my home. Jasmine. I was visiting my sister in Belgium. We were having coffee and cake in a coffee shop in Bruges when I looked up and saw a well-dressed couple walking past. I recognised Daniel immediately. He had grown heavier but it was him. She had gone up in the world, with a fur jacket and jewels and his arm around her shoulders. I pushed past the waiting clients and rushed outside but I was too late. They had already caught a taxi.'

I sat back, stunned by her simple, straightforward account. So it was all true. With Nicky gone, Jasmine had opened her arms to Daniel. The stylish young couple on the streets of Bruges were destined to be Dominique's parents. Nanny Hoogendoorn had told me enough. As my layers of not-knowing had peeled off, the sprightly old woman had wilted before my eyes.

'Thank you, I said, as I rose from my kitchen chair. 'You have given Daniel de Luc a past.'

There was a noise at the door. Astrid spoke.

'Mams, you should tell her about het kind.'

'What child?'

'Astrid, let sleeping dogs lie. None of that has anything to do with her missing husband. It is over.'

'How do you know, Mams?' She walked into the kitchen and sat down at the table with us, her eyes locked onto her mother's. 'Tell her. Then it will be over.'

I left them arguing and went into the small lounge, trying to making sense of the rapid-fire Dutch. Individually, the words were not so different from Afrikaans but their whispers were difficult to follow. Nanny Hoogendoorn was saying 'Nee. Nee,' in a low voice.

What do I not know?

At last Astrid came to find me.

'My mother will talk to you now.'

It was one of those time-immemorial stories. Two years after she had left his employ, Mr van den Bogen called on Nanny Hoogendoorn here in Amsterdam. He asked her to go to Paris to collect a six-month-old baby girl. Daniel's love child, he had said.

What an archaic phrase that is. A love child. The small kitchen was the quietest room on Earth.

The mother had contacted Mr van den Bogen with certain threats and demands. Nanny Hoogendoorn had never seen Jan van den Bogen so upset, not even at Nicky's worst escapades.

'Why did he believe her?' I couldn't quite take it in.

The single mother claimed to have met Daniel through an underground organisation that encouraged natural conception. This matter could remain private if a sum of money was deposited into her bank account each month. Mr van den Bogen railed about gossip magazines getting hold of the story and destroying Daniel's future and, on top of that, dragging the van den Bogen name through the mud. Jan van den Bogen was an intensely private, proud man, Nanny Hoogendoorn explained. That was why he'd paid the blackmailer but now, finally, the unstable mother had agreed to a deal that involved the child being adopted by a third party. Nanny Hoogendoorn was the only person he could trust with the transfer of the child.

Astrid shifted in her chair, gazing at the snow-flaked windows as her mother talked. *In insurance terms, we are liable for the damage that happens on our watch. In human terms we are culpable.*

'The new parents lived in a mansion behind walls outside Paris. I told myself she would be well looked after – only God knows how often I have prayed that she has been. The baby reminded me of my own girls, with her fair hair. For a foolish moment I considered keeping her, Marie's granddaughter, hiding her away, but I knew it would be impossible.' She used her apron to wipe her cheek.

'The new father saw my affection for the child. He asked me to stay and look after *la petite*, but I could not do it. I did not have the courage to face that child's future with her. I put her into Monsieur Sarrazin's arms and left her there.' She sat with her hands clasped in front of her. 'It was not right,' she acknowledged softly. Astrid stood up, kissed her mother's forehead and then left the room, saying she was late for a class.

All the roads lead to Sarrazin.

With Astrid gone, Nanny Hoogendoorn sat slumped in her chair, exhausted and with nothing more to tell. When I asked for the mother's name, she said tiredly she had never met the mother. An elderly woman had acted as a go-between. She had handed the child over with a bag of her things; perhaps there were some documents inside. She herself had preferred not to know any more than she had to.

It made me uneasy to think of the faceless blackmailing mother still out there. But what difference would it make to know? I thought about the Limbo Files – the seven graces, Jasmine and the others – it seemed entirely likely that Simone's mother was among them.

Jasmine. That name pulled me up short. The photographic threesome on a hot summer's night. Surely it wasn't possible. *Pull yourself together, Paola. Wild, unsubstantiated theories are not helpful.* In a city the size of Paris, there must have been so many random acts of conception that long-ago European summer that a photo and a date proved nothing.

Everything comes round. I remembered how I'd delivered Lady Limbo's message to Nicky so triumphantly, buoyed by an overwhelming sense of self-importance and invulnerability. Nanny Hoogendoorn had followed the dictates of love and loyalty. As if she'd read my mind, she spoke up, her voice sharp.

'Mr van den Bogen compensated me well for my time. I thought my daughters and I could start a new life in a better suburb and one day they could have studied at the university, but Astrid heard everything – she came home early from school with her asthma – and because of her I gave the money back.'

At the door I extended my hand, and she took it.

'When you find him, tell him Carolien Hoogendoorn wishes him well.'

'I'll do that. Say goodbye and thank you to Astrid for me. You are fortunate to have such a strong relationship.'

She nodded. 'Yes, she is a good daughter. She was born with a smile in her heart.'

With that we parted. I left my imprints on Astrid's slippers in exchange for a chapter of Daniel's history and the careful story of a baby girl left to fend for herself. It seemed clear to me that Nanny Hoogendoorn knew more than she'd let on.

It was snowing outside. Flocks of snow fell around and over me as I walked. Undeterred, the citizens of Amsterdam continued with their daily lives. Cyclists rode past me ringing bells to warn pedestrians, dogs in stylish coats and foot mittens took their owners for walks, and red-cheeked children in colourful pompom hats rushed ahead of their mothers, as if we were all playing in a great snowy park. A door swung open and closed and an enticing fragrance of freshly brewed coffee and baked cakes reached the street.

* * *

Less than a month before, I'd met Nicky's mother at a coffee shop back home. The overweight bleach blonde who tottered into Mozart's Café on unsteady legs and with smudged red lipstick was hardly recognisable as the glamorous man-eating Mrs van den Bogen. In her version, tears springing to her eyes, her husband had never treated Nicky, his only son, as well as he had treated Daniel, a stranger's child, and they (Nanny Hoogendoorn and her own husband) had conspired to keep Nicky away from her. She had never trusted Daniel and his mother. She had grown up with that kind; they only knew how to survive from one day to the next. To gold diggers like them, the van den Bogen money was a honey pot.

'You mustn't blame yourself too much.' She'd grabbed my hand with hers, blue veins standing out against the withered fair skin, slurring her words. 'My Nicky was a charming boy but a philanderer, just like his father. I told him to be careful, always to use contraceptives. Sometimes there's a kind of blackmail where the man must pay forever. But he told me other women weren't important; he wanted to marry you. You're an attractive girl. And intelligent. I was never intelligent.'

I'd jumped in and raised the subject of Nanny Hoogendoorn, expressing a desire to look her up now that I was actually going to Holland. I'd said I would, at the funeral.

'Ah, yes, the funeral,' she said, leaning forward, her voice suddenly clear, the washed-blue eyes hardened to pale quartz. 'That seems so long ago, doesn't it? We all behaved so impeccably. I thought I played the distraught mother part rather well but you, oh, you were the showstopper.'

She had never looked so much like Nicky as in that moment, her son's mouth twisted into a sneer of contempt. He had come back from the dead to accuse me.

'You didn't realise, of course, how you gave yourself away, only having eyes for the friend who was in excellent good health. A handsome but vain boy. What did you do to him, my dear? He seemed very eager to avoid you that day. He *was* with you? Among others I dare say.' She took a small silver flask out her handbag and drank from it. 'Cheers!' I could smell whisky. When she looked at me again her eyes were bright with tears. 'I thought I saw him the other day. They say murderers always revisit the scenes of their crimes.'

I'd stared at her in astonishment. Was it possible that intelligence made one blind and that Nicky's airheaded mother had seen things clearly? She continued with her ramblings. Her husband had accused her of having an affair; now he had found a younger woman. Perhaps if she'd shown an interest in his rusty old swords … She bored him. She filled the time with dance lessons and tennis. Occasionally she took a lover.

In the end I didn't tell her I was married to Daniel.

* * *

In retrospect, I think she must have sensed something of what had been done, but her husband would not have told her. I wonder about the car that came out of the Parisian fog and hit Jasmine. The car that was never found. What Elijah would call 'a loose end'. I think of the infant left in a mansion with a strange new family. Another 'loose end' roaming the planet. All the adults who had made their choices had ignored the rights of the unborn children involved. It seems to me that loose ends are the flipside of consequences. Marie would have said that chickens come home to roost. I reach the tram stop in chilly Amsterdam. A woman climbs on ahead of me, her arms laden with a bounty of crayon-bright flowers with strong green stalks. She shakes a dusting of snow gently off the perfect blooms as she walks down the passageway. Other travellers, men and women, climb on at later stops, and some of them also carry bunches of cheerful hothouse flowers. The passageway glistens wet with melted snow. A straw-haired boy with a hooded jacket glides into the empty seat in front of me next to a girl with long raven tresses and a Peruvian knitted cap with ear warmers on her head who looks like a traveller from far away.

'Do you speak English?' he asks almost immediately, with a Dutch accent and a disarming grin. The girl holds two fingers parallel with a very small space between so he switches to clumsy Spanish and the girl giggles, the woollen red and yellow tassels of her cap flying as she shakes her head firmly, responding in fluent

Dutch. She is older than Simone. After that they chat quietly in Dutch. Outside a snow blizzard has started.

Lean Away from
the Mountain

TWO DAYS LATER, I was part of a wave of delegates pouring out of a heated Amsterdam conference hall for the morning tea break, mobiles clutched to ears as we caught up on half a morning's news from information technology workplaces spread across the globe. The hallways hummed with the palpable static of communication. Personal messages were stored for later listening. The close quarters also provided a superhighway for the spread of the flu virus. I looked around me as I blew my nose.

Heads rose above the hubbub like satellite dishes. They belonged to hardened IT professionals who had clawed their way up career ladders by being one step ahead of everybody else. They were totally familiar, these glittering-eyed power apostles hungry for success, calculating how best to capitalise on the opportunity for exposure. In spite of assertions to the contrary, the main reason why IT companies pay huge sums of money for consultants to attend far-flung international conferences has hardly anything to do with increasing the knowledge base, and just about everything to do with the deals that are struck in the shadowy chandelier-lit realm of conference halls. The conference delegate who aspires to the next rung of the career ladder fully recognises the advantage of the networking opportunity.

The über-power hustlers were already in position, huddled in tight conversation rings and exchanging business cards like piranhas nibbling at each other's tails. But at that moment I needed a quiet lounge.

'I can hardly hear you. Hold on, Elijah.'

A babble of languages followed me, through the banquet hall of laden tables into a lounge area with muted lighting and mobile reception.

'I found him, Paola.'

The strangest thing happened. I left the hotel lounge and the throng of two-thousand-and-something delegates and flew far away to the summit of a sand dune that stood in my past with all the glorious enigmatic power of the Sphinx.

The sun is setting over the sea, a fiery blood-orange orb is sinking behind the horizon, I am a flesh-and-blood lightning rod surrounded by a sky of pure, undiluted blue and I have my arms stretched out. I'm having a fourteen-year-old moment and God is everywhere. It's the closest I've ever come to believing. I start to turn like a spinning top and I only stop when I'm so dizzy that I collapse onto the soft, cool sand. Now I stand on that same hilltop of white sand and my heartbeat is strong and regular. Daniel is the still point of the turning world. I am exactly where I belong. Faith has found me.

'Paola, are you listening? There's this sanatorium in Switzerland.' Another pause. 'Are you there?'

'Yes. I'm here. When can I fetch him?'

'These places are like the Treasury Department,' Elijah said. 'They wouldn't let me in. I followed one of the nurses to a bar.'

Why did something not feel right?

'Elijah, what are you not telling me?'

There was a terrible dead silence on the other side. Panic began to overwhelm me.

'I just missed him, Paola,' Elijah confessed in a low voice. 'He walked out of the place a couple of weeks ago.'

I sat down on the closest chair.

'It's a long story,' Elijah said quietly, giving me time to recover, 'but that Enid Lazzari of yours and Patrice Musso had him stashed away in this fancy sanatorium in the Swiss Alps to recover from so-called exhaustion. By the way, Patrice is his uncle, the husband of Mirabelle, Marie's sister, and he really is a publisher. And the full name on Mr de Luc's passport is Lucien Gabriel Montaigne. That's why we struggled to trace him. Nathan knows someone at South African Airways. He agreed to help for a fee. I checked hundreds of computer printouts until I found an entry showing a Lucien Montaigne had flown out of the country four months after Mr de Luc disappeared. That's why Patrice's payments stopped. Anja – that's the nurse – has been finding out things and passing them along.' Elijah grew more and more animated as the story continued.

'Elijah, did we discuss this? Are you in Switzerland right now?'

'You bet I am. That Hoogendoorn woman gave us leads. I just had to fill in the missing pieces. You were out of the country so I hopped onto the first plane to Zurich.

'I've always wanted to try my hand at skiing. It turns out Anja has a brother who's an instructor at a ski resort in the mountains so I've had some lessons in-between. She set the whole thing up.'

'Astonishing how quickly a relationship can flourish,' I said testily. 'What is she getting out of it?'

'She didn't have to help, Paola,' Elijah replied in a hurt tone. 'She only agreed after I told her the whole story. We'll work the finances out. I've been saving for a holiday anyway.'

Ashamed of myself, I tried to make amends. 'Sure. So, how was the skiing?'

'Well, it took me a while to get the hang of it. The secret is to lean forward, away from the mountain. Anton – that's Anja's brother – explained that one's natural fear response is to lean back, away from the downhill slope but leaning back is what makes you fall so you have to change your mental conditioning. Funny, isn't it? It took me a while to get the hang of it but then I didn't want to stop. Can you believe it? Elijah Bloom, skier!'

I visualised Elijah, a projectile in one of those tomato-red ski jackets that ski shops hire out so that learner skiers are easily identifiable as potentially dangerous obstacles on the slopes. But my mind was a blizzard. Chilling winds swirled and blinding snow fell.

Why couldn't he just stay put?

'Elijah, how did you track Daniel down to this place?'

'I had a bit of luck there,' Elijah crowed. 'The young gentleman who works as PA for Patrice Musso has an elderly mother who suffers from Alzheimer's and requires expensive private nursing care. He was willing to keep me informed on Monsieur Musso's movements for a certain fee once I'd supplied him with my credentials and assured him no harm would come to his employer. Simple, really.'

'Yes, I suppose so.'

'How's the conference, by the way?'

'Great. Just great. Nothing I haven't heard before. Clients want projects implemented faster and cheaper to keep their shareholders happy, the scourge of AIDS is cutting a swathe through highly trained personnel from Africa and Asia, and Indian outsourcing companies are taking over the IT business by remote control.'

'Hey, why so glum? We've got a breakthrough here!'

'Elijah, where is Daniel right now?'

'No leads at this time,' he replied solemnly. 'Anja doesn't know. Says they don't have to leave a personal forwarding address if everything's paid for, and in his case he had a benefactor. She presumed this to be the relative who accompanied him on his arrival, a Monsieur Patrice Musso, but – wait for this – he had a visitor who answers to Enid Lazzari's description, so if that scheming woman wasn't in on it, she certainly knew about it.'

I couldn't say a word. I wished I was on another planet just then, the planet Daniel and I had inhabited before my relations with disappointment became so intimate.

Elijah hurried on, filling the gap. 'This is all good, Paola, we've never been this close before. A couple of days after this woman's visit, Daniel asked to sign the release form and left in a taxi. Swiss law doesn't allow them to keep a patient against his or her will, except in very specific circumstances. I'm guessing her visit triggered his decision. I'm going to hang around for another couple of days and see what else I dig up. If I can find the taxi driver maybe we'll know where he went, but it's a long shot. He phoned for the taxi himself and no one remembers what taxi company it was.'

'Do you think he's returned to South Africa?'

'Maybe. It's possible. I don't want to get your hopes up too much, but maybe Enid Lazzari filled him in so now he knows those Sarrazins are in custody.'

'Why was he there?' I asked dully. What did it matter any more?

'They have strict security clearance protocols for patient records. She couldn't tell me much except to say that he'd arrived in a general state of exhaustion but by the time he left he was much recovered. She said he was a model patient and spent most of his time reading. Get this – apparently the room's balcony overlooked the lake. Just like your sister-in-law said. Anyway, you can sleep well tonight. Your man's alive and well.'

The crowds around the tea urns were beginning to thin as people started drifting back into the conference hall. 'Do you have any news on Simone?'

'She's doing well. It's tough on such a young girl. Those skunks should be drawn and quartered.'

'I should be there.'

'She's a great kid. Monica had to visit her mother in the hospital so I took Simone on a beach expedition with my metal detector.'

'What happened?'

'Nothing. She went running up and down like there was no tomorrow.'

'Not to Simone. What's happened to Monica's mother?'

'The end-game with emphysema is not a pretty sight. Ask me: my grandfather drowned in Lexington Creek. They've got her on a ventilator.'

I must get home.

'Hey, Simone found a Portuguese coin. Can you believe it? I'm getting a friend at the museum to have a look at it and give us a date. I don't know what it is but beginners always have all the luck.'

'She must have been over the moon. Thanks, Elijah. It's important to keep her occupied so she doesn't get up to any mischief.'

'When do you get back?'

'The day after tomorrow.'

'I'll let them know. Any messages?'

'No.' I was the last delegate left in the quiet lounge. 'Elijah?'

'Yes.'

'Have you ever been married?'

'Once,' he replied promptly. 'She was eighteen, I was nineteen, we were both fresh in the city, straight out of school. Her name was Ellie. I thought she was the prettiest girl I'd ever seen. She fell in love with a stuntman and asked me for a divorce about a year later. That was it. My doomed experiment with True Love.'

'I'm sorry. Sorry I asked, I mean. It's none of my business.'

'Don't be. Marriage didn't suit me. I hated sharing my toothpaste and I couldn't stand the way she was too lazy to get her own towel out the cupboard so she always used mine. I was secretly relieved when she asked for the divorce. Her family didn't even know about the marriage and there were no kids, so we just walked away from it. There were no regrets.' I had to smile at my PI's enviable tranquillity. 'It wasn't like you and him,' he said.

'Elijah?'

'Yes?'

'You're the best PI a girl ever had.'

'The pleasure's all mine. I haven't had so much fun in a long time.'

I spent the night tossing and turning in the enormous double bed that came with the Hilton Hotel room. The phone call was probably recorded using the sanatorium conference facilities. Had he thought of me as he looked out at that Swiss lake? They'd done it to make us think he was alive in the city and to stop me going to the police. Instead I'd gone to RMI and selected Jack. All those men I followed in Paris … That old witch Enid Lazzari knew where he was all the time.

On the flight home, exhaustion finally kicked in. I wrapped myself in the KLM blanket and woke up the next morning as the breakfast round began.

As I unpacked back in the flat, I listened to the messages on my answering machine.

One was an enthusiastic report back from Monica. 'It was a breeze, honey bunch! She's a great kid! We *bonded*. I took her to La Senza. They've just launched their new summer Ultimate Lingerie range. Colours to die for, girl! I bought the teeniest weeniest itsy bitsy jungle tangas you ever saw in a shade of acid lime and she bought herself a set of panties in tutti-frutti ice-cream shades. I gave her some money and said that's it, not a cent more. I could get used to this aunt thing. Call me as soon as you get in. I want you to meet Paloma properly. *This* is *the* woman I've been waiting for!'

I groaned, not at all sure whether taking an eleven-year-old ex-shoplifter to buy lingerie on her day out was a good idea and wondering what new sorrow Paloma would bring. Nothing about her mother, but that was typical Monica. Her mother was her business and nobody else's. I made a mental note to go round after work the following day.

There was also a message from Esmeralda.

'I've got all the documents ready for you to sign so we can get the adoption process going, if you're still serious about this. In the meanwhile, if you want to take her home as a foster child, she's all yours. It's been approved. Let me know.'

When Elijah eventually returned from the Swiss slopes, he was glowing with sunburn and *joie de vivre*. I'd almost guessed right. A framed photograph of Elijah in a tomato red one-piece snowsuit and outlandish goggles now graced the attic desk.

'My mojo's back, Paola. I can feel it. Right here!' He tapped his chest with a closed fist. '*Whoosh, whoosh,* you should have seen me do my curves.' My scalp prickled. I had the fleeting impression of watching Elijah roll down a slope in his red outfit, a snowball gathering more and more snow down an endless run. When I looked again, Elijah was still sitting there.

'But you want to know what I found out,' Elijah said, all at once serious.

His persistence had finally paid off. A longstanding member of the security staff who shared his interest in galactic phenomena of an alien nature had assisted with access to the sanatorium's electronic visitors' system, allowing Elijah to confirm that Daniel's visitor had indeed been Enid Lazzari. Moreover, he had discovered that she had top security clearance and was a frequent visitor to the institution, where she was highly regarded as a specialist psychotherapist in the difficult field of night terrors.

The sanatorium incorporated a separate dream research facility for the applied investigation of dreams and dreaming. The patients included rich and famous celebrities with extravagant lifestyles and a precarious sense of reality, who came back to the sanatorium at regular intervals to be treated for a 'sleep deprivation disorder' or 'exhaustion'. Elijah acknowledged it was all hearsay, but if one put all the puzzle pieces together, it made sense. Enid had herself told me that Daniel had gone to see her about his nightmares.

I had to talk to Simone and then I would go and find Enid Lazzari.

The Queen
of Cats

I PICKED HER UP FROM SCHOOL at the usual time, waiting under a tree to escape the heat. After the cold of Amsterdam, the February heat in Cape Town was a shock. *When the sun comes out, snow melts.* Simone showed no interest in where I'd been for the past ten days. Instead, she asked pointedly why Monica hadn't come, before announcing what her plans were for the day.

'The new *Pirates of the Caribbean* is showing at the Waterfront.'

'No movies today. We're going to the circus. There's a matinee performance.'

'Borrring,' she pouted, and folded her arms tightly shut against me. 'Do I look like I'm five years old? Everyone at school is going to see *Dead Man's Chest* and you're taking me to the circus? I've been to the circus a *million* times. God, you're embarrassing.'

Inwardly my resolve almost crumbled but I refused to let the little madam have the satisfaction of making me miserable so I talked brightly to myself all the way to the circus site, praying she wouldn't refuse to get out of the car. The elephant that sprayed our car with dirty water saved me. She must have decided the universe was on her side at that point because after doubling up with loud laughter at the sight of my unimpressed face, she sauntered along behind me to get tickets. It wasn't the same without Daniel. The acts were tired and provincial and the costumes were tatty and outdated but she giggled at the clown's antics and from the look of stupefaction on her face when she was watching the trapeze acts I could tell she hadn't seen a million circus shows.

On the way home, she started moaning about the film again after seeing a poster at a bus stop, so I stopped off at the 7-Eleven to buy a packet of popcorn kernels. About five minutes into the whole popcorn-making exercise, she'd forgotten the movie and started enjoying herself, insisting on lifting the lid to let stray popcorn kernels shoot out in random directions. From the way she acted I guessed she'd never made popcorn before.

Popcorn was a diversion to buy time. I'd reached a decision about our future without telling her. She sat on the high stool, happily munching buttery salted popped corn while I cleaned up. I couldn't stand it any more.

'Simone, I want to adopt you.'

The blue eyes turned on me.

'But it could take months, so I applied to act as your foster parent so you could come and live with me here. It's been approved. What do you think?'

'When?'

'We can get the rest of your things tomorrow.'

She turned back to the important business of eating popcorn. 'You said you'd tell me the story of the talking cat some day.'

I couldn't see her eyes, only her stooped head and arm at an elaborate angle as a hand trailed its way through popcorn. The last time I told a story to an audience was in Grade 1 because Mrs Meyer needed to keep the English half of the class busy.

'Now's good, I suppose.'

She looked up, her lips curled. 'You don't have to if you don't want to.'

'No. Really. Why not? This is a good time. The right time.'

So, we went into the lounge with the bowl of popcorn and she lay on the couch under a blanket, waiting for me to tell her the story of the Queen of Cats. I dug around in the LP box until I found the circus music, Daniel's victory spoils from a scuffle with another would-be pretender at the Sunday flea market.

You loved this silly burlesque music.

I took my time, lighting some candles and closing the curtains against the daylight before I gently set the needle at the start of the track. A tinny circus-band routine with clashing cymbals and rousing trumpet flew out over our heads into all the empty spaces of the lounge, drawing us into its scratchy thrall, and soon it no longer mattered if we were the mirrors and it the smoke of a grand illusion. We were at the circus. It was just like the old days – the world-famous lion tamer induced terrifying roars with a lash of the whip on the lion's stool; a master horseman of Romany gypsy blood hung by one stirrup off a jet-black Arabian stallion as it galloped around the sawdust ring; the knife thrower opened his act with a tame tiger as his petrified assistant. It was all gloriously decadent and electrifying and quite beyond the bounds of political correctness.

Before long, Simone was sitting upright, a pillow hugged to her chest. I cleared my throat and began.

Ladies and Gentlemen, Children, I give you, the One, the Only, Igor Shashenok! Master of Cats! Apologies to my geek friend, Igor, I thought, for plucking his name out of the ether to assist me in this silly game. *All the way from Siberia,* I continued, *land of ice and bears, with his troupe of performing cats to amaze you with tricks that will keep you on the edge of your seats! A big hand for Igor and his cats!*

As I began the story, I thought I could make out Daniel's voice, the cadences and resonances from another time and place, telling me the story imparted to him by the cat master from Siberia while we sat on the carpet and I sipped red wine. He was very strict with himself, refusing to imbibe a drop while he lived and breathed the cat master of Siberia. I remembered what he'd said: for a good story the storyteller must become the story, and the story must become the storyteller. So I abandoned the last vestiges of inhibition and tried to invoke the cat master himself.

A shabby introduction! I disdainfully declared in my best Russian accent. *It gives no hint of the marvel I, Igor Shashenok, have brought with me. Can you feel the thump of the circus band, smell the popcorn and sawdust as it rises to the stalls, hear the giggles and shrieks of the children? This was our world, Anastasia's and mine.* Another name shamelessly borrowed as I was swept along by the story. A story about a peasant boy from a land of snow and hunger who held fireside conversations with his mother's cats. Conversations where one remained silent and the other knew his thoughts.

Felines are a mysterious and intelligent race, Igor intoned, *with their delicacy and finesse. In our little cottage we were content, our cats and my mother and I. When the day came for me to leave Russia, my mother hugged me fervently to her breast and begged me to return. There was such a fussing by my feline family as you could not imagine.*

The cheerful young Igor was taking shape under my conjuring hand. He travelled the world, learning the magic of the circus from masters around the globe. Wilkie's, the Moscow Circus, Cirque du Soleil. Meanwhile, his mother took to training the cats and it was on his return from Prague one spring that he discovered she had succeeded not only in simple matters of hygiene and etiquette, but that one white kitten with an unusual blue sheen had begun to walk on two legs.

I saw this with my very own eyes, Igor cried, *hidden as I was in the grandfather clock. Indeed, I am not certain she did not know I was there, since she stopped and stared upwards with enchanting mischief in her eyes.*

The next marvellous breakthrough was when it was established that the kitten listened to conversations. *I tested her on a simple question: 'Would you like some fish?' Yes, yes, yes. Anastasia nodded at me. I was so delighted with her cleverness that I began to practise simple words with her, such as 'yes' and 'no'.* Anastasia grew into a beautiful, accomplished young lady and Igor took her on a grand circus tour. Anastasia and her friend Igor conquered the world. She even had her own personal caravan with heating and a human admirer who read her poetry and brought her caviar.

Anastasia the Talking Cat! Her vocabulary grew in leaps and bounds. Words like 'water' and 'food', were quickly followed with longer, more complicated ones, like 'pickled fish', 'anchovies' and 'caviar'. *How foolish we were not to foresee the consequences of her fame and glory,* Igor said.

Anastasia grew contemptuous and vain, then took to moping, and, before long, she was overtaken by an exquisite ennui. She reclined in the sunshine on her doorstep in her ermine cloak and diamond tiara and refused to enter the big tent. *She let me understand that she was most sick and tired of performing and wanted to spend some time in the sunshine.* One day, she went missing and to Igor's shame and horror it turned out that her human admirer was a rascally catnapper. A talking cat would fetch a fabulous sum! The Paris gendarmes launched a massive secret rescue operation. *As soon as I was informed of her rescue and good health, I left to make some travelling arrangements.*

When Igor told her they were going back home, Anastasia sat up, licked a paw very delicately and meowed.

We were back in Siberia within the week. I was never to hear her talk again, I said in Igor's voice as the circus music faded away.

Simone had sat transfixed through my improvised version of the magical circus tale Daniel had once imparted to me. It took a moment for her to snap her mouth shut and muster the usual insouciance.

'Anastasia was *so* totally right. Why would anybody want to be a human being?'

'I can't imagine,' I said, myself returning from a pleasant trance. 'Maybe because human beings get to do fun things like eat popcorn?' I suggested facetiously.

The blue eyes regarded me with haughty disdain. 'She was a cat. She had to go back to being a cat otherwise she couldn't be happy. We can't be something we're not.'

'Right. Of course. So it's fine to be a human being if you're born that way?'

'I guess *so*.'

'Well, thank goodness for that.'

She flounced back onto the couch. 'Still, in my next life I *so* want to be a cat and sleep as long as I want!' Then she bounced up again as a radical thought hit her. 'Can we get a cat?'

This was good. Even if feline feel-ups and urinary odours were not my thing. I could tell, right where my epiglottis flapped gently over my windpipe and kept me breathing, that this question was a good sign. Still, I groaned inwardly as I packed the vinyl disc away and played for time. *A cat?* What had I expected, telling a silly story like that?

'A cat? I suppose so,' I said, opening the curtains and letting the daylight back in.

'*I suppose so*,' she said sneeringly, exposing my weak noncommittal response for what it was.

So what if Mrs Shimansky and the Sandkasteel body corporate would want 'extenuating circumstances'? I'd give them a briefcase of the stuff. I jettisoned caution.

'Fine. Yes. Absolutely yes.' Boldly, I ventured deeper into the tundra of parenting. I was making life-changing decisions on the fly, without the parachute of a plan or training manual. It was peculiarly addictive; there was a deliciously reckless feel about it. It was akin to taking a sudden detour off the main highway sans map or GPS. 'We could get a Siamese kitten!' I pronounced brightly. At least Siamese cats were supposed to be easy to train.

'No, it has to be an *old* cat.'

'An *old* cat?'

'A cat that somebody doesn't want. A cat that doesn't have a home,' she explained with withering logic.

'Right. That's settled. We'll get an old cat then. *The* cat that absolutely no one wants. The ugliest, oldest cat on death row. Will that do?'

She nodded sanguinely as her hand reached out for the television remote. I left her in the lounge, switching channels with dizzying speed.

It was all very contrary and not in any way the result of a

deductive reasoning process, but that was how my daughter gave me permission to be her mother – on her terms – and I accepted, with Daniel in the room.

The Death of
the Little Prince

HOW NAIVE I WAS TO TRY and hold the forces of evil at bay with a fable. Of course somebody had to pay. They weren't going to let us off scot-free.

I was there when it happened.

Elijah had called me at 5.30 pm to ask if I could meet him at his office in town.

'Is it important Elijah? I have to finish something off ...'

'Can you come *right now*, Paola? This isn't going to wait. And you have to bring your laptop.'

He sounded tense and quite unlike himself. Under my influence, Elijah had started to grasp the endless possibilities of the Internet, cautiously venturing forth into unexplored territory. I jumped into the car and rushed over, imagining an online detective picking up Elijah's missing person description. I visualised a grey, waterlogged body shrouded in kelp. That was always the first thought, ever since Enid had told me Daniel dreamt about drowning.

When I arrived, the bookshop was already closed so I went up the back stairs. It was very quiet. I knocked on Elijah's door and walked in without waiting, as I'd done many times before. After that, everything happened very fast. A huge man in a balaclava grabbed my free arm and twisted it behind my back, before relieving me of the laptop. He forced me to stumble over lever arch files and papers strewn all over the floor and sit in the visitor's chair. Elijah was slumped in his chair, his face swollen and deathly pale. There was a gash on his forehead and a trickle of blood running down his face onto the checked collar. A second muscleman in a balaclava had a gun barrel jammed against Elijah's forehead.

'I'm sorry, Paola. I'm not very heroic, I'm afraid,' Elijah said, his voice hoarse but steady. 'They want the computer files you told that RMI operative about, the ones you *said* your husband left behind. They said if I didn't call you, they'd have to ask Simone.'

I followed Elijah's lead.

'There are no files,' I said slowly, rubbing my arm and watching the gun in disbelief. 'It was all in my head. I made it up on the spur of the moment. That's why I couldn't give you the files.'

'Isn't that what I told you?' Elijah said jocularly, looking up at the man holding the gun. 'I said she had an over-fertile imagination and you were wasting your time.' He made it sound as if it were all a silly mistake. Only I could read the approval in the owlish blue eyes. *Good girl, whatever happens don't admit to having those files. And get out of here alive.*

'That's enough, shut him up,' the one behind me said. Whoever he was he enjoyed garlic in his food. He held me back with a single black-gloved hand around my neck.

The other one obeyed, laying the gun down on the desk before jamming a cloth between Elijah's lips and yanking it tight like a horse's bit so that Elijah's eyes bulged and his face contorted into a grimace of pain. Then he grabbed Elijah's hands and started tying him to the chair like a trussed chicken. Elijah shook his head at me, entreating me not to do anything stupid with his eyes. *Simone needs you.*

'Stop it!' I yanked myself away and tried to get across the desk but the man behind me was faster. This time my arm was twisted up so high I screamed in pain.

Taking advantage of the diversion, Elijah made a superhuman

effort, head-butting the thug in an attempt to wriggle his way out of the ropes and get to the gun. But it was futile. I heard the crack of metal against soft tissue and bone. When Elijah dragged his head up, his mouth was bloody and his jaw hung slackly to one side.

'Why don't you go after someone who can defend himself, you prick?' I couldn't believe they'd actually *hurt* Elijah. I had my own problems; the hulk had tied my hands behind the chair.

The next thing that registered was Elijah and chair being spun around to face the blue sky outside. The thug pressed Elijah's face up against the glass. The one next to me spoke.

'How do you like the view, Mr Bloom? For your sake I hope your predicament jogs the pretty lady's memory. Real stylish, isn't she?'

My PI and I had held so many discussions gazing out of that low alcove window, with its unencumbered view of pigeons on ledges and Long Street going about its business. Now there was an old office chair on wheels spinning round and round across the room, faster and faster, gaining a terrifying momentum. It was the silent one who casually redirected its spinning path, sending it bumping into walls and filing cabinets as if it were empty. Elijah doubled up in pain as he hit an open drawer and I could do nothing. Once, the careering high chair hit an obstacle and fell sideways, Elijah's head hitting the ground with a sickening thud. The thug yanked it up, slapped Elijah's face a few times in a horrible parody of concern, and set it off on another interminable pirouette.

Why doesn't the damned thing break? Oh dear God, let it break. My frantic pleas for them to stop reverberated in the loft room, bouncing off the low eaves and walls. But the cruel game distracted them, allowing me to loosen the rope cutting into my wrists. Occasionally, the bastard next to me shoved the chair back to his partner with a hard kick.

Finally, Elijah's tormentor halted it at the last minute with his foot so that it teetered dangerously close to the window. For a few merciful seconds the spinning stopped. Elijah sat with his head bowed, his body slack in the chair. I couldn't see if he was still conscious.

'You sick bastards! Let him go! He hasn't done anything.' If I could keep them distracted we had a chance: the ropes were slackening. If I could just get a hand free.

'That's where you're wrong Mrs *Dante-de Luc*.' He made it sound as if I was Marie Antoinette and he was the guillotine man. 'He's been nosing around in matters that don't concern him. Haven't you, Mr Bloom?'

The other one slapped Elijah on the head to make him pay attention.

'You'll pay for that, Bozo! Leave him alone!' I said through clenched teeth, trying to shake off the icy gloved fingers stroking my neck, willing the teetering chair to stay on this side of life.

'My boss wants his files. So why don't you tell us where they are and we can all go home? Or maybe they're on the machine?'

The big man spoke in an odd affected way, as if at one stage he'd trained for the theatre. I told myself to remember that voice. The reek of garlic made me want to gag. Act natural, be patronising, that's what they'll believe.

'I keep telling you, there are no files. Think about it logically for a minute. Not even my cheating fuck-up of a husband would leave contact details of his women for me to find. He's discretion incarnate, I'll give him that!' I gave the performance of my life, a bitter, hysterical laugh, scraping the bottom of the barrel to locate the almost-truth. 'Look, I need that laptop. If you take it I'll lose three weeks of work.'

The chair was careering across the floor once again. *Helter skelter.* How long might we have played our parts in that unreal dance, the game at stalemate? All I can say is that I did not believe they would do it and I obeyed the imperative to protect Simone.

It was Uriah, the red-lipped bookshop assistant and random agent of chaos, who tipped the scales onto death's side when he shouted nervously from the bottom of the staircase.

'Elijah, are you there? I've called the police, they're on their way!'

Uriah had returned to his parked car after a drink with a friend, only to notice that the lights were on in the bookshop. So he'd let himself in and heard me scream. I would relive those few seconds over and over again. Uriah's voice echoing up the stairwell. Elijah's swollen face jerking upright. Two pairs of cold eyes communicating. The smooth-talking brute next to me aiming the chair at the window. The neat sidestep of the mute joker as he let it fly by. Or did he help it along, impelling Elijah towards infinity without so much as a backward glance, before readying his weapon? I would never know for sure.

Once again I was to hear the sound of breaking glass.

It happened in a heartbeat. I saw the weighted projectile crash through the glass, hang suspended in the air as if it were a bird freed of all earthly restraints and then drop out of sight. Shards of glass rained down.

'*No!*' I yanked my hands free. Tears blurring my vision, I launched myself at the thug with the gun, pummelling him away in a desperate fury, somehow believing I could turn the clock back and stop what had already been done, throwing myself at the gaping hole, scraping at thin air. Maybe he landed on a ledge … But the hulk took hold of a chunk of my hair and dragged me away from the window over the carpet of broken glass. Out of the corner of my eye, I saw Elijah's baseball bat lying on the floor. Just a little closer … I grabbed it with both hands and swung it with all my remaining strength. It hit him on the shin. He gave a howl of fury and pain but I had to sink my teeth into his arm before he finally let go of me. I ran for the door but the other one blocked my way, the little pig eyes enjoying themselves.

I will survive! I can control my fear! I will overcome any threat with courage! The warrior's mantras coursed through my head. All the self-defence lessons I'd ever taken, all the breathing exercises, were worth this one moment, whatever it was going to cost me.

'Hey, watch this!' I yelled at some imaginary person to my right as I approached, and in the split second the thug looked away, I thrust my knee into his groin with a feeling of near-glee. My rage was my fuel. It was just a pity that I couldn't see the look of stupefaction on his dumb face. The bastard crumpled into a little heap at my feet, whimpering like a girl. Next moment I was flying through the air – the hulk threw me against a filing cabinet as if I were a stuffed doll. I heard a dull *ping* right close to my ear and a brief scuffle, and then the talker said, 'You heard the boss; only the carrot-head. Let's get out of here!'

Later, the forensics team would find the bullet that ricocheted off the filing cabinet in the opposite wall. It had missed me by a couple of centimetres. Through a cloud of pain, I could hear police sirens. Uriah reported that they'd made their escape with my laptop through the back a few minutes before the cops arrived. They'd taken Elijah's hard drive as well. All that was left of Elijah was a contorted bloody heap of man and chair splayed on Long Street.

It was on Cape Talk Radio the next day when Klaus Knappman picked me up after my overnight stay in the hospital. He wanted to switch it off but I stopped him. It was 'top of the news on the hour': the manager of the bookshop W&W&W in Long Street, which dealt in esoteric literature, had been killed after intruders broke into the shop after hours, possibly not expecting to find him still at his desk in the attic office. It was not known whether he had been thrown out of the window or had lost his footing in a struggle, but in his plummet to Earth he had bounced off the bonnet of a car before coming to rest on the tarmac. The driver of a car that narrowly missed driving over his inert body had called emergency services but he was declared dead on their arrival. Police were investigating the possibility of the death being linked to a devil-worship cult after receiving an anonymous tip-off. Staff members were being interviewed by police.

'We fed them that cock-and-bull story,' Klaus said quietly. 'They don't know about you.'

Klaus drove me straight to the police station. After I'd called Monica to make sure Simone was safe, I told him what had happened. But first I extracted his promise that what I told him would remain between us. In my written statement, I gave an abbreviated version of events that said nothing about them wanting the files.

I had a cup of tar-black coffee in front of me and every inch of my body ached: I was covered in cuts from the glass that had been lying everywhere, a deep gash across my midriff had required stitches, a few ribs were badly bruised. Nothing was broken. I'd refused painkillers and tranquilisers. The only wound that mattered was one that couldn't be bandaged or anaesthetised. I deserved to feel pain, my body's discomfort made my sorrow bearable.

'They think you know something. Bloom was executed so you won't give anybody the information. They wanted to frighten you. It was a message,' Detective Knappman elucidated patiently. 'That means they're real professionals,' he mused. 'The bullet won't help; it came from Bloom's gun.'

'He's dead, Klaus.' Something in me snapped. I swept the coffee off the table with the back of my hand, outraged at what they had done. I could not discuss it academically, as if it were a police exercise. 'Elijah is dead! He was my friend! What if they try again?'

Detective Knappman stood up, towering over me, before he grabbed some sheets of the newspaper on his desk and tried to clean up his floor.

Somebody knocked. A policewoman stuck her head around the door. 'Kan ek …?' She replaced a box and departed with another under her arm. Elijah's boxes and files were stacked against a wall of Klaus's office; his precious collection of newspaper articles was now in police hands.

Somewhere in one of those boxes was the picture of the street child standing next to the graffiti wall.

I HAVE OF
LATE, WHERE
FOR I KNOW
NOT, LOST ALL
MY MIRTH

I knew now that it came from *Hamlet,* and that Elijah's mission had been to recover lost mirth.

'Have you found anything?'

Klaus sat down heavily. 'My people are going through everything. It's like looking for a needle in the sand.'

'You mean a needle in a haystack,' I said. 'What can I do?'

'I mean it's a hell of a job, that's what I mean,' Klaus said irritably. 'You can help by staying out of trouble.'

In the car on the way home he said, 'I'm going to assign two detectives to keep an eye on you and Simone. We'll play it safe.' I didn't argue. He even offered to have one of the detectives pick Simone up after school every day and bring her back to the apartment. A newspaper banner flashed past. MISSING GIRL, 7, RETURNED TO HER FATHER.

'What's going to happen with Elijah's papers when you've finished with them?'

'It all goes into storage.' Klaus glanced over at me. 'I'm serious, Paola, stay out of it, otherwise I'll take you in for questioning as a material witness and get social welfare to arrange foster care for Simone – for her protection, of course. Unless you have something you want to tell me?' There was a harsh glint in his eyes. Klausie was growing up.

'You've become so suspicious. I can't believe it,' I said. 'Okay, okay, I get it.'

Later Nathan fetched me. He was in a black tracksuit and slops and he looked as if he hadn't slept or shaved in a week. His hollow eyes took in the plasters and my hobbling walk.

'We can do this tomorrow,' he said.

'I'm fine. It's just bruises and cuts. There's nothing broken,' I mumbled, not able to look him in the eyes. 'I want to do it now.'

But once we were in his car he couldn't hold it in any longer. 'What the hell happened up there, Paola?' he asked, holding onto the steering wheel as if he might never let it go.

'They killed him, Nathan, and I couldn't stop them. What else do you want to know? Can we just go and get this over with?'

He punched the steering wheel with his fist and swore under his breath.

We eventually traced the body to the Diep River police mortuary.

Were we family? No, we were friends. Only family was allowed. Nathan replied that Elijah's parents lived in Sutherland. His father was a retired astronomer. He'd suffered a stroke so he didn't travel any more. I realised that I knew nothing about Elijah Bloom. He had left my life with the same suddenness as he had come into it. We'd been pulled into each other's orbits by the circumstance of my husband absconding from life.

'Many people wouldn't let you in, friends isn't enough, but the dead don't tell tales, do they?' We watched mutely as he signed the necessary form. 'Righteo, in you go. First left, ask for H1019,' he said, returning to his sandwich. The gatekeepers to the chambers of death pride themselves on not being your average squeamish human beings.

Once again I found myself identifying a dead man.

A falling body will be crushed by the incredible force of abrupt deceleration. The Little Prince was only recognisable by the mop of red hair that stood on end as if a massive electrical discharge had passed through his follicles at the moment of impact. Where pale blue eyes gentle with curiosity had once looked back at the world was a grotesquely distorted face, the features realigned by broken bones and snapped sinews, his throat a gaping wound, a shard of glass still inside, his right cheek and ear a raw, pulpy mess after his second landing on the tar. Staring down at Elijah through a veil of tears I understood what drove me to identify bodies. All my life I'd hunted down certainty as the be-all and end-all; the certainty of mathematical equations, the certainty of digital logic, the certainty of the long sleep that is no longer part of the equation of life, the certainty of the black box of absolute zero. There is nothing more eclipsing, more certain than death. Death is the big full stop.

* * *

Elijah had called me a week before. He'd asked me again about the files. I said aloud what I'd thought to myself when I first thought the whole thing up.

'Elijah, stop worrying. Project Hadrian is the ideal Trojan

horse; it's the safest place in the world for those files.'

'Tell me those names again. The women in the Limbo Files.'

'Grace. Hela. Isabelle. Jasmine. Rita. Tamara. Veronique.' I counted them off wearily, sick to death of my husband's amiable liaisons.

'Why those seven?' Elijah muttered, thinking aloud as the pencil scribbled to keep up.

Perhaps they were the seven handmaidens who transported him to the sensual bliss of the seventh heaven.

Elijah had called back the next day, a note of urgency in his voice. 'You said something yesterday about a Trojan horse – that got me thinking. Maybe the Internet was Jasmine's Trojan horse.'

I sighed loudly. 'Elijah, what exactly are you talking about?'

'Get this, Paola. Four of the seven names in the Limbo Files tie up to the newspaper articles: Veronique, Grace, Hela, and Isabelle. I don't know why I didn't think of it before.'

'Think of what before?'

'Veronique was a modified second name and Grace was a nickname – Sunday's child is full of grace – that's why I didn't make the connection at first. But I did a search on the names together with the date of death and there they were in the tributes on the memorial pages the families set up for the women; amazing what you can find on the Internet these days. Helène Depardieu, a rising star in French politics, was called Hela in her private life – she was the most high-profile. The police said it was a suicide by prescription drugs but the family paid for a private autopsy. The report showed she had been tied to her bed and actually choked on the pills somebody had stuffed down her throat.

Hedwig Veronika Haas was the wife of a truck driver who was found drowned in her bath, electrified by a portable radio that her husband said was not hers.

Isabelle – it's such a common name – didn't just fall out of her open apartment window ...' Isabelle on the ledge. I remembered the article well. The brother hired a PI after he listened to her mobile messages. Some guys delivering furniture saw a man going into her apartment just before it happened; he was never found.

370

'There's more,' Elijah continued, 'Grace, actually Sophie Kahlo-Chevalier – she was eight months pregnant, by the way – died with her husband and the entire crew in a fire on their yacht. There's no article on Jasmine – and I have a theory on that – but we know how she was killed: hit and run. That makes five out of seven. Your husband had information on these girls, meeting times. It must have something to do with that wacko Real Man organisation.'

'You think Jasmine was murdered by RMI? Why?'

But Elijah was off on his own track. 'These are not nice people, Paola. That operative Jack practically told you those girls were murdered. You have to watch yourself. I can't link Rita or Tamara. I'll try the Internet again using a different angle. Possibly date of birth. Can you get those dates to me?'

It didn't seem the right time to remind Elijah about his reservations regarding the Internet. 'It's just circumstantial, Elijah – they're just character outlines with names attached. He used Isabelle's death for his book. Maybe Veronique isn't Hedwig Veronika whoever –'

'And maybe she is,' he interjected firmly. 'The way I see it, Jasmine gets wise to RMI, maybe a girlfriend winds up dead, so she starts cutting out newspaper articles on women's deaths around Paris. Later, the sister finds them and sends them to Mr de Luc together with the threatening letters – the folds on the early clippings match up and two different fragrances still linger – but she's careful not to send anything on Jasmine. Mr de Luc figures it out, so he collects his own articles on RMI clients he's been with that die in suspicious circumstances and he starts the Limbo Files, and now Jasmine's in, she's one of them.'

'Elijah, this is all total conjecture.'

'If something happens to me, get hold of Olmi. Ask him to check if anyone fed the police information to do with the child smuggling rings the year before Jasmine was killed.'

'Elijah, you're getting paranoid. What's going to happen to you?'

Why hadn't I believed him? Those other women had died so far away; their deaths blended into a background of Parisian murder statistics and sensational international headlines. But Elijah had looked out for me. He'd stepped inside the Trojan horse for me, believing the information inside those files was dynamite.

* * *

Nathan's face was mashed grey with grief. He left the room abruptly, saying he needed some water. I found him in the corridor, his shoulders shaking with dry, silent sobs. He said he was going to visit the crime scene himself; he knew somebody who would get him in. I'd been a fool to think Nathan would believe my edited version of what had happened there. The next day he called me, his voice jagged.

'They wanted the files.'

'How can you know that?' I asked, my heart skipping a beat.

'The bookshop was vandalised to make it look like a robbery. But his office had been meticulously searched. They were professionals; they didn't miss a trick. He used to keep a cash box in a wall recess behind the pin board. He had a gun taped under his desk in case he ever needed it. He didn't get the chance to use it. They took the money and the gun but they carried on looking instead of getting out of there. And then they made him call you. They were looking for something specific. Something small, like a CD you said was in a safe place.'

'Nathan, Elijah was my friend too.'

'Maybe you should have thought about that before you put his life on the line. All he was worried about was your safety; he put the surveillance CD of your night on the town in a security box at the bank and left the password with me but he couldn't safeguard himself against something that doesn't exist.'

'The files exist.'

'If you had any real information you'd have tracked those women down. That's the kind of obsessive-compulsive behaviour you've exhibited all along. You think the whole world revolves around you. Beats me how an intelligent woman can get herself so mixed up over a man. Underneath that cool businesslike exterior you really think Daniel de Luc might come back if the planets line up just right. That's why you hired Elijah. Then when he'd found out everything you needed to know, you threw him to the wolves. Sleep on *that*, Mrs de Luc.'

The line went dead. Obsessive-compulsive behaviour?

Later that evening, I knocked at Sharon's door.

'Elijah's dead.'

'Oh my dear, come inside.'

'I was right there and I couldn't do anything. Nathan says I'm obsessive-compulsive and should have handed over the files. I thought they were bluffing. I can't tell him Elijah died for nothing; there's nothing in the files.'

'Of course you're obsessive,' she said, leading me gently into her living room as if I were the sightless one. 'Love makes no sense at all.' She steered me towards the couch. 'I heard it on the news. You've had a terrible experience. Sit down and I'll make you some camomile tea so you can sleep.'

A picture flashed through my mind of that shelf of bottles in her kitchen with the beaded ribbons that she used to tell them apart, but I was no longer afraid of a blind woman's concoctions. I realised at that moment that I liked Sharon and would trust her not to harm me.

'Sharon, you were wrong.'

'About what, dear?'

'*The Bridge of San Luis Rey* isn't about the importance of love. It's about the stupidity of love. I'm going to be an old maid still wondering if he's out there somewhere.'

'Drink it up, you'll feel much better.'

I drained the cup, feeling as if I was drinking a potion of hemlock, letting the bittersweet liquid run down my throat while she patted Miss Potter's head and smiled serenely at the wall. My bereft, aching body finally gave in to the mercy of sleep. I woke up once to find my head on Sharon's lap, her fingers slowly stroking my hair with the delicacy of night moths beating their wings as they fly through nocturnal gardens.

Simone's birthday party on 21 March was a subdued affair. I ordered a granadilla cake decorated with her name, 'Simone', and '12' in white icing and rushed back from work early on the Wednesday to collect it. Monica and Sharon and Miss Potter and Kiki joined us for a cold drink and cake. I kept on hearing Elijah greeting her with a big, sloppy grin when he came to visit us: *Hey, kiddo, are you up to it?* And then they'd disappear to the beach with his metal detector in tow, like two accomplices on a secret mission. He'd been planning to get her one of her own (*I know someone who's got a second one he doesn't use*) for her birthday. She must have been thinking of him too because she said, 'This is for you, Elijah!' then drew a huge breath and blew the twelve candles out as if she were the cleansing wind from the north.

* * *

The verdict was death from non-accidental causes. The autopsy findings correlated with my version of events.

Oh, Elijah, with one wing-beat; and you dreamt of inter-planetary flight.

Elijah was given a traditional send-off at the Jewish cemetery although the police had kept the body for longer than twenty-four hours and as far as I knew he'd stopped practising his faith. At the funeral service, attended by his elderly parents and a host of uncles and aunts and younger relatives that had come down from Johannesburg, it was easy for Nathan to keep his distance from me. It was difficult to see Elijah in any of his family – the smart-mouthed cousins with slick haircuts looked like stockbrokers; even in a wheelchair his high-browed father had a fastidious air about him; and his stern beak-nosed mother didn't look like the fantasy-story type. I wondered how Elijah had known for sure his sister had run away.

Most of the mourners wore buttons with torn black ribbons and the eulogies seemed never-ending. We duly took our turns to fill the grave with three shovelfuls of soil. It was surreal. It could not be true that Elijah Bloom was to depart the world in a pine casket. A mourner in a black suit with dark shades and long grey hair to his shoulders did not come forward. Could he be another Intergalactic Detective? Heidi stood alone to one side in her trademark trench coat and stilettos, with sunglasses and a black scarf over her head, a faceless mourner in the bright sunlight. I found myself wondering if she wore her shimmering white hot pants under that belted, high-collared public garment she chose to wear in the outside world. I left Simone with Monica and went over to the family to pay my respects. Heidi appeared noiselessly at my side.

'Are you okay?'

'I think so. Thanks for asking.'

'What's up with you and Nathan?'

'He blames me for Elijah's death. He thinks it was expedient for me to sacrifice Elijah.'

'Nathan's an idealist. The world is full of those.'

She slipped away as silently as she had arrived. I watched her walk out the cemetery gates alone, her tall figure casting a shadow like the hand of a sundial over the pathway.

Nathan sauntered over, his lips curled in a sneer.

'So, do you feel like a widow yet? Are you happy now?'

The goading was so unlike the urbane Nathan I knew that a clutch of fighting birds locked beaks in my throat. But in the enraged, bloodshot, alcohol-blurred eyes I saw the ashen shape of sorrow and found my voice.

'That's a strange question, Nathan. But yes, in a way I do. As if I've lost someone who'd become part of me. What would you have done in my place?'

'Handed those files over instead of playing games with people's lives.'

From across the grave, I could see Simone watching us, her eyes narrowed. This time I was ready for him.

'Hindsight is an exact science, Nathan. Who would I have handed them over to? Elijah? You?'

He turned on his heel and walked away from me without another word.

Elijah is dead. Nothing can change that. I must carry on alone. A waiting police car followed us home. Klaus wasn't taking any chances.

More than the
Sum of Parts

I CALL ENID LAZZARI but there is no reply at the number I have for her. I try several times through the night. The next morning, I rush over to Harriet's between meetings. I park on a yellow line because that's the only space there is and ask a parking attendant to come and call me if the traffic police arrive. I question the young man behind the counter about a very small orange-haired woman dressed in a Chinese gown who comes into his coffee shop. He shakes his head lethargically, he's seen weirder things than a Chinese midget, and I want to shake him.

'This is important. It's a matter of life or death. The police are involved. Is there anyone else who might know?'

He's only looking after the place for his mother, Harriet, who's away today. I should ask her. His mother knows all her customers. I say I'll be back tomorrow.

'What do I do if the cops come?'

'Tell them what you told me.'

The eponymous Harriet recognises my description of the midget woman instantly. 'She comes in occasionally. She's a strange one. She lives just around the corner. I've seen her leave the building.'

Enid Lazzari stares at me through the peephole and then opens the door partially, leaving the safety chain on. She snarls at me to leave before I bring the police here. 'You seem to like the police.'

I manage to jam my foot in before she can shut the door in my face. But I know I don't have much time. She'll get a broomstick soon and poke me in my aching ribs. 'Enid, I must talk to you. You were right about the police. I was wrong.' I am prepared to grovel. 'Please open the door. I'll sleep outside your door the whole night if I have to.'

It's enough to make her take the safety chain off and open the door. She lets me in and bolts the door shut behind me, putting the safety catch back in place. I'm standing in a double-volume, high-ceilinged apartment that has been done up to look like something out of the last Emperor's Forbidden Palace. The mysterious lighting is provided by numerous lamps, some hanging and some standing, and the chairs and couches are opulently upholstered in brocades and silks with deep tantric shades like saffron, vermilion, and peacock blue. Tall ceramic and copper vases stand around like sentries – some of them taller than their mistress – and my feet sink into the thick woven carpets with intricate oriental patterns that cover the floor. It's a dark, eerie cavern full of ancient treasures, the home of an oracle in the city. The sitting room must have spectacular city views behind the thick curtains but not a chink of natural light is allowed in. Hundreds of wind mobiles made up of small glass ornaments and cut pieces of glass in myriad colours hang everywhere. As we walk, the wooden floors creak and groan beneath our feet and the glass tinkles constantly, the sound following us, opening up and closing behind us as we pass.

Dressed in similar cloths and colours to the décor, Enid is difficult to locate in her sitting room, even though she is coiffed with her orange helmet. She has a disconcerting way of flitting around behind the large pieces of furniture like a capricious child playing in a whimsical maze of her own design. She appears out of nowhere in front of me and indicates where I should sit, at a black lacquered Chinese table with four straight-backed chairs, and then sits opposite me. She seems to have composed herself after her snarling words at the door.

'I'm going to adopt a child. A girl.' I hadn't actually known what I was going to say but now it comes tumbling out.

Most people would think I'm mad to come bursting in and announce such an intention but not Enid Lazzari. Her eyes widen. 'This is good. Wonderful. Yes, wonderful news.'

'I'm not doing it to get Daniel back. Not any more. I've more or less given up on expecting him to walk in at any moment. I don't think anyone can help him, and especially not me. But I keep seeing her face, everywhere I go, whatever I do. It's as if it was meant to be. As if Daniel's disappearance had a point to it. She's a damaged child. I will have to work hard to gain her trust.'

'The child Dominique.'

I am done with asking questions. If she knows about Dominique then she probably knows about Simone too.

'No, not Dominique,' I say deliberately. 'She belongs in France. A family who have lost a daughter have applied to adopt her. I am going to adopt Simone.'

Her face contorts as if it is a rubber mask.

'Ah, the sister. So, Paola Dante hopes to make amends and put the world to rights. You would be well advised to take care. The limbo dancer's sinful blood courses through the veins of her abandoned firstborn. You are letting the devil's daughter into your home.'

I have long suspected Jasmine of being Simone's mother as well. All paths lead to Lady Limbo. Enid Lazzari's theatrics no longer intimidate me. Daniel has taught me that we can all be many things. I struggle against an emotion that is new to me. A fierce desire to protect something defenceless, something oddly precious to me. I speak firmly. 'No. She is a damaged child who acts the role of tough little minx, but she is not the devil, and she is not evil. She is the progeny of two confused human beings. Daniel wanted me to help her. He led me to her. We are both damaged; perhaps we can help each other. Simone has the right to be a normal teenager. You have to leave it to me now. You have to back off.'

Enid Lazzari's eyes have not left my face. 'You speak with

passion.' Then her gaze flits to the lacerations on my arms. 'You have been through much.'

'Why? Why didn't you tell me you knew where he was? Maybe Elijah would still be alive.'

'It would have changed nothing. It would not have saved Elijah Bloom's life or brought Gabriel back. The forces were unleashed a long time ago. The imperative was for Gabriel to go. As it was for you to search.'

I feel a searing rage at this jumped-up little guru woman with her orange wig in her faux opium den. What gives her the right to impose her pseudo-wisdom? 'It was necessary for you to suffer,' she drones on. 'Through suffering we learn our true heart.'

In my true heart I hate Enid Lazzari. I see now that what I felt for Jack was not hate; it was a kind of trumped-up derisive fury directed at myself.

'You knew all about RMI,' I accuse her.

She doesn't bother denying it.

'You're big on theory but not on the practical side,' I taunt. 'For future reference, it doesn't work the way they do it.'

'You didn't want to have a child. You ignored your dates,' Enid pronounces serenely.

'That's not true,' I splutter. 'They were practically red-letter days. How come you know so much about RMI anyway?' I stare at her, understanding dawning. 'You work for them.'

'I only work for myself,' she says, her eyes flashing. 'But it is an interesting organisation. I was approached because of my longstanding relationship with Gabriel.'

Daniel. Daniel. Daniel.

'Daniel is coming back.'

'You don't believe that or you wouldn't be here.'

'Daniel is the son of a poet. He has to write to live. When he's ready he'll come back.'

'Daniel is the son of a married circus performer,' Enid Lazzari says calmly. 'Marie Montaigne was a spinster who wanted to have a baby. She created a story that she could live with and she brought her son up on it.'

I don't remember how I got out of there but I remember saying, 'You know how to get hold of me if he ever wants to look me up. For a different kind of life. I'm still at P&P, running projects and crunching numbers, it's what I do. That's who I am.'

'We all have it in us to be far more than the sum of our parts,' she calls after me from her cave. 'You are fortunate to have come so far so quickly. Some never reach this stage of their soul's journey. You were, of course, given a marvellous opportunity.' Enid's voice follows me down the corridor, into the lift, out through the dingy entrance hall, into the street, past the car guard, and into my car. All the way home I consider her words. Driving home over Kloof Nek it seems important that I should have become more than the sum of my parts. As if I have crept a little closer to God.

But the feeling of euphoria is transient. Enid Lazzari's doomsday warning has its desired effect. Her remark about the sins of the mother being visited upon the abandoned firstborn has penetrated to the bone. The devil is always in the wings. The dark side is not yet vanquished; I must protect my adopted daughter. In this determined mood, I tell Simone that we have to go through the motions of a legal process to give her a new name so that she can start a new life untainted by the old. I even propose the name Carmen (a name I consider full of possibility). But Simone will have none of it.

'One day I will live in a house in Heaven with my real mother!' she yells at me in pale-faced defiance.

I stare at Daniel's daughter in horror. What have I done? I have tried to take her name away. Simone believes her name is all she has left of her real mother to carry her through life; I have tried to take her real mother's place. I can do neither of these things. We do not know exactly what we are to each other.

For a while, it feels as if we could as easily give up on each other as keep on going. At least one of my injustices is easily redressed and that is how we start again: I tell her that she will keep her name, and she smiles beatifically at me. It is the first smile I have seen from her in days.

But soon we have another fight because I confiscate her mobile after the school complains about her disruptive behaviour in class.

'One day I will live in Heaven with Daniel and Jasmine,' she screams at me as if her heart will burst.

I stop dead in my tracks. There is ice in my veins. I turn around and stare at her. A little stranger in my home. In the last few months Simone has lost some of her puppy fat and she has grown a few centimetres taller. She has full lips and thick, shining hair.

'How did you find out about Jasmine?'

Her smooth child-woman's face crumples and her mouth trembles. 'Daniel told me my mother's name was Jasmine. He said one day I would be pretty, just like her.'

I walk over and take her in my arms and to my surprise she doesn't resist. I hold her for a long time as she sobs and sobs, huge heart-rending sobs that shake her body. I find there are tears running down my face too. I have not cried this way since the night I saw my father's body on the mortuary slab, his head blown away by his own gun. Even when my body cried for Daniel, the tears would not come, even when I brushed tears away over Simone's cache of Smarties it was out of sheer exhaustion and relief. Now I cry for all of us, I cry rivers for what cannot be changed. My daughter and I fall asleep on the lounge couch in each other's arms.

This at last is the grief that follows loss.

A Daughter

IN THE WEEKS THAT FOLLOWED I tried to unravel the story. There was no one left to ask. They were all dead. Or missing.

I called Gi and asked her what the date of Dominique's birthday was. She had it right there on the birthday calendar: Dominique was born on 31 May 1997. Why did I want to know? I told her that according to her birth certificate Simone was born on 21 March 1995. I believed Jasmine was the mother of both girls. Gi considered this. Yes, she concluded, there were long periods when Celestine and Jasmine did not see each other so it would be possible that Celestine had not known of an earlier child.

I told Gi that in his manuscript Daniel had written about a ground stewardess, not about a dancer. It was a small, silly detail but why would he have done that?

Gi sighed softly as if she had expected my question. She should have told me long ago but she had not thought it would make a difference. So many people had been hurt. But now that I had taken on the care of Simone perhaps it was best that I knew.

Celestine and Jasmine were both intelligent women, she explained. Like many single women of their generation, they often talked about ways in which women could have genetically outstanding children without having to submit to the complications of marriage. Wasn't that why evolution had blessed us with large brains? To optimise our long-term reproductive success? Wasn't that what Darwin had bequeathed us? Reproductive sex on demand?

It was astonishing what Jasmine learnt from infatuated clients – it was her idea to put the Lady Limbo notice on the new online messaging system that was becoming all the rage. The message had been surprisingly effective, even in those early days of the Internet. But it was mainly men who responded, eager for unusual entertainment. Of course, the sisters already knew the address of RMI. Now Jasmine proposed offering it for a price to the men and women who replied to Lady Limbo. Celestine had vehemently opposed it. RMI stood for the emancipation of women from the chains of religion and society. The two sisters never resolved their differences over the matter.

I removed the envelope with Celestine's letter from the drawer where I had put it. There they were, Nicky, my boyfriend, with his dazzling grin and an arm around Jasmine. Daniel, his best friend, with the enigmatic eyes and the half-smile that I knew so well. I had never asked myself who the photographer was. Probably an obliging tourist. Now I realised it must have been Celestine who had choreographed the scene. I had found Lady Limbo: she had two heads. What a merry, merry dance she had led us all.

Klaus Knappman kept me informed about progress in the Sarrazin case. The more I learnt about Sarrazin, the more I was able to unravel the facts of Simone's disrupted life.

Albert Sarrazin was well known in the porn industry but he also owned several nightclubs, of which Pompadour was only one. His business dealings spanned continents, his particular predilections being the pornographic movie empire inherited from his father and child-trafficking in all its forms of predation. Albert Sarrazin had met his wife, Nada, a Czechoslovakian hooker and cocaine addict, on the movie set of a film he was personally directing. Two years after marrying her, he bought a child, apparently to distract her from her addiction. And that was how Simone came to the Sarrazin home, delivered in the capable arms of Nanny Hoogendoorn. Jasmine's blackmail of Jan van den Bogen would have ended there, and when Daniel looked her up after Nicky's death there would have been no sign of the infant girl conceived the previous summer in the shadow of the Eiffel Tower. By the time Dominique was born a year later, both sister and father were long gone. I could hear Celestine's voice as she tripped along at my side: *Remember my sister's early life before you judge her.* How history repeated itself in infinite variations!

I could only speculate about the life a small, defenceless girl would have lived in the Sarrazin home. After six years, Nada Sarrazin fell pregnant with her own child and by the time the family moved to South Africa, their son Sasha was three and Simone was nine years old.

Klaus Knappman had called me to say they were interviewing Sarie Abrahams, the housekeeper. Did I want to come and watch the interview through one-way glass? I hesitated, but I told myself that the more I knew about my daughter's past in that house, the more I could face whatever she was going to throw at me, so I went along and listened to the testimony. Once the housekeeper understood that she herself might be charged with child abuse she co-operated fully. She told the detective that Meneer Sarrazin had not involved himself with Simone's upbringing but it was he who had ordered Simone to be locked in her bedroom at night after she ran away. It was Mevrou Sarrazin who made the arrangements with Sarie for Simone's daily care but she was a busy businesswoman and hardly spent any time with her daughter. Dit was altyd maar net oor die seuntjie Sasha, she said. The mother of five and grandmother of eight confessed with much wringing of her handkerchief that occasionally Meneer would tell her to get Simone ready. She would wash her pretty yellow hair and bath her, and then she would bring her to where the films were made. Afterwards, the child would stare at the ceiling and not eat that night, but Sarie swore – *Die Here is my getuie!* – that she did not know what went on beyond the closed doors. As God was her witness.

A medical examination had shown that Simone's hymen was

intact, so her participation had been limited to sexual titillation, no doubt thanks to Albert Sarrazin's plan to auction her as a child virgin on the World Wide Web. The police psychologist who worked with such matters convinced me it would be best if I did not ever see the films, so that I would not prejudge her behaviour or limit my own capacity to treat her as a normal child.

Not surprisingly, Simone had become increasingly rebellious. Apart from her experiences in front of the cameras, a part of Simone must have resented her adoptive father's indifference to her and the favouritism he displayed towards his natural son. She was ten years old when she was detained for shoplifting after trying to leave a department store wearing lingerie for which she had not paid under her school uniform. Subsequent offences ranged from spray painting a neighbour's wall and scratching a teacher's car with a nail to stealing a bicycle, which she claimed to have borrowed for a few hours. She was repeatedly let off for reasons of insufficient evidence. Simone told me herself that she had never spent longer than an hour or two in a cell. Her adoptive father's fancy lawyers always arrived to take care of everything. Her activities must have finally brought her to Sarrazin's attention, as she had probably subconsciously intended. It was entirely likely that, faced with mounting lawyer's bills and the possibility of exposure, Albert Sarrazin decided to kill two birds with one stone by saving her for a fate worse than starring in a porn movie.

At some point Simone had contacted Daniel.

The way Simone told it, one day an envelope had arrived with a note containing a name and address purporting to be those of her real father. The Sarrazins had quickly removed it but not before Simone had read the contents and pocketed the head-and-shoulders photograph the anonymous sender had thoughtfully included. In her letter, Celestine had written that she had first learnt about Simone from Nathan, who had reported seeing Daniel with a schoolgirl. Had someone else engineered the first meeting between father and daughter? There was no reason for Celestine to have lied. Who else might have had an interest in Simone's relationship to Daniel?

I wanted it all behind us. The loose ends were terrifying to me. I missed Elijah and his step-by-step, level-headed approach. I even missed his pencils and the shavings he left behind him all over the place.

Also from Simone I learnt how she first met Daniel. She had informed him in a note left on his windscreen that he was her father and summoned him to a meeting at a restaurant in a shopping centre. Listening to her describe how she'd walked up and down a few times in front of the table where he sat waiting, I was reminded of a terrifying conversation I'd had with Monica after my return from Holland. I'd asked her how sexually mature she thought the average twelve-year-old was.

'Listen, honey bunch,' Monica had said, not taken in for one second by the casualness of my question, 'your girl's savvy about the birds and the bees, make no mistake about it. She probably knows more than you do. You just have to look around you next time you go shopping. They all copy the music and fashion channels and *Heat* magazine, and they pass around sex videos on their phones that would make your hair stand on end.' She eyed me sympathetically. 'I get the idea that underneath the big show Simone's wary of men. Still, I'd keep an eye on her – she's a stunner.'

I'd watched enough schoolgirls at shopping centres to know what Monica was talking about. They rolled their uniform skirts up and their socks down, and they wore their shirts half-in half-out, their young tits lifted high beneath the thin, white fabric. Often, they pulled their long hair up and let it tumble down, or wore it loose, and occasionally I'd spot a real Lolita wearing make-up that made her eyes and mouth look huge.

With horror, I imagined Simone flouncing to attract Daniel's attention. 'But he just ignored me,' she continued petulantly, 'so I went up to him and gave him a note that said "R50 for a blowjob".' She was so forthright, so shockingly honest, that it took a single drawn-in breath for me to realise that for twelve-year-old Simone, life was already full of irony. She was looking back at her precocious ten-year-old self, a child whose knowledge of the aberrations of human sexuality had been far beyond her years. She noticed my dismayed expression immediately.

'Geez, I was just joking,' she said, rolling her eyes and tossing her ponytail for extra effect. She went on to assure me with a superior air that she had never, *ever*, done such things but she knew plenty of *other* girls who did BJs for extra pocket money, or just because they wanted to be popular. At that moment I could see what arrested men and boys around her, the beguiling blue eyes gave it away: the intimate knowledge of dark carnal matters forced upon her by depraved adults. The chilling secrets that were hers alone. I didn't know what to say so she continued with her naive teenager act. One girl who worked in a men's clothing shop in the holidays made three times her daily wage just by giving the customers blowjobs while they were in the change cubicles. There was something immensely touching about her attempt to protect me from what she'd been through. I couldn't let her down. So I laughed with her at the thought of Daniel's discomfort.

'Men want girls that look like dolls they can break. That's why they always go for girls who wear those silly doll's shoes,' Simone said trenchantly with heartbreaking insight. Her stubborn resistance to girly footwear finally made sense.

She was tall for her age with long coltish legs. She could have passed for a sixteen-year-old. Daniel had been furious with her; he'd told her she was destroying her life. She'd reminded him that it was a bit late for him to be playing father. They'd both been a bit tense after that, but he'd asked to meet with her again. It was easy for me to imagine the ten-year-old conducting herself with far more composure than Daniel.

I played the scene over and over in my mind. How could Daniel have known for sure that Simone was his daughter and Jasmine her mother?

There was enormous publicity around the Sarrazin case. It captured the imagination of the international community with daily reports on all the major TV networks reaching every corner of the globe. Detective Knappman called one Saturday to let me know a senior official at the French Embassy in Cape Town had contacted him. This woman, after reminding him of her diplomatic immunity, told Klaus about a conversation she'd had with a French national who claimed that the Sarrazins were using an underage French child, their own adopted daughter, in porn movies. But the man had refused to make a written declaration and his allegations appeared so bizarre – the Sarrazins were well-known business people in the French community – that the matter had died there and then. A few months later, she had received a phone call from the same Monsieur de Luc but she had cut him off, thinking he was a madman.

So you did try to do something. You didn't just leave her there. There was ice in my veins as I put the phone down. The need to know exactly what had happened on that last day overwhelmed me.

I barged into Simone's bedroom without knocking. 'You were in the car with Daniel on the day he left.'

She lifted a headphone from one ear. 'What?'

'You phoned him that day. That was why he went out. Everyone thought it was a woman, but it was you.'

She removed the headphones and sat up, nodding, almost as if she'd been waiting for me to work it out. 'Yes,' she said. 'I'm hungry.'

It was an overcast windy day so I made us two mugs of real hot chocolate, the way my father used to do, melting a slab of dark chocolate and swirling it with just enough milk and a tiny knob of butter in a small saucepan. On our big comfortable couch, surrounded by cushions and sheltered from the outside elements, Simone started talking about what had happened on the day Daniel disappeared. She had arrived home from school at about 4 pm, after netball practice. Albert Sarrazin was waiting. He confronted her about the secret meetings with Daniel; he'd had her followed. Terrified of a man she knew to be capable of anything, Simone refused to tell him anything. He slapped her twice and threatened her, saying this was not the end of the matter. When he went out half an hour later, she slipped out of the house on a pretext, grabbing one of Nada's hats from the hat stand and using a barrette to pin up her long hair as a kind of disguise. She called Daniel from a payphone a few blocks away. She was close to crying, afraid of what would happen to them both. He told her to wait where she was and picked her up about twenty minutes later. They drove out to a viewpoint on Chapman's Peak.

'He kept looking in the rear-view mirror,' she said. 'There was a white car following us. It had dark windows.' Daniel stopped where several other cars were already parked waiting for sunset. He hit the steering wheel while she recounted Sarrazin's bullying tactics but otherwise he said very little. A while later, he drove back the same way, glancing frequently into the rear-view mirror. After stopping briefly at the apartment on the way, he dropped her off around the corner from the Sarrazin mansion. 'He hugged me and told me he'd find a way to get me out of there, but in the meantime I must be brave.'

Did she know what time that was?

It was about 6 pm. She ate supper together with Sarie as usual. That was the last time she had seen Daniel. As he'd pulled away, the white car with the tinted windows had slipped into the traffic behind him.

'Why did I do it?' she wailed into my hair, till I was damp with her grief. 'I think Albert wanted me to phone Daniel. He wanted Daniel to come. And then he had my father killed.'

'Don't cry, Simone. Don't cry like that. I'm sure he's not dead,' I drew her closer to me.

Daniel had called me at 4.10 pm and asked me to spell 'hippopotamus'. I'd been so complacent that afternoon. Life was good: my career was progressing well, the weekend was nigh and my husband was in an amorous frame of mind. In a different part of the city, a sick creep slapped a defenceless young girl and the world as Paola Dante knew it rocked on its axis. Within a couple of hours, it would be turned upside down.

* * *

With the assistance of Interpol and a set of excellent bookkeeping records, the Special Crimes Unit managed to uncover a web of deceit and sleaze that went back years before Jasmine and Daniel met. Sarrazin's bookkeeper bought his freedom by telling the authorities where a second secret set of his ex-employer's records were kept. These went back all the way to Sarrazin's youth, implicating him in a web of shady financial transactions. The meticulous process, designed to safeguard Sarrazin from the amoral scum he did business with, ultimately proved his downfall. With the help of names and bank details, the international child-trafficking agencies were able to make connections to other big players in the international illegal trade of children. A series of high-value transactions with various offshore companies in Barbados, Hong Kong, Mauritius and Dubai came to light. But there was no mention of a company called Real Man Inc.

I was in the kitchen early one morning when my eye caught the visuals of a building burning on BBC News; the brick structure was a raging, glowing furnace. I caught the words 'gas explosion, old quarter of Brussels, no one injured'. As the firemen charged with their hoses, the camera zoomed in on a familiar brass plaque at the front door: Research Management International. I was watching RMI go up in flames. The devil's forge. The roof caved in before my eyes, moments after firemen had evacuated; huge flames licked the night sky and smoke belched out of every corner. Damn. Damn. Damn. The belly of the monster was rumbling and roaring, destroying all evidence of its existence. But the sins of the flesh don't need a fixed abode.

'What's wrong?' Simone's curious voice cut into my thoughts.

'Nothing. Let's have breakfast.' I switched the television off.

Klaus told me later that the SA Police, with the assistance of Interpol, had obtained a court injunction in Belgium granting permission for a combined operation to raid the offices of Real Man Inc. and remove all computer and paper records held there. Before they'd been able to act, the central headquarters had been razed to the ground. As Madeleine – mysterious RMI Châtelaine of whom no trace could now be found – had once pointed out, the organisation existed in people's minds. It had many offices in many parts of the world.

I seethed with frustration. I longed for answers. Apart from the lost proof of RMI's existence, I could not accept that Simone's past had simply been obliterated. I would find someone who had proof of her identity. It was at that point that I decided to speak to Nada Sarrazin, desperate to fill in some of the gaps.

There was another reason I needed to speak to Nada. I had found a brand-new electric-blue bra and matching briefs in Simone's wash basket. She claimed she had bought them with Monica months ago but had just never worn them before. I must have looked sceptical or scared, or both, because she said with a hard little smile, 'Don't you believe me? Maybe you should just send me back. I don't care. It's boring here in this stupid flat the whole time. At least I wasn't bored with Nada.' Her words were serrated carving knives intended to sear and gash all at once.

What was Esmeralda's original advice, delivered with a pitying look? *When in doubt, resort to the truth.* 'I'm new to this whole mother thing, Simone. I don't know if I believe you or not.'

'What*ever*. It's your problem,' she said and flounced out of the room. At supper, we both acted as if nothing had happened.

There were other lies. Lies about make-up that appeared in her room, money that disappeared, lies about where she'd been, why she was late. The final straw came when Sharon rang my doorbell to ask if I knew where Miss Potter was. She said she'd left the door open while she went to get the mail – sometimes she liked to go down on her own – and when she returned she called and called but Miss Potter wasn't there. It was most unlike Miss Potter; she never went anywhere on her own. Perhaps Simone had seen her? She'd passed her in the corridor. Simone denied any knowledge of the dog's whereabouts but offered to go and look for her immediately. Sharon thanked her profusely, wringing her hands in a state of agitation. Two days and many phone calls later, Miss Potter was finally returned to her relieved owner. A woman had brought her in to the local SPCA after finding her tied to a pole on the beachfront.

'Did you do it?'

'I did her a favour.'

'Why, Simone?'

'She acts as if she can't live without the stupid dog.'

'She loves the dog. It's all she's got. It's specially trained to look after her.'

She shrugged. 'I went to look for it afterwards. It was gone. I knew she'd get it back. People always pick up abandoned animals. That way they feel good about themselves.'

'What happened to the girl who wanted an old cat that nobody else wanted?' The subject of getting a cat hadn't been mentioned again. I'd decided it was one of those teen ideas that came and thankfully went. Now, in spite of myself, I'd raised sleeping cats from where they rightfully belonged. A cat came with a smelly cat box.

'Did you think I meant it? I just said what you wanted me to say.' Her voice was almost gentle in its terrible implication.

I stared at her, horrified. Some detached part of me considered her allegation while my stomach churned and my throat clenched. Was she right? Had I put the words into her head, had some subconscious part of me wanted her to respond to the cat master's story in a certain way, and she'd picked it up with the razor-sharp antennae of youth, honed by her experience of adults? Had I sought to manipulate her, just like everyone else?

I didn't tell Sharon. I couldn't. Instead, I suggested an evening walk all together. I suspected Sharon knew but she said yes anyway, and she gave Miss Potter's lead to Simone while she held onto my arm. Simone took the lead nonchalantly, yanking it a little to show who was boss. I bought a tennis ball at Pick n Pay and we played with Miss Potter on the beach. There was plenty of excited barking to begin with but eventually the dog got the idea, running away with the ball up the beach with Simone chasing behind, kicking up beach sand in her barefooted wake. Sharon's sightless eyes followed the sound of Simone's raucous giggles and Miss Potter's yaps, her ears tuned for sound like an antenna. After that, Simone took Miss Potter for a walk on the shoreline while

Sharon and I sat on a bench and chatted.

'I believe Robert's son went into the merchant navy and his daughter became a journalist for CNN,' Sharon said quietly after a while. 'Then there was something about the son leaving the navy and buying a pizza restaurant. I always wondered what our children would have been like. I've come to think of Miss Potter as the closest thing I'll ever have to a child.'

'I'm sorry about what happened.'

'It was a terrible shock, but it made me realise I could manage without Miss Potter. I was becoming overly dependent on her. I'm thinking of attending that swimming-pool exercise session the Institute for the Blind have invited me to so often. What do you think?'

Life was full of surprises. 'I think it's a marvellous idea.'

'You can fetch Miss Potter any time you want, Simone,' Sharon said when we left her at her door. 'She hates being cooped up with an old blind person the whole time.' The dog did its one excited bark routine to let everyone know it completely agreed with the sentiments expressed.

'Maybe,' Simone shrugged. Later I convinced myself I must have imagined it, but for a moment I thought I saw her fingers brush against the dog's ear.

'If that works out, maybe I could leave her with you when I go for my swimming lessons once a week?'

'If you want,' Simone agreed nonchalantly. At that moment she looked like any other twelve-year-old, her face flushed with exercise and sea air. She sang at the top of her voice in the shower that night. '*Old MacDonald had a farm, ee-ai-ee-ai-oh! And on that farm he had three pigs, ee-ai-ee-ai-oh!*'

An African
Story

One night, Detective Olmi phoned. He told me to sit down and listen carefully. 'Elijah Bloom's death has achieved one thing. Nathan Khan and his sister Heidi …'

'*Sister*?'

'Mais oui. Heidi is the sister of Nathan.'

It is an African story of dispossession and diaspora. A young girl flees her burning village and her torn country. This courageous young refugee makes her way south, getting lifts and doing what has to be done in order to stay alive. After many months, she finds an older brother again, the rest of the family all dead. Together the brother and sister decide that it is better others do not know because in their village their father was an important man.

It was a good thing he'd told me to sit down. I saw the horrific scene again: a mother and sisters raped and disembowelled, brothers slashed with machetes, the rivers of blood baked into the African soil by the pitiless sun. Nathan had not witnessed the massacre but he'd experienced it all through the eyes of Heidi, the only remaining member of his family. I could see the young girl watching, tears streaming down her face.

Annie, my psychic sister-in-law, knew all along. And I didn't.

'Are you there, Madame?'

'Oui.' My voice was a small croak.

Detective Olmi, calling long after normal working hours from the Hotel de Police in Villegny, France, went on to tell me that Heidi and Nathan had voluntarily offered their services as state witnesses in the case against Sarrazin. Based on their signed statements, the police now believed that Albert Sarrazin, king of porn, was behind my *hosband's* disappearance. Nathan was convinced that the reason Daniel had been forced to disappear was that he had foolishly threatened Sarrazin with the exposure of his criminal activities if he harmed Simone. Many of the young women who worked in Sarrazin's club had been brought into the country on false pretences, naively believing promises that they would be trained as hairdressers or beauticians, and been given false papers. Nathan had observed several angry exchanges between Sarrazin and Daniel at Pompadour, and had on two other occasions come to Daniel's assistance when he was attacked by Sarrazin's thugs. At a certain point, Daniel must have decided his only course of action was to disappear, banking on the fact that Sarrazin would not harm Simone or me for fear of attracting attention to himself. Nathan and Elijah had kept the full story from me. They reckoned that my natural behaviour was my best protection: the more I acted like the proverbial bull in the china shop, the more it would convince Sarrazin that I had no idea where Daniel was. In Detective Olmi's opinion, it all made sense. He had undertaken to inform me before the newspapers got hold of the story. Mention was made by Nathan of incriminating files in my possession.

'It was a bluff,' I said. 'There was nothing in the files that could have identified anybody. My husband is a writer; he does not have a criminal mind.'

'Ah. A *bloff*. But he is a writer of thrillers, is he not? Where are the files?'

I noted the present tense – was it tact or did he know something more? But I could not help him.

'I deleted them by accident,' I said.

'Merde. Of course you did.' After a pause he said, 'I could get a court interdict and have the computer seized.'

'You would find nothing.'

'Your husband is a fortunate man, Madame de Luc.'

I had first requested permission from her lawyer to visit Nada Sarrazin soon after I heard my application to foster Simone had been successful. She had repeatedly refused, saying she had nothing to say to me. Out of the blue, her hotshot lawyer contacted me to say his client had agreed to see me; a good report from me on the witness stand might increase her chances of a lenient sentence. He suggested I take a packet of Gauloises in with me; it made the smokers more relaxed and talkative. *Don't forget an ashtray – tin, not glass – the guards don't like it if the visiting room gets dirty.*

On Tuesday, 22 May 2007, I went to Pollsmoor Prison, straight from a project meeting. Nada Sarrazin had startling almond eyes and spiky, black-tinted hair with fading platinum blonde highlights. In the deep rasping voice of a heavy smoker, she asked if I had a cigarette. I passed a cigarette and a tin ashtray under the mesh barrier that separated us, leaving the open blue packet on the ledge where she could see it. As she leaned forward for me to light the cigarette, I noticed a small scar above the full lips. That seductive mouth had once had a starring role in her husband's films.

'I want to know about Simone.'

'Why?' she asked, blowing smoke directly at me.

'I want to adopt her.'

She removed the cigarette from her mouth and scrutinised me coolly.

'What is she to you?'

'My husband has been missing for well over a year now.'

'Je suis desolée.'

Appealing to her humanity wasn't going to work. Those mocking eyes challenged me to tell the whole truth, nothing but the truth. 'He wanted me to look after her. I don't know why.'

She nodded as if satisfied with my answer. 'So little Simone's dark cloud has a silver lining. And what will happen to little Sasha?'

'Your son? I can't tell you that.'

'I will tell you. Sasha will live with my parents in France. No one will know he is Albert Sarrazin's son: they will be given new identities in a safe town. The public prosecutor has offered this deal in exchange for my testimony. I will have no way of knowing if they are keeping their side of the bargain. You will visit my son once a year and bring me news.'

So that was why she had agreed to see me.

'They will expect your testimony to put your husband in jail for a very long time. Your own safety can't be guaranteed.'

'I am prepared for that. You will bring me proof that Sasha has a new life. Those are my terms. Yes or no?' Her voice was very calm. She blew a smoke ring upwards as she waited for my answer.

'Who will pay for the trips?'

'That is your problem. All our funds have been blocked, thanks to you.'

I made a quick decision. 'In return, you will tell me everything I need to know. If I should find out that you have misled me in any way our agreement ends.'

'Everything you need to know, Paolita,' she agreed sardonically. I didn't like her tone or the Mexicanisation of my name. But with my co-operation assured, she settled back and started to talk.

'Albie brought her to our home outside Paris one day.'

Hearing that name made me recoil. 'You mean your husband, Albert?'

In Daniel's *Lady Limbo* comic, Albie was the name of the man who corresponded with Lady Limbo, the man who possibly killed her.

'Albert, Albie. What is it to you? Are you listening or talking?'

'I'm listening.'

'So I tell you how she arrived. I didn't want her. What is an addict supposed to do with a bébé? I told him to take it back to the mother. He laughed and said he didn't think the mother would give his money back.' She exhaled slowly.

'Did he say the mother's name?'

She waved a hand as if she was swatting a fly.

'For weeks I didn't touch her. Albie and I fought a lot. Comme toujours. Albie would drink too much and then he would slap me around till I begged forgiveness. After that, we'd fuck. But one night when I told him again to take the brat away he grabbed her by the armpits and held her over the balcony railing. She started crying.'

How much does a small child remember? Does it come back later in dreams?

Nada Sarrazin paused, rubbing her upper lip where the scar was with a finger. 'I told him to stop fooling around and give the bébé to me, but he just laughed. He told me to go down on my knees and beg – all the time she was crying louder and louder, it was making my head hurt – so I went down on my knees and begged. He let her fall into my arms and said I could have la petite putain.'

The little whore. She didn't stand a chance.

She watched me with a tight smile. 'Should I carry on?'

'Did you ask about the mother?' I repeated coldly. Each of us had been brought to this room by circumstances we'd participated in, now we were locked in this game as combatants.

She ran a thumb along her bottom lip as she considered my question. 'Albie knows many people: artists, writers, filmmakers. When we first met, I asked him when he was going to make proper films. He became angry and said proper films don't make you filthy rich, but with filthy rich you become famous.'

'Could we stick to Simone?' I snapped.

'You have the impatience of your kind. Bien, as you wish,' she shrugged. 'We were starting on a new film. I was to wear a chinchilla fur coat Albie had brought from Hamburg.' I let her talk. 'A few days before the shoot, we went for a walk around the city centre – to break in the coat, he said. I was naked under the chinchilla fur – oh là là, it was extrême! – we made love against a concrete pillar, just around the corner from the Arc de Triomphe.' She leaned forward, her mouth so close to my face I smelt prison food on her stale, warm breath as she stage-whispered, 'Have you ever had sex in a public place, Paolita?'

Amoral, unashamed slut that she was, she instinctively knew I was a voyeur of her antics; I could see her pressed up against the wall, her nails dug into his shoulders through his shirt, the violent push and shove of him into her, the convulsive orgasm with its saturated cry. The foetid prison air of our confined meeting space was redolent with the odour of sex. I, Paola Dante, who practised total control in the face of all provocation and abhorred female tactics, felt a hot tell-tale flush creep to my hairline.

She watched quietly, the mocking eyes enjoying my discomfort.

'Carry on,' I said through gritted teeth.

'Alors. During the shoot, with that soft fur around me, I asked him about the bébé's mother. Talk about his other women always aroused me. La jalousie, c'est aphrodisiaque.' The almond eyes smouldered. 'As we filmed, he talked about Jasmine, a dancer in a club on the Champs-Élysées. A woman like her dazzled men, he said – she made them crazy.'

A door clanged shut in the corridor of arrival as I fumbled in my handbag. An armed prison guard escorted another visitor into the visiting room. A heavy-set man in a suit with a briefcase nodded to me in greeting as he sat down on a chair at another booth.

The black lace knickers I'd worn as Mata Hari and grabbed on my way out of Jack's city loft chose that moment to emerge, limpet-like and slickly synthetic. *Shit*. That's what happened when you changed handbags. I disentangled my hand and shoved them back, promising myself savagely that I'd bin them as soon as possible. *Slow down. Focus.* I finally found what I was looking for. The picture was a close-up of Daniel that Nathan had taken with a telescopic lens. I put the picture up against the mesh.

'Do you know this man?'

Her eyes took in his face as she slowly exhaled.

'Even in a picture he can make a woman's knees turn to jelly. Every woman knows this man. He is a man who can make a woman weep with pleasure,' she said huskily. The blood was wrung from my heart. I felt physical pain.

'Should I carry on?' she taunted. 'For such a man lovemaking is an art …' She grew suddenly tired of her game. 'But if I knew him then I have forgotten him.'

So that's the way she wanted to play it. 'I'll take that as a no,' I said, changing tack, determined not to let her get to me. 'Let's stick to your husband. Do you think he had anything to do with Daniel's disappearance?'

She shook her head, the almond eyes narrowing. 'That's not Albie's style. He's a sadistic son of a bitch. He prefers making people suffer. His master plan was to have Simone in his movies. He brought her in to watch the filming even when she was very young.'

'You let him?' I rose to my feet in fury. 'What kind of a woman are you to let something like that happen to a little girl?' I battled to maintain control. Murderous thoughts flooded my head. If the steel mesh hadn't been there I might have throttled her.

'You want to judge me? Bien. You think there was someone to protect me when I was her age? She never had to go on the streets. I did what I could. Because of her I stopped the hard drugs. I kept her away from him. I invented an infection that wouldn't go away. He called a doctor to examine her. So I paid the doctor to lie. Do you want to know how I paid the doctor? No, of course you don't. Nice girls like you don't want to know how bad girls like me get by. When we came here to South Africa matters became worse; she started to do naughty things. A few times, Albert went into a rage and beat her with a belt. Sometimes she managed to slip out and run away. One time, I drove around for days until I found her with the street people who live under the bridge. Other times the police brought her back. She endangered us all; we had to change our plans.'

'You mean, that's when you both decided to sell her to the highest bidder,' my voice grated.

'Fuck you, Miss Perfect. Why are you here? Look at yourself. You're nothing but a cocksucker in a businesswoman's suit.'

I sat down shakily, struggling to recover myself.

'What about a birth certificate? She must have had papers to travel.'

She watched me with those unnerving eyes, the scar above

her mouth twitching, pulling the upper lip towards it. That small movement echoed in my groin – I saw the huntress in her, I detected an odour that drew my flesh to her. She was unashamedly irredeemable. I understood how a man would want to make this woman do unspeakably erotic things. But she remained broodingly silent.

'If I'm going to help with your son, I want answers.'

'Perhaps that is why your Daniel has gone away; you are so busy being perfect you are hardly a woman any more.'

We glared at each other.

'You want to know? Bien, I will tell you. Albie came home with a birth certificate one day. He said it was some dead child's certificate with the name changed. That way there'd never be any questions asked,' she shrugged. 'What does it matter anyway? I wouldn't worry if I was you. Genetics are a funny thing. If you ask me, Simone looks more like Albie. From the way he talked he was screwing the same woman your Daniel was. Makes one think, doesn't it?'

'Go to hell!'

'Not just yet, Paolita. My lawyer says I'll get ten years max, then I'm out. Remember our deal, or I'll come and find you.' She crushed the cigarette out as if it were my nice-girl head she was smashing to a pulp and rose from the chair.

'Hey, your cigarettes! I've still got some questions.' She rapped loudly at a window next to the door, ignoring me.

But my stint in limbo had taught me something.

'Poor little Sasha – everybody will be looking for him.'

She turned round slowly, her face expressionless.

'As I said, I still have some questions.' The silver Porsche Carrera. 'And for little Sasha's sake, I suggest you skip the bullshit. What were you doing at our apartment?'

'I don't remember,' she sneered.

'Try harder,' I suggested. 'Did you have your people trash my things?'

'Your Daniel is a stubborn fool,' Nada Sarrazin said, spitting words at me like bullets. 'Albie was in a rage that Simone had contacted him. I warned him not to interfere.'

I almost believed her. Still, I wasn't about to let her off the hook.

'I will come again at exactly the same time next year. And you will give me all the information I want before I give you news of Sasha.' I spoke softly, tunelessly, savouring a delicious sensation of power as I contemplated my hands. I finally had her full attention. When I looked up, the almond eyes were watching me, glittering with hate. 'A year can be forever, or it can be a minute.' A guard opened the heavy door and let her pass.

At the last moment she turned around. 'A futon is so hard. I would change it.'

Our audience was over.

Did you seduce her on our bed? Do I love you a little less with each discovery? Is that how love ends? By a process of subtraction?

My chair ground back across the concrete floor; my teeth were gritted in place. The lawyer-fellow glanced across, stopping his conversation with another inmate mid-sentence. He came across to me.

'Mrs de Luc?'

'Yes,' I mumbled, deeply uncertain of why I had come to this depressing, airless place. What had I expected? Soothing answers?

'I've heard about your story. Hans Merensky at your service. I'm a family lawyer. Here's my card.'

Through the enlarging porthole of the magnifying glass, Albert Sarrazin is a flaccid pink-skinned man with sandy-coloured hair around a balding, shiny crown who wears what I take to be a real panama hat when he faces the media. He has the incongruous look of a Scottish confidence trickster on the Italian Riviera.

I place Simone's picture between Albie's and Daniel's and zoom in and out, scrutinising their physiognomies with the dogged determination of a scientist searching for topographical clues to life on distant planet surfaces. In the end, I am forced to admit there is no telling. The huge blue eyes with irises like starbursts survey the world with a knowing expression that takes without giving anything away. Her mouth has something of Daniel's expression; the long-limbed body may also be his contribution to the information encoded in her genes. It is irrefutable that her hair colour, with its strawberry blonde tint, is most similar to Albert Sarrazin's, but I know this is not a definitive genetic marker. Besides, he probably lightens his hair. Finally, I conclude she looks like herself, with Jasmine's long black lashes against the fair skin, and the thick, shining hair and wide, sensual mouth. The unknown father has left few outer traces of himself.

Driving along the road, I spot a teenager with jeans hanging perilously low on her boyish hips, showing off three laughing dimples in a charming triangular arrangement on her lower back. For a while, I turn into a sniffer-dog hunting down physical attributes that lie hidden under clothing. I make excuses to go into the room while Simone is changing. I barge in while she's showering on the pretext of looking for my shampoo. I discover another tattoo, a red rose with thorns, on her hip bone but no dimples, no birthmarks, only the brown mole on her cheek. Simone's soft girl-child's skin holds all its secrets intact. It gives no clues to her origin.

There are biological fathers and fathers of the heart. It would have to be enough that Simone believed Daniel was her father.

For my part, I accepted that motherhood was something I would have to work at. I was alone in an open boat on the psychic equivalent of the Bering Strait. I knew only that in another world the reach of a hand away, she was easy prey and I was all there was between her and the predators of the night. Time is the great equaliser. I decided that I would let time instruct me, do nothing in a hurry. For once, I rejected the safe harbour of a plan with a schedule. I could learn slowly as I went along. I could let my daughter show me what she needed from me.

What was it Enid Lazzari had said? *It is not necessary for a child to be of one's blood for one to love that child.* I heard something in that echo I had not heard the day Enid Lazzari spoke the words: she had put herself into the words. She was speaking from first-hand knowledge.

* * *

Hey, honey bunch, where are you hiding yourself these days? Guess who's selling up? Remember you telling me about the billionaire Dutch guy that owns oil platforms? The one who took Daniel and his mother in when he was a kid? Well, a few days ago, this old-school guy in a yellow Lamborghini pulls up in front of our offices. It's him – Jan van den Bogen. He came to put the Llandudno family home on the market. His wife Cecilia lives there. It's part of a divorce settlement. I met with Cecilia yesterday. She's off to Majorca as we speak. Strange old goose. It got me thinking. Maybe Daniel went to stay with them for a while? I'm doing a show house there next Sunday. Why don't you come and keep me company? Call me.

* * *

A few days after my interview with Nada Sarrazin, on a blustery Saturday afternoon, Detective Olmi again called from France.

It now seemed certain that Albert Sarrazin's low-key profile as a soft porn movie producer in sunny South Africa was a successful front for the more lucrative business of heading up the European child racketeering gangs. He was most certainly one of the masterminds in a vast international child-trafficking organisation. If they could cut a few heads off the Hydra, it would be a major setback for the racketeers. Who knew if it might not break the monster's back?

So, why can I still smell the monster's stinking breath?

They had an important witness in a safe custody programme – a French lawyer who was implicated in many of Sarrazin's deals, including the adoption of several babies. The French law enforcement agencies were now reinvestigating the whole Sarrazin case. With this lawyer's evidence and the meticulous bookkeeping records Albert Sarrazin had himself insisted on, he could be linked to almost all the women in the later newspaper articles. These cases were being reopened as proper murder investigations. Each of the women had once sold a child for adoption to Sarrazin via a third party. The sale of the children was conducted by Sarrazin himself. No records had been kept of their whereabouts. Unfortunately, the records did not extend as far back as the earlier deaths.

This is for you, Elijah. I can't think why else I'm asking this question.

'Can I ask you something?'

'Naturally.'

'What made you investigate those women's deaths? Why didn't you think they were accidents, like everybody else did?'

His fatigued voice finally replied. 'I had my reasons. An informant. But it is now a police matter, part of this investigation. I cannot tell you more.'

Could it be that you were right, Elijah? Did Jasmine want to make amends for helping to create a monster?

'Can you tell me who the other women are? The ones you can't link to Sarrazin?'

Olmi was silent for a moment. 'Perhaps you will remember something that will help us so I will tell you. We have nothing on the train death. An English schoolteacher who lived alone on a modest stipend. She is an enigma. The other woman – the Verbier skiing accident – was the opposite: a cover model for many fashion magazines, even for *Vogue*. A young woman who had everything. Galia Ustinov is not her real name; it is a stage name. Her father is a politician in Russia.'

'What is her real name?'

'Tamara Abramova.'

Tamara. She is the long-limbed warlike daughter of a Cossack.

'After we put some pressure on him and he spoke to his lawyer her partner has had a change of heart. He has confessed all. She was over-friendly with her ski instructor. In a fit of jalousie, her partner challenged her to ski the infamous Tortin black piste with him. When she slipped on the ice and fell hundreds of metres to the bottom, he panicked and left the scene. But there is no suspicion of murder. We French understand un crime de passion. He is a wealthy man. A little son awaits his father. The judge will be lenient.'

'The camel can take so much and then you add a single straw and its back breaks,' I heard myself say into the telephone. 'I've read that it's true. At least that the camel won't go on. It refuses to continue one second longer.'

'And by this you mean?' his puzzled voice came back.

'Who is looking after the child?'

'He is with his paternal grandparents.'

'Paternal? I don't think so.' I heard myself laugh, a raw sardonic laugh.

'You are implying that he is not the father?'

I remained silent. Olmi could work it out for himself. I was weary of it all. So many children in compromised situations.

'An RMI child that she refused to give up? Diable! Why did we not think of it! Perhaps it is murder, after all,' Olmi sighed. 'But our hands are tied. There isn't a judge in France who will agree to a DNA test. When the court asks – where is the evidence that this RMI ever existed? – qu'est-ce que je peu dire?'

RMI exists. There is a surveillance recording that proves it.

'I'm sorry. I can't help you,' I said.

I have to think. I grab my rain jacket and head for the beach after telling Simone I'm going for a walk. Klaus's unit is too short-staffed to spare detectives for protection duty so I've approached Heidi. Since her previous employer is now a fugitive from the law, Heidi has moved on to start her own company, which hires out trained female bodyguards ('like the Russians do'). She has taken to wearing black pantsuits of a high-shine fabric, her glistening body seeming even more explosive in the new costume. And her shoes, for those who look, are always black snakeskin. I've checked with her whose side she's on right now and she says she's always been on Simone's side so I don't need to worry.

In the lobby, I ask the bodyguard Heidi has provided to watch TV with Simone while I'm out. Samba Nyerere nods and goes up in the lift. She has teenage children of her own so she knows how to handle Simone. We've grown used to having her around.

There are rock pigeons foraging in the littoral zone, close to where the big waves come ravaging up the shoreline to reclaim what is theirs. Today is an off-day for the tourist-brochure designers. The sea is not tranquil or azure; it has the wild aggression of a gangster with foul-smelling breath. There are mounds of kelp stockpiled between the damp sand and green grass, long coils of seaweed bunched like a nest of vipers. Under my footfalls, they are surprisingly tough and springy.

On a good day, this beachfront shines as warmly bright as Paradise. On a bad day, you notice the peeling walls of the tidal pool, the overflowing waste bins and the folded white plastic deckchairs that look decrepit, unloved and unsalvageable. The sage waves thunder in. An outcrop emerges from the turbulence with the calloused back of a whale. The odour of decaying plant life hangs over everything. Tomorrow is another day.

Huddled in my raincoat on a giant boulder surrounded by a roiling sea, I call Nathan on the mobile. It's our first conversation since the funeral.

'I want you to take the surveillance recording to Olmi in France and deliver it to him personally. I'll pay for the trip. Will you do it?' I ask without ceremony.

'You don't have to do this,' Nathan growls. 'Give him your husband's files. Goddammit, Paola, why are you still trying to protect Daniel?' I close my eyes. At least he hasn't put the phone down. The deep voice sounds close by.

'The recording proves that RMI exists. Olmi can use what Jack said to convince the judge. The files won't do that.'

Nathan stays silent but he's listening.

'I was walking on the beach, trying to work out why the thought of total strangers listening to it upset me so much. It seemed cowardly. Love feels a lot like loyalty sometimes.'

'I can't figure you out. You watch Elijah get killed over some files that any normal woman would have handed over long ago and then you hand this French detective your personal life with a can opener attached. What happens if Galahad comes back?'

'You know what? I've thought about all that. I don't know what happens then. But it still feels as if it's the only thing to do.'

'I said some things about you that were pretty harsh,' he says eventually. 'I was out of line.'

'Don't apologise, Nathan. It's funny, you know? I took a gamble that they'd think I hadn't shown the Limbo Files to the police because I didn't want anyone to know about Daniel's other women, and then I nearly covered up the tape's existence.'

In the end he agrees. He will collect it from the security box using the password only he knows and take it to Olmi.

'I do some insane shit for you, you know that?' But I can hear that he approves of what we're doing with the tape.

I walk back to the apartment feeling lighter than I've felt in months.

Let's see you wriggle out of this one, you child-trafficking, murdering bastards.

* * *

Towards the end of May, in the week of my thirty-first birthday, my mother invited herself to lunch to meet 'that girl of yours face-to-face', as she put it.

Twenty-seven scented yellow roses in a silver bucket. Twenty-eight scented yellow roses in a silver bucket. Twenty-nine scented yellow roses in a silver bucket. *Mon amour, a birthday is a celebration!* Dancing in his arms around the apartment on bare feet to the slow Parisian beat of Édith Piaf and *La Vie en Rose*.

I had been about to let the occasion slip by without acknowledgement. In that way, he could walk in the door any minute and it would be as if our lives had been interrupted for a moment and then everything had started up again. But it seemed I had no choice in the matter. I told my mother not to bring a present or make a fuss because Simone knew nothing about it and it would only embarrass her. We were all nervous.

Perhaps she was trying to find a subject more interesting to a young girl than the gallery or her latest protégé when she started telling us about a naturopath she'd been seeing who'd suggested colonic hydrotherapy as part of a detox diet to get rid of her migraines.

My mother had always relished matters relating to human excretion and waste, believing they were good grounding subjects.

'Ugh. Gross,' Simone said. Taking this as her cue, my mother gave an explicit explanation of the process as we consumed cold meats and cheese and a huge salad. Simone's eyes went wide and she spluttered over her food.

'TMI,' she gurgled as she rushed from the room. I found her screaming with laughter on her bed. Too much information! My mother was still taking delicate mouthfuls of food, seemingly unfazed by the helpless giggles emanating from the bedroom. Her response to Simone's arrival had been more muted than I'd expected. No telephonic recriminations, no snide, abusive comments. I'd contacted her when the newspapers picked up the story, telling her everything on the phone, silently daring her to interrupt, but she hadn't. My explanation was met by total silence. She was probably calculating the number of months I'd been deceiving her about Daniel's disappearance.

Now she sat opposite me, for once not implying with her body language that I was responsible for the mess my life was in. Out of the blue, she asked if I ever played the piano. It had been my father's idea to buy it, she said; he'd wanted us to learn to play because he'd never had the opportunity himself. I stared at her, nonplussed. Why was she telling me now? I didn't remember it that way. I'd always believed she'd bought the thing with the purpose of turning me into a concert pianist. I was still absorbing this new knowledge when she hit me with the next question: Did I think Daniel would come back now? I told her I had no idea but I hadn't given up on him, and lifted my glass of white wine to hers. She chinked her glass against mine and we looked into each other's dark eyes, something we had not really done since I was five years old, or thereabouts.

When it grew quiet between us, I got up to wash the dishes. She said she'd go and see how Simone was doing. Half an hour later they returned arm-in-arm and Simone served us pudding as if nothing had happened. She'd made the trifle herself from a recipe she'd found on one of the biscuit packets. My mother asked for seconds. Simone had a highly chuffed air about her as she ladled out another helping.

'Why don't you play something for us, Paola? While I make us some tea.'

'You said you can't play,' Simone said, turning to me, eyes accusing. 'You lied.'

'Of course she can play. It's something you never forget, like riding a bicycle,' my mother said, ignoring my expression.

'Cool. Can you show me how to play?'

'You want to play piano?' I asked carefully.

'I guess. Debussy is cool. And Rachmaninoff. They're like … masters of the universe.'

'They are?' Where did she come up with this stuff? 'I was going to tell Romy she could take it.'

'Romy wants Storm to play the trumpet,' my mother said, waving all negativity into the ocean. 'It's Simone's piano now.'

I turned to look at her. *It is?* For the second time that day, my mother held my gaze.

When I'd finished my impromptu performance to a standing ovation, I asked Simone if she'd like to try. *Do! Re! Me! Fa! So! La! Ti! Do!* Watching those schoolgirl fingers with the chewed nails carefully pick out their first tune, it struck me that the objects of our lives carry our history deep within the cracks and seams of their inanimate beings, and this piano, touched by everybody I had once loved, still loved and now loved, was the equivalent of a powerful tribal totem in my lounge.

Before she left, my mother took Simone's hand and wrapped it gently (é molto fragile!) around an object in tissue-paper, then she hurried away, not looking back. Simone opened her hand. The pink tissue paper sprang apart and we both saw a perfectly preserved white icing-sugar swan. It was left to me to tell my adopted daughter about the Swan Lake birthday cake, how I had never seen a cake like it, before or since, how my mother had taken one look at my face before swooping in to rescue the one remaining elegant swan from the party predators. This then was the only surviving swan of my thirteenth-birthday cake.

'Rad!' Simone said. 'Your mother's pretty cool.'

She left me encrypted notes like 'C U @ scul @ 4'. She asked me how fast I could say 'supercalifragilisticexpialidocious'. Roxy, a sun-streaked school friend, arrived to stay the weekend with two surfboards in tow. 'You're *sooo* lucky to live on the beach!' Roxy exclaimed. I asked Roxy how she'd started. She said her mom and dad had taken her with them on the board when she was still a toddler. Her dad had chosen her name. Simone was going to use her mom's old wetsuit. They spent the weekend out in the waves. On Sunday, I went to see what progress had been made. I watched Simone's fearless rush into the jaws of the sea, how she climbed up and fell off into the churning white water, time and time again, Roxy shouting encouragement as she paddled furiously alongside. When she managed to maintain her balance for a few seconds and streak through the water with wings, before being catapulted head-first into the waves, my body stopped all breathing reflexes until her head and the surfboard bobbed up several metres away. I was still lightheaded when she came rushing up the beach, jubilant and out of breath.

'Did you see? I stood up! *Yes!*' She punched a fist into the air. 'That was so cool! Did you bring something to drink?' She drank thirstily and ran back, not giving me a backward glance.

* * *

Once the story was all out, or what we were able to piece together into a semblance of reality, her citizenship was resolved. She was now legally under the guardianship of the South African state. It had not been easy, but with the evidence of Nat the Bear and his sister Heidi, and Klaus Knappman the young detective, and Esmeralda the social worker, and Hans Merensky who had ironed out all the legal issues and ensured that the best interests of the child prevailed, we had straightened matters out to the satisfaction of the authorities.

The Sarrazins co-operated from their cells in the men's and

women's blocks of the high-security prison used for high-ranking sexual offenders. They signed a document admitting the illegality of the adoption and giving up all their rights as adoptive parents in the hope of having their sentences reduced. This was merely a technicality, Hans assured me. Just a safety measure in case the absence of documents ever made a judge uncomfortable or the Sarrazins were ever found to have rights under a future French law or government. It was simply a matter of dotting the i's and crossing the t's. With all the necessary documentation in place, she was declared a ward of the court to allow the judge time to reach a decision.

After a trial period of twelve weeks, which went better than anyone had expected, the court finally concluded it would be in Simone's best interests to live with me as a parent on a permanent basis. I was granted permission to officially adopt her.

'Life has given you another chance, young lady,' the magistrate intoned ominously, glaring down at Simone. With her shaggy grey hair and piercing eyes under fierce eyebrows, she looked more like a witch on her broom blown off-course by the South Easter than a high-ranking officer of the law, but Hans assured us we were lucky to have been assigned to her court: she made decisions quickly and she had an open mind. For a moment, in the whirring of the overhead fan, I heard Elijah's voice: *An open mind is always good,* and I imagined he was squeezing my hand in a brotherly way. Magistrate Ponting pointed a stubby warning finger at Simone. 'Don't mess it up by doing something silly, young lady. No more shoplifting or vandalism. No fancy lawyers are going to stop you going into a reformatory next time. Am I being clear? Do you *get* me?'

'Yes, Ma'am! Yes, Judge, I mean. I will do my best. I definitely won't shoplift or scratch cars again. I get you.'

The adults in the room hid relieved smiles. I was wondering if the feeling of terrified joy would ever leave me.

'And you, young woman.' I snapped to attention. She was talking to me. The terror-inducing judge of my dreams. Judgement Day was upon me. 'Do you understand the responsibility you are taking upon yourself? Do you understand that this child's trust has been repeatedly broken by the adults around her, and it must not happen again? Do you freely take this child to be your daughter? Will you stand by her in the good times and the bad?'

'I do your worship, I do. I do. And I will.'

'Very well, off you go. I don't want to see either of you here again. Make it work,' the magistrate said, looking down at her papers as she waved us away.

As we all troop out obediently, I dare to take Simone's hand and she does not pull it back. One day she will have a woman's hands – slender hands with long, strong nails. Jasmine will breathe in her daughter's ear in my house, and I will put up with it because I am on Earth and she is somewhere else. I thank all the guardian angels who stuck around.

Simone sings a French children's ditty as she skips along next to me:

'sonnez les matines, sonnez les matines,
DING! DANG! DONG!
DING! DANG! DONG!'

I will love you with my last breath, I tell Daniel as I hold on to her.

The
Anteroom

THERE I AM. IT IS AN OLD, pleasant daydream. The unmistakable
aroma of pasta alla carbonara greets me as I come out of the
lift. I fly as light as an evening moth on the air that brings me
to the front doorway of our apartment. The door stands open;
I only have to float towards the light. Daniel stands there in an
immaculate white apron and chef's cap, holding a pan out, the
pancetta sizzling. Simone waves a handful of knives and forks,
her lips quivering with laughter, her beloved face turned to me in
rapturous anticipation. The table is being laid for three.

'Bien venue, ma chérie. What took you so long?'

* * *

Another year has passed. A cold, wet winter has come upon us
early. Simone has officially been in my care for almost a year and
there is still no word of Daniel. I live one day at a time. I take
nothing for granted. It is the oddest thing but now that Simone
is here with me I sense him everywhere. I put the words 'not yet'
and 'already' to the test: It is now *not yet* three years since Daniel

disappeared from my life. It is now *already* two years since Daniel disappeared from my life. Every time she hums a tune I turn around to look. I see now that my fears were unfounded and that all the sour grapes fermented into mischief shall not poison us after all. The resemblance to Daniel is uncanny, more in the gestures, in the playful tone of her voice, in the solemn beauty of her eyes, in the way she tilts her head at the mynahs, in the way she likes to sketch scenes of people busy with their lives with a common soft pencil. She looks at things with his inner eyes although she is a child and she has led a different life. I see Jasmine, too, and I marvel how one human being can carry so much genetic information in her slight frame.

I have not slept properly since Sarrazin was granted bail of half a million rand. They put a picture of him leaving the courtroom with his team of silks on the front page – a dapper dresser in a white suit with a navy-blue silk shirt and white leather shoes. Nada Sarrazin has cut a deal with the prosecutor and is in a witness protection programme. One morning, the newspapers scream the news: SUSPECTED INTERNATIONAL CHILD-TRAFFICKING KINGPIN JUMPS BAIL. Everybody blames somebody else, but the upshot is they let him get away. He hadn't pitched for his daily visit at the police station so the cops went to the residential address on file, only to find the mastermind not at home. The tamper-free electronic surveillance bracelet he'd been issued with lay on the hall table next to the phone. He'd slipped out of their hands like water. The monster's stinking breath can be smelt everywhere.

I change my routine to take work home instead of staying late at the office. Samba Nyerere is back with new instructions. She is not to let the young lady out of her sight when I am not around. It is the end of May 2008.

A week after Sarrazin jumped bail, I drove home, glancing in my rear-view mirror, trying to make out if the car one behind me was the white Opel Corsa I'd spotted a few times in the last three days. Klaus had called when the news broke – they were pulling out all the stops to put Sarrazin back behind bars, but I should keep my eyes open and Detective Knappman himself was available 24/7.

Ever since surviving my encounter with RMI's goons, I'd felt strangely invincible. The murdering scumbags would have killed me then if they'd intended to; it's not as if I hadn't provoked them. I reasoned that we had a tacit deal made long ago via Jack: as long as I didn't hand over the files to anyone, Simone and I stayed alive. RMI's *raison d'être* was founded on a guarantee of confidentiality. When I looked again, the white car was no longer in sight.

A man in a green rain jacket stepped into the road at a pedestrian crossing, forcing me to stop. Impatient to get home, I pressed the accelerator a little, letting the pedestrian know I was in a hurry. When I looked up, sensing the man's fleeting glance through the softly falling rain, he had already raised his collar and looked away, heading for the beach. What was he doing in the rain on the beach? I was on the wrong side of the road. No matter. I had become subject to odd spontaneous impulses that I no longer repressed or attempted to control. I double-parked the car, ignoring the hooting, and ran after the fleeing figure of my delusion. The green rain jacket slipped into a cleft between some giant boulders to the left of the bay. I had instantly surmised it was Daniel. Was he living in some kind of a shelter on the beach?

I don't know exactly what happened. They tell me I ran across the road without looking. A minibus taxi braked but a white Opel Corsa travelling at high speed overtook him and struck me with so much momentum that I was thrown up in the air like a crash test dummy, bounced off the bonnet of a parked car and landed splayed on the tar road. Thanks to the minibus driver, who had the presence of mind to pull his taxi to a stop in front of my limp body, no one else rode over me. The Opel Corsa raced away without stopping. According to eyewitnesses, it had no number plates. I was rushed to hospital strapped to a stretcher with suspected internal bleeding, multiple contusions and fractures and possible spinal damage.

The doctors had me on the operating table for several hours. They did all they could to stabilise me, but at 9.41 pm, after being returned to the intensive care unit, I flatlined. The scientists who study these things will tell you that a near-death experience is the result of a loss of oxygen to the brain. I am a scientist myself, so I respect their view. I can only tell you that I hovered between this world and the next, uncertain of whether to go or stay, one metaphorical foot already in the next world, the siren call of the non-living almost more than I could resist. But in my recent travels I had learnt that in limbo one has the time to look around and reflect; a brief moment in the time and space of a galaxy is time enough to see everything with blinding clarity. I saw it all. I saw the Paola I had once been. And I saw Simone Dante-de Luc, the daughter of my heart, sitting in a hospital chair next to my bed, her hand holding my hand. I heard her trembling voice, repeating the same words over and over again, holding death at bay with her fear and a prayer. She resorted to the ancient rhythms that were sealed in her blood.

Maman, ne me laisse pas seule. J'ai peur.

How could I have contemplated leaving my newly found daughter alone and afraid? My medical chart recorded that the patient resumed breathing at 9.42 pm.

When do I know we will make it? Simone unfolds a white cotton cloth and hands a small, black leather journal to me, her eyes filled with grave intent. I take it from her slowly, in the way of one who has awoken from a deep sleep between two worlds, my arm muscles still slack and uncertain. My favourite nurse looks around while she takes the blood pressure of the stroke victim that arrived in the night, her calm face swivelled towards us as if she has sensed a disturbance. I turn the cover page. On the inside front cover of the journal it says simply: 'Pour Marie mon amour Antoine de Luc'. Simone explains in a soft voice that her father gave it to her on that last day when he dropped her off. He said she must keep it safe for him, that he would come back to get it from her one day, when he could. She has used her rusty French to read all the poems. They are love poems.

'Who is Marie?' she quizzes me, quite certain that I know everything about her father.

Daniel had given his most prized possession, the journal of love poems his father had bestowed upon his mother as an act of everlasting love, to Simone for safekeeping. For a moment, I am blinded by tears. I want to pummel my pillow like a ten-year-old, I want to put my face into the pillow and weep rivers. A year ago I would have resented this precious gift to an unclaimed daughter, but now I see it: he has given her the only thing he could, and to me he has given this child for safekeeping. I pull her into my feeble arms and speak unintelligible words into her sunrise-gold hair while tears course silently down my cheeks, the healing rivers of knowledge and pain I have struggled against for so long. She strokes my hair gently as if I am the child and she is the mother.

The nurse turns back to her critically ill patient, satisfied that all is well in our corner. I blow my nose and then I tell Simone the little I know about Marie and Antoine the circus performer and she listens enraptured to the end, her luminous eyes never leaving my face.

'He will come back,' she says with absolute certainty. 'That is why he gave the book of poems to me, so I could give you the message. He must come back to get the book from me and then he will stay.'

And so we are reconciled.

Monica popped in on her own one afternoon during visiting hours. Her mother was doing better now that she had a professional nurse looking after her at home. 'Hey, honey bunch,' she smiled, 'when are you going to tell me what you've been up to?' So I told her about Real Man Inc.

'Sexy name,' Monica said. 'It's the kind of name a woman would dream up.'

A woman? I stared at Monica in a kind of mortal funk. 'What if you're right?'

'What if I am? I like being right. Is there a problem with that?'

'What if it's her and not him? What if he's just a low-down skunk porn producer and she's the brains?'

So I told her the rest of the story.

Once I am out of hospital, I contact the minibus driver who defended my limp body from those who had wanted to move it. I heard the story from a young man who was on ambulance duty the night I was run over. He told me the driver had put a blanket over me and stood guard, refusing to let anyone touch me until they arrived. If I had been moved, my spine would have been severed. Monica drives me to the beachfront where he plies his trade. We meet at the service station twenty metres from where I was run over. I shake the hand of an enormous, paunchy black man in a beige windbreaker with Scottish tartan lining and say thank you because what else is there to say? He's impressed by my plaster casts. I learn that he has completed two first-aid courses with St John's and wants to do a third one, and that he is part of a volunteer group that fights fires in Imizamo Yethu, the township in Hout Bay where he lives. Across the front of his vehicle, above the windscreen, are the words that have made him easy to trace: *ALL IS WELL*. He beams at me and does not let my hand go, as if delighted that he has been proved right on so many counts. Guardian angels come in all shapes and sizes.

Monica decides I need to rest in a coffee shop. When I'm safely seated she says, 'I have something for you, honey bunch. It's a present.'

She hands me a package. When I open it, there's a rectangular object wrapped in brown paper inside.

'What is it?' I ask, suspicious of the self-satisfaction she oozes. My fingers fumble at the string.

A framed photo emerges.

I can't make out what's happening. I'm looking at a picture of Simone posing for an unseen cameraman, playing the coquette, her lovely eyes laughing, the charming mole on her cheek giving her a sophisticated air older than her years, the strawberry blonde hair blowing in the wind a pale shade of off-grey in the monochrome picture.

'It's Simone,' I say in astonishment. 'Where did you get this?' In some strange way I see Simone as existing in a parallel dimension to ours, her lost identity out there somewhere, waiting to be plucked from thin air, waiting to be stolen from me.

'It's not Simone,' Monica says smugly. 'It's Cecilia van den Bogen. Look.' She opens the frame without any trouble and shows me the back of the photo. *Cecilia Rastoff 1957.* 'Remarkable resemblance, wouldn't you say? I noticed it immediately when I met her. I had plenty of time at the show house so I looked around. Oh, by the way, I sold the house to an Arab sheik.'

'This is not Simone?' I whisper. My mouth is as dry as a shard of bone. The wings of the lost daughters of limbo are beating frantically against one-way glass.

'Nicky's her father?'

'Paola? Waiter, bring us a glass of iced water! Put your head on the table.'

When I've recovered, she takes a white envelope out of her bag.

'She won't miss it; she's got others. I found them under her lingerie.' She tips the envelope and a photo falls out. 'And she's probably forgotten about this one.' It's a close-up colour picture of a fair-haired baby with a rosebud mouth, very blue eyes and a small blemish on her right cheek. All that can be seen of the woman holding her is a piece of brown coat with a big button. Was this one of the last photos Jasmine took of her baby daughter before keeping to her side of the bargain?

Cecilia van den Bogen knew all along her grandchild had been left to the wolves. No wonder she drank like a fish.

Memoirs of an
unDutiful Daughter

A DOG WALKER AT SEEKOEIVLEI reported a white Opel Corsa dumped in the lagoon. The owner was in Mozambique doing business. His seventeen-year-old unlicensed son was taken into custody but, unsurprisingly, witnesses who saw the car with darkened windows speeding away failed to recognise him at a line-up parade. Life began returning to normal. There was no way of knowing if the hit-and-run episode had been by accident or design. Heidi reassigned Samba Nyerere to other security duties and I convinced Nathan he couldn't sleep on our couch forever.

Almost ending up a suspicious death myself had been curiously liberating. I'd written Piet a letter from hospital. In theory, P&P could have taken the opportunity to be rid of me – anybody who had lost her husband (literally) and acquired a teenage daughter overnight was no longer entirely sane and could not be relied on to put her career before her private life. But Piet understood alternative scenarios that benefited everybody. A corporation is the sum of its parts, and the consulting manager has extensive decision-making powers. P&P allowed me to take all the paid leave owing to me and an additional six month unpaid leave of absence in order to put my personal affairs in order.

I used the time to recover and to help Simone and me settle down into our new life as mother and daughter. The way I looked at it, I wasn't going to win any mother-of-the-year awards any time soon, but I couldn't do much worse than the Sarrazins.

So there I was, smugly congratulating myself that we were cruising when the gods punished my complacency with a well-directed *klap* from the heavens.

I'd left her having an ice-cream while she kept an eye on the grocery trolley. On my way back from the bank, I passed two men in overalls, one up a ladder and one on the ground, all productive activity halted as they stared in that slack-jawed, tongue-hanging-out-of-mouth way that signals male arousal and predatory inclinations. Simone was leaning playfully over the shopping trolley, one foot on the back of it and with the other pushing herself around. A strong wind from the sea lifted her pleated school skirt and held it aloft, exposing a pair of pink nylon briefs caught in the cleft between two naked bum cheeks. Time's tempo skipped a beat. There was something heartbreakingly innocent about that schoolgirl figure hugging the trolley like a toddler in a supermarket, but at the back of my mind was the treacherous lurking suspicion that circumstances had turned her into an overly sexualised child with a confused sense of boundaries. There was *no way* she didn't know what she was doing! I speeded up to a run.

'Simone, get off that trolley *now*!' Adrenalin pumping, I took her by the arm and yanked her off. There was a startled yelp and then my daughter's terrified eyes turned on me. A split second later I felt an excruciating pain in my lower leg. I should have known the well-aimed kick to my shin came from some deep well of terror and that it was a survival impulse, but I slapped her hard in a moment of misdirected fury.

A woman buying ice-creams for her kids gave me a filthy look as she hurried them away. An elderly woman walking past said loudly, 'Sies! 'n Groot mens moenie 'n kind klap nie!' No, of course a grown woman shouldn't slap a child.

423

'*I hate you!* I'm not staying with you any more. I'll tell Esmeralda you hurt me!'

Then my dazed eyes met the only eyes that really mattered. She stood there panting, glaring at me. I saw everything in those clear young eyes: the primal urge to run, the calculations she was making on how to get away from me and where to go, the defiance mixed with shock and confusion. It wasn't the words so much as that accusing look in Simone's eyes, the composite whole of it, which stopped me in my tracks and saved us. I unclenched my body, my hand still tingling, and stepped back away from her. It was probably one of the hardest things I'd ever done; all I wanted to do was grab her with claws of steel, like some android with a human strain, and not let her go.

Tell her the truth. She can handle the truth. You can't lose her now.

I spoke as calmly as I could. My mouth was as dry as a sand dune. 'I'm sorry. I overreacted. I was wrong to slap you. Those men over there were watching you.' She followed the direction of my gaze and then looked back at me, her body still poised in that state of bolting from a rabbit hole. I carried on babbling. She hadn't run yet.

'Your skirt was blowing up in the wind ...'

'You're so *archaic*. So *what* if the wind blows my skirt up! Those guys are just pervs.'

Her eyes were still wary but the old insolence was back. I could handle insolence.

'That's not the point. The world's not a safe place. Come, let's go home.' All I wanted was for us to get back onto solid ground.

'It's not *my* home, it's *your* home. I'm not going with you.' I almost smiled. I remembered saying similar words to my mother on more than one occasion.

'You heard the magistrate, Simone. I'm your last chance. We have to make it work. You can choose to have a good life or you can mess it up. It's up to you. We all have a choice.' I was practically begging.

'Why should I listen to you? You'll just hit me again!'

I took a big breath. 'You're right, but I'm not proud of hitting you. My father slapped me once when I was even older than you – I'd said something rude about my stepmother. It never ever happened again. I think he probably felt like I do now.'

I took her stubborn silence as a hopeful sign. Just when it looked like we were on the home straight I overreached myself.

'It's not your fault. You've grown so tall in the last few months; I should have seen it. Tomorrow we'll buy you some new underwear. And when we get home we'll ask Kiki to help with your hem. Now, let's pack the groceries.'

'Stop speaking to me as if you're my mother!' she screamed, shoving the trolley straight at me, before taking off. Winded and caught by surprise, I fell hard on the paved walkway. I tried to get up and run after her but my ankle gave way under me. A security guard picked up the groceries and returned the overturned trolley, which had careered into a concrete post. Simone was long gone by then. As the pain subsided I considered my options.

Heidi.

She roared up on a huge motorbike, dressed top-to-toe in skin-tight black leather. I don't think I've ever been so grateful to see anyone in my whole life. She removed the helmet and assessed the situation in the blink of a long-lashed onyx eye. 'Do you have any idea where she's gone?' she asked, totally ignoring my physical state. I'd been going over our conversations while I waited, trying to organise my jumbled thoughts and stay calm. 'She once told me she liked swings and that she used to meet Daniel at the kid's park in Woodstock sometimes. That's all I can think of. You have to get her back before they find her.' I sounded desperate. I was desperate.

'I'll handle it,' she said, climbing off the motorbike and handing me her helmet. In front of my astonished eyes, she walked nonchalantly over to a car parked two bays away. I saw her lean down, fiddle a moment near the handle and then slide smoothly into the driver's seat. Next minute, she'd drawn up next to me in the black Hyundai. She laughed when she saw the expression on my face, a loud, gutsy, devil-may-care laugh. 'You stay put. I'll bring her to you. Tell the owner I went the other way.'

Heidi was as good as her word. After the doorbell rang and I opened the door, Simone brushed past me without a word. She smelt of wood smoke.

'How did you get her to come back? Where did you learn to pick locks like that? What are you going to do with the car?' I asked nervously. I couldn't believe I was an accessory to car theft.

'We talked about my village on the river,' Heidi said casually. 'It's a crap car, no power. I wouldn't want it anyway.' And motorbike helmet in hand, she sauntered off towards the lift. 'You were right about the swings,' she called back.

I am not her mother. I am something else. But this is where she belongs.

I left Simone in the shower and knocked on Kiki's door. Kiki the Jungle Queen, in that wacky, beatific way of hers, suggested a ritual; she called it the old hemline ceremony. I asked Kiki to go in and talk to her and waited nervously in the lounge. Five minute later, the two of them emerged, Simone studiously ignoring me, and disappeared into Kiki's apartment, giggling like schoolgirls with a secret. An hour later, Sharon and I were called in to see a newly practised dance routine. Simone followed Kiki's lead, imitating ultra-cool rapster moves, her body and hands jiving in oddly staccato undulating motion to a piece of rap music. Simone wore the errant skirt with her white school shirt and as she moved her head back and forth like a turtle coming out of its shell in time to the beat, a multitude of tightly braided thin plaits swung on the breeze. Dressed in Simone's other school uniform, Kiki looked like a full-breasted sixteen-year-old, the Rasta blonde mane a luminous halo in the late afternoon sun. When the piece of music finished, they collapsed onto the carpet in a paroxysm of laughter.

'What are they doing now?' Sharon asked in a puzzled voice.

'Well, if you can imagine beetles on their backs cycling, with plenty of high-fives between, something like that.'

After some juice and ordered-in pizza, they sat together at the dining-room table. Under Kiki's patient expert tutelage, Simone undid the old hem, marked a new hemline with a white marker, tacked the pleated fabric to its new length and, after practising on a scrap of fabric, sewed the new hem with neat hem stitches aided by a silver thimble on her finger. This entire operation was conducted with great gravity, the pink tongue peeping out from the side of her mouth a tell-tale sign that she was in a state of deep concentration. Before Kiki left, she made sure the new hemline was ironed into place.

When I went in to say goodnight, her eyes were closed.

'I never learnt how to do a hem. I'm proud of you.'

She let me suffer, then she opened her eyes. 'You don't have to *whisper*. I'm not asleep. I only did it because Kiki said the really cute rich guys don't go for the skanky look.'

She grinned at my expression. 'Just kidding, *mom-person*.' She only ever called me mom-person for special sardonic effect; the rest of the time I was Paola. Then she changed tack. 'Why didn't you like your stepmother?'

'I blamed her for taking my father away.'

'Did you love your father a lot?'

'Yes, I did. I loved him very much.' It's harder to admit love aloud than one might think.

'Night, Paola.'

'Night, Simone,' I replied, closing the door gently behind me.

And so we went on, gradually growing accustomed to each other. Maybe we needed that day, to know we could go all the way to the brink of hopelessness, to the edge of the abyss where love is flown, and still pull back; maybe we needed to know we'd get through the bad days, too.

* * *

I arranged to visit Igor with Nathan and Simone. Simone said, 'That's the name of the cat master,' and I didn't disagree with her. While she made some of the cats in the lounge dance with a mynah feather hanging off a stick that she brandished like a wand, we grown-ups talked. I told Igor she was the girl I'd informed him about and Nathan was the person she owed her life to.

Only Igor and I would ever know what we had done. Even gallant Nathan who monitored the auction sites never found out. The night after Nathan gave me the URL of the auction site, I'd gone to see Igor. I'd offered him a substantial sum of money if he was able to find where the auction had moved. Once he had done that, he was to make a very high offer on the blonde virgin child, supplying Jan van den Bogen's name and bank account details, which he would have hacked by checking major Internet deals involving antique swords. The amoral swine who had sold a tiny infant girl to a porn king would unwittingly save her life. I calculated that the Sarrazins, already nervous after Nathan's break-in, would accept the highest bid on the table and prepare to move the girl. The scary thing was Igor said he put in a ridiculous figure and somebody topped it. We had almost lost her.

Perhaps Nathan and Igor could work together in the future.

Simone and I left them to it. Finally, the forgotten daughters of limbo let me sleep through the night without waking.

* * *

My mother called to say an old friend of hers, Domenica de Nobrega, a world-renowned Spanish sculptor, was exhibiting in the city. She was a guest lecturer at the Michaelis School of Fine Art for a year and she'd be doing adult courses in the evenings. The exhibition opening was on Friday evening. She'd pick us both up at 6 pm. Simone seemed to enjoy the various cultural excursions my mother came up with so I went along with it, no longer unduly embarrassed by our rapprochement. The exhibition was titled *Memoirs of An unDutiful Daughter*. The brochure acknowledged the allusion to Simone de Beauvoir. The bronze female figures demonstrated various measures of pain and beatitude and longing and fear and somehow it was possible to tell the mothers and daughters apart. Hanging against a vast wall was a floor-to-ceiling installation of the artist's mother, with her hands closed over a wooden cross, viewed from the foot of her death bed so that she appeared to be standing with her eyes closed but watching over us. That bed and its occupant hung over the exhibition visitors like a crucifix. My mother introduced us to the artist briefly and then wandered off with Simone in tow. I told Domenica de Nobrega how much I admired her work, that it touched me in my gut. She asked to see my hands and then surprised me more by her next question. Had I ever sculpted? I replied that I had not; one art devotee in a family was enough.

'Ah, we are all undutiful daughters at some stage of our lives, even your mother. Who knows why it is easier to show love to an aunt than to one's own mother? You have good strong hands. If you wish, there is still a place for the Monday evening class.'

'But you don't know if I'm any good.'

'I have never been wrong about a student,' she said simply. 'Shall I put your name down for Monday?'

'Yes.'

On the way home, Simone sat next to my mother and babbled away about the über-cool art crowd at the exhibition and the snacks that were rad and the background music that was *insanely* retro. Once I caught my mother's eyes resting on me in the mirror but she looked away so quickly I could have been mistaken. Someday, I'd have to ask about my grandmother, her mother, and in exactly what ways she had herself been an undutiful daughter.

* * *

Occasionally I had the feeling that somebody was watching us, especially when Simone and I were together, as if wings were brushing the skin of my face, unseen. As the winter chill set in, the feeling became stronger. Each time I looked around there was nothing there, but it was no longer entirely no one, it was as if a shadow flitted out of sight. One rainy day towards the end of the cold season, something happened. It was nightfall and I was closing the curtains, when through the sheet of rain I glimpsed a man standing across the road gazing up at our lit windows. By the time I had hobbled down the two flights of stairs and pushed open the heavy front doors, he was gone. I searched the street in both directions, dragging my stiff leg in the pouring rain, and encountered only a bedraggled cat that made a dash across my path. I returned to the apartment exhausted and drenched to the bone. But I knew what I had seen.

I went to see Enid Lazzari one more time. This time the door was open, as if I was expected. I stepped through to find her already sitting at the lacquered table.

'Is he dead? Why do I keep feeling as if I'm seeing his ghost?'

'He has gone away, perhaps forever. What you sense are residues of regret.'

'Do you get so involved with all your patients?'

'I have something to show you,' she said, a small, plump hand beckoning me as she stood up and flitted away. I followed her to a door that opened into pitch darkness.

'My living quarters are upstairs,' she observed, switching on a light.

A wooden staircase stood at the far end of a dimly lit corridor. Each cross beam that traversed the passageway had been stencilled with archaic gold lettering so that when read consecutively, like a spiritual filofax, the wooden trusses read: *'I PRAY THAT I WILL LIVE AND LIVE AGAIN IN THE GREAT CIRCLE OF LIFE.'*

The glinting eyes watched me in the gloom, a queer, mischievous look I couldn't decipher.

'You were part of the cult,' I said, realisation dawning. 'The one Marie Montaigne ran away from. That's how you know him so well.'

'Ran away? Hmm,' she said, in that infuriatingly enigmatic way of hers. 'I had already left France. Marie came to me for assistance. It was not the right place for a child like Daniel. But my belief persisted. It has become my life's work. Dreams are a pathway to the subconscious. One day I hope to prove to science that reincarnation exists.'

'You were studying his dreams? That's why he came to you?'

'Yes, he understood my interest.'

'Will he ever come back?'

Enid Lazzari's face contorted in that odd way it had of displaying emotion.

'He has passed through one doorway. Another is yet to come. Life is a game of hazard. Not even the gods know.'

I let myself out, and it seemed to me that the world around me had lost its sound. I could not hear my own footsteps walking forward.

* * *

It was during that long recovery period that I received a letter from Eveline Kaas, the woman who had told Celestine she was a receptionist at RMI. She reminded me of our meeting at the cemetery on the day Celestine was buried.

Before the fire swept through her employer's offices, she had been able to save some documents. She enclosed something that was among them.

It was a birth certificate for a girl, born to Jasmine Nothomb at the Bruges Maternity Hospital. The name given to the newly born infant was Simone Nothomb. The name of the father was given as Nikos Jan van den Bogen. The date and time of birth were recorded as 15 April 1995 at 1.33 am.

I pondered what Evelyn Kaas's debt to Jasmine could have been and the coincidence of the authorial pseudonym Gabriel Kaas. Love is a strange beast, borne with a stubborn tenacity that knows no bounds. Perhaps she saw herself as a bereaved member of some greater sisterly band. We are all deluded.

As far as Simone was concerned, she was bossy Aries born on 21 March. I could not give her true birthdate back without explaining how I'd come by it, so on the small matter of a birthday sleeping dogs would be left to lie.

But on the much larger matter I did not hesitate for a minute. Jack had let it slip so long ago: *If he's 'one of us' … then he checks the classifieds*. I placed an advertisement in the classified births section of all the major South African, English and French newspapers, and the *St Helena Tribune*. I also couriered a copy of the classified supplement to Enid Lazzari and Patrice Musso.

---

101 Births. SIMONE, 3.45kg, born to Jasmine Nothomb & Daniel Gabriel Montaigne-de Luc on 21 March 1995, 5.17 (bossy Aries), at Bruges Maternity Hospital.

The only person whose opinion mattered was out there somewhere. I saw it now: Daniel had known all along she was Nicky's daughter; he would have seen the resemblance to Cecilia immediately. He would understand why I had done it. We had become the guardians of our dead friend's daughter. It was the only way to keep her safe. Besides, Simone believed Daniel was her father and there didn't seem to be any reason to disillusion her.

An appointment with Hans Merensky sorted out the rest. If anything should happen to me, he would know what to do. For now, everything that could be done had been done.

IV
PROTECTION

Cape Times, Friday May 22, 2008

ISLAND MYSTERY
BODY OF ALLEGED CHILD TRAFFICKER FOUND FLOATING OFF ST HELENA

Police have confirmed that the body of a man found floating two nautical miles out to sea from St Helena Island is that of Albert Sarrazin, the Cape Town business tycoon and nightclub owner whose high-society lifestyle ended abruptly when he was charged with child-trafficking.

Sarrazin, who is rumoured to have made his considerable wealth as a kingpin of the European pornographic film industry, disappeared while out on R500 000 bail.

His naked body was found by local fishermen, tied to a life ring from the RMS *St Helena*. Dental records were used to identify Sarrazin following an anonymous tip-off.

In December 2007, Sarrazin was taken into custody by the Special Crimes Unit of the South African Police under charges of violating the Sexual Offences Act for forcing an underage minor to participate in pornographic films. The child victim's identity may not be revealed.

Racketeering charges were later filed by the Organised Crime Unit after Sarrazin was linked to a crime syndicate that ran an Internet auction site that exhibited children as young as three years old. This was widely regarded as an important test case for the tough new child-trafficking legislation recently enacted in South Africa. Sarrazin, who was under house arrest, disappeared from his home before the case was heard in court.

The case continued to make international news after a French court turned down a request from French police to have Sarrazin extradited for the murder of five young women in his home country, citing insufficient evidence linking him directly to the killings.

His wife, Nada Sarrazin, who agreed in a plea bargain to testify against her husband, was sentenced to eight years in a South African jail for her part in the child auctioneering racket that shocked the world. If she wins her appeal to be extradited to a French prison, she could be released after having served as little as two years. The court accepted that undue influence had been exerted by her husband.

Speaking under condition of anonymity, a private detective associated with the case said the killer had done everybody a favour by taking Sarrazin out. 'The fact that the body was tied to a life ring suggests that the perpetrator wanted the body found and everybody to know the scumbag was dead,' the detective said. Police are investigating the theory that it was a 'lone ranger' killing, perhaps by a fanatic linked to the anti-child-trafficking lobby group. All leads are being followed but no suspect has yet been detained.

435

Epilogue

Lady Limbo.
By Gabriel Kaas.
Pocket Policier Books, Montreal, 2008

HIS BODY SLIPPED INTO THE BLACK WATER UNSEEN. The ship's swell lifted the man's body high, and for a moment, to anybody else watching from the deck far above, it could have been a seal hunting far out at sea, the sound of pounding water earthly music in its ears. The sky flared with electric white moonlight. The waves took up the offering and rolled him over and over. He was part of the churning mass, a tooth in the monster's maw that had become dislodged.

The eyes of the exhausted man on the deck did not let go of the receding flotsam until the night had swallowed it up, his shoulders heaving with each breath. It was done. The white moon alone had seen and she was not going to tell.

The wind whipped his hair. His hands still gripped the aft rail. They were safe: his brave mercurial wife and the precocious girl who could have been his daughter were safe at last. This had been the only way. Long ago, he'd found her shining and bold on the threshold in front of him, his best friend's woman. He'd accepted from that moment that he would die to protect her.

When he closed his eyes he could imagine she was here with him now, in his arms, heading for some remote undiscovered shore.

Mon amour, comme tu me manques …

In the end, it was a line from a late-night film uttered by a small, talkative child that had decided him. 'Everybody needs protection, even grown-ups,' she'd said with eerie conviction. After that it had seemed obvious. Getting rid of Albie was the only way.

The undulating ocean breathed around him. *Rien ne dure*. His mother's favourite saying came to him. Nothing lasts. Later, he'd imagined they could make it work, once he'd put Amélie and Paris behind him and convinced her to become his wife, that the past was safely in the past, and they were the future. He'd imagined their love could keep the nightmares at bay and their happiness could fill the dark pockets of his mind.

But nothing lasts and the past had come to find him.

The corn-haired girl was a surprise. In the photograph slipped under his door, she wore a pretty floral summer dress and a straw hat with a yellow sunflower. She was sitting demurely on a chair, with both thin straps off the slim shoulders and a few buttons left undone. The startling blue eyes were wide-open and innocent. He had the impression he was being laughed at.

He saw instantly that it was a threat – they would never let him go. He'd never allowed himself to think about the children, but he knew even before he lifted the photograph from the floor that the challenge in this child's eyes would follow him to hell. There had been other photographs after the first. In the end, there were enough for a small bonfire.

Beneath his hands on the rail, the man could feel the throb of the engines urging the vessel on, powering its prow as it carved the sea, heading south-east to the Cape of Good Hope. He hoped for nothing. Albie might be drifting in the mid-Atlantic where gulls would peck at his guts, but he'd have to watch his back. La Reine Noire had lost her mate. Her rage would stretch to the far corners of the globe. She would come looking for him.

To his wife he had become as a man behind glass. He was not sure he could ever reach her again. All he could do was watch. The rain would drip from his hair like the streams of his own yearning as he watched. The fingers of his longing would caress the air around her as she walked.

So he hoped for nothing. He only knew that it was done.

The
Old Cat

SPRING HAS CREPT UP ON US UNAWARES; the balmy days are longer and the mild nights shorter. A pair of Indian mynahs has migrated southwards to warmer climes and set up residence on a corner truss of the balcony ceiling. I remind her they are regarded as an invasive species but Simone will not hear of their removal. Their raucous cries and daily scuffles become part of the background noise of our lives.

One day, a parcel arrives. Sender unknown. The red ribbon (a nice touch) does not entirely deliver on its promise but the epilogue is a surprise. I cannot help being glad of the protagonist's act of protection, but it makes me shiver for him. Evil lives on. He can never come home. I sit on the balcony for a long time, hugging his book to my chest. Then I hide it away from Simone and contact Daniel in the only way I can.

---

120 Personal. CHOCOLATES, I have eaten the chocolates that were in the chocolate box. Forgive me, they were delicious, so sweet and so cold.

On the weekend we visit the animal shelter. Simone selects a moth-eaten black cat that goes by the unlikely name of Petruschka. The woman on duty tells us she was rescued from a sinking houseboat after her aged mistress drank hemlock and pulled the plug. Simone holds the old cat in her arms and whispers in her ear. *Truschka.*